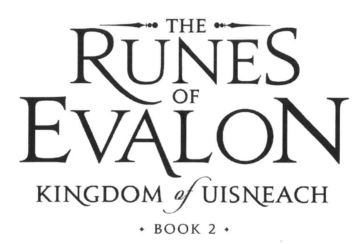

THE RUNES OF EVALON

KINGDOM *of* UISNEACH

• BOOK 2 •

HEIDI HANLEY

Printed in the United States of America
First Printing, 2019

Sword and Arrow Publishing NH, USA
Charlestown, NH 03603
heidihanleyauthor.com

E-book ISBN-13:978–0–9982736–2–4
Paperback ISBN-13:978–0–9982736–3–1

Editor: Jill Shultz
Cover Design and Formatting: Damonza
Author Photo: Cecile Lackie
Uisneach and Hill of Uisneach Map: Donna Therrien

Lovingly dedicated to Joseph—
king of my heart.

ACKNOWLEDGMENTS

To my family—Your sacrifice and support means the world to me. Thank you for letting things slide and giving up time so that I can pursue my craft.

Marsha Downs (a.k.a. Magdrael)—Thank you for staying the course. You remain my number one cheerleader.

Jase Hartly—Thank you, Wribu, for your eye to detail, honest comments and new tools! More importantly, thank you for your friendship and the cyber coffee klatch.

Donna Murray—I am so happy that you agreed to be the Irish consultant for this book. I can rest easy knowing that I haven't inadvertently offended anyone in the country I love so much. It was a big task I gave you and you answered the call brilliantly!

Sue Church—Your enthusiasm and love for this story is such a confidence boost during times when I doubt myself.

Lava Mueller—Welcome to the team and thank you for your immediate enthusiasm and encouragement.

Jill Shultz—You are proof that professional commitment and skill is only enhanced by kindness and humor.

Donna Therrien—Your generosity in bartering for the maps is much appreciated.

Justin Moffat—Thanks to you and the Hill of Uisneach gang for the photos and permission to use the website map as a guide for our own version.

A holler out to those who follow and support my efforts on social media. Your "likes" and "loves" mean the world to me!

AUTHOR'S NOTE

Welcome back to Uisneach! I'm delighted you've decided to continue following Briana's journey. For your convenience, I have included an updated glossary in the back of this book. Some terms or names in this book are fictitious or based loosely on Irish words. Please keep in mind that regional variations in spelling and pronunciation abound in Ireland. As much as possible, I held to pronunciations consistent with the usage in Ulster.

⁓

I hope you enjoy *The Runes of Evalon* and would gently remind you that as an indie author, I rely on you to help spread the word about my books. Feel free to share links, posts, etc. on your social media page and please, consider writing a review on Amazon.

If you would like to join the Kingdom of Uisneach community to receive updates and behind-the-scenes information and join in conversations about your favorite characters, there are several ways to be involved:

Website:

heidihanleyauthor.com

Facebook:

https://www.facebook.com/heidihanleyauthor/

Instagram:

https://www.instagram.com/heidi_hanley/

Goodreads:

https://www.goodreads.com/author/show/17657691.Heidi_Hanley

Twitter:

Heidi Hanley @HeidiAuthor

https://twitter.com/HeidiAuthor

Pinterest:

https://www.pinterest.com/heidihanleyauthor/

For more information about the Hill of Uisneach, go to their website:

www.uisneach.ie

My heartfelt thanks to each and every one of you who support The Kingdom of Uisneach. *Beannachtai Ríocht*! (Kingdom Blessings.)

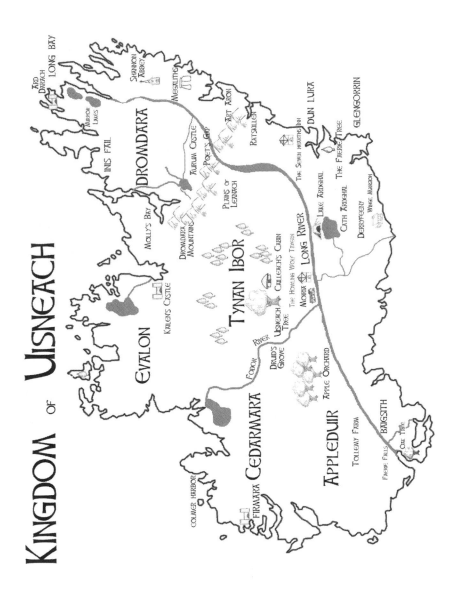

THE MAGICIAN AND THE DEER

Katrina, Brennan home, Camden, Maine

Candlelight flickered across the table in the pre-dawn hours. Wind tousled the trees outside the window, but Katrina's energy was grounded in the tarot cards laid out in front of her. Because the cards had laid out the same way for weeks, she knew when she turned the last card that it would be the Eight of Vessels, indicating a time of rebirth, healing and new possibilities. She scanned the other cards. Deer represented Briana. Beside them fell the Archer; the King; the Wanderer; the Journey card; reversed Lovers; Six of Bows; and Eight of Vessels. She was about to put the deck down when an eighth card fell out of the deck into her empty hand, hot enough that she dropped it. The card landed face up on top of the others. The Magician.

"Oh, this is new," she said, shaking fingers still warm from the heat of the card. "Universal power divinely inspired but grounded by earth. A conduit for magic. Strong and determined, he understands what needs to be done and does it. Interesting. Who are you? Why are you here?"

She pulled the deer card from the layout and held it lovingly in her hands. "And you, my sweet, gentle, Briana, what are you up to?"

CHAPTER ONE

THE BURNING OF INIS FÁIL

Briana, Inis Fáil, Dromdara, Uisneach

Thick, gray smoke blocked what should have been a bright sun and clear blue sky over Inis Fáil. Crows scattered around the decimated village below her. The smell of smoldering thatch, wood and, Maker, how she hated to think it, the flesh of humans and animals, assaulted Briana's nostrils. She blinked away the sting in her eyes and choked down a cough. *We're too late*, she thought, surveying the grim array of dead or dying bodies, the handiwork of the Gray Military at the orders of Lord Shamwa. Sorrow and rage battled within a heart already primed for grief by her parting, perhaps forever, from Silas of Cedarmara, the royal bard, the man who shared Briana's soul. He'd left this morning on a quest through the tree portal in Appleduir to Maine, where Briana Brennan had come from only a few months before. At least they hoped he would make it there and find the hidden Runes of Evalon that would help restore magic to Uisneach. She shook her head. Though crucial to their plan, for now, that had to take a backseat. What was Shamwa's point in attacking this helpless village? A show of power? To destroy more faerie trees? The wanton destruction made her ill. She looked to her husband, King Brath Taranian. Anger blazed from his eyes, but when he spoke, his words were focused, his tone even.

"They could still be around," he whispered to Lord Marshall Sigel, who nodded. Using hand signals, Sigel directed the Taranian and Winge soldiers to fan out along the ridge encircling the hamlet.

"Where are the faerie warriors that King Kailen promised?" Briana asked Brath.

He shook his head and shrugged. At his whistle, soldiers streamed down into what was left of Inis Fáil. They discovered no evidence of Lord Shamwa or the Gray Military. Nor, did it seem, were there any survivors.

"Come on, Bri, but stay close to me," Brath said.

Briana's legs automatically tightened against her mare's ribs. Banrion surged forward. She followed Brath down the hill. Dara, Briana's wolf-hound, growled, drawing her attention to luminescent orbs moving among the trees down into the village.

Brath tried to shield her from the worst atrocities, but she gagged as they skirted the sight of a woman's twisted and bloodied body tossed carelessly against an apple tree like an abandoned rag doll.

She blinked back tears, and tightened her grip on Nuada, her magical sword. Warmth radiating from the hilt filled her hand. She kept her eyes on the moving lights. *These orbs must be allies because Shamwa has no magic.*

Her designated squire, twelve-year-old Jonathan Stark, Queen's Protector, moved close to her side with his bow upright and an arrow nocked.

It wasn't until Briana and Brath were in the middle of a circle of knights and warriors that the light-filled orbs expanded and the thousand twinkling lights morphed into a thousand golden faerie warriors. Unlike the Taranian troops, no mud dulled the faeries' golden leggings and knee-high boots, which shone brightly, as did their tunics and the breastplates that reminded her of an elaborate insect carapace. Briana sucked in an awe-inspired breath. Golden armor. *Armor would be good right about now,* she thought, not for the first time since coming to Uisneach. The best the warriors of Uisneach had was heavy leather jerkins, poor protection against arrows and swords. She'd pestered Brath for the last month to have the smith learn to make armor. Maybe these guys could provide the prototype. Each faerie carried a massive sword, at least half a dozen small blades, a long bow and a full quiver of arrows. They moved into formation. She gauged them to be about seven feet tall. *They'd have to be big to pack all that weaponry.* They seemed nearly identical with long, blonde hair and intense crystal-blue eyes. One warrior stood out from the rest, both in height and demeanor. He stepped away from the group and bowed before Briana. Briana moved Banrion a step closer to Brath on his bay stallion, Ruark.

"High Lady Briana, Tuathla of Evalon and Queen of Uisneach, allow me to present the Royal Faerie Army of Evalon. I am Captain Aya'emrys, at your service. My sincere apologies that we did not arrive in time to help the people of this village."

She stared at the warrior in wonder, incapable of speech.

"Neither did we," Brath responded steadily, as though he greeted giant faerie warriors every other day.

Briana was still trying to find her voice when Sir Glendon assisted a terrified old man into the circle of soldiers. She cringed at the soot-covered bruises and cuts over his torso, visible through a shirt that was nearly flayed off him.

Brath slipped to the ground beside his stallion. He stepped forward and placed a hand on the man's hunched shoulder. "Are there other survivors?"

"A few, yer Majesty, in what's left of the tavern. We hid the women and children in there soon as the Gray Military were spotted in the area."

Brath nodded to a group of men who immediately headed for the tavern. Turning his attention back to the old man, he asked, "What happened?"

"Lord Shamwa hisself came with his Grays aiming to collect taxes. We told him that now you was alive, we be sending our taxes to Ard Darach. Course we knew he wouldn't like that, but we never expected him to go beserky. Sumpin's changed him, Sire. Might be it has sumpin' to do with his evil horse."

"What horse?" Briana asked, finally able to speak.

"Terrible vicious. Huge black beast with bloody red eyes and puffin' smoke out his nose. Sumpin' like ye'd see in a nightmare."

Briana frowned. If true, this was the first time Lord Shamwa, the ex-prime minister, had led his Gray Military himself. His modus operandi had been to stay safe in his garish and well-protected Aurum Castle. This was also the first she'd heard of any red-eyed, smoke-breathing horse.

"What happened when you refused the taxes?" Brath asked.

"Like I said, Sire, he went crazy. Din't bother to negotiate or nuthin'. Ordered his men to set fire to every buildin' and kill anyone, men, wimmen or children who tried escapin'. The crow soldiers got here with the men ye sent, but there was just too many Grays. They was cut down quick and the town left to burn. I killed a few; my son did too, before he was grabbed and..." He looked beyond the circle and Briana followed his gaze to where a middle-aged man lay on the ground near the well, eyes open, staring at the sky.

"I'm sorry for your loss, man," Brath said quietly.

The man met his eyes, sorrow replaced with a hunger for vengeance. "Don't be sorry, King Brath. Be determined to repay Lord Shamwa for what he done to Uisneach. Every one of us still able will follow ye and fight for the Taranians."

The king clapped the old man on the shoulder. "Be assured, sir, Inis Fáil and all those who have suffered under Shamwa will be avenged."

Taranian soldiers returned with no more than a dozen women and children, their tear-stained faces a sign that they already knew the fate of their menfolk. The women immediately began the task of collecting the dead.

Briana moved close to Brath. "This is a good opportunity to gain the people's trust and affection by helping them clean up."

He nodded and Sigel gave the order for half the men to help collect and bury the dead, and the others to set up camp.

Barely half an hour later, Dara's furious barking alerted Briana, who was comforting a grieving widow. She looked up at the ridge where a colossal black stallion stood just beyond the stone arches on the road leading out of Inis Fáil toward the Dromdara Mountains. The rider astride the beast, looking every bit as sexy as the last time she saw him, even with those red eyes, was Lord Shamwa. *Red eyes? Sweet Maker, the horse wasn't the only one with freaky eyes. What the hell?*

"Brath!" she yelled.

Brath and Sigel were already in motion. "Line up! Shields up!" bellowed Sigel.

Briana's squire immediately moved in front of her to create a human shield, temporarily obscuring her view.

"Mr. Stark, get back, you'll be killed!"

Without taking his eyes off Shamwa, he retorted, "Better me than you, Your Majesty," with more machismo than she was sure he felt.

Briana growled at the ancient ethic that allowed a child to be in the heat of battle, adjusting her opinion slightly when he backed her away behind the line, keeping his shield up in front of them until he had her in a safer position.

Behind her, survivors of the first attack hustled back to the tavern, led by a few Taranian soldiers. Suddenly, a battalion of Gray Military soldiers appeared across the ridge, surrounding Shamwa. The Winge army of shape-shifting crows were in fully human form, prepared for battle. The faeries stared in her direction with their shields up, seemingly unaware of what to do. Why weren't they responding?

"They're waiting for your orders, Briana," she heard Brath shout to her. "They're *your* army!"

She stared at them, dumbstruck, before yelling at their leader, "Do whatever he says," she ordered, pointing at Brath, who responded with a smile and wink before giving Captain Aya'emrys the order to make a second line between the queen and the first line.

"Bows ready," Brath ordered the archers.

"Brath Taranian, I denounce you as the king of Uisneach!" Lord Shamwa called out from his cocoon of soldiers.

Brath laughed. "Denounce away, Shamwa. It gains you nothing."

"You're a dead man, Taranian."

"Really? Seems you tried to kill me once before and failed. For what you've done to this kingdom, Shamwa, I will gladly meet you in battle and end you."

Shamwa responded by ordering his men to fire. Under the rain of arrows, Briana watched helplessly as a handful of Taranian soldiers were hit and fell. She heard Sigel's battle yell and saw the first line move in to defend rather than forge uphill after Shamwa, which would've been suicide.

"Squire Stark, get your queen to safety," Brath ordered. "Artanin, too."

She opened her mouth to argue that she wanted to help, but if she had learned nothing from her short time with Brath, it was to not argue in the middle of a battle. She and the druid Artanin helped other survivors limp as quickly as they could to the tavern.

What was left of the tavern's door rattled shut. A haze of smoke settled down over Briana from the smoldering thatch roof, most of which had already burned away, leaving the tavern open to the sky and layering the floor with ash. Jonathan and Dara posted themselves between the door and the current inhabitants, an old woman, Her head bent low, a younger woman who moaned and held her arm at an unnatural angle against her chest, two squirming toddlers and a teenage girl doing her best to settle them.

"Would ye help me, Missus?" the woman with the dislocated shoulder asked weakly.

Briana went near and felt the affected area. Grimacing at the swelling under her fingertips, she warned, "It will hurt."

"Aye, it's popped out before. I'll be all right."

Before the woman had time for dread, Briana anchored one hand above the injury. She wrapped her other hand around the woman's upper arm and pushed firmly.

After a brief yelp, the woman took a long, relieved breath. "Thank you, Missus… what's yer name, then?"

"Briana."

"Queen Briana?" The woman's eyes went wide. "Aye, I've heard yer a warrior *and* a healer."

"Yeah, jack of all trades, master of none," Briana replied with a twisted grin and a wink.

An increase in the noise of battle drew her attention to the window where she saw Brath, surrounded by soldiers, fighting his way toward an opposing group of men protecting the prime minister. The black stallion reared up, smoke and flame blowing out its nostrils. Brath pressed forward. Gray soldier after Gray soldier fell at his sword.

She wheeled around to where Artanin stood like a dead gargoyle in the corner. "Help me cover them in a protection spell," she urged him. He began mouthing words and she turned back to the window, reciting her own words of protection around the Taranian army and this huddle of survivors.

Shll… craaacckk. The crash and splinter of wood broke her concentration. Nua rose up without invitation. "Dara, protect them," she said, nodding at the widows and children. The wolfhound obeyed without hesitation.

Jonathan was giving his all to prevent the warriors from getting to his queen. From her peripheral vision she saw Artanin cower in the corner, his mouth still working silently.

"I don't think it's working," she hollered at him. "Get up and give us a hand," she ordered, before lunging fiercely at the one Gray who'd slid past Jonathan. Then she kicked at another who leapt over his mate. The roundhouse kick she had perfected in gym workouts back home in Camden, Maine, met the target's gut, but the target responded with a well-placed kick in return against her temple, birthing stars in front of her pupils.

And then it was silent. Briana drew in a gasping breath and prepared to defend, half blinded by the twinkling lights. When her vision cleared, she saw the Grays dead on the cottage floor and the impressive golden height of Aya'emrys, the faerie captain, in front of her.

"Brath?" she asked.

"He is fine, High Lady. It is over and he wants me to bring you to him."

She and the others were led into the town square, now flooded with Taranian men. She ran to Brath and visually searched him for any obvious wounds. Finding none, she relaxed and waited with the others for orders. The number of bodies on the ground had multiplied significantly. Thankfully, all wore gray uniforms.

"Shamwa?" Briana asked.

"Escaped. What the hell is that horse-thing he's riding?"

Heads shook all around until Aya'emrys said, "Dark magic. Somehow he has tapped into something evil."

"That much is obvious," Sigel muttered, wiping red and gray gore from his sword.

"All right, men, back to original orders. Set up camp!"

"We're not going after him?" Briana whispered to Brath.

He shook his head. "That's what he'd like. Split us up. Probably has a legion circling around us while we talk. I've sent crows out to see what he's doing. We have another problem. He's got magic."

"Hmm, right. What will we do about that?"

She felt the air around them swirl as three crows flew in to the village. In a macabre transformation she was growing used to, they twisted and morphed from black-winged corvids to black-uniformed soldiers.

"Sire," one reported in impeccable English, "The majority of Lord Shamwa's troops are en route to Aurum Castle. He has, however, sent smaller units in other directions, presumably to destroy more faerie trees."

"No doubt," Brath agreed. "We'll stick to our plan."

"Brath, if he's allowed to continue murdering faerie trees, we'll soon have no magic at all. We have to stop him," Briana said.

"Begging your pardon, High Lady, but the king is correct. The sooner the prime minister is stopped, the easier it will be to save and replant the trees."

"But even with Shamwa gone, the Gray Military will keep destroying trees," Briana argued.

"Might I suggest a different plan for your consideration?" the faerie captain asked.

Brath put an arm on Briana's shoulder. "We're open to ideas."

"Lord Shamwa has somehow tapped into magical power. You must fight magic with magic." At Briana's skeptical look he continued. "You have more power than you realize. You only need to learn how to use it."

"I'm all for that," Briana said, "but we don't have much time."

"I can help," he answered.

Brath agreed. Tents were erected quickly, the king's first. Briana took her place beside Brath as they hashed out their strategy.

"Lord Shamwa's strategy is simple," Artanin said. "He believes the people of Uisneach are no smarter than sheep and that if he can kill the king, queen and lord marshall, the people will agree to anything he proposes."

Sigel snorted. "It may sound simple to him, but he's out of his mind if he thinks he can defeat us."

"You're outnumbered," Artanin pointed out.

"Yeah? Whose side are you on?" Sigel growled at the druid.

"Enough," Brath said firmly. "If the crows' reports are accurate, then it's true we have only two thousand troops to his five thousand. However," he said looking directly at Artanin, "bigger doesn't necessarily mean stronger. We have to think more strategically and, as Captain Aya'emrys has pointed out, we have magic." He turned to look at Briana. "We need to figure that out.

"We also have something Shamwa doesn't have—a healthy vision for Uisneach. While Shamwa is working to create a dictatorship, we are offering the citizens a monarchy with a parliament of their peers. In our Uisneach, the people have a voice. How much decision-making power will they have under Shamwa? We need to get this message out through the whole king-dom, as quickly as possible."

"Parliament of peers," Briana repeated. "I like the sound of that."

Brath nodded and smiled at her before turning back to the group. "Our strategy must be founded on political goals rather than military ones. We will… What's wrong, Briana?"

She frowned at the sight of the druid, now shrunk into a corner, silently mouthing words. "Artanin, what are you doing?"

He jumped and stopped his incantation. "Just strengthening the protec-tion spell around the camp."

"You already tried that at the battle without any success," Sigel said.

And at the tavern, Briana thought.

"Get him out of here," Sigel ordered a guard. He turned to Briana. "I still don't trust him. He shouldn't be in here when we're planning our strategy."

She didn't argue. Something about Artanin's behavior bothered her.

Brath paused while the druid was escorted out.

"To summarize, we want this to be a politically motivated plan with the following specific goals. First, humanitarian aid to Inis Fáil. The survivors will be escorted to Ard Darach until we can rebuild the village.

"Secondly, because we need all of Uisneach behind us, we'll send small teams throughout the realm to explain that Shamwa has made the people of Uisneach dependent on him while we want to bring them into a future of shared prosperity, offering them a say in their own governing. We've already started the process by choosing representatives for the EU Council.

"We'll keep the main force of the Taranian army at Ard Darach and use the Winge army for reconnaissance. Any skirmishes should be limited in nature. Prisoners will be taken to Winge Mansion, where we'll do our best to turn them into allies or spies."

"If they can be trusted," Briana muttered.

"Well, spies are untrustworthy by nature," Sigel said, "but sometimes it's worth the risk." He glanced at the curtain covering the tent opening that Artanin had just gone through. "And sometimes it's not."

"The faerie warriors?" Briana prompted.

"Your Majesty," a guard said, outside the door. "There's a young boy just come in to camp, frantic for a healer."

11

"Send him in." Brath stood as a small boy, no older than eight, tumbled into the tent. Brath beat Briana in helping him to his feet.

"Sire, sir, sorry I am te trouble ye, but me Mum is 'avin a baby and it's comin' ard. I need help, sir. I heard the queen's a healer. Can ye come?" he said, giving Briana just the kind of look she couldn't refuse.

"Where do you live, boy, and where's the midwife?" Brath asked.

"In the woods on the road to Molly's Bay. Soldiers just buried the midwife, sir."

Brath looked at Briana. "I know your mother is a midwife, but have you ever delivered a baby?"

"No, but I've helped Mom with a few deliveries. I think I have to at least see what I can do."

He sighed deeply. "Nothing can be simple, can it? Aya, would you send enough of your troops to guard? I need you here to continue finalizing our plan."

"Aya'emrys, if you please? It is my name."

"My apologies. Aya'emrys, would you…"

"Of course, Your Majesty." The captain left the tent perfectly calm and poised.

By the time Briana grabbed her satchel and gave Brath a quick kiss good bye, two dozen warriors were waiting to chaperone her and the boy to his home.

As they journeyed through the forest, she learned the boy's name was Samchea Molloie. His father, Sean, was killed fighting the Gray Military in their cabin. The stress of the attack apparently prompted his mother's, Aileen's, labor, since she wasn't due for a few weeks.

She'd been in labor for more than twenty-four hours now. Briana grimaced. Lengthy labor and premature babies were tricky enough in modern times. How on earth would she deal with the scenario here?

Maker of all, whether by magic, medicine or common sense, please help me bring this child into the world safely and help this family, Briana prayed silently as she entered the dark cabin of the Molloie family. She was pleased to see a fire already going and the cabin clean and well-tended. Agonizing groans from the corner led Briana to where Aileen Molloie lay on a bed, glassy-eyed, drenched in sweat and holding her clenched belly.

"Aileen, I'm Briana. I'm here to help." The soaked mattress underneath the woman indicated that her membranes had already ruptured. "May I examine you?" She took Aileen's growl for consent. Feeling around her abdomen provided a grim clue to a second problem. *I think this baby is breech.* After setting the boy to fetch clean supplies and boiling water, she gently eased the woman's legs apart to see if she was dilating at all. She was. *Okay, unless magic is going to turn this baby around, I'm going to have to rely on brute force.*

"Aileen, the babe is not in the right position in your belly but doesn't seem to have dropped into the canal. Do you understand?"

"Not... good..." she ground out, as another hard contraction hit her.

"Do you think you could turn over and get on your hands and knees if I help you?"

The woman might have been trying to laugh but it came out more a growl.

"I'll take that as a no." She was simply too exhausted and weak. "Okay, Aileen, I'm going to try and turn the baby by pressing on your abdomen. It will hurt a bit."

"No... more... than... now."

Briana waited until the contraction stopped before again feeling the baby's position. Sometimes babies would turn on their own during delivery. Not in this case. With as much gentleness as possible, Briana compressed Aileen's lower abdomen, something she'd observed her mother do once. Nothing happened. Briana sighed and sat back on the stool Samchea had brought her. *Mom? Help? What do I do now?* No answer. She waited the next contraction out. She was one of two dozen faeries in and around this house; surely there was something they could do to help Aileen? *That's it! Maybe Aileen can't turn on her own, but a couple of faeries could turn her.* "Samchea, go outside and ask two of the men to come in here."

Minutes later, a pair of seven-foot-tall golden warriors assisted the laboring woman into a position on her hands and knees, supporting her from either side. No time for gentility or modesty. Briana placed her hands on Aileen's abdomen, waiting for something to tell her the baby was responding. Finally, after what seemed an eternity, Briana felt something shift.

"Oh, sweet Maker, that's better," Aileen whispered. She dropped her head weakly.

"Okay, guys, ease her back down." Briana immediately palpated to verify that indeed, the baby was now properly positioned for the journey into the world. "Okay, Aileen, now we let nature take its course."

It took hours. When Aileen dozed, Samchea made tea and he and Briana talked quietly about his family, how his father faced the Gray Military bravely in support of King Brath. Sam was worried about his family's future. Briana assured him they would be fine, that she and King Brath were bringing the survivors of Inis Fáil back to Ard Darach until they could get back on their feet. She was already thinking about space in the keep and an unused cottage near the castle that could be used to foster families.

Altogether, six hours passed before nature took its full course, the supreme effort interrupted by a few rest periods. Aileen was drenched in sweat from the physical exertion, while Briana's wet armpits and chest came more from nerves. The moon was nearly full, shining its light through the window when, with one pitiful moan and weak push, a blue-faced girl child entered the world. Briana quickly wiped her face and blew several breaths into her lungs, but there was no life-sucking wail. Briana tried a second and third time. The infant remained flaccid and breathless. Briana checked for a pulse but there was none. She glanced up at her mother, who was looking at Briana with dread in her eyes.

The woman dazedly turned her face to the moon in the window. "She should have a name. I'll name her Luna."

"I'm so sorry, Aileen," Briana managed to say past the lump in her throat.

"Aye, tis not for yer lack of tryin,' Yer Majesty. You did yer best. Yer known to be a fine healer, and so ye are. Wee Luna was not meant to be. Sam?" The boy made his way beside his mother, his face streaked with tears. "Ah, Samchea, 'twill be all right, son. We'll wish the lassie's soul well and go on about our lives." She turned back to Briana. "Would those kind men who helped me be willin' to bury Luna for us? I can't do it and don't want Sam to be burdened with the task."

Briana nodded, humbled by the woman's calm acceptance of the still-birth, the loss of her husband, and her uncertain future as a single mother. Swallowing her own grief, Briana set about cleaning the infant and then Aileen, making her comfortable, then bringing her a cup of tea.

When mother and son were settled with little Luna wrapped in her mother's arms, Briana slipped outside. After asking the faeries to bury the child when Aileen was ready, she leaned against the side of the cabin and breathed in cool night air, feeling tears spill down her cheeks. Could she have done anything differently? Was there nothing that could've allowed that innocent babe to live? Birth in Uisneach was a dangerous and uncertain affair that held the potential for death to infant or mother. She slid down the wall and buried head in her arms. *What am I going to do? My responsibility to Uisneach is to bear its next ruler, but there's no way I want to have a child here.*

"High Lady," said one of the warriors, his voice void of emotion.

She looked up, wiping her tears. "Data."

"Pardon me?" he asked, his voice coming from far above her.

"I just realized who your voice reminds me of. It's Data, the android from Star Trek."

"I do not understand."

"No," she replied wearily, reaching up a hand for him to help her up. "I don't imagine you would."

She allowed the faerie warrior to walk her back through the woods to the center of the Taranian army camp, where her tent stood. Brath was still awake and working from the looks of it, maps and writing tools scattered across the surface of a small table. He stood as she entered. A half-empty cup of something she hoped was whiskey caught her eye. After accepting his kiss, she nodded at the cup.

"Don't suppose you've enough to share?"

"Of course," he said, handing her the cup. She drained it in two gulps and coughed. He reached for a flask and poured more of the strong spirit.

"Rough night?"

"Yeah, but I don't want to talk about it yet. What happened here after I left?"

"Well, the bad news is that Aya'emrys believes the horse Shamwa was riding is that of the Dar Morch."

"The Dar Morch? What on earth is that?"

"It is a very bad faerie. So bad in fact that he was exiled to Scáil Meanoiche, or what you might call the Underworld, in ancient times, by Urelian, the first faerie queen, when he rose against the faerie kingdom after being seduced by a goddess of the Moherians. His banishment was supposedly eternal and had become more a myth than a real dark power. Seems he's real after all and is supposed to serve only the tuathla. And, more bad news—he can fly and breathe fire."

"Damn. If he is supposed to follow only the tuathla's orders, how is it he's escaped the Underworld? I sure didn't call him up!"

"Don't know. Aya'emrys believes it does have something to do with you being inaugurated as the tuathla of Evalon. The thing is, someone with magic had to have called him and that someone is clearly working with Shamwa."

"Great. Being made Princess of Evalon has called dark magic to Uisneach. As to who called him, I'll bet my money it's Ealga. You did hint there might be some good news."

"Hmm... sort of. The Dar Morch might be less willing to use his powers to destroy faerie trees since losing magic would be to his own demise."

"Ahh. That is good news."

"Aya'emrys also believes there is a pool of magical waters in Evalon. Our Evalon, not the faeries' realm." He reached for the cup they were sharing and took a long sip.

"Minimal good news, Brath. There are a lot of places that could hide a magical pool in Evalon. It would be like looking for a needle in a haystack."

He shrugged and swallowed the whiskey. "Isn't Silas basically doing that?" His voice held a tinge of jealousy. "If he can go searching for needles, so can we."

She felt a pang of guilt. Brath was a good man and she did love him. Just not the way she loved Silas.

"Silas doesn't have Shamwa breathing down his neck."

Brath smiled wearily. "Well, it so happens that we do have one small clue. This Pool of Queens is behind a waterfall, and there are only three in Evalon. One of them is at Kailen's Castle. Seems likely they'd build a castle for a queen next to a queen's pool. Guess I will get to take you on a honeymoon after all. Oh, and the ring they gave you would have its power enhanced by the pool. You'd probably have more magic to work with."

She looked down at the red and white stones set in a gold band carved with runes that King Kailen had given her on the day he told her she was his granddaughter. Not just part faerie, but the High Lady, Tuathla of Evalon, the faerie princess. She had noticed no evidence of magic so far. "That would be an awesome upgrade." Her words ended in a yawn.

"Hey, I'm sorry, Bri. You must be exhausted. Let's get you to bed." He set the cup down and led her to the thick pile of furs. She slid her trousers off, leaving her tunic on, and slipped under the covers. Brath eased in beside her and blew out the candle before sliding an arm underneath her shoulders and gathering her close. He kissed her temple but did nothing to make her think he wanted to make love. She relaxed gratefully in his comforting gesture; sex was the last thing she desired now. Oblivion, yes—the potential for pregnancy—no way!

"You ready to talk about the baby?"

She meant to say no and much to her horror, burst into tears. Though she was trying her damnedest to conquer the tendency, tears were still her first response to sadness or joy.

"Shh, love. I'm here. Tell me."

"What if we don't find the pool? What if Silas doesn't find the runes? What if Shamwa wins and we lose? What if Uisneach is lost to a dictator?"

She could almost hear his confusion in the silence that followed. Choking back a sob, she blurted, "What if I get pregnant and I die, or the baby dies?"

"Ahh, so the baby didn't live." he said quietly. "I'm so sorry, Briana."

"It was awful. Breech presentation. I was able to get the baby turned with the help of the faeries, but it was too long and too much stress on the baby and she was blue and I couldn't revive her and Aileen took it as a matter of course, like it was no big deal, and the faeries buried her and now it's just Aileen and Sam 'cause her husband was killed by Shamwa."

Brath held her, caressing her shoulder as the words tumbled out, accompanied by a torrent of tears. When she was done, she buried her face in his chest and he stroked her back.

"Oh, Bri, you've been through so much. So many losses. Your father's death, being ripped away from your mother so suddenly. Not to mention being thrown into a world so different from your own and then having someone you love leave, and now this tragedy. Cry all you like, love. I suspect you've held this in way too long."

The fact that he understood her grief, even about Silas, was validating enough to end her tears in a short string of hiccupping sobs. But would he understand when she said she didn't want babies?

"Briana, do women always have live births where you come from?"

"No. Some babies don't survive."

"Why does this seem so much harsher to you?"

"I, I don't know. Maybe because I felt so helpless trying to save her. Or, maybe the fact that in my time we have so many more tools to prevent or save high-risk births. Women here are far more likely to die or bear dead children. I don't want that to be me."

"Well, neither of us can pretend it isn't possible, but many, in fact most babies, are born just fine. Perhaps in time you'll see that and it won't be such a scary thought. Still, I am truly sorry about what you went through."

She couldn't imagine the images of dead little Luna or the sorrow in the Molloie cottage ever being replaced by a hopeful wish for children, so she said nothing. He continued to hold her and just as she was drifting off, she heard him whisper, almost to himself.

"I have no intention of losing to Shamwa."

CHAPTER TWO

KAILEN'S CASTLE

"Behold, Uisneach," said Brath.

"I've never seen anything so beautiful," Briana replied, turning in a full circle to take in the panoramic views of Uisneach in all her splendor.

They stood on top of the last hill in the Dromdara Mountain chain. To the east lay the blue expanse of Molly's Bay, glinting with early morning shards of sunlight. The Dromdara Mountains stretched south like green spikes on a dragon's spine. Blanketing the west and north were the mysterious and magical forests of Evalon, birdsong echoing in its canopy.

She turned back toward the bay. "Cailleach told me about Molly, but I would love to hear your memory of her."

Nostalgia softened Brath's eyes. "Molly grew up with us. She was a little older than me and a bit younger than Sigel, but I think they were in love by the time she was out of nappers. Everyone loved Molly, including me. She, however, had eyes for only Sigel, and he for her. They married, and he was taking her to Cedarmara shortly after the wedding when they got caught in a nasty thunderstorm. When lightning split a nearby tree the horses panicked and Molly's slipped on a stone and fell over the cliff. There was nothing Sigel could do. It all happened in an instant. Since that time the bay has been called Molly's Bay."

"How sad." She was quiet a moment, then asked, "Do you think he never married again because she was the only one for him?"

Brath studied her for a moment before answering. "Maybe, but we both know it's possible to love two people at the same time. Maybe he just hasn't found the right woman."

She looked away at his reference to their love triangle.

Last night's emotional storm and his tender care during her meltdown had cleared the air between them. She was humbled by his understanding of grief she hadn't fully acknowledged. He bravely broke down the walls holding it back and then wrapped her in love as she shattered into a million pieces. *For that alone, I will always love you.*

Her heart, relieved of the burden of sorrow and pain, felt ready to move on. She agreed with Brath that they needed some time alone to grow stronger as a couple. Well, maybe not totally alone, as the cadre of golden warriors surrounding them suggested. Odd how such large and powerful beings could be both present and on high alert and nearly invisible at the same time, so silent and unobtrusive that she sometimes forgot they were there.

The forest here differed from other parts of Uisneach, the trees older and the stones draped thick with moss, reminding her of the grove where the Uisneach Tree, and its guardian dryad, Nionon, lived. This forest had the same tangible feeling of magic in the air, an ancient, vital energy flow. Dara also seemed sensitive to the energetic difference; his ears and nose twitched incessantly. Rabbits bounced among the brushy rowan bushes. Occasionally, the twitter and trill of a songbird and the screech of a raptor broke the periods of silence that rested easily between the two of them.

"Come back here, Dara," she called, when he bolted down a ravine and dove into a downed tree trunk.

"Have you tried any magic?" Brath asked, pulling up on Ruark's reins while they waited for Dara.

Briana looked around. Seeing an old oak, bent by weather, streaked black from a lightning strike, she focused her intention and imagined it in its former youth and vigor. Energy welled up inside her, nearly to the boiling point. She forced it toward the tree. Slowly, the tree began to straighten. Black streaks faded to the dark brown bark of its younger years. Leaves popped, green and satiny.

Feeling the waning of energy within, Briana took a deep breath and sat back on Banrion to survey her handiwork. "Seriously? I did that?"

"You did. More specifically, you successfully manipulated energy to return life to something that was dying."

Briana's jaw dropped at the implication. "I just raised the dead?"

"Well, sort of."

"Sweet Maker," she whispered. "If only…"

"Don't go there, Bri. You did everything you could. Magic won't be the answer to everything."

Dara bounded back up the rough slope and barked out his readiness to proceed.

They took their time riding through the beautiful landscape, pausing here and there for Briana to collect herbs, mushrooms, nuts and a variety of other things that might be useful for cooking or healing.

"Hold up," Brath said, coming to a clear stream that sparkled with bright green- and red-speckled brook trout. He jumped off Ruark. Briana followed suit. Reaching in his pack, he produced line and hook and dropped it into the water. Faerie warriors silently surrounded the king and queen. Briana walked a bit upstream to fill their water bags, then took the opportunity to stretch and drink in the pine-scented air. The balsam was heady, or perhaps it was the new lightness of her heart. She stared up through the branches to the bluest blue sky she'd ever seen. The contrast was magical. High on a limb, a squirrel raced across one branch and soared across a remarkable expanse to another. She giggled with delight. A toad plopped on her foot, drawing her attention. Apparently deciding her boot was not where he wanted to be, he hopped away into the open end of a rotted tree trunk. Her eyes feasted on the colorful flora, tiny purple flowers co-existing with broad ferns, communities of mushrooms and endless carpets of moss.

"Ready?" Brath said next to her.

"Mmm hmmm," she agreed, beaming.

A look of pure relief swept over Brath's face. "It's good to see you smile."

With one step, she was close enough to smell him. The earthiness and smoky residue from last night's campfire couldn't hide the scent of bergamot that identified him. She put a hand on either side of his face and touched her lips to his.

"I've missed you," he said, before taking her lips with a hunger that made her knees weak.

When he released her mouth, she laid her head against his chest. "I've missed you too."

Dara bounded around impatiently until he bumped against Briana hard enough to separate her from Brath.

"Guess it's time to go." He laughed.

They remounted, but not before Brath stole one more kiss. Twirling his finger overhead, he cued the warriors, who fell into formation.

They crossed the brook easily before turning in to deeper forest. The water sounded louder as they moved farther away from the brook.

"That makes no sense. We've just left the brook and yet the sound of water is getting louder."

"Patience, wife," Brath said, leading Ruark along a narrow trail through a dense copse of trees. She ducked a few odd branches before coming out of the trees beside Brath. He pointed below them, toward a natural amphitheater watched over by a ring of boulders covered with moss and lichens. The tributary they'd just crossed forked into a small river whose main flow fell into a hundred-foot waterfall that dropped in rippling silver sheets into a pool. Water spilling onto stone echoed across the forest.

"Oh, Maker, that's gorgeous!" she exclaimed. "The source of the river and this waterfall is a lake a little farther north. Maybe we'll hike up there one of these days."

At the top of the falls she could just see a familiar purplish color.

"There's a faerie tree!" She pointed. "Let's go check it out."

"We will, but I want to show you something first, through those trees." He pointed to a stand of birches separated only by the hint of a path that meandered through them. Her eyes first noticed the movement of a buck with his doe meandering along the side of the ampitheater's bowl, but then something else caught her attention and stole her breath. In the middle of the forest stood a structure of wood and stone, a cross between a mini-castle and a hobbit house. The dwelling, adorned with an abundance of small windows and turrets, a timeworn wooden door and stone chimney, was surrounded by ferns, mosses and a smattering of tiny woodland plants. A waterwheel turned in the stream that flowed from the falls. Pure enchantment.

"Kailen's Castle?" was all she could manage.

"*Your* castle, my lady."

"I don't know what to say. Thank you seems wholly inadequate."

"The look on your face right now is more than enough thanks. Come on, let's go in."

She paused. "What about the—" She couldn't finish the question as the faeries she'd meant to ask about were gone. All except Captain Aya'emrys. "Where'd they go?"

The captain spread his hands around the forest, where hundreds of tiny golden sparks floated amidst the trees. "We will still be here protecting you, but you will not see us."

"Don't you need to eat or something?"

Aya'emrys offered her his odd, not quite human smile. "We will fend for ourselves. Your husband can manage quite well from here on, but if any threat presents itself, we will appear instantly." He bowed and began moving away.

She looked at Brath. "This is crazy stuff."

Aya'emrys was now a shimmering gold dot that wafted into the forest.

Briana and Brath made their way down the path to the door of the castle and tied the horses to a post. She noticed a small paddock that looked new.

"I'll explain that later, come inside," he said, as he pushed open the carved wooden door. She walked into *her* castle and was overwhelmed once again by a great room where kindling stood ready next to a large stone fireplace, logs and peat blocks neatly placed and waiting for the strike of flint. Or magic.

"Care to try your magic here?"

With barely any effort she blinked and sparks lit the dry tinder. In seconds the fire was burning and the smell of dry oak welcomed them home. She grinned at Brath with a little shrug. "What can I say?"

While she explored the main room, he filled pots of water from a barrel and hung them near the fire.

Looking out a window, she noticed a stone sluice that ran from the waterwheel through the castle's wall into the large barrel next to a copper sink. A tight-fitting stone plug in the sluice, just a few feet away from the wall, stopped water from coming into the house when it was not needed, probably to keep the barrel from overflowing. Once the plug was removed, water would flow easily.

What an ingenious method, she thought.

A handhewn and polished oak table and four carved chairs sat at one end of the room, a couch at the other, covered with thick blankets and a smattering of colorful handsewn pillows. A tall, wide window on one wall offered a magnificent view of the forest. Near the kitchen, a smaller fireplace served as a cooking hearth and the heat source for that end of the castle. She found a well-stocked pantry, everything needed to set up housekeeping and Brath said there was a cold cellar outdoors, behind the castle.

"Brath, this looks like someone set things up for us. How is that possible?"

"Let's just say it's faerie magic," he replied mysteriously. "I'll need to hunt, but we've meat enough for tonight, thanks to the fish."

She looked around her and then at him, shaking her head. "I can't believe it."

"We're not done." He took her hand and led her up an ornately carved set of stairs. Examining the staircase and railings on the way up she was delighted to see faerie history carved into each step and the branches that made the railing. Scenes of battles, images of faeries and a king, presumably Kailen, sitting on a throne. Evalon, the faerie realm, appeared as a hill leading to the soul-reflecting pool. Other symbols—crows, a sword, the Uisneach Tree, tall standing stones, a cat, arrow, and mouse—depicted elements of the prophecy. At the top of the stairs she found an image of the Runes of Evalon, held lovingly by Catriona as she entered the magic oak tree. This was her genealogy, carved by her ancestor's own hands. She studied the carvings carefully, caressing the lines and images. Her eyes grew moist.

"This is supposed to make you happy," Brath teased, wiping away the single tear that had slipped down her cheek.

"Oh, my Maker, it does, Brath. It's fantastic. Hey! I think I found a clue to the Queen's Pool! Look here." She ran the tip of her finger along the carved image of the very waterfall that she'd seen just outside the castle. Somehow Kailen had carved the image of a pool behind the falls, with the jeweled ring she now wore superimposed over it.

"Well, maybe our needle won't be so hard to find," he said.

"I wonder if this is the meaning of the line in the prophecy, 'when two worlds collide'?"

"Possibly. Faerie world and human world, through you." They spent a few more minutes appreciating the extraordinary carvings.

"Ready to see the rest?" Brath asked.

She grinned and nodded like a kid being asked if she wanted to open another present under the Christmas tree.

At the top of the stairs a balcony diverged to connect three rooms along three sides of the castle, the railed edge overlooking the great room. He took her into the last two rooms first. Light filled charming spaces that contained no furniture or decoration. Then he led her back to the first room and she sucked in her breath. The turret room was completely furnished with a large bed graced with a thick colorful quilt and fluffy pillows. On one side of the bed was a neatly piled bundle of blankets—Dara's bed. Dara circled around and fluffed the blankets to make it his own. On top of a small table was a hand mirror and brush. Inside the armoire she found a few dresses, tunics and trousers hanging on pegs. A small fireplace would provide enough warmth during the cold nights here.

"Is there anything the faeries didn't think of?"

"I hope not. If we don't have it, we don't need it. But before we settle in, I should take care of Banrion and Ruark."

"This is incredible," she said, following him back down the stairs. "Incredible and magical. Brath, I don't know how to thank you or Grampa Kailen."

"Your pleasure is thanks enough, my love," he replied, kissing her hand before turning away to lead her back outside.

My love? She was grateful that he looked away and missed her reaction to the endearment. Her insides turned soft at the idea that he loved her. Not only loved but, despite her impulsiveness, inexperience and mistakes, trusted her. Humbled and speechless, she followed him through the door.

They quickly fed and secured the horses in the paddock. Brath looked up through the forest canopy to the sun, still holding onto the day. "We've plenty of time to explore the falls."

"Don't have to ask me twice," Briana said, already two steps ahead of him.

They followed the stream to the base of the falls where a path edged up the side and disappeared behind the falls about halfway up the slope.

Brath took her hand as they negotiated the narrow, damp ledge behind the cascade.

"Oh, Brath, there *is* something here," she exclaimed, raising her voice over the sound of the falling water. Holding tight to his hand, she drew him through the narrow entrance of a cave. Daylight made little difference beyond the first few feet of the entrance, but the very old and very dry rush torch would change that. Brath produced flint from his pocket.

Dara plopped himself down across the front of the entrance, earning an appreciative pat from his mistress. "Fine. You be the guard."

Briana breathed in the earthy scent of wet moss. The dry rushes caught quickly, illuminating the space. The grotto was immense, with a high ceiling and a floor composed of a singular slab of nearly flat stone. "Oh, my Maker," Briana said. In the corner, a tiny ribbon of water cascaded from a high ledge to a pool of water that in turn emptied into a narrow stream along the side of the wall, finally disappearing into a hole near the mouth of the cave, where they stood. Beckoning tendrils of steam rose from the pool. "A hot spring?" Briana walked to the pool and kneeled, dipping her fingers in. She skittered back when a ripple of green luminescence appeared in the water. "What was that?"

Brath secured the torch nearby and went to Briana's side. He dipped his hand in with no such effect. He frowned, then stood and in one decisive movement, stripped off his shirt. He was stepping out of his trousers when Briana had the wherewithal to ask what he was doing. "I'm going in first to make sure it's safe."

"But…"

Too late. He walked down a few stone steps into the water and waded across. The pool appeared to gain depth as he approached the other side.

Briana held her breath, but nothing happened. Well, nothing but the rush of desire that hit her when her magnificently built husband returned and stepped out of the pool dripping water on the stones beneath their feet. Suddenly, a dip in the pool seemed less desirable than the idea of tackling this man and having her way with him. Something in her expression must have communicated her thoughts.

26

One side of his mouth curved knowingly. "Your turn, darling."

She reached for the hem of her tunic, but he moved her hand back.

"Allow me," he said, his voice turning husky.

She stood still as he lifted her tunic as though lifting a veil from her face. He didn't speak, but the warmth in his eyes and the sound of his breathing spoke volumes about his own desire. Yet he was holding back. At first, she didn't understand why. He held her hand while she stepped out of her pants, standing naked before him.

"Whether this pool holds magic or not, it is a pool of queens because it is an Uisneach queen who enters it," he said softly.

Holding firmly to her hand, he led her in. The second her foot hit the water, the green luminescence reappeared; the farther in she went, the more it spread across the pool. Soon the entire grotto was filled with green brilliance. Tiny candlelike lights magically appeared throughout the cavern. It didn't feel like faerie magic. Of course, Uisneach had magic of its own.

"It's beautiful," Briana whispered, looking at Brath who was staring at her in awe. "What?"

"You're shimmering."

"Oh, that's the faerie in me. It happens when I go to Evalon too."

Brath swallowed convulsively. "I'm not sure what to do with this."

"Well, that's a first. King Brath not knowing what to do. I never thought I'd see the day."

"I'm serious, Briana. You are not exactly human at this moment."

"I do feel odd, like I'm being filled with energy. But I am very human, Brath, and I know exactly what to do."

"What's that?"

She moved through the water toward him and wound her arms round his neck.

"Briana, I don't know. Maybe that isn't allowed here. This seems like a pretty sacred space."

"I'm sure it is *exactly* what we need to do. Someone, something, wants us to consecrate this. I've never been surer of anything in my life."

Wrapping her legs around him brought them skin to skin. "Brath, what could be more holy?"

"You have a point," he murmured against her ear.

The hand that stroked her back moved to coil in her hair and cup her neck. His mouth captured hers, opening it and drinking of her sweetness. When Briana thought she would die of need, he curled his other hand around the curve of her bottom, lifting her tight to his body. Water and skin slid against each other in a natural dance of love.

As though his lovemaking was not enough for her body to contend with, something else was sending currents coursing through her, from head to toe. Power. Strength. Magic. She was a human Vesuvius, ready to erupt. She couldn't breathe so she stole breath from this king who was doing all he could to match her power. He would fail. In this moment, she was the strongest force on Earth or in the heavens.

She felt the change in him. Felt his need reach its peak. That force could be resolved only when the earth gods and goddesses gave permission. Now she understood, it was Uisneach itself guiding them. Brath and Briana held each other in a state of suspension that neither could control.

"I want all of you, Briana. Your body. Your magic. Your heart and soul."

Not our soul, an inner voice contested. Her soul was not hers alone to give.

"I give to you all that I have to give, Brath and I give it freely, for Uisneach. For us."

She heard the words as though from far away, saw the scene as though from inside the looking glass. A smell she associated with meditation rooms invaded her consciousness. Sandalwood. Green from the water flashed and raced around the grotto, spiraling into the center of the king and queen. Heat infused her body from head to toe. The stab of burning pain she felt on her hand seemed inconsequential compared to the rapture Briana felt in her core. Pure energy snaked up her spine to the delta of nerves and fibers throughout her body, burning a path up her torso and neck and wrapping her head in fire. She felt brilliantly alive. Feral. Free.

Brath's gasp stabbed through her dissociated state. He stared at her with what she interpreted as awe.

"Don't let go of me," she said.

"I'm not sure I can hold you."

"Don't let go." He was the only thing grounding her. If he let go, she feared she would erupt into the ethers and never return.

Together, they rode the tempest until she knew it was time to complete this magical mating.

"Now." She let herself go as Brath filled her. Ecstasy bound their cries as the powers of Uisneach were satisfied, the land sanctified by the king and queen. She knew of ancient Celtic rites that included a ceremonial marriage and consummation between the king and the goddess of the land, during which the king pledged to protect the land and its people. For her part, the goddess was the guardian of the natural world. It was she who held the beating heart of the earth in her hands and her power that transformed the kingdom from barrenness to fertility. Was this sexual union a way to receive the blessing of Uisneach as well as to revive the kingdom? Had Uisneach judged them both worthy of such a responsiblity?

Briana fell against Brath's chest, trying to catch her breath. Eventually they moved together to a ledge in the pool, which allowed them to rest in the water, still warm, and luminescent green.

"Brath look at my hand!" She looked down at the back of her hand where she'd felt the burning in the water on her ring finger. The Tuathla ring itself didn't look any different, but winding around her ring finger and up the back of her hand to encircle her wrist was a raised vine-like scar, the color of English ivy. She ran her finger along the length of it. She attempted to remove the band, but it didn't budge. It had fused to her during the power surge.

"What does it mean?" she asked.

He held her hand, turning it every which way to study the pattern and the feel of it. "I don't know, honestly. It's magic. Do you feel any different?"

"This is going to sound strange."

"Really?" he said, glancing pointedly around him and at her face with wide eyes.

She chuckled for a moment, then her voice turned grave. "I know I've been changed. I guess we'll see how at some point."

⁌

Back in the castle, Briana said, "I'll fix something to eat," eyeing the fish on the chopping block, wondering what she could prepare to go with it. She rifled through her satchel and pulled out the assortment of edibles. "You don't suppose there are potatoes or something lying around?"

He bowed to her. "Your wish is my command, Your Majesty. I am very sure there is something in the cellar." He walked out to the cold cellar, the swinging door ushering in a brief blast of cool air that the hearth fire immediately swallowed up.

He returned with potatoes, wild onions and apples. Dumping those beside her, he headed outside again. This time, he returned holding a jug of wine in each hand.

"Outstanding," Briana said, grinning. "Pour us a drink? I was thinking maybe we should take advantage of this time alone."

"Yes, just you, me, Dara and a thousand faerie warriors," he said, handing her a cup and lifting his. "*Slàinte!*"

She tapped her cup to his. "I have a feeling I might have more power. I'd like to practice and see what I'm capable of."

He grinned mischievously. "I'd like to see what else you can do too."

She took a step toward him.

He backed away. "When you don't smell like trout."

She wiggled her hands but paused in mid-air. She couldn't seem to stop looking at this symbol of… of what? Royalty? Magic? It was insanely bizarre, but she had to admit, super cool. *I wonder what the point of it is?*

"I'll hunt tomorrow. Good thing you can cook. Hey, I'll bet you could use magic to have that supper cook itself."

She let her hands drop to her side. "Perhaps, but tonight I'd rather pretend we're a normal husband and wife and cook your meal for you, anyway."

While their supper cooked over the fire, they sipped a red berry wine that didn't have as much finesse as some she'd enjoyed in Maine, but it was hearty and warmed the belly. Conversation was light, devoid of any mention of armies, evil prime ministers, grief or even magical grottos. They sat at one end of a much too large oak table and enjoyed her home-cooked meal and a second cup of wine. She cleared the dishes while Brath poured hot water from the kettle into the copper sink.

"Clever folks, the faeries," Briana commented, as Brath added cold water into the bucket over the dishes.

Briana let the dishes air dry and joined Brath on the couch. The evening passed easily between them, talking about faeries and hunting and whether it was possible for waterfalls to reverse direction, everything but

Lord Shamwa or the war that awaited them outside Evalon. When she yawned, he rose and reached for her hand. "Time for bed, sweetheart."

That endearment made her think of Silas for the first time in hours. He always called her *a mhuirnín*, the ancient Uisneachan word for sweetheart. Her stomach dropped. She followed Brath upstairs, pushing the bard out of her head once more. There wasn't room in the marriage for the three of them. Brath was right about that.

Pulling the quilt over them both, he pulled her close. They made love again and Brath fell asleep. She watched him sleep, happy for the smile that rested on his lips. Eventually she blew out the candle. In the deep dark of night, she allowed herself a few minutes to think of the two men she loved: Silas was sunlight and joy, Brath the moon, dark and moody at times, methodical, the complete opposite of Silas' carefree, creative nature. One brought her soul completion while the other fulfilled her supposed destiny. *They bring out completely different sides of me.* Brath brought out the nurturer in her and inspired her to compassion and selflessness. With Silas she felt secure, loved and playful. She missed the affection and passion she shared with him. *Really? What you just shared with Brath was extraordinary. Admit it, you didn't think of Silas once. Nor should I*, she reminded herself.

She molded to Brath's body, searching for the place where she fit. She matched his breathing and willed her heart to synch with his. Peace and contentment eventually carried her to her dreams.

"Are you going to wake up today?" asked Brath, his voice deep and rich.

She rolled over. Sun now poured its warm rays in through the window, landing with vigor on her face. She stole a glance at Brath, still beside her. "Goodness, I must have slept half the day away."

"Well depends on whose standards you use, but if you don't get up soon, your first meal will be supper."

She laughed. "You could at least have started a fire."

"I thought you might do it."

"Okay," she said, giving him an odd glance as she pushed the covers back.

He stilled her hand. "With magic."

"Ahh. Hmm..." She focused on the nearly dead ashes in the hearth. In her mind's eye, she imagined a cozy peat fire and a warm room. Heat coiled in her chest and sent runners into her arms and down into her hands. She sniffed in the scent of sandalwood and felt a little woozy. Briana forced herself to remain focused despite the surprise she felt. Seconds later, something told her to raise her hand and flick her fingers toward the fireplace. Her finger warmed along the new scar and the stones of the faerie ring sparked. Flames appeared around a few peat bricks. Briana dropped her hand.

"Very nice, High Lady. I can see that being married to a faerie will have some advantages. I'll never have to get up in a cold room again."

"Only part faerie, but yes, if this is any indication of what I can do, magic is awesome!"

As the room warmed, they talked about strategies for dealing with Shamwa.

"There must be some way for you to get control of the Dar Morch."

"I think I need to talk to Teaguen about it. Which means I need to get to the faerie tree."

Brath groaned and pulled her close. "I hate it when you do that. You look practically dead when you go to Evalon, and the last time you came back in tears."

She didn't comment. They both knew she came back upset because she learned Silas would be leaving Uisneach.

"Well," he sighed, "might as well get up. If I expect a hot meal tonight, I best go find something to cook."

"What I wouldn't give for a slice of cold pizza right about now."

"What's pizza?"

She explained.

"It sounds good," he said, removing his arm from beneath her and getting out of bed. "However, the best I can do is maybe a rabbit or squirrel. Or if I'm lucky, a willing deer will offer itself for supper." His voice took on a huskier tone as he watched her slide her naked body out of bed. Quickly she reached for the dress hanging over a chair and put it on.

"I was thinking that I should work on the animal magic more. They could be valuable allies if we could communicate better," she said tightening the laces on the bodice of the dress.

"If you're intent on talking to animals, you might want to come over here. This owl seems to have something on his mind."

Briana joined him at the window. "Good morning, sir." She hoped her greeting was acceptable to the raptor.

"Evalon will be pleased to see you," he said, before lifting off in a flurry of pewter and white feathers.

"Well then," she said, turning to Brath, "now I really do have to go."

"I suppose you do," he replied grimly, and headed out of the room.

She followed him downstairs. While she poured tea, he produced some of Moira's scones. Just the sight of the delicious cakes made her mouth water. "Where'd you get those?" she asked, delighted.

"Kept a few in my pack. I figured the rest of the troops would have them fresh when they got back to the castle."

They ate slowly. He seemed to be in no hurry to leave her.

"Your eyes," he said, staring.

"What's wrong with them?"

"Nothing. I just keep marveling how they change. The other day, when you were mad at me, they were like the blade of your sword. When you were crying, they were like the ocean on a cloudy day. Now, they remind me of a summer rain, kind of misty and peaceful."

"Wow, such pretty words. Sure you're not a bard?"

The innocent remark made Brath stiffen. "Well, darling, what can I say. You inspire me." He moved away from the table and gathered his pack and bow and arrows.

"Will you be gone long?' she asked, sorry to have spoiled the moment. "I really do want to get to the faerie tree."

"I don't plan on staying out too long, but I do think it would be good to have some game. A venison stew would be nice tonight, or maybe rabbit. What will you do?"

"Maybe a little more exploring around here. I might clean up some of those hanging vines outside."

"You'll keep Nuada close?"

She was surprised. She'd assumed they were safe here. "Am I in any danger?"

"With Shamwa on the loose, you're always in danger, Briana. Don't underestimate him, ever. Even in Evalon."

"I have Nuada and Dara. And a golden faerie army. I'll be fine."

She moved their dishes to the sink. He came up behind her, putting his arms around her waist. Snuggling into her neck, he whispered, "Thank you for last night."

She turned in his arms and was surprised at how easy it was to kiss him. "Maybe we'll have a repeat performance tonight."

He squeezed her tight. "Or sooner, if the deer cooperate. Please, Maker," he looked to the sky, "bring food quickly so I can get home to this gorgeous woman."

Briana swatted him. "Get out of here, oh great hunter."

He kissed her once more and opened the door to leave. "What the…" he exclaimed nearly tripping over the brace of dressed-out birds laying at the door.

Briana looked over his shoulder and glanced into the woods. "Seems the faeries have been busy."

He lifted the trussed birds. "I guess you'll get to Evalon sooner than planned," he said.

She wasted no time in changing from the dress to breeches and tunic. Brath was waiting just outside the door with Dara. His loyalty to her and Silas had made him wary of Brath, but this morning the wolfhound gamboled enthusiastically around him. The sun was bright in a cloudless blue sky, the air cool. Briana pulled her cloak tighter, keeping the hilt of Nua handy. Her instinct to explore her surroundings and clear out some of the tangled vines around the castle, as well as her attempt to persuade Brath to take the diverging path into the cave, made the excursion to the faerie tree at the top of the falls a lengthy one. It was hand-in-hand in places, but she easily made her way up, proud of how far she'd come since her first days in Wellsland, when the gnomes trained her for just such excursions across Uisneach. Eventually they made their way closer to the small tree. Palpable tendrils of energy reached out to her the closer they got to it. She continued, focusing all her energy on maintaining her awareness despite the dizziness starting to woo her. Bells. Uilleann pipes. Drumming. She felt the pull, the kinship with the tree. Climbing over the last boulder, she sank into the mossy ground next to the tree. Dara whined and sat down next to her. Brath took her hand.

"Are you sure about this?"

She smiled and nodded, then relaxed with a deep breath and allowed herself to be taken into the heart of the tree.

Evalon. The land of ten thousand faerie trees. She sprinted down the stone steps to the lake where she knew Teaguen would be waiting for her. She glanced at herself, expecting the blue dress she wore on her last visit here, only to discover she was draped in voluminous red silk with shiny garnet earrings and a weighty garnet necklace encircling her throat. Cardinal feathers were woven into her braided hair and her toenails were painted the same color of red. No shoes allowed in Evalon, better to feel the moss beneath her bare feet, easier to dance. She waved to the faerie with the short spiky, silver hair and cornflower-blue eyes who waited on a green marble bench.

"Nice dress, Teaguen. Thanks," she said, twirling and loving the feel of the red silk as it swirled around her legs.

"Greetings, High Lady. It is good to see you again."

Briana shivered at the title. She'd never get used to this. Queen in one world, princess in another. *Crazy stuff.*

"I'm happy to see you too." She held out her hand, showing the scar. "Do you know anything about this? Is it from the faeries?"

"Of course. You must have found the Queen's Pool. These are the markings of faerie royalty."

"Do they give me more magic?"

"When magic is fully restored, I suspect you shall find yourself more powerful than anyone in Uisneach."

From across the pond, firefly lights gathered and swirled around in a phantasmic ballet before shifting into more physical forms. Faeries, she had learned, came in a myriad of shapes, sizes and appearances. Some appeared hobbitish, some like the stereotypical beings from the faerie tales of her youth, with a translucent glow and diaphanous wings, and some, she now knew, appeared as giant, golden warriors. In a few minutes, a large group stood around the two ladies. Briana greeted them warmly, many of them by name. Following a short ceremony to formally greet the princess, the faeries moved on about their business, leaving Briana alone with Teaguen. The inspirational music stopped when everyone was in more physical form. The only sound now was the tinkling of the waterfall and the soothing sound of wakes created by giant black swans drifting along the shore of the lake, chatting amicably with one another in swan language.

"What brings you to Evalon, from Evalon?" Teaguen asked with her bell-like giggle.

Briana smiled. It *was* strange that there was the part of Uisneach called Evalon and a whole other magical dimension that was the true Evalon, home of faeries. Only those of faerie blood, who felt the energy near a faerie tree, could visit this enchanted world.

"First, Brath and I wanted to thank you or King Kailen or whoever made all the arrangements at the castle."

"You are more than welcome. We want Uisneach's monarchs to be well and happy."

Briana didn't respond at first.

"Are you? Well and happy?"

Briana sighed. "I have to admit, I am. You, of all people must understand how shocked I am by that little confession."

Teaguen nodded. "I know, High Lady."

Briana waved her hand. "Can we agree to dispense with the formal titles and all, while it's you and I?"

"Of course. As you wish."

"Brath has been so good to me," Briana continued. "I find myself becoming more… fond of him with each day. And he's a magnificent king who loves this kingdom. His determination to govern fairly for the good of everyone is stunning. His strength and compassion…"

Teaguen giggled.

"What?" Briana asked.

"You sound like one who has discovered love."

"Well, I… I just know he's a much better man than I could've imagined and that he can conquer the evil plans of Shamwa and bring magic back to Uisneach."

"With Silas' help. Do not forget, the runes need to be returned and all four treasures safe in Uisneach before magic will truly be restored."

Hearing Silas' name made Briana frown. "I do miss him. And I worry about him."

Teaguen nodded. "It is normal to miss someone you love when they are gone. You cannot *unlove* him. But, you must focus not on what was or will be, but what is. The Wheel of Life is ever in motion, always circling around. It serves no purpose to dwell in the past or the future. Allow yourself to be present for the kingdom and for your husband. There is enough challenge and enough love in this moment to keep you busy. You must embrace and nurture what is happening now. Silas will be fine, and I believe he will be successful in his quest."

Briana nodded. "I know. Silas will always be in my heart. He is a part of me forever. But you were right; love has many faces and I believe there is room in my heart for Brath. I must tuck Silas away for now and focus on my marriage and on the security of Uisneach."

Teaguen hugged her close. "You are evolving and maturing, Briana, and it is beautiful to see. Speaking of Uisneach's security, I believe that has much to do with why you have come here now."

Briana told her about Inis Fáil.

"We are aware of the tragedy. Captain Aya'emrys told us."

"Brath has plans to help the survivors and deal with Shamwa. Did Aya'emrys tell you about the Dar Morch?"

"He did advise us that the Dar Morch has somehow been raised. Tell me, what happened to you in the Queen's Pool?"

Briana told her what she could about the magic, leaving out the personal parts. "I was even able to start the hearth fire this morning using magic. Brath says he'll never have to wake to a cold castle again."

Teaguen giggled. "What man would not wish for a wife who could keep hearth fires lit?"

"Teaguen, seriously, what is the meaning of this scar and the ring?"

"It is a form of consecration, the traditional way that faerie royalty is initiated. It also means you have stronger magic."

"Even though magic is dying in Uisneach?"

"Even with that," Teaguen confirmed. "It may not be consistent because of the loss of the faerie trees and the missing faerie treasure, but you will certainly have more than you would have otherwise. You have been accepted as a faerie princess." The faerie's eyes were bright with excitement.

Briana studied her finger and its new markings, turning it around to see the different angles. "Too bad I didn't have this when the baby was born."

Teaguen's smile faded. "Captain Aya'emrys told us you assisted a woman in birth. I am sorry that the child did not live."

"Me too."

"Something troubles you."

Try keeping something from a faerie. "I'm supposed to be a healer *and* I supposedly have magic. Yet there was nothing I could do to prevent that baby from dying. What good is having the skills and power if I can't do anything with it?"

"Do you think that saving the baby is the only evidence of healing? Of magic?"

"Isn't it?"

"Assuming too much responsibility for life and death is a form of arrogance."

Briana felt herself turn red.

"Tell me, Briana, how have you experienced healing and magic in your life?"

Immediately she thought of Brath's comforting arms around her when she cried through her grief, and of them making magical love in the Queen's Pool. Neither of those involved life-or-death situations, but were, in their own way, healing and magical. With Silas… *Don't go there*, she cautioned herself. Applying the lesson to her experience with Aileen Molloie, she realized that her calm and caring presence was a sort of healing.

"I get it, Teaguen, but sometimes I have crazy power. I was able to bring a dead tree back to life. As hard as I tried, I could not revive the baby. It's not fair."

"The universe does not necessarily behave in ways that are, or at least seem to be, fair. You are simply a conduit. Although you hold the potential to heal and resurrect, everything is born and everything dies in its proper season as ordained by the Wheel of Life. You must learn to trust Maker."

Briana responded with a grunt. "See, this is why I don't go to church. I can't buy into a deity that thinks it's okay to let babies die."

Teaguen placed a calming hand over Briana's. "I did not mean to suggest that Maker would save some and not others. It is more accurate to describe

Maker as a force or energy that holds all within itself and allows each soul to follow its own wisdom and path, for the highest good of all."

"What possible good can come from that baby's death?"

"That is not for us to know. We can only do our best to follow the path we are on. Which you are doing."

Teaguen sat calmly in the ensuing silence, giving Briana time to absorb the insights. Serious thoughts gradually lightened as Briana took in the wonderment of Evalon. The black swans continued to drift by on the glassy lake that changed from royal to turquoise to sky shades of blue, with cotton candy reflections of the pale pink clouds above. Two green- and red-striped snakes glided past, their tongues flickering to each other, oblivious to anyone or anything around them. Orchid bats with silver wings shared space with giant monarch butterflies. A multi-colored heron landed only a few yards from where Briana and Teaguen sat, then squawked and lifted again in a frenzy of color.

"Was it something I said?" Briana laughed. "Oh, that reminds me. This morning an owl showed up at my window and told me to come here. I wondered if, since I can communicate with animals, I could use them to help us get to Shamwa?"

Teaguen adjusted herself on the bench. "Not in the way I believe you mean. Forming military troops would not be possible. Animal communication, even for faeries, is largely based on whimsy, although they always seem to be present and talking when there is a real emergency. You would be well advised to hone your intuition and magic, which you will find are much enhanced from the pool and even more so when near faerie trees and the warriors. Your hands, and the ring, hold power. You should find you can use any elemental to your advantage with the magic you now possess, even without the return of full magic."

"By elemental, you mean water, fire, earth and air?"

"Exactly."

"Well the fire thing has been working out well."

"Water, too. Remember when you looked into the soul-reflecting pool?"

"I've done lots of scrying, come to think of it. Guess water's covered."

"Restoring the tree is earth magic," Teaguen reminded her.

Briana nodded. "I need to work with air."

"Your intuition will be much stronger."

Intuition. Psychic. Telepathic. *No*, she chastised herself mentally. *I will not reach out to Silas*. Better to maintain the barriers as they agreed.

"Teaguen, is there a particular code of ethics I'm bound by in the use of magic? I didn't get any inkling of that at the pool."

"Just the usual rules about not using magic for selfish gain at the expense of another. Never use magic to exact vengeance. Respect the power you carry and do not use it frivolously; well, that one is a sort of gray area. You are not forbidden to have fun or bless another with it. If you always use magic for its highest good and with a heart of compassion, you will not err."

A blue-billed raptor screamed overhead. "Greetings, Tuathla," it screeched as it zoomed by. Briana waved.

"One other question," she asked. "Does King Kailen live here? Why have I never seen him except in Uisneach?"

Teaguen smiled. "I wondered when that question would arise. I wish I knew how to explain better, but I can only say that in Evalon, there are layers of dimensions. This is not all there is. King Kailen is, as far as I know, the only faerie currently able to travel through all dimensions."

"Well, oookay," Briana replied, wishing she hadn't asked. She was none the wiser, but clearly, she would only see King Kailen on his terms. Teaguen was truly the emissary.

"Have you any other questions?"

Briana shook her head. "I better get home to Brath. He'll be worried if I'm unconscious for too long."

"I am pleased to hear Brath's name mentioned so often. I hoped you would bond with him, and it seems you have."

"We are a work in progress."

Teaguen hugged Briana, signaling her departure. Pipes and drums began the anthem that called all faeries to gather and sing blessings as she and Teaguen walked back to the tree.

"Oh," Teaguen exclaimed, claiming Briana's arm and leading her away from the path. They stopped in front of the soul-reflecting pool where Briana had learned much about herself and her relationship with Uisneach. "Let us see what, if anything, has changed."

Briana stared at her reflection in the water. The heart-shaped face and gray eyes were unchanged. The dark ash-blonde hair that had earned her the nickname Mouse remained long and lush, although the wild curls that so often plagued her were now drawn up into braided loops and knots, fit for the High Lady, Tuathla of Evalon.

"I hardly recognize myself," she said, drawing in her breath at the changes that had come over her since her first trip to Evalon.

"Look closer."

Briana focused, took a few deep, cleansing breaths and looked deeper into the soul mirror. "Something is different," she mused. "I've been changed. The pool?"

"The magic may be part of it, Briana, but it is more than that. Accepting the changes in your life and binding yourself to your husband and the goals of Uisneach has matured you and made you wiser."

"There's something else, though."

Teaguen leaned in and her lips bowed into an uncharacteristic frown. "Ah, that is fear. Fear that you must confront and overcome. Your next task, perhaps. Come, dear friend. We must get you back to your husband."

Pausing before the small door in the ancient tree trunk, Briana hugged her faerie mentor once more and thanked her for the advice.

Teaguen touched her face. "I know you have heard it many times, but we all owe you so much for making the sacrifice to save Uisneach."

Briana shook her head. "You know, Teaguen, I've thought about that a lot. And the truth is, I'm not the hero of this story. The real hero is Silas. I would've given myself to him a thousand times, probably ended up pregnant and *unfit* for the king, destroying Uisneach's chance for survival. Had he asked, I would've run away with him. But he never did. He stayed loyal to the prophecy and he is the one who is now risking his life to find the runes. Without them, Uisneach will be lost. If you want to thank someone for saving Uisneach, thank him."

A thoughtful look came over Teaguen. "There is some truth to that. It takes a great deal of courage and commitment to deny oneself something that means so much, for something greater than themselves."

"Enough serious talk," Briana said. "Gotta go, girlfriend. I don't know what's happening on the other side of this tree, but if I don't return soon, Brath will totally freak out!"

The faerie bowed, smiled and waved as Briana turned back to the tree, opened the door and stepped inside.

≈

"Briana. Briana. Wake up. Please, wake up."

She came instantly awake and alert. "Hi." She was lying with her head on his lap. Dara stared over his arm, not the least concerned.

"Hi? That's it? You scared me to death." He continued to stroke her hair and her face gently, as though to assure himself that she was alive.

"I'm just sleeping here, but I assure you, I am very much alive there. I love that place!"

She eased out of his caress and sat up, stretching and yawning. "It's actually quite rejuvenating. Oh, Brath, I wish you could see Evalon. It's lovely."

"Did you see Kailen?"

She tried to explain about the dimensions but ended up failing. "Bottom line—none of us will see him unless he chooses to come to us."

"Hmm. Odd way to run a kingdom," Brath mused, finally calming down. "Can we go home now? You've been out long enough that I'm ready for you to make us something to eat."

She gave her best attempt at a glare. "Where I come from, the wife isn't always the one who has to cook."

"If you wish me to cook I will, but you may be sorry."

"Right. I'll do the cooking."

They headed down the side of the waterfall and didn't speak until they reached level ground. Then she told him most of what she and Teaguen talked about.

"Briana? Promise me you won't go to Evalon unless someone, namely me, is with you to keep your body safe. You truly are vulnerable in that state."

"I'd like to agree to that, really I would. But if I get close to a faerie tree, it's like I'm compelled to go. I may have no choice, even if I'm alone."

He shook his head, sighing. "You'll be the death of me, Briana, surely you will." A shiver ran up her spine. "But, I'll die a happy man."

His grin made her forget everything else. She planted a kiss on his lips and headed for home with him hot on her heels.

❦

"Are you ready to go home to Ard Darach?" he asked, handing her Banrion's reins.

She nodded. "I've truly enjoyed this time, Brath, and I know five minutes after we leave, I'll be wishing we were back, but we need to go after Shamwa and I'm eager to get those wheels spinning."

"By Maker, no one can accuse you of not being committed to Uisneach."

"I love Uisneach. It means everything to me and I will do whatever it takes to rid it of Shamwa's terrorism. However, I think we've accomplished a lot these past few days."

"Me too," he said, wrapping an arm around her waist and kissing her cheek.

"Seriously, Brath. Evalon's updated, we have a plan to go after Shamwa and I've been able to practice magic."

"All kinds, of magic," he said with a wink. "Hopefully, our magic has resulted in a smaller version of us."

Her stomach clenched, but she forced her smile to remain intact. "You're incorrigible."

Dara seemed eager and restless after so many days of lying around, chasing squirrels and eating. He paced back and forth between Brath and Briana. She put a foot in the stirrup but was gently pulled back.

"Wait. One more kiss."

"Brath, trust me, you will get plenty of kisses from me."

"One more kiss *here*. I have no idea when we'll get to come back. Honestly, I wish we didn't have to go and face the real world. I would be content here alone with you forever."

"You would not! You'd be bored to tears, missing your meetings with the knights and planning the next battle."

"Not so, my lady. As long as I have you, I will never want for anything ever again."

She stepped into his embrace and rested her head on his chest. "I hope I never give you reason to feel otherwise." Tilting her head, she accepted his kiss, which began as tender and quickly turned to fire.

"Uh, Brath."

"Hmm…" he whispered against her earlobe.

"We'd better go or we'll have to open the house again."

He looked around them. "Why would we need the house? There's plenty of room to…"

She giggled. "And what do you suppose Captain Aya'emrys and his warrior guard would think about that?"

"Sweet Maker, I forgot about them. Perhaps you best let them know we're leaving."

At the sound of his name, Captain Aya'emrys appeared, transforming from a shimmering light to a very tall golden warrior on his way out of some trees. "Tuathla."

"We're going home, Captain. Are your men ready?"

"We are." Twinkles of light appeared and surrounded her.

"Aren't they going to become, you know, warriors?" she asked.

"If need be, yes. Your journey will be less conspicuous if they remain as they are. If your security is threatened in any way, they will immediately take form."

"Masters of camouflage," she muttered.

"Bloody brilliant," Brath said.

Banrion pawed at the ground and Briana mounted, then took one last look around the castle and their forest hideaway. She thanked the spirits of the land and the faeries for this beautiful home and for the peace she'd found here. She looked up to the top of the waterfall and blew a kiss to the faerie tree, promising in her heart that nothing would ever hurt this place or that tree. With a nod from her, Captain Aya'emrys shifted back to light and moved to the front, leading the way to Dromdara.

CHAPTER THREE

MEANWHILE, BACK AT THE RANCH

While they traveled, Briana had practiced her air magic and while in Evalon, was able to stir up a few minor tempests. However, outside of Evalon, her magic seemed less powerful. As they neared Ard Darach, the warm still air became a light breeze at best.

"The farther away from Evalon we get, the weaker my magic is," Briana said.

"Well, we knew that was a possibility, right?" Brath reined Ruark at the convergence of two paths.

"I thought what happened in the pool would make me stronger."

"It did, Briana, in many ways. Be patient. It will likely take some practice."

Sweat dampened her neck as they rode down into the plains around the castle. Briana winced when they passed the boulder at the crossroads, the site of two separations from Silas; but this time, she said a silent prayer for his safety and moved on. Except for Captain Aya'emrys, the faerie troops floated into the tree line as they came out of the hills. Ard Darach lay peacefully before them. They were barely across the moat when Sigel met them.

"Welcome home. Any success?"

That's a loaded question, Briana thought. The success of this trip could be determined on many levels. She caught Brath's knowing wink and smiled.

Sigel didn't miss anything and rolled his eyes. "Did you find the pool? Do you have any magic?"

"I do, but it apparently comes with conditions." She showed him her hand.

"What in all the Five Blessed Realms is that?"

The aura, as she now called the feeling of shifting consciousness and the smell of sandalwood, began to come over her. *Is there really no warning and no controlling this?* Spotting a barrel of staves nearby, she pointed a finger at the nearest stick and made a motion to lift it out of the barrel. The wood moved, but with such force it knocked the entire barrel over. "Oops," she said. "I don't seem to have a lot of control yet."

The lord marshall shook his head. "We'll need to work on that. In the meantime, there's been a development here."

Briana grimaced, fearing Lord Shamwa had sent his troops to Ard Darach before the Taranian army could make it back from Inis Fáil. "What's happened?"

"Ripparivendar Tollemy was here when we returned to the castle. Apparently, the lad ran away from home and made it clear across Uisneach to help his queen."

As though understanding that there was a new boy to play with, Dara raced under the portcullis and was gone from sight in seconds.

"Sweet Maker, how was Rippa not killed?" Briana said, stunned that he'd do such a thing. "His parents must be frantic!"

"A crow's been sent to let them know he's here and safe. We'll either need to send him home with an escort, or honor his plea to join the king's army."

"He's only ten years old."

Brath shrugged. "We've trained squires younger than that. He made it across Uisneach on his own, and he once saved you from Shamwa's goons. He must have some skills if he did that?"

"Yeah, he can fish, sing, play a fiddle and play with dogs." Briana said sarcastically.

Brath raised an eyebrow. "Perhaps he can replace our bard, at least temporarily."

"He needs to be home with his parents."

"We can't afford to send anyone back with him. Besides, he was lucky to get here without running into the Gray Military. I don't think we should push our luck."

Inside the middle yard, a groom appeared to take the horses. Briana dismounted. Captain Aya'emrys stood silently beside her, awaiting further orders.

"Aya," she started, but the captain interrupted.

"Aya'emrys."

"Yes, of course. Sorry. Captain Aya'emrys, you may stay here in the castle if you wish, so that you would, you know, be handy if we need you."

"I will be ready in an instant should you require me, even if I was with my guards. However, being a part of the staff at Ard Darach on a day-to-day basis might be useful, so I accept your offer."

Briana stared at him, not knowing quite how to respond.

"We'll have Mrs. Flannigan prepare a room for you, Captain," Brath said smoothly.

Sigel pushed open the door to the great hall. In addition to the smells of bread baking, meat roasting, mead brewing and burning braziers infused with pine needles, there was the hubbub of staff scurrying around, bringing refreshment for the king and queen. Gael, her lady's maid, appeared out of nowhere asking if Her Majesty would like to bathe and change into a gown. Emmett Ryan, the king's personal attendant, did likewise for Brath. Both declined. First things first.

The contrast of Jonathan Stark's glorious blonde curls and Rippa Tollemy's black mop caught her attention. They stood side by side in a corner of the hall, apparently already bonded by youth, anxious to discover how the queen would respond to Rippa's arrival at the castle. Dara was wedged between the boys and looked as apprehensive as they did.

"Well, come here Rippa, Mr. Stark," Briana said, using as commanding a tone as she could muster.

The boys stepped forward obediently. Briana turned her attention to Jonathan first. "Mr. Stark, I believe Banrion could benefit from your attention. I'll speak with you later." Dealings with Rippa should not occur in front of his peers.

"Yes, my lady. I mean, Your Majesty." Jonathan Stark turned to go.

She opened her mouth to speak, but Brath elbowed her, so she closed her mouth. The title thing still rankled, but her husband faithfully reminded her to allow staff to follow the protocols they were used to in dealing with royalty. She sighed and turned to Rippa, who stood, head hung, before her. He was barefoot. "Rippa?" He looked up nervously at her and his blue eyes and freckles slayed her. "Oh, Rippa," she repeated. "I'm so glad you're okay, but what on earth possessed you to run away from your home and come here?"

The boy looked toward his king as though wondering if he should answer.

"Speak freely, young man," Brath said, with an encouraging nod.

Rippa inhaled. "Once youz was gone, Pa put me back to work with the crops. I was mizrable jus' tendin' borin' vegetables and such. One day, a group of Grays came to the house an' threatened Ma and Pa if they din't pay taxes to 'em. Not only that, but them bastards—sorry, mi'l—uh, Yer Majesty, took most of our food. I knowed right then that I couldn' stay an' do nuthin'. I wanted to help youz get Lord Shamwa.

"So, one night, I prayed to Maker and knowed what I had to do. I put up a pack with some of Ma's good bread and meat an' headed for the river. I knowed it would bring me to ye. Youz said ye'd give me a job at the castle. Youz said I could be yer protector." He raised an eyebrow at her. "I see ye din't waste no time givin' that job to someun else."

"Rippa, I said that someday you would have a place at the castle. I was pretty clear that you were too young yet and that your parents needed you."

"You said I was Sir Ripparivendar, Protector of the Queen. I kin be more help te youz here, goin' after that evil Shamwa." He thrust his chin forward and met her eyes. "Are ye gonna send me home, then?"

She regarded him, torn between his loyal courage and her belief that he was too young to serve in the army. She looked to Brath, conflicted about her options.

"Young man, if the queen wishes, I believe we can put you to work here," Brath said.

Rippa's eyes lit up. "Thank ye, sir. I told Jonathan ye'd not send me packin'. Youz will have two good guards."

"Hold up, Mr. Tollemy. The queen has all the protection she needs. You'll not serve as a squire to her. However, you have a knack for storytelling, which," he glanced at Briana, "could be *cultivated*." At her somewhat reluctant nod, he continued. "I suggest we assign you under Steward Donnelly's tutelage and train you as bard."

"Hanroi isn't a bard," Briana pointed out.

"But he can help you, Rippa, with learning the ways of court and with Queen Briana's help, you could start learning how to turn the events around you into stories and songs to share with the rest of Ard Darach. In return, we will house and feed you and provide a small stipend each month. What do you say?"

"Sir, Sire, Your Majesty." Rippa grimaced, clearly confused about how to address his king.

"Sire or Your Majesty is fine, Rippa," Brath answered.

"Sir Rippa," Briana corrected. "I, uh, kind of made him a knight when I was in Appleduir."

"You did, did you? Then you must've been sure you were going to marry me and become the queen."

"At the time, I thought I would be." His eyes lit up.

He turned back to Rippa. "I suppose I must honor your promise to our young friend. Sir Rippa, it is. And it is proper to address your queen as Your Majesty or ma'am, not as my lady. She is only *my lady* to me," he said, winking at Briana.

"Yes, Sire. I understan'."

"Good. Now, if you and Briana, agree to this arrangement and if you're willing to accept the terms of being employed at Ard Darach, then we can conclude this meeting and ready ourselves for dinner. Oh, and Steward Donnelly will get you some shoes."

"Brath I'm in *if* his parents are agreeable," Briana said.

Sigel had been standing back silently until now. "Your Majesty," he said, addressing Briana, "if you wish to write a note, I'll see that it gets sent."

"Thanks, Sigel, uh, Lord Marshall Sigel," she replied. They would all have to attempt the formalities in public if the lad was to learn proper etiquette. "I'll do that right away. In the meantime, Rippa, Sir Rippa, you may do as you like. Perhaps go find Mr., uh, Squire Stark, and help with the horses. I imagine dinner will be in a couple of hours and you will need to be cleaned up and dressed appropriately."

Rippa didn't race off.

"Is there something else?" she asked.

"Well, Ma'am, it's just I understan' about the proper way to address ye, but fact is, I feel sort of funny bein' called sir, when I's so much smaller than the real sir's. I don' wanna be disrespectin' of ye, but could ye just call me Rippa, as ye always have?"

"Perhaps in private, but the others must learn you're a gentleman of the realm. They will only do that if we treat you as such." Briana empathized with his discomfort.

"As you wish, Your Majesty," he replied in perfect English before turning and leaving Briana and Brath with their mouths open and Sigel laughing outright.

Dara, apparently satisfied, returned to Briana's side and followed her and Brath upstairs.

⌁

After changing their clothes, Brath and Briana met with Sigel and the knights in the great hall for an update.

Survivors of the massacre at Inis Fáil were being fostered out. Lady Seraphina, Silas' childhood friend and Briana's new one, had taken in the young woman with the three children that Briana met in the tavern. The old woman was settled with another family. The old man occupied a room in the keep. With so few survivors, plans to rebuild the village were on hold.

Crow messengers found no evidence of the Gray Military planning to attack Ard Darach directly. Curiously, small contingents of Shamwa's military were scattered across the kingdom, making it hard for Brath to decide where to focus his attention. Shamwa was back at Aurum Castle, heavily protected by the Gray Military and a protection spell that was most likely enacted by Cailleach's sister, Mother Ealga, the spiritual leader of Shannon Abbey. The added complication of the Dar Morch made it difficult to pinpoint his activities.

"If Shamwa now has more magic at his disposal, it'll be even more challenging to get to him. Briana's magic has been strengthened, but is less strong away from Evalon or the faerie trees."

"We could lure them to Evalon to gain magical advantage," Sir Niall Harkin offered.

50

Swatting at a fly that had made its way into the castle, Brath shook his head. "I don't want to risk having them close enough to Evalon to destroy the trees there. I'd rather meet them elsewhere, like the Plains of Leanach."

"I agree, one big battle, wipe out the Grays, get to Shamwa and end this thing fast," Sigel said.

"We don't have time tonight to fully develop a plan, but one thing is certain. We'll need to leave a fairly hefty troop here to protect Ard Darach and the queen."

Briana's head swiveled in his direction. *What? He doesn't plan on taking me on the campaign?* What was the point of having magic if she couldn't use it to fight Shamwa? Before she could challenge him, he looked at her directly.

"Briana's magic will be useful at some point, but at the moment, it's rather unpredictable. She'll stay here, where she can work on strengthening it."

She gritted her teeth, but if he thought she would accept this without question, he would learn otherwise when they were alone.

Reilly Doherty, the butler, appeared in the hallway. His dignified stance and the ringing of a bell indicated dinner was ready to be served.

"Time for supper, men," she casually announced. Brath stood, giving the men permission to move to their tables.

Others soon filled the room and the sounds of chatter, clinking cups and grunts of culinary appreciation changed the atmosphere from military matters to social matters. Briana was prevented from speaking with Brath by the hordes of people who wanted his attention. She turned instead to Sigel.

"If I'm to strengthen my magic, I need to start sparring. Would you work with me?"

Sigel rubbed pointedly at the scar on his arm, inflicted by their last sparring. "I'm not sure I want to subject myself to that again."

She stared at him defiantly. "You asked for that one. If you hadn't goaded me…"

"I'm teasing you. Why not work with Brath?"

"No. I have to prove to him that I'm good enough to go with you guys after Shamwa. I don't want him to see what I'm capable of until I'm actually capable of it."

"There is plenty for you to do right here at the castle. There really isn't any need for you to go into battle."

"Don't you start. I am not staying home baking cookies while my husband and friends risk their lives. Sigel, please, you said I was a good warrior; will you help me?"

He searched her face. "I suppose I better, or you'll do something foolish on your own. Meet me in the training yard first thing after breakfast."

"Not the training yard. I don't want the others laughing at any mistakes I make. Let's go somewhere more private."

He shrugged. "As you wish, Your Majesty."

⤚ꝏ⤙

The next day dawned pearly gray, the air heavy with the scent and feel of rain.

"What are you doing?" Brath asked sleepily from the bed.

Startled, Briana nearly dropped Nua, which she was starting to slide into the scabbard.

"Sigel is going to spar with me today."

"Is he? Is there a reason you were trying to be out of here before either the sun or I are up?" He rose on one elbow, watching her, looking more amused than upset.

"No. I just want to be ready."

"Bri, seriously, Sigel is not even going to be awake yet. You've plenty of time. Why don't you come back to bed with me for a bit?" Seeing the look on her face, he sighed. "Very well. Let me get dressed and I'll come and have breakfast with you."

She waited quietly, not wanting to make waves.

"I'm not taking you into battle, Briana."

"I didn't say you were."

"I know you think if you can prove your magic is strong enough, I'll change my mind."

"Then what is the point of me having magic?" she countered, her tone rising with her frustration.

"There are endless ways magic can be useful to us, but it is my intention that you use it within the protected confines of Ard Darach. I hope this can be a cut-and-dried campaign that ends quickly with Shamwa's death."

"You can't guarantee that, Brath. I don't want to sit here, twiddling my thumbs and worrying about you."

He stepped in front of her, slipping an arm around her waist and drawing her close. He pushed a stray lock of hair behind her ear and nuzzled her. "So, you would worry about me?"

"Of course, I would." She meant to sound irritated, but the sound trailed off as his lips slid down her cheek to her lips for their first kiss of the day.

Pulling apart, he rubbed the same spot with his thumb. "As I would worry about you in the midst of battle, where I can't afford any distractions. I'm sorry, Bri. It's in our best interest for you to stay put."

A knock at the door prevented further discussion. "Come in," Brath growled. "Sigel, you made a liar out of me. I told my wife you wouldn't be awake yet."

The lord marshall was fully outfitted with weaponry that Briana knew would challenge her. "Yes, well, I thought if I wasn't ready when the cock crowed, the queen would be in my room, pushing me out of bed. When she gets something in her head—well, you know."

"I do," Brath said, running a hand through his hair. "Might as well go see if Moira has anything ready for breakfast yet."

"Come on Dara." Briana canted her head in the hound's direction. "Let's go eat."

Kenna, the kitchen maid, was just setting out bread and a hot pot of tea when they entered the great hall. She curtsied and left quickly to bring out the rest of their breakfast. Dara followed the maid, knowing she was the key to his breakfast.

Conversation revolved around Sigel's plan to combine the Taranian, Winge and Evalon faerie troops into one large army, leaving a substantial unit at the castle for protection. Briana remained silent, still hoping she could prove to Brath that she would not be a liability.

Dara's return and whine at his mistress' side prompted the end of the discussion.

"Well, little warrior, are you ready?" Sigel asked, before swallowing one last drink of his tea.

Briana jumped up and was halfway to the door when Brath stopped her. "Ah, Briana, did you forget something?"

She glanced down at herself and knew she had everything she needed. When she looked up, he was pointing to his lips. She smiled and scurried back to plant a lingering kiss on his lips before following her mentor out the door.

"Thank you, dear wife," Brath called after her.

"Where are we going?" Briana asked, when they were through the portcullis and halfway across the drawbridge.

"There's a spot up beyond the crossroads that you can't see from the main road. We won't be interrupted by any curious eyes. Dara, you'll be lucky not to feel Orion's kick, if you don't get out of the way."

Banrion exhibited her usual extraordinary patience with the wolfhound's eager antics, but Sigel's stallion laid his ears back and snorted as Dara crisscrossed in front and behind them.

As always, Briana sobered at the boulder marking the crossroad. Sigel didn't miss the change in her demeanor.

"We've not been alone since your wedding, so I haven't had an opportunity to ask how you're feeling about things."

Briana considered what to tell him. Determination to be a faithful wife, good queen and technically, Sigel's boss, should guide her words.

"Briana, you're like a daughter to me. We've been through a lot. I respect your efforts to put the past behind you and stay committed to the present situation, but I want to make sure you're as content with your decisions as you seem to be. You may be my queen, but I hope you will always feel I'm someone you can trust."

"Of course you are. I just wasn't sure how much I should say."

"You and Brath seem to be doing well."

Her lips curved, thinking of the past few days. "You can't be surprised by that?" she said, remembering his words of assurance during their journey to Ard Darach.

"Not surprised, but relieved to see it so. You're happy?"

"As happy as a queen who is in the middle of helping to plot a war can be."

"And Silas?"

"Is on a quest and may, someday, return. Or not."

He stared at her.

She met his gaze. "Nothing has changed except that I accept our responsibility to Uisneach and find it not as insufferable as I supposed."

Sigel shut one eye and trained the other on her. "Not insufferable at all, by the looks of things."

"Not where Brath is concerned, though I admit, I miss Silas and I worry for his safety. I'm sure you do as well."

Sigel nodded, thoughtfully. "I pray for the lad every day," he said. He nudged Orion behind the boulder where a path lay well hidden behind the pines. The trees opened into a wide glen with gently sloping hills on three sides. A shallow stream curled beside a flat space in the middle that was perfect for the kind of practice Briana meant to engage in. They tied the horses, then Sigel walked toward the stream. Dara seemed to understand something momentous was occurring and sat on his haunches near the horses, watching them.

"Show me what you can do," Sigel said.

Briana looked around and saw a scraggly, dead shrub. She stood straight, cleared her throat and closed her eyes. Visualization seemed to enhance her magic. Painting her inner vision in shades of red and orange, she called up images of flames. There was no accompanying aura, but she continued to focus her energy on fire. Something was raising in her, different from the aura, hopefully something she could use. Opening her eyes, she pointed her finger with the faerie ring at the bush. It sputtered and sparked before bursting into a small flame.

"Not bad," Sigel commented, moving toward the burning bush to extinguish it.

"No, wait!" Briana had an idea. Turning to the nearby stream, she visualized the water gathering itself into a ropelike stream that rose out of its source. Repeating the action of her finger, she guided the hose of water to the fire and dowsed it. She released the vision and the water dropped to the ground.

"Bravo!" Sigel looked truly impressed.

Briana was warmed by his praise. Success encouraged her to look for something else to do.

"Find something to use as a weapon," he said.

Briana chose a hefty bough, recently departed from its mother yew tree. "What do you want me to do with it?"

"Can you make it attack me on its own?"

She bit her lower lip and stared at the branch in her hand. Again, using the power of her mind, she willed it to fly at Sigel's leg. Tree energy vibrated in her hand for a few seconds before pulling out of her grasp and whizzing away, far too high to strike his legs. Sigel jumped sideways but not far enough. The thick end of the limb clubbed his shoulder. He swore.

"Oh, Sigel, I'm so sorry," Briana said, hurrying to his side. He waved her off, rubbing his shoulder.

"Give it another go," he said. "You almost had it."

"Are you sure? Maybe I'm not ready."

"Of course, you aren't ready. That's why they call this practice. Do it again, only focus more on the aim."

She retrieved the stick, stepped back and brought up the same image. "Strike true," she chanted in a whisper before opening her hand and letting the branch fly. Sigel looked prepared to protect any part of his body and Briana grinned as the branch seemed to be projecting in the right direction. Without warning, it reversed on itself and boomeranged back in Briana's direction, whizzing over her head as she ducked to avoid the direct hit.

Sigel laughed outright. "Oh, ho! Your magic plays fairly. Let's try something different. See those vines?" he pointed to a ropey vine twisted around some elder bushes. "Maybe you can get those to travel to me and bind me up."

"I like that idea. And then I can torture you for every mean thing you've ever done to me."

He put a hand to his heart and frowned. "What mean things have I done to you?"

"Let's see, there was the time you goaded me into fighting you in front of all the men."

"You needed to get your anger out."

"There was the time you yelled at me for kissing Silas."

"Well, that was wrong of you."

What started out as joking was quickly fueling Briana's ire. She began to truly imagine the vine wrapping itself around the lord marshall. "And let's not forget you telling me that Brath was going to kill us if he found out, so you sent Silas away."

Sigel's expression grew serious. "You both needed to cool off," he said firmly. "You were acting dangerously."

"Except that I asked Brath about that and he said he never would've killed us." Her mind filled with the image of Sigel, bound and begging for mercy. She pointed. Nothing happened.

Sigel stood with his hands planted on his hips, smirking. "Maybe your magic doesn't work when you're using it to get revenge against your friends."

The teasing light was returning to his eyes. Briana lost the fuel for her own anger as well.

"Maybe I need spells or rituals for some of this."

"I can't help you there," he said, walking toward her. "That's Cailleach's expertise." He pulled his short sword from a scabbard. "I'm going to attack you and I want you to evade the strike using nothing but your mind."

"What if I fail?"

"Then you'll be stabbed, sliced or otherwise maimed."

She took a deep breath and focused on all parts of him at once. She needed to anticipate his move and visualize herself jumping out of the way. The first one was easy. She saw his hand tighten on the grip and his left leg shift. The blade would come from his right side. She jumped to her right as he jabbed at her.

"Good," he said, jumping forward with barely a breath. She visualized herself jumping backward. Her body was propelled back so fast she hardly had time to screech as she hit the stream.

Sigel laughed hysterically as he reached a hand down to pull her out. "Are you hurt?" he asked, wiping tears from his face.

Dara was at her side, sniffing her all over.

Briana rubbed her backside. "And if I was, would you still find it funny?"

"Nah," he said, clapping a hand on her shoulder. "Lesson learned—know your environment."

Banrion's whinny distracted Briana from the next maneuver. Sigel's sword glanced off her arm. She was relieved to see no evidence of injury and looked to where the horses were tied. Nothing seemed to be amiss, but she did notice the darkening skies.

"It looks like rain."

Sigel nodded. "We should head for home."

"Before we do, I watched you jump on Orion without using stirrups. That would be a useful skill to have in battle. I want to learn how to do that. Surely magic could help me there." Before Sigel could argue, she untied Banrion and led her away from the tree. "Stay put, my lady," she instructed the mare. Stepping back several paces, she focused her attention and breath and took off at a dead run. She told her legs to leave the ground but instead of flying into the saddle, she slammed into Banrion's side, rocking the horse on her hooves and dumping herself unceremoniously onto the ground.

Almost afraid of what she'd see, she turned to find Sigel standing with his arms crossed over his chest, biting down on his lip to avoid laughing.

"Don't even…"

He raised hands in front of him.

Briana stood and dusted off her breeches.

"Enough for one day, Briana. We should go back before it rains or you kill yourself."

"One more try," she said, already getting into position.

"As you wish, Your Majesty." He stepped back, leaned against a tree and hooked one leg in front of the other. "Give it a go."

Briana gathered her wits, closed her eyes and saw herself flying onto Banrion's back. She felt the air underneath her and visually swung her leg and… she opened her eyes just as she left earth and flew—not onto the mare's back, but completely over it. *Thud!* The landing pushed all the air out of her lungs, making it impossible to cry out. She lay still only as long as it took to regain her breath and assure herself she wasn't broken. Sigel was at her side by the time she was on her feet. She pushed him back.

"I just overestimated. I can do this." She limped back to her starting position as the first plops of rain fell. Sigel looked at her with a grimace, Dara with a look of encouragement and Banrion with a look that said, *Enough already!* Briana went through the visualization again and ran toward Banrion. Up, up and *thunk!* Her bottom met the saddle perfectly. She threw Sigel a victorious smile. "Okay, now let's go."

✧

She barely had time to change into dry clothing before Gael entered to tell her lunch was ready.

"Have you seen the king?" Briana asked her lady's maid.

"He's been sent for, ma'am. I believe he's been in the stables this morning."

Briana and Dara entered the great hall at the same time as Brath. Even coming in from working with horses, he looked as though he belonged on the cover of GQ. Did he never get dirty or mussed?

"How was the practice?" he asked, pulling her chair back before sitting down at his own.

Briana had been contemplating what to tell him. She didn't want to lie, but she also wanted to instill confidence in him. Sigel entered just as she was about to answer. He gave her a game look.

"Well, Briana, how do you think it went?"

"Thank you, Reilly," she said to the butler as he set a basket of bread between her and Brath. "I'm happy to say that we made some progress. I didn't feel any aura today, but with some adjustments, I was successful with a few things. I am now able to jump on Banrion without stirrups."

Brath glanced sideways at her while slathering creamy yellow butter on his bread. "Isn't that more a skill of horsemanship than magic?"

"Well, when you're as short as I am and your horse is tall, it takes a fair amount of magic to accomplish the feat."

Brath paused, staring at her. She evaded by buttering her own slice of bread. He turned to Sigel. "So, it was a successful session?"

He started to speak, and Briana used her eyes to plead with him to say something positive.

He finished chewing before answering. "Everything with Briana is magical. This was no different."

Nice answer, Sigel.

"Thank you, Sigel."

"That's terrific, Bri." Correctly reading her hopeful expression, he added, "I'm still not taking you into battle."

She started to argue, but decided silence was the better part of valor and took a sip of her wine instead. "What have you been up to?"

"I spoke with the smithy about your idea of metal armor."

"You did? Can he make it?"

"He might. He'll have to work out what kind of metal should be used and where we can get it. He'd like you to draw him an example."

"I will do that, right away. Thank you, Brath. I think it could be a lifesaver for our army."

The hall was filling with people. Jonathan and Rippa came in together, laughing. The knights took their places and began feeding their appetites without diplomacy. Artanin appeared in his usual silent, eerie way. Conversation was a blend of male bravado, political opinion and bets on who could fart without the queen knowing who'd done it. This she assumed she was not meant to hear. She did, however, have other senses that alerted her to the offender's general direction.

The sound of rain grew louder. Most everyone drifted off to their rooms after the noon meal ended, except Brath, who remained in the hall to talk with Emmett Ryan about Ard Darach's financial status.

Briana gave Gael the afternoon off and shooed her out of the room. When the door was closed behind her lady's maid, she gathered a dish of water, a candle and settled herself in front of them. Forcing the tension, aches and noise of the day out of her muscles with deep breathing, she stared at the water and created an intention to communicate with Cailleach. Seconds after she called the woman's image up, she was there, her silver hair and kind eyes staring back at Briana.

I need you, here, Cailleach. Bring spell books if you can. She repeated the thought a few times before allowing the image to fade. The effects of relaxation lingered, leaving her in a reflective mood. Magic was becoming more and more a part of her being, even if it was yet imperfect. But what was her purpose in achieving proficiency in magical skills? To fight Shamwa? That went without saying. To secure power over the Dar Morch and either turn him to her side or send him back from whence he came? Yes, that would be an excellent use of magic. But that kind of paranormal power could potentially do so much more. She could connect with Silas. Ahh, that would be wonderful. They already possessed the kind of magic that could cross time and allow them to communicate or even make love. Guilt infused her cheeks. *Stop it,* she berated herself. *We made a promise not to use the telepathy.*

Forcibly shoving Silas out of her mind, she transferred the romantic possibilities to her husband, calling up images of making magically enhanced love with him behind the waterfall. Heat traveled from her cheeks to below her waist. Making love in the queen's pool was awesome. *Yeah, right, making love with Brath anywhere was awesome.* That line of thinking created a dilemma. While she was totally into sex with her husband, she still worried about getting pregnant.

Hearing voices outside, she went to the balcony and found Captain Aya'emrys and Sigel deep in discussion, oblivious to the steady rain falling around them. She caught a few muffled words—strategy, warriors, magic.

Magic! Of course! Why hadn't she thought of it! She needed Aya'emrys to train her, not Sigel! Grabbing a cloak, she raced out of her room, nearly tripping over Dara, hoping to catch him before he disappeared somewhere.

Jonathan appeared out of nowhere as she left the great hall. "Where are you going, Your Majesty? Wait up, I'll go with you."

Briana saw Sigel coming toward her and the faerie warrior walking away toward the middle yard. "Aya'emrys," she called out, trying to stop him before he got too far. "Not going, anywhere, Mr. Stark," she shot back at her protector, dismissing him with a wave of her hand.

"How am I supposed to protect you if you never let me stay around you?" he complained. He stopped following her, but remained nearby, watching.

To Sigel's questioning glance, she said, "I just want to ask Aya'emrys something." She pulled the hood of her cloak up against the rain and joined the captain.

"I need to talk to you," she said. "About magic. You said you could teach me how to use it."

"Let us move out of the rain," the golden warrior suggested, taking her elbow with an unexpected lightness for a being of his size and power. Once they were under the protection of the walkway's roof, she told him about her fiasco with Sigel.

"Do you know why sometimes this ring works and sometimes it doesn't?"

"No, I do not. Whatever power that ring holds is for faerie royalty alone. Only another princess or a queen might have the answer."

"Well then, would being near a faerie boost my abilities in the same way being near a faerie tree does?"

He was quiet for several minutes. His response, when it came, was not what she expected. "You are a faerie, at least partially, so I believe the magic is already within you. You are putting all your faith in the trees, when what you need is faith in yourself and a bit more education in the mental craft. A few trustworthy spells would not hurt either."

"I've summoned Cailleach to bring books."

"That is a fine beginning. You also need a faerie mentor. I think that is what you are asking of me."

"It is. Will you help me?"

"Of course, Tuathla. I am at your disposal, although I would recommend waiting until the skies have stopped blessing us with all this water."

She squeezed his arm. "Thank you, Captain. Maybe tomorrow. Come, Dara, let's go find the king."

Briana couldn't get used to the absence of Silas' music and storytelling during dinner. Rippa was not near ready to take his place, though she'd heard him singing to himself when he thought no one was around. Much of his time was spent tagging along with Donnelly, learning the ins and outs of castle life. It was quiet in the hall tonight. She caught snippets of conversations but suddenly understood what it meant to be lonely in a crowd. Brath and Sigel were deep in conversation about how they might capture Shamwa. Sir Jameson and Jonathan were huddled over a game of ríocht. The other knights wandered in.

The scent of herbs and spices wafting in from the kitchen was the only thing remotely soothing about the hall tonight. Briana's mind wandered to thoughts about how she might best Shamwa, assuming she ever got the chance to challenge him. She barely noticed Moira Flannigan, the head cook, and her assistant Fionn enter the great hall laden with covered trays. It wasn't until one of the trays was set before her that she realized it was highly unusual for Moira and Fionn to deliver meals themselves. The cook was beaming as she stood in front of her queen and lifted the cover from the tray. Briana became aware of the silence around her and looked to see

Brath staring at her, a strange, hopeful look on his face. Briana looked to the tray and her hand flew to her heart.

"Pizza! How on earth… Brath?"

"I did my best to explain it to Mrs. Flannigan. It appears you were successful, Moira. Thank you."

"Yes, thank you," Briana echoed, barely able to refrain herself from attacking the Uisneach version of her favorite comfort food. "And thank you," she said, turning to Brath and planting a kiss on his cheek. "I can't believe you did this."

"You'll have to show us how to eat it," hollered Sir Faolin McPhee, looking at the pizza from every angle.

"You can cut it into bites, or…" She ripped off a piece from the pie and bending it slightly, bit into it. She closed her eyes and moaned as the herby cheese and tomatoes filled her mouth and her senses.

"Can you possibly chew that any more?" Sigel teased her.

"Oh, my Maker, this is to die for. Oh, Brath, how can I ever thank you?"

He winked at her wickedly. "I'll think of something."

They ate leisurely, everyone except Rippa, who practically wolfed his food and then, picking up his fiddle, began to play a lively melody that changed the whole tone of the room.

"He catches on quick," Sigel commented, wiping stringy cheese from his beard.

"I'm telling you," Briana said proudly, "he's a natural entertainer. He told me he was practicing at home, knowing he would never be big enough to be a warrior, but *reckoned* he could be a bard."

"I'm becoming more convinced he's the boy for the job," Brath said.

"It's a sad day when a child has an easier time getting in the king's army than a fully grown and magically enhanced queen."

Brath leaned into her. "I would hate to lose a single man to Shamwa, but the loss of the woman who keeps my bed and heart warm and who will bear the next king of Uisneach would be devastating." He nipped at her ear before sitting back in his chair, focusing on Rippa.

As Rippa effortlessly moved from music to storytelling, Briana and Brath held hands under the table and shared intimate glances. Suddenly, Briana had a shameful idea. What if she could use magic to persuade Brath to take her on the campaign? Not by showing him she had magical battle skills, but what if she could use sexual magic to convince him he couldn't go anywhere without her? Cailleach's words about the appropriate use of magic sounded a warning in her head: "used for one's personal advantage, it can result in unimaginable heartache." *Yeah, but she also said I might be called upon to use magic that might seem like interference, but is really part of the plan.* She slid a sideways glance at her husband and formulated a plan.

Catching Doherty's eye, she motioned him over. He leaned down and she whispered, "Could you have Moira send a plate with some of the leftover pizza to our chambers? And a jug of wine?"

The butler tried and failed to hide a grin. "Of course, Your Majesty, as you wish."

She forced herself to sit through Rippa's story about her abduction before forcing a loud yawn. "My goodness, I'm tired. Brath, if you don't mind, I'd like to go up to bed."

He stood. "Certainly. I'll go with you."

She had a moment of panic; she needed time alone. "Oh, no, please stay. Ask Rippa to tell you about when he first met me." She kissed him quickly and left before he could ask any questions. Dara, realizing his mistress was about to leave him, barked and bounded to her side.

Briana saw Gael standing near the door to the upper floors and twitched her head subtly upstairs.

When they were behind the closed door of Briana's chambers, Gael burst out, "Okay, what are you up to?"

"We need to hurry before the king comes. Find me the sexiest nightgown I have." She snorted, "It shouldn't be too hard." She had images of Victoria's Secret in her mind, but what Gael handed her was more like something from the Vermont Country Store. She wrinkled her nose. "Where's the chemise I wore under my wedding gown?"

Gael opened a trunk and rifled through the contents. Finding the undergarment, she handed it to Briana, who undressed and slid the fabric over her body. *Well,* she thought, *it ain't Paris, but it's probably the closest thing to sexy I own. At least it has laces on the front. That's useful.* "Remind me to have Donla make a visit soon. I need to do something about my frumpy lingerie."

Gael answered the knock at the door and took the tray from Kenna, the kitchen maid. She arranged goblets and wine on the small table, then turned down the bed. Briana brought out the ríocht set and staged it on another table near the fireplace. Looking around the room, she nodded. Everything was ready. "Thank you, Gael. I think I'm set."

The girl smiled innocently. "If you'd like me to come back and…"

"Uh, no, that won't be necessary. Good night."

Gael chuckled all the way out the door.

Briana took her place at the ríocht table and adjusted her position so that the chemise hiked up her thigh, revealing a long, toned leg. Looking down at her chest, she pulled one shoulder of her chemise down, revealing not only her shoulder, but a generous portion of her bosom. *That's what I'm talkin' about*, she thought. "Dara, go lay down. This has nothing to do with you." With an affronted shake of his hairy body, the wolfhound padded to his bed, circled a few times and plopped down with an insulted grunt. All that was left was to take some centering breaths and invite the magic she wished to use into the space. With the magic came a warming, not of her hand but of other parts of her body to the point she feared she might have to go downstairs and drag her husband back here.

Footsteps announced his imminent arrival. Inhaling and exhaling deeply, she pretended to be focused on the board in front of her. The sound of the door opening and closing sent a ripple through her belly. Butterflies. Her neck tingled when he pulled back her hair and leaned over to kiss her. "I thought you were tired?" he whispered against her goose-bumped skin. She felt her nipples harden to diamonds. *Who's working the magic here?*

"I had a second wind and felt like a game of ríocht," she said huskily.

"Is that so?" He ran his teeth slowly up each vertebra on her neck.

She sucked in her breath. "Won't you have a seat."

"Sure," he answered, taking his seat. He studied the board.

She wished he hadn't agreed so quickly, but bit her lip and forced herself to visualize the magic she meant to create.

Each made a few random moves, accompanied only by the sounds of sputtering candles, crackling fire and their breathing, growing heavier with each move and glance at one another.

Brath leaned back in his chair. "Is that a nightgown?"

She narrowed her eyes and didn't answer. Instead she stood and walked around the table to his side. His look dared her. Holding his gaze, she lifted one leg over his lap and straddled him.

"It's like that, is it?" he said, adjusting his position. She felt the effect she was having on him. His hands moved up her ribcage to the soft curve of her breast and stroked the fabric that barely covered her.

She pulled out one lace and heard him sigh. Another lace loosened and he stared at the swell revealed beneath it. One more and she watched his eyes dilate and heard a faint moan. "Do you like what you see?" she asked, attempting to sound sultry, thinking maybe she sounded ridiculous.

"Very much," he whispered, as he pressed his lips to the tender flesh she was exposing ever so slowly.

She pulled away slightly and he frowned. When he moved toward her, she shifted back as though to get off him. His hands gripped her waist and pulled her back. "You may be powerful, but I'm stronger."

"Define power and strength."

He paused momentarily and shook his head. "Maybe you are more powerful. You have totally bewitched me, Briana. I can't imagine my life without you."

She rewarded him by moving in again, deliberately adding pressure to the slide. He sucked in air. She leaned in, allowing his mouth access to what she had just taken from him. His lips and teeth explored every curve they could reach, reducing her to a quivering mass. Both were breathing fast and hot. If she wasn't careful, she'd forget the purpose of her seduction. He gave her a dreamy-eyed look.

"Just to be clear, I know what you're doing here and although I am a willing victim, your manipulation won't change my mind about taking you with me."

She sighed and gave in to her own raw desire. "Well, I sure as hell don't want to stop now."

❦

Aya'emrys waited patiently in the middle yard. Dara automatically moved out of the way. Jonathan Stark had once more been asked to stay back. He wasn't happy, but Briana wanted privacy and reminded the squire that she was well protected by the faerie captain. *I'll have to find some opportunity for Mr. Stark to be involved. He's becoming rather sulky lately.*

"Okay, Captain Aya'emrys, I'm ready." She withdrew Nua from her scabbard.

"You can put that away," he replied. "We'll be working with a different weapon."

When Nua was secured again, he led her to a tree stump in the middle of the ring. "Much of your power comes from within. Centering and focus is critical."

"I have been doing that."

He nodded. "I hope to help you go deeper." He sat down on the stump himself and pulled her in front of him and raised her hands to settle on either side of his head.

Instantly she grew dizzy and subsequently agitated.

"You are faerie, High Lady. This power is yours as well." He pulled her hands away and traded places with her. The disconnect momentarily reduced the intensity of sensation, leaving a cold void. Moving behind her, he placed his hands on her temples. A deep thrum started underneath his hands, the low vibration travelling to every fiber of her being, creating a power surge that nearly knocked her over.

"Relax. Breathe in our combined energy. Do not resist. Breathe."

She forced her body to calm and follow the stream of energy. Bands and swirls of color whirled inside her, filling her with energy. She knew each by its name. Intuition. Intention. Grounding. Power. "Ahh…" Slowly, Aya'emrys removed his hands so that the energy she was using was all hers.

"Focus on a single wild rose in that bush," he instructed. "When you are ready, direct a stream of power toward the flower with the intention of destroying it." At her sound of distress, he reassured her. "Do not fret. You will restore it to perfect health."

It was half an hour before the pink petals drooped and then fell limp against the thorny bush in its death throes. Regret welled up and Aya'emrys seemed to know it.

"Sorrow will not revive the plant. Use the same energy with the intention to heal and you will see what happens."

Briana gathered her thoughts and imagined what the rose had looked like in bloom. She imagined the sweet smell and the pollen that beckoned to the bees. Time ceased to have meaning as she filled her heart with the sole intention of reviving the rose. Before her eyes, it lifted slightly and then a bit more. Flat, brownish petals plumped and pinked and then the rose was as perfectly beautiful as it had been before she killed it.

She was drenched in sweat and felt weak. Aya'emrys moved beside her. She leaned into him.

"At first it will leave you depleted," he confirmed, "but as you grow more adept, it will be less draining. Remember that the magical stores must be constantly renewed."

"How do I do that?"

"Eat well. Get enough rest. Spend time in nature, especially around faerie trees."

She giggled, and the faerie warrior frowned. "I'm sorry. I'm just surprised it's that simple. I've heard that advice all my life in terms of generally taking care of myself."

"That is precisely the point, High Lady. Magic is intrinsic to your nature, but is supported by a sense of well-being. I recommend that as much as you may be tempted to practice this on a constant basis, you must pace yourself." He paused and looked around as though trying to remember something. He smiled, and Briana was awed by the transformation. His usual bland robotic appearance became more human and warmer, making him quite handsome. "Using magic empties the well. Do things that will replenish the well."

"I've heard that too, Captain. Thank you. I promise to follow your advice."

His advice was quickly forgotten when they came across the full regiment of men practicing battle skills in the training ring. Briana and Aya'emrys made their way to stand near Sigel, who was directing the war games.

"Archers, step forward!" the lord marshall ordered in his deep, commanding voice.

Jonathan Stark joined six other men in a line. None of the knights were particularly expert in archery, so they stood back to watch with respect.

"Raise your bows."

At once, all bows were lifted into position.

"Arrows nocked!"

To a man, they were proficient in pulling an arrow from their quiver and setting it in the longbow.

"Loose!" Sigel bellowed. Seven arrows flew to the targets. Sigel inspected the marks. "Well done, Mr. Stark."

The action was repeated several more times and each time, young Jonathan Stark hit closer to the bull's eye than any of the other men.

"Well, Mr. Stark, it appears you've been practicing."

"I have, sir," he said. "I haven't had much else to do lately," he grumbled, looking pointedly at his queen.

"Enough for today. The rest of you men best put in a bit more practice if you don't want this *boy* to show you up again."

As the group disbanded, Sigel walked toward Briana and the captain. "That young man is going to give Silas a run for his money."

Briana nodded. "I hope he gets the chance," she said quietly.

Brath entered the training ring. His knights gathered around. "Hope I didn't miss sword practice," he said, pulling a short sword out of his belt and swinging it in perfect arcs in front of him.

"Nearly so, but the archers were on time, so they went first," Sigel said, giving the king an accusatory look, which Brath ignored.

"Briana, want to spar with me?" he asked, wiggling his eyebrows.

She smiled at his boyish enthusiasm. She was glad to see his playfulness despite the dire circumstances they were all in. His good humor went a long way to lifting everyone's spirits. He had an innate ability to use authority and camaraderie in proper measure, just one of the reasons he was so beloved and respected.

"No thanks, I'll sit this one out. I've already had my training session."

He meandered over and hooked an arm around her waist, drawing her next to his body. "I can teach you things Aya'emrys never can," he whispered in her ear. "You recall the last time we sparred?"

She did and nearly swooned again at the memory of him trapping her against the wall with his body and his sword. Her temperature rose several degrees, which must have been apparent in her face.

Brath chuckled and stepped back before bowing deeply to her. "Very well, my lady. Another time, perhaps."

"Perhaps," she croaked in a voice barely above a whisper.

"If you're done flirting with your wife, Your Majesty," Sigel said, "perhaps *we* can start training?"

Briana watched as the men sparred one-to-one and then in small groups with short swords and longswords. *This might be a good time to practice my protection spell*, she thought and mentally walked herself through a process that would cloak each man in a protective shield. It wasn't until Sigel nudged her that she realized the men were helplessly flailing their weapons in the air and no one was able to make a direct hit.

"Oops." She immediately released the spell.

Brath jabbed his longsword into the ground and leaned on the pommel, looking at Briana. "Helpful, love, but not enough to buy you a spot in the army."

She glared at him. *Oh, why can't you just disappear?* No sooner had the thought risen than she felt heat shudder through her hand and heard the ground crack next to the king, dangerously close to his foot. Brath jumped back to avoid tripping into the small crevice. His eyes grew nearly as wide as the crack that threatened him.

Briana paled, and her hand flew to her mouth. "Oh, my Maker, Brath, I didn't mean…"

"Now, that kind of magic might be helpful," he said, his mouth split in a shocked grin. "Imagine opening the earth big enough to swallow the entire Gray Military!"

CHAPTER FOUR

GOBSMACKED

Silas, Brennan home, Camden, Maine

The smell of earth and pine mixed with something heavier and less pleasant tickled Silas' nostrils. Birds warbled from leafy branches. A dog barked in the distance. This forest looked disappointingly like Uisneach. *Damn it. I didn't make it through.* He turned, expecting to see the gnomes and Cailleach standing next to the magical oak tree. He was alone. The door he'd come through wavered and then disappeared. He looked down at the front of his breeches, certain his balls had retreated into his bowels.

Whirring overhead, like the sound of a giant eagle flapping its wings, caught his attention. Instantly, his bow was up and an arrow nocked. His eyes bulged at the big black thing that flew across the sky. It didn't seem to be a bird, exactly, but he had no idea what it was. His throat went dry. Could the thing see him? Would it come after him? He held the bow steady. The noise faded as the monster passed by. He leaned against a nearby tree and took a breath.

Briana had tried to prepare him for what he would find in her hometown of Camden, Maine in the twenty-first century—if this was her world. Truth was, they didn't know for sure where he'd end up. Scuffling in the leaves drew his attention. *Ah, a wee chipmunk.* The familiar creature was comforting, as was the *caw* of a crow in an old oak. The sun's position told him it was mid-morning. Briana had said that if he came out in the same place she entered the tree, he should find a stone wall and follow it to a road. Her home would be across the road. It was a strange description she'd given of the place and he hoped he'd recognize it.

His heart raced as he shouldered the longbow and readjusted his rucksack. *Which way?* She said her home sat in the shadow of a small mountain, Mount Battie. The terrain behind him traveled up to a rounded shoulder of a hill. Supposedly, there was a tower at the top. He headed in the opposite direction. Sparse grasses and a few wildflowers carpeted the forest floor, served by a small army of bees, buzzing at their work. It wasn't long before he saw a stone wall and an open space beyond. A hard, black surface ran in a straight line. He paused. Was this the road she described? He stepped over the stone wall and started onto the black road when a loud sound and a stinky smell made him look up. A monster was speeding toward him. His heart flew into his mouth and he jumped back, nearly falling over the stone wall.

"Sweet Maker!" *That must be a car. No way could Briana prepare me for this!* He took a deep breath and straightened his spine. *Buck up, lad, she gave you far more preparation than she had comin' to Uisneach.* Looking both ways, he saw nothing else coming and tried again. Once he was on the road, he could see a dwelling on the other side, sitting beside a small stream in a grove of trees, surrounded by shady gardens and a well-constructed stone wall. He paused a moment, listening to the babble of the stream and the tinkling as something that hung from a tree moved in the breeze. *Quack. Quack.* He searched and found the pair of ducks on a small pond. It had to be Briana's home. It looked just as she'd described it. *No wonder she's done so much so soon in the garden at the castle. She's very good at this.* His heart swelled with pride at her creativity and hard work.

A few more steps and he was standing in front of a grand cottage that looked nothing like either Cailleach's cabin or a castle. A petite woman knelt in a garden, digging around some flowers with purple petals. She glanced up at the sound of his footsteps on gravel. The sight of her took his breath away: same dove-colored eyes, small features and bow-shaped lips. *Briana.* Or rather, Briana as a mature woman. *Beautiful.* He was in the right place and this was Katrina Brennan.

He knew he must have presented quite a sight in his Uisneach clothing, leather breeches, tunic and boots. *Good thing Cailleach suggested I leave me sword behind. I'd probably send this poor woman screamin' into her house if I were carryin' that!*

To her credit, she didn't panic. She smiled gently and stood, almost as though she'd been expecting him.

He put a hand up in a gesture of peace. "I mean you no harm, Mrs. Brennan."

He could see her trying to work out what she was seeing, but she didn't move a muscle.

"I'm a friend of—"

"Briana's," she said, her voice shaking slightly.

"Yes. May I speak with you?"

"Of course, Mr. ...?"

"Silas," he said, stepping forward and offering his hand, as Briana had instructed.

She slid off a floral- and butterfly-patterned glove and extended a small, graceful hand.

"I'm sorry to startle you, comin' out of the woods like that."

"I'm not startled." Her eyes continued to study him with curiosity. "Where's my daughter? I can feel her all over you."

Warmth curled in his belly at the thought. "That's a long story, but she's relatively safe."

Katrina's eyes narrowed and her hand flew to her chest. "Relatively?"

"Well, at the moment, she's likely battlin' Lord Shamwa, but I know King Brath will protect her." He couldn't hide the tension that he felt at that.

Her eyes narrowed to slits. "Battles? King Brath? I have all the time in the world to hear about this."

He nodded, adjusting the bow on his back. "Aye, and I mean to tell you all, but do you suppose I could trouble you for a cup of water? Me throat is sorely parched."

"Of course. Follow me."

She bent down to pick up her gardening tools and dropped them in a basket along with the gloves. Silas was reminded again of Briana, digging in the gardens of Ard Darach. Katrina had lighter hair and was obviously older, but Briana definitely took after her mum, in looks and in the graceful way she moved. Silas followed Katrina up the stone walkway leading to the place Briana had called home, so different from the homes of Uisneach. It was made of wood, he guessed, not stone, although it was gray, as was the roof, made of something other than thatch. Windows of different sizes were trimmed white. It had all kinds of triangular projections and several doors, two that attached at a cocked angle to the house with much wider openings. The stone walkway swept past a few blooming bushes and through four slender pillars to a large, white door which Katrina pushed open. Silas' eyes adjusted to the lower light of a walled entryway.

"You can set your things down there, for now," she said, pointing to a bench.

He was taken into a spacious room, flooded with natural light from many windows.

"Have a seat, Silas, and I'll get you a drink." She indicated a couch behind a low wood table upon which sat an arrangement of colorful flowers. As he lowered himself onto the furniture, he grabbed at the arm wondering if the couch was sturdy enough to hold his weight. It was. Katrina was gone from the room before he relaxed enough to take a breath. *Soft. Comfortable*, he thought, adjusting to the unfamiliar cushiness of the modern bench. His fingers stroked the textures of the small pillow next to him. Suddenly, his breath caught in his throat when he spied an image of Briana on a nearby table. She was sitting in the middle of a garden, her lap filled with cut flowers. Her eyes lit up and her smile suggested she knew he was looking at her. He was up in a flash and went over to the likeness. *How is this possible*, he thought, lifting the framed object and turning it over and around. *I thought I would never see her again, and here she is.* He swallowed hard. Hearing a sound behind him, he turned to find Katrina entering the room with two see-through containers of water. He quickly wiped the tear that had formed at the sight of Briana.

"That's one of my favorite pictures of her," she said, handing him the cold container, before sitting on a chair opposite him.

Picture? "How the bloody hell did you get her in there?"

Katrina studied him. "Where are you from?" she asked reluctantly.

"I come from Uisneach."

"Ireland?"

"Uh, no. That's me destination. You may find this difficult to believe, but the kingdom of Uisneach is on the other side of a tree in the woods across from your house."

Katrina stared at him blankly. She stood again and walked to a sideboard, picking up another container holding an amber liquid that he hoped was whiskey. "I think this is going to require more than ice water." She poured and handed a clear cup to him, her eyes raised in question. He accepted the drink and smelled it. The heady smell of barley delighted him. "Ah, whiskey. Thank you, Mrs. Brennan. Just what the healer ordered."

"Please, no more Mrs. Brennan. It's Katrina."

He chuckled. "Why doesn't that surprise me? Briana hates bein' called milady or Your Majesty." His smile wavered as the royal title rolled out of his mouth. "She tried to make me promise I'd never call her that."

"Your Majesty?" Katrina repeated.

"Aye, she's the queen of Uisneach, married to King Brath of the House of Taranian."

Katrina's eyes grew round. "What! You're kidding me!"

He nodded, "No, it's the truth, though I really ought to start at the beginnin'."

"Silas, does this have anything to do with an old woman with silver hair who was dressed like a witch? She visited me the day Briana was born."

He grinned. "Cailleach! Yes! Exactly! Do you remember about the prophecy, then?"

"I remember there was a prophecy, but I never knew what it was. I was supposed to tell Briana about it, but there never seemed to be a good time and to be honest, I didn't know what to tell her."

"Ah, so that's it. She wonders why you never said anythin' about it."

Katrina sighed deeply and started to pour more whiskey.

He held up a hand to stop her. "Gettin' drunk so soon after meetin' Briana's mother would be the height of poor manners."

"Do you think so?" She laughed with the same musical sound he'd heard from Briana a million times, winding his stomach in knots.

The light had changed drastically and the decanter and glasses, as they were called, were half empty. The spirit seemed stronger in Briana's time; he felt a bit woozy. He also had to piss in the worst way. He and Katrina had both been so absorbed in his story that neither had moved, eaten or relieved themselves in several hours.

He leaned forward awkwardly. "Katrina, I hate to be improper, but could you direct me to the privy?"

"Privy? Oh, the bathroom. God, Silas, I am so sorry. You have been drinking and talking for hours. I imagine you do need the bathroom. And food. I'll show you to the bathroom and order delivery pizza."

"Pizza! One of Briana's favorite foods."

"All food is Briana's favorite," she said, with her musical laugh.

"Aye, the woman does enjoy her victuals."

He followed her down a hall to a small room of unfamiliar appliances, colorful textiles and an assortment of mysterious things. He studied the three largest objects before him. "Let me guess: toilet, sink and bathtub," he said, pointing to each respectively.

Katrina nodded.

"Briana tried to teach me all the things I would need to know." He leaned over to get a closer look at the toilet. "I believe I'm to do somethin' with this each time I use it."

Katrina took in a deep breath. "This is going to be interesting," she muttered. "Okay, then. When you're done, you know," she made a wild gesture with her hands that he interpreted as doing his business, "you flush the toilet by pressing down on this handle. Then," she moved to the sink and turned on the water, "you wash your hands here, but be careful that you don't get the water too hot and burn yourself. Then you can dry your hands with this towel." She paused. "We'll deal with the shower later. One thing at a time, I think."

He managed the toileting procedures without any difficulty. When he returned to the living room, Silas heard her talking to someone about pizza. He took the opportunity to look at other photographs of Briana. She was a cute little girl. One image showed her on horseback in some kind of competition. Her expression held the same determined spirit he'd seen on the battlefield and at her wedding. A picture of her in a black cap and gown showed a young woman ready to embrace whatever her future held. *Little did she know.* The one that moved him most was of her sitting under a tree with a book in her lap. She was gazing off, lost in thought and unaware that she was being photographed. Was she thinking of her red archer? Longing for something that eluded her? "Ah, Briana, *a mhuirnin*, I miss you so," he whispered to the framed image.

"She was so beautiful," Katrina said quietly beside him.

"She still is," he said wistfully.

"You love her."

It was not a question, but it gave him the opening to share his grief with someone who might understand.

He faced Katrina, meeting her eyes. "I love your daughter with all me heart and soul."

"Does she share your feelings?"

"She married another man," he said, knowing he must sound bitter.

Katrina didn't respond, but held his gaze as if waiting for more. He realized how unfair that was and sighed. "She said to tell you that you were lookin' at the man who held her heart in his hands." He looked away.

"And yet, she married another man."

"Well, she had to. The prophecy foretold her savin' and marryin' the king."

"So she had no choice?"

He looked at the photo again. The longing in her eyes was evident. That longing hadn't been for a king; it had been for the red archer, the bard. "If not for the prophecy, we would have married and I would've been the most blessed man in Uisneach."

"Then she doesn't love Brath?"

He paused and sighed again. "If she doesn't already, she will. He's kind, smart, handsome and completely besotted with her, of course. I could never blame her for fallin' in love with him. I want to hope for it and be happy for them both, but..." he trailed off helplessly.

Katrina put a hand on his shoulder. "I don't know about this King Brath, but I know my daughter and I can tell you that I can't imagine anyone more suited to her than you, Silas. I believe she meant it when she said you held her heart. I hope that's some consolation."

He looked at this woman who might, under different circumstances, have been his mother-in-law. "Thank you, Katrina." Being around her, a constant reminder of Briana, would be hard. Perhaps he would get to Ireland quickly. Suddenly, he remembered it hadn't been so long since the woman's own husband died.

"Briana told me about your husband's passin'. I'm sorry for your loss, Katrina."

Sorrow passed like a shadow over her face.

"You must miss him terribly. I know Briana misses her father." He paused. "Although I suppose Sigel has kind of stepped into that role for her."

"Sigel?"

They talked until the pizza arrived and Katrina showed him how to eat it, both with utensils and his hands. He chose the latter and wolfed down three slices before Katrina had finished her first.

"I guess I was hungry."

"So, while you're here looking for these magical runes, Briana is trying to do away with this Shamwa character. Is she in any danger?"

"Well, I suppose she is—everyone is, as long as Shamwa's drawin' breath. Brath will do all he can to protect her, but knowin' her, she won't make it easy. Oh, did I tell you the part where she killed several men savin' me life?" He watched Katrina grow pale. "Sorry, but she did, and got herself a nasty leg wound."

Katrina set her plate down, her fingers shaking.

"Oh, she healed up fine, not to worry. Cailleach is a skilled healer. I have to say though, Briana didn't think much of bein' laid up. She fought Cailleach tooth and fist to get out of her room and one night she... What's wrong, Katrina?"

She held up a hand. "I'm having a difficult time imagining my daughter on a battlefield, killing men, sustaining horrible wounds and arguing with witches. Could we, for a moment, fast-forward to how we help get her out of there?"

Silas leaned back against the back of the couch.

"Get her out of there? I don't believe she wants to leave Uisneach."

"Of course, she does. Briana is not a soldier or accustomed to living in primitive circumstances. I imagine she would be quite happy to be saved, brought home, marry you and have lots of grandchildren for me."

Her pale face, wringing hands and tremulous voice indicated a rising level of distress. Should he ease up on the details of Briana's life in Uisneach, or help her confront reality? Deciding no useful purpose was served by hiding the truth, he leaned forward and took her hands.

"Katrina, I know this is all shockin' to you. Briana said it would be. But if we are to help her, the best thing we can do is find the runes, and to do that, you'll have to accept the fact that Briana is not only a capable warrior, she is a queen. She was offered the chance to return here and rejected it." He let that sink in.

"She chose not to come home to me?" The words came out in a whisper.

"She chose to accept her destiny and save a kingdom."

"As the witch said she would."

"Aye."

The only sound in the room was the whirring of something Silas couldn't identify but had heard since his arrival, and the ticking of what Katrina had told him was a timepiece called a clock. He stayed silent, understanding that the entirety of what he'd told her was just now hitting her. He allowed her the time to grasp it.

Finally, Katrina spoke and Silas heard the same determination in her voice that he had heard in her daughter's when she decided to marry Brath and accept her role in fulfilling the prophecy. "Well, then, you'll stay here until we can figure out how to get you to Ireland. My parents live there, so you'll have a place to stay, but there are legal implications of getting you there. Unless of course, you have some magical means of getting to Ireland without identification and a passport?"

"I don't understand half of what you just said, but I don't have any magic."

She rose from her chair and reached for the empty plates. "I think that's about enough for one night, Silas. I am, as my father would say, gobsmacked, and if you aren't feeling the same way now, you soon will be. I think it would be best if I showed you how to operate a shower and got you settled in Briana's bedroom." She motioned Silas to follow her to the kitchen. The whirring sound he heard earlier came from this room.

"What is that sound?"

It took Katrina a minute to determine what sound he meant. "Oh, the refrigerator." She spent a few minutes showing him the basics of a kitchen.

"You can't learn everything in one night." They moved to the bathroom, where she set out towel, washcloth, soap and shampoo. Looking at him, she nodded. "You'll want to shave I expect, and I have nothing here for you to use. I didn't keep Edwin's razor. Tomorrow we'll go into town and get clothes and whatever other personal items you need. Now then, you turn the water on first and adjust the temperature where you like it. Then…"

Silas jumped back when the water came out of the nozzle in a torrent. "Katrina, you've a bloody waterfall in your privy! And you say it's warm? I'd be tempted to use this every day."

Katrina chuckled. "Yes, Silas, we usually do." She turned the spray off.

"Use this to wash your hair," she instructed, pointing to the bottle of Pantene. Setting her hands on her hips, she looked around. "I think that's it. You should be all set."

When she left, closing the door behind her, he shucked off his clothes and faced the shower. Turning the handles as she'd instructed, he marveled again at the power of the water coming out. He stepped in and let the water sluice down his body. *Amazin', but maybe a bit too warm.* He studied the device, trying to remember which way to turn it. *I think it's this way.* He turned it and then shrieked as hot water hit bare skin. He grabbed the towel and flung it around his waist, holding onto the edges with one hand. He threw open the bathroom door to find Katrina on her way down the hall. She halted, her jaw fell open and her faced turned a raging shade of red.

"I can't turn the hot off," he blurted. "I was nearly scalded. Can you help me?"

She seemed frozen.

"What is it, Katrina?"

She shook her head. "Nothing. Nothing. Silas, you can't just walk around like that."

"Can we please set decorum aside for a moment and focus on the fact I was nearly boiled alive? I'm covered up, Katrina. Would you please just help me?"

She waved him aside. "Never mind, I'll show you again." She quickly showed him the adjustment. He heard her mutter on her way out, "Some things you just can't unsee."

When he returned to the living room, it was filled with light, but he saw no candles or braziers, only a few decorative objects that seemed to produce light without fire. Katrina was sitting calmly, writing something down on paper. Without looking up, she asked, "The heart necklace you wear—is that about Briana?"

"She gave it to me." *Two hearts together, unbreakable.*

Katrina continued to stare at the paper.

"Katrina, I'm sorry about…"

She looked up shaking her head. "No need. It just took me by surprise, that's all." She inclined her head to the warrior bones at his throat. "For what it's worth, I'm glad she found love, even if it came with pain. 'The course of true love never runs smoothly.'"

"I suppose not. What are you writin'?"

"Well, if the only thing we can do to help her is get to Ireland and find these hidden, magical runes, then I need to make a list of everything that needs to be done. Do you have any idea where the runes are and how long it will take to get them?"

"No idea whatsoever. It could be a week or a year. All I know is that the druidess Catriona supposedly hid them on the Hill of Uisneach in Ireland. Even that is more legend than fact, but it's as good a place to start as any."

"Do you think so?" She nodded slowly. "And this Catriona is my grandmother?"

"Briana believes they are one and the same."

"I just can't understand why, if she was, she didn't tell Mum about the runes. Or maybe she did. I'll find out in the morning when I call."

"Call?" Silas bit his lower lip, thinking, then snapped his fingers. "Ah, yes, the telephone. Can you not call her now?"

"Anxious to get started, are you?" At his nod, she shook her head. "Not so fast, nor will it be easy. First, I can't call her now because in Ireland it would be about one o'clock in the morning. There's a time difference." At his look of perplexity, she waved a hand in the air. "I'll explain that later. Secondly, Silas, you have a gargantuan learning curve. Let's say, worst-case scenario, it does take a year to find the runes. You have to live in this world, and in order to do that, you have to learn about this world. That is going to take some time. I have a lawyer friend who used to work for the department of justice in the witness protection agency. Robert might be able to help us get you an identity."

"I believe I have an identity. I'm Silas of Cedarmara, Royal Bard to the House of Taranian in the kingdom of Uisneach."

Katrina stared at him a moment, then smiled slightly. "Well, Silas of Cedarmara, that may be so, but here you will need a real last name, a birth certificate and a passport, none of which can be obtained with the information you just gave me. We have a lot to do and I suspect you will need to remain here with me for a while before we can even get to Ireland and start looking."

"How long?"

"A month or two."

He groaned.

"Don't worry. You'll be busy. The time will fly by."

His response was a huge yawn.

"Tired? I bet you are. I am, too. Let's get you settled in Briana's room. You can get your bow and backpack and store them in there."

He followed her down the hall again, grabbing his belongings on the way. Entering Briana's domain raised the hair on the back of his neck. Apparently, it was kept just as she'd left it, the slightly crumpled bed where she must have slept the night before entering Uisneach, a backpack slung carelessly over the back of a chair, her guitar leaning against a bookcase filled with the books she treasured, and the photos and trinkets she'd collected. *She's here, all around.* He searched for the figurines she described to him and found them arranged as if on a battlefield, the queen well-defended by warriors and… the red archer. He picked the figure up, turning and examining it. Yes, he could see the blonde hair underneath the helmut. He smiled.

"I doubt Briana would even remember this, but when she was a little girl, she used to tell me that she was going to marry a man with long blonde hair."

"She remembers."

"You are the spitting image of the man she described to me as a child. I often wondered about that, especially given what Cailleach told me. She kept a journal and after she… left, I read through it; she'd kill me for that, but I needed to see if there were any clues to her disappearance. I don't believe she had any idea she was leaving. However, there are hundreds of drawings and dream reflections of that archer… of you, Silas. Somehow, she knew of you."

Have I ruined everythin' for us by comin' here? For the millionth time, he reminded himself that if they were meant to be together, Maker would find a way. He ran a hand through his hair and replaced the archer in front of his queen.

A strangled noise from Katrina spun him around. The first tears she'd shed since Silas' arrival made a sudden appearance, Tears wet her cheeks, the first she'd shed since his arrival.

"Katrina, what is it?"

"Oh God, I miss her."

Battling his own sorrow, he put his arms around her, hoping that it wasn't terribly imprudent of him to do so. "I know," he said. "She misses you too, very much."

"Will I ever see her again?"

He rested his chin on the top of her head. "I don't know, Katrina, if either of us will see her again."

"How could you have left her?"

There was no accusation in her voice, only concern.

"I had to go. Not only was it impossible for her to move forward as Brath's queen with me in the way, it was killin' me to watch her try. Besides," he said, attempting to lighten both their moods, "someone had to come and get the runes that will save Uisneach. If I'm successful and go back a hero, well, she'll wish she'd married me!"

His ruse worked. Katrina giggled past a sniffle and stepped out of his embrace. "Thank you, Silas. Sorry to cry all over you. Now I'm really acting like Briana."

He laughed. "Katrina, she believed she could communicate with you through magic and that you would get messages through your wee cards. Do you think you could get a message to her, or at least to Cailleach, that I've arrived safe?"

Katrina put a finger to her lips thoughtfully. "There have been moments when I thought I was getting something from her. I'll try."

Silas picked up one of the figures and sighed.

"It's hard to know what to say to you, Silas. I suspect we both need time to process this, but I'm glad you're here and very glad to know that Briana has found such a deep love in her life. I cannot believe that God will let this just evaporate as though it were nothing more than morning mist on the garden. There will be a happy ending here. There just has to be."

"That's a lovely thing to say, Katrina, and I hope you're right. Briana and I have talked much about happy endin's and our hope that we'll have one. In the meantime, thank you for everythin', milady. I understand now why Briana's the way she is. Well, except you aren't quite as, uh, emotional."

"She is a bit of a drama queen sometimes."

They laughed as she wished him a good night and left the room. Thinking about Briana, he wandered around her room again, seeing little things he'd missed before. He picked up her guitar, a Gibson J-35 that her father had given her on her thirteenth birthday. He experimented with the instrument, different from what he was used to. Strumming soothed him, and words arose to the melody he found. "Surrounded and protected by the guardians of time." *My Maker*, he thought, *something in her knew—knows, and she doesn't even know she knows*. He looked for other clues of what she knew. A book with "Songwriting Journal" handwritten across the front caught his attention. Flipping through the pages, he was enchanted by her words. He jerked in sudden recognition of one entry:

> "Across the veil a sign appears
> A hero's call to arms...
> A journey made from future times,
> To ancient royal mound.
> Raising sword with steady hand,
> To prophecy she's bound...
> Pick up your shield and make your stand
> For home and kin, now we strike."

"It's true," he whispered. "We really do share somethin' that makes us think along the same lines." This was a song he'd also written some years back in Uisneach. He and Briana sang it as an anthem and call to arms when they were traveling across Uisneach. It was how they discovered their gift for what she called telepathy.

Feeling the weight of fatigue settle over him, he set the instrument down, slid into her bed and turned to stare at her picture. The feeling that she was there with him was so strong; he could smell her, for Maker's sake. True, she had spent her whole life in this room—of course her scent, her energy, would be all over everything. He turned off the light and pulled the covers up over him, allowing himself to relax into the feeling of her. Words to another song began to form in his mind:

"Come closer, Briana, and lay by my side
Let me tell you I love you, deep into the night.
Let your magic surround me, till dawn's early light
One body, one heart, open, nothing to hide."

He stared into the darkness. *What would happen if I let me wall down? Would I find yours already fallen, Briana? No, it wouldn't be fair. We promised we wouldn't. We didn't promise not to think of each other, though.* He imagined her beautiful face, her long, silky hair, her strong, lean body and delicate breasts. His pulse quickened. He felt her next to him, her head tucked into his shoulder, her small fingers tracing the tattoo on his chest. One hand went to his necklace, fingering the place where the two warrior's hearts were connected. *Good night, Briana.* Peace replaced longing as his soul travelled to the ethers where they were once reunited as one.

CHAPTER FIVE

A BRAVE NEW WORLD

Silas woke to the sound of several voices that seemed to originate in Katrina's living room. What had happened? Had she had a change of heart and called someone to come and remove him? He lay still, trying to make out the words, but none of the bits of conversation he heard made sense. *Political will… Congressional failure… The US is ending a weapons ban concerning Vietnam… Severe weather hits Kansas and the Midwest. Tornados possible…* Music cut in and then he heard, *Ladies, if you want your man to get and keep an erection…* His eyes went wide. What on earth was going on out there?

He jumped out of bed and into his breeches. Quickly pulling on his tunic, he took a deep breath and opened the bedroom door. Creeping around the corner of the hallway, he was relieved to find the living room empty of people. It took a couple of seconds to realize this must be the television Briana spoke of many times. He stared, horrified, as a woman wearing practically nothing pulled a man into her bed just before the image changed to a little, round blue tablet. *Good Maker, have these people no shame?*

He heard Katrina's voice in the kitchen.

"No, I'm not afraid. I trust him, Mum. I don't believe there's a malicious bone in his body. He knows everything about Briana and clearly loves her."

She stopped talking but there was no answering voice. He drew his eyebrows together.

"Yeah, he's handsome. He's very tall, has this amazing long, blonde hair and eyes the color of the ocean. He dresses like, well, like a hunter from an ancient kingdom? Like an old soul. What? Mother! He's Briana's age! I don't know, that's the only way I can describe him." Her description ended with a chuckle. "Best not tell her about him coming out of the shower," he heard her mutter apparently to herself. "Nothing, Mum."

One side of Silas' mouth curved up. *Why is she talkin' to herself that way?* A pause.

"Yeah, he sounds Irish but swears he's from this place called Uisneach. You're sure your mother never told you she was a druidess who was married to a faerie?"

He put the pieces together. *Ah, she must be talkin' on the telephone.*

"Well, I know, but something like that… Do you think so?"

Not wanting to eavesdrop, Silas tried to focus on the scantily clad woman and shirtless man cavorting on a bed in the box.

"Just like I never told her about the witch coming to the hospital room when she was born. I certainly regret that. She must've been terrified. God, part of me wants to go in the woods, find this tree and go get her."

A longer silence.

"I know, Mum. Well, the bottom line is that I need to figure out how to get him legal and on a plane to Ireland. I think Robert might help with that. Thanks for being willing to have him stay with you when he gets there. I'll keep you posted."

A cupboard door shut.

"I love you, too. Give Da a kiss from me. Bye, now."

He heard a click, the sound of something being poured, and then soft footsteps in his direction. He stared at the screen and forced a yawn.

"Good mornin', Katrina," he said brightly when she entered the room holding a cup of something in her hands, tendrils of steam rising and swirling up around her face, which was now turning a delicate shade of pink.

"Uh, how long have you been awake?"

"Just woke. Came out here and saw this. A television, I presume?" He pointed to the screen.

Katrina watched him for a moment before turning to the television.

"Meet your new best friend, Silas, at least for a while." She raised the cup to her lips.

He stared at the box, then at her, dubiously. "What's *erectile dysfunction?*"

Katrina's free hand flew up to avoid spewing her drink all over the floor. Pale pink became rose red on her face and neck. "Never mind," he said, "maybe I don't want to know just yet."

She cleared her throat. "As shocking as what you'll see is, this is the quickest way for you to learn about this world you've entered. Would you like tea or coffee?"

"Tea, please."

"Milk and sugar?"

He nodded, sitting down and then rising again. "Perhaps you should show me where things are and how to make it so I can do it meself."

And so, his education began. After figuring out the process of making tea, which he was delighted to find was not so different from Uisneach's method, he went back to the living room, drank his tea and watched the news, making clucking noises and shaking his head every so often.

Katrina was in the process of making a list of things to teach him. "There's the first fifty things," she said setting the pad of paper down. "Do you like scrambled eggs?"

He nodded. "Dara likes them too."

"Who's Dara?"

"Oh, I forgot to tell you she has a dog. We found him injured on the way to Cailleach's. Sigel and I warned her not to get near it. We were going to, uh," he ran a finger across his throat to demonstrate.

"Let me guess. Briana had a fit."

"Forbid us. Said she could heal it, and by Maker, she did. He's been at her side ever since. She calls him a wolfhound. She said to tell you she finally got her dog."

One corner of Katrina's mouth curved. "We never had dogs when she was growing up because Edwin was allergic. She adores them. After he died, I thought it would be good for her to get one. Her response, every time I mentioned it, was that she didn't know where she'd end up, so it didn't seem fair for her get one that I might have to care for." She leaned back in the chair and sighed. "That message from her, more than anything you've said yet, convinces me that she is where she wants to be and has no desire to come home. Oh, Briana…"

They sat silent for several minutes, sipping their tea, until Katrina patted the side of her chair and stood decisively. "Well, breakfast won't make itself and we've lots to do."

He followed her to the kitchen, eager to watch how cooking was done here.

"Does she still quote from fairytales?" Katrina asked, cracking eggs into a bowl.

Silas smiled broadly at this memory of her quotes. "Oh, aye, at least she did at first. It was one of the things I loved about her, always sayin' somethin' funny and then tellin' the story. As time went by, she did it less and less and now rarely does." His expression turned sad. "I asked her once why she stopped and she said it was because she no longer believed in fairytales."

Katrina put down the whisk and looked at him. "That's sad, Silas. Is she that broken?"

He answered carefully, "It would be nearly impossible to break Briana. She's a strong woman."

Katrina raised one eyebrow.

"She is. Certainly, she cries at the drop of a cloak, but…"

"Hat," Katrina interrupted. "Here, it's 'cries at the drop of a hat.' And that she certainly does."

He tipped his head in acknowledgment. "She has faced every challenge with the strength of five warriors. On the battlefield and in matters of the heart."

Karina turned back to the stove, laying out bacon in another pan. "Briana has had her fair share of boys and men wanting to date her."

"No doubt," Silas murmured.

"She went out occasionally, but inevitably, it was one or two dates and that was the end of that suitor. I accused her once of being too picky, and she responded that they were all boring. I asked her how she ever thought she'd marry if no one could meet her expectations and her answer was, 'There is a man out there for me, just one, who is everything I could ever want, and I will wait for that man if it takes forever.'"

Silas had to grab on to the countertop to keep from losing his balance. He looked at Katrina with pain-filled eyes. "I guess Brath is that man."

"I wouldn't be so sure about that. My point is that Briana *is* a strong woman who perhaps needed to go to Uisneach to discover her strength. If she believed that marrying King Brath was serving the highest good, she would commit herself to that duty, but it wouldn't necessarily distract her from what she feels in her heart. It may be that you must live with being the man who lives in her heart."

⌘

Silas was fine with the car until Katrina put it into gear and headed out onto the street. He held his breath as Katrina maneuvered through Camden and onto the highway, toward a village she called Rockland. When they were away from Camden, she drove at a much higher speed. He clutched the arm of the door and gasped. "Slow down, Katrina, you're goin' to kill us!"

"Silas, I'm not even going the speed limit."

"This is insanity! Bloody terrifyin'!"

She laughed, then apologized. "Once you get used to it, you might fall in love with cars and speed."

He adamantly shook his head. "Never! I'll never like this! I want me horse back!" Every time they went around a curve or passed a car, he closed his eyes and held his breath. The size of Rockland shocked him into breath-lessness. "Oh, Maker, what have I done? I think I'd better go back to Uisneach. This village is so much bigger than any place in Uisneach."

"Wait until you see Dublin." Katrina paused. "Silas, you can't go back. We must find the runes. This is all coming at you so fast, it's bound to be overwhelming. Give yourself time to adjust."

The color returned to his face. "Briana was right about one thing. It probably was easier for her to get used to Uisneach than it will be for me to get used to her time. It's loud here, and fast and wild. It's a wonder you all don't go beserky."

"Who says we haven't," she joked.

They went to one of the chain department stores and with Katrina's help, Silas was outfitted with pants and belts, shirts, underwear, socks, shoes and an electric razor. He even found a tweed driving cap that Katrina insisted he add to the pile in the cart. "It looks great on you!" she exclaimed.

After drawing an odd look from the cashier, they got back into the car and Silas groaned. "Must we do this again?"

"Yes, but this time, I want you to watch carefully *how* I drive this car. You'll need to drive yourself, so pay attention. We still need to go to the grocery store. Oh, by the way, I made an appointment with Robert O'Shaughnessy, the lawyer I told you about. I'll meet with him tomorrow and if he thinks he can help, I'll have him over for dinner to introduce you."

"Katrina, I'm so sorry to have brought all this trouble to you. I guess I didn't understand how much work it would be. And cost. Somehow, I need to repay you for what you've spent. I'll get a job and…"

She patted his hand. "Don't worry about it, Silas. Please. You can't get a job until you have some form of ID, and as far as the cost, well, I see it as helping my daughter's cause. Never fear, I'll find some things for you to do to earn your keep."

He nodded eagerly. "Just tell me what to do."

After loading a cart with food, Silas watched the transaction at the checkout line. He would ask Katrina later about the plastic card she used to pay. Next, they stopped for fast food. She demonstrated how to order. His eyes widened as a voice answered from out of nowhere. As they drove around the side of the building, she whispered, "I don't often eat in places like this. It's not very healthy, but quick. You might find it handy sometimes."

He noticed she used a different kind of money for this, paper bills with the faces of different men on them. *Why can nothing be simple in this place?*

She pulled into a parking space at the harbor, where they ate. Some of the ships were masted, like the ones in Cedarmara, but the more modern ones fascinated him. "Do you think I'll really get used to all of this?"

"Of course you will. Briana got used to Uisneach."

"What's that?" he asked, pointing to a wall that jutted out into the harbor, ending at a wee house.

"It's the breakwater lighthouse. You can walk all the way out to the lighthouse. I'll bring you back when we don't have a car full of groceries."

Once home, they put the food away. The afternoon was spent rearranging Briana's bureau and closet a bit to make room for Silas' clothes. She handed him a book with blank pages, much like the one Briana wrote her songs in.

"I thought you might get an urge to write down your thoughts, or your own songs or poetry."

"Thank you, Katrina. That was thoughtful of you." He mentioned the book he'd found on medieval armor. "Briana has been badgerin' all of us to have armor made, but no one knows quite how to do it. Would it be okay if I take that back with me?"

"Of course. There might be other things that would be useful or meaningful to Briana. We'll load you up."

He nodded toward the figurines. "I think havin' these would make her happy."

"It sure would."

Next, she showed him the wood pile out back. "Thank Maker," he exclaimed, "somethin' I actually know how to do."

"Well, dear man, this all has to be split and stacked over there. I was going to hire someone to do it, but I think this is something you could do that would help both of us."

"Consider it done." He started to pick up the ax, and she put her hand on his arm to stop him.

"Not today, Silas. There's time enough in a day or two. We have other things to focus on."

The rest of the afternoon went by in a blur. After explaining the modern monetary system and introducing him to the internet, Katrina called it good enough for one day and suggested he watch music videos while she fixed dinner. While they ate tacos, Silas fired off a million questions: What's a mosh pit? How big is the world? Have people really walked on the moon? Can anyone buy a Lamborghini? Did she think there was a way they could get modern bows and guns to Uisneach?

"You'd know better than I?" replied Katrina. "Is there?"

He screwed up his lips. "I doubt it. The tree seems to have a mind of its own. The faeries probably wouldn't think much of guns. Too violent." He bit his lip.

"Hmm… Do you think so?"

"The real question is whether or not it would be good to bring weapons to Uisneach at all. On the one hand, they would give us an advantage. I can only imagine what I could do with a crossbow. But should Shamwa or the Gray Military get hold of them…" He made a clucking noise.

"I want to do whatever we can to help Briana, but I understand your concern. You've seen on the news what happens when guns are used for the wrong reasons."

"It seems to me," Silas said, "that the weapons we have in Uisneach are more than enough to provide food and to aid us in a fair fight. Guns aren't really what's needed to get Shamwa. Magic is the weapon we need."

"Do you think so? I do have a gun here. Edwin kept one. If you want to learn how to use it, I'm at least competent to show you."

"It won't hurt to see how it's done, when we have the time."

They did dishes together. Katrina dimmed the lights before wandering into the living room with a bottle of wine and two glasses. She showed Silas how to work a corkscrew, and handed him the bottle, letting him pour them each a glass. "Do you want to watch TV or talk?" she asked.

"I think I've had enough of that bloody box for one day."

"Good, because I haven't heard near enough about Uisneach. Tell me about Sigel. He sounds rather important to Briana."

"Aye, they're fond of each other, though sometimes you wouldn't know it." He handed Katrina her glass of wine and set the bottle on the table between them before leaning back in the chair and stretching his long legs out in front of him. Katrina wrapped a colorful, handknit throw over her shoulders as he began to talk of King Brath's lord marshall.

"You must understand that Sigel is as dedicated to Uisneach as they come. He takes his job very seriously. His family have been the king's marshalls forever, and next to the king himself, he has the most authority. Sigel and Brath grew up more like brothers than king and subject. It was due to their practicin' with swords as boys that he, Sigel I mean, got the scar that runs down the side of his face." He told the story of their fight on the wall, how Sigel fell through the tree, earning the gash that would leave him with a vicious scar. He described the dark-haired warrior in bold terms so Katrina would have a clear image of the man who was in charge of her daughter's security.

"He sounds rather dashing."

"Briana says there are no homely men in Uisneach. Not that she thinks of Sigel that way." He laughed. "Sigel and Briana get on each other's nerves at times, but there's a definite bond between 'em. He's a good man and will take care of her."

Katrina raised her eyebrows. "Won't that be her husband's job?"

He snorted. "I suppose so, but I like knowin' Sigel is there for helpin' her cope with things Brath can't."

"You mean like your absence?"

"Aye." He took a sip of the wine before continuing. "Sigel was initially our guard dog—that's what Briana called him, and I know for a fact that Sigel would never let anyone hurt her, includin' me, when it came to it. He'll watch over her." He sipped his wine and closed his eyes for a minute.

"And then there was the time I told you about when she damn near died durin' our first battle with the Gray Military. One of the bastards—oh, sorry, one of Shamwa's men—sliced her leg badly when she was in the process of runnin' him through with her sword while he was tryin' to kill me. She saved me life, Katrina. Your daughter can be fierce when she needs to be."

Katrina turned white but she held her tongue as Silas told the story. He yawned and reached for the wine bottle, then put it down again.

"Time for bed?" she asked.

He nodded. "If you don't mind. I'm a bit tired."

She collected the bottle and glasses, stopping next to his chair to lean down and place a motherly kiss on his head before heading for the kitchen. "Thank you for the stories tonight, Silas. It means so much to learn about her life now."

"There's lots more to tell, but it'll take a bit, I think." He yawned again.

"I imagine. Sleep well. It'll be another long day tomorrow."

"Good night, Katrina. Thank you for everythin'."

He went into Briana's room and sat on the edge of the bed. The things he shared with her mother tonight brought Briana so clearly to mind. Words arranged themselves in his head and he reached for the empty notebook Katrina had given him.

> "In my mind, I feel you.
> My hands, they want to touch you.
> I hear your voice call across the void."

The pencil was flying across the page.

> "Closer than a heartbeat, further than the sun."

"Will I ever sing these words to you, *a mhuirnin*?"

⚜

"This tropical depression has intensified and is now the second named storm of the season. Tropical storm Bonnie is sporting winds of forty-five miles per hour. It is not expected to evolve into a hurricane, but we will keep you posted as developments occur." The weather forecaster disappeared, replaced by a toothpaste commercial.

"We won't get that rain, though it is overcast," said Katrina. "What's the weather like in Uisneach? Do you have hurricanes and such?"

Silas swallowed his tea before answering. "At the moment it's like it is here, all the time, though that isn't normal.

One of the changes since magic is wanin' is that we have no winter. It's like spring and summer all year round. When magic is restored, the seasons will also return."

The ring of the doorbell ended the conversation.

"I'll answer that," Silas offered. He was up and away before Katrina could stop him.

Two young women stood on the doorstep, laughing. At the sight of Silas, they became instantly mute. The dark-haired woman stepped back and glanced at the number on the house.

"Hello," Silas said.

"Well, hellooo…" said the dark-haired one, with the look of a cat licking cream.

"Uh, we were looking for Katrina," the other said uncertainly.

"She's—"

"Debbie. Samira," Katrina interrupted, coming to the rescue. "How are you? Come on in."

Silas stepped back and the two women entered, neither taking their eyes off him.

Katrina laughed. "I haven't had time to tell you that a friend of Briana's is here visiting. Samira, Debbie, this is Silas. Silas, Debbie and Samira, Briana's best friends."

He reached out his hand and the two girls took turns shaking, neither of them yet in control of language skills.

Debbie was the first to compose herself. "Does this mean Briana is home?" she asked hopefully.

Katrina shook her head. "No, she's still on assignment." She shot Silas a look that warned him to say nothing.

Samira asked, "Are you on assignment with her?" Katrina responded, "Samira, you know we can't share that with you. His status is also classified and really, you shouldn't even know he's here. So please, keep it on the Q.T." Her face had taken on a very serious expression that made Silas want to laugh, but he nodded, maintaining an air of solemnity.

"Can I get you girls something to drink?" Katrina asked.

They shook their heads in unison. "We wanted to ask if you would make a pie for the bean supper at the church next week? I know it's short notice, but we've discovered we're short a couple of pies," Debbie explained.

Katrina agreed to make her famous peanut butter pie. "In fact, I'll make two, so you won't have to ask anyone else."

"Maybe you'd like to bring Silas to the supper," Samira invited slyly.

That would be nice," Silas replied.

"If Silas hasn't returned to Briana by then, we might, but we're waiting to hear from some officials about that."

Silas darted a confused glance at her that went unnoticed by the girls.

"You sound Irish," Debbie guessed.

"Aye, I might be, but I suppose I'm not at liberty to confirm or deny now, am I?" He gave them a conspiratorial smile, starting to get into the role he was supposed to be playing.

"Well, can you confirm or deny that you and Briana are just friends or more than friends?' Samira asked.

"Samira!" Debbie scolded.

Understanding finally dawned on Silas and he grinned. "I'll tell you what, Samira. I will confirm to you that Briana and I are more than friends, but that is absolutely all I can say."

She frowned and shrugged. "Well, we'd still like to see you at the church supper if you're around."

Silas was saved from responding when Debbie slapped her head. "Oh, I'm supposed to tell you that Tara Smith thinks the baby's dropped."

"Wonderful," Katrina said. "I'll call her. She's due in a couple of weeks."

"She's so lucky to have you as her midwife," Samira gushed.

Katrina smiled and asked when they wanted the pie ready. After finalizing the details, the girls finally left, but not before Samira moved her eyes up and down Silas appreciatively and said, "Briana always was the lucky one."

Debbie said nothing, but Silas noticed the deep scrutiny behind her smile.

When the door was shut, Silas started laughing. "That was interestin'," he said. "I suppose you better tell me what you've told people about Briana's disappearance so I'm prepared next time."

Katrina sighed. "I figured her disappearance had something to do with the prophecy, so I didn't dare call the police and start an investigation that could go nowhere. I told people she had been sent on a covert government assignment of an undetermined period. I thought that if she didn't come back in a couple of years, I would just have had to say that she died."

The smile disappeared from his face. "That must have been awful, Katrina, not knowin' for sure where she was or if you would ever see her again."

She nodded. "It was, but I was seeing it in the cards, so I was relatively certain she'd gone to the crone's kingdom and had not been abducted. To lose her and Edwin so close together was rough, but at least I could believe that Briana was alive and that she might come home again. Just before you arrived, I thought she might be coming. The cards were telling me that some big change was about to happen, and I hoped it might be her."

"I'm sorry," he said quietly.

"At least I know now what has happened to her. And we can both hope that she comes home again soon."

"On this Memorial Day, remember to thank our veterans," the announcer said one last time as Silas and Katrina left the tree-shaded amphitheater where they'd spent the last two hours listening to band music and speeches about the ultimate sacrifice made by warriors committed to preserving the country's constitutional freedoms and liberties. Silas was quiet, contemplating the ritual honoring of war and peace at the same time. Katrina led him across the street to the harbor, to the grassy hillside above the water where historic schooners and huge modern yachts shared slip space.

"Ducks and gulls."

"What?" Katrina glanced at him, flicking out a blanket for them to sit on.

"That's one thing that's the same." He shaded his eyes against the sun as he followed the trajectory of the gray-and-white birds across the harbor. A blaring sound made him jump. "What's that?"

"A horn. It's how boats communicate with one another to announce they're coming in or going out of the harbor."

"Hmm..." he said, leaning down to straighten his side of the blanket.

They ate sandwiches and drank fresh lemonade from a thermos. Neither said anything for some time. Silas studied the children rolling down the hill, the adults taking pictures of the harbor and walking dogs or sitting and talking. He watched a young couple walk up the hill to a bench under a group of low-hanging birches. A statue of a woman stood nearby, a romantic guardian for the young lovers. Longing filled his chest as the young man put an arm around his lady and she leaned into his embrace and kiss.

"You miss her."

He closed his eyes, trying to swallow past the lump in his throat, and nodded.

"One kiss," he finally said.

"Pardon me?"

"That's all we had. One magical kiss in the moonlight. I relive it in me mind every night."

"Perhaps it won't be the last. This story is far from over."

Silas looked away from the lovers and back to Katrina, who looked so much like Briana that his heart wanted to break. "Honestly, Katrina, suddenly Uisneach seems very far away, like a place I dreamt. Perhaps it is a dream. I wonder about me goal. I wonder if I will ever see Uisneach or Briana again."

He saw understanding in her eyes, but for a long while neither spoke. Only the honk of a duck overhead and the *whishhh* of its landing in the water at the edge of the harbor broke the spell.

"'There sound will sleep the traveler, and dream his journey's end,'" Katrina said, quoting Edna St. Vincent Millay, whose statue Silas was once again contemplating.

CHAPTER SIX

SILAS O'MARA

"You broke my heart, through no fault of your own. Forbidden love, don't touch, can't have. Reckless kiss is all we have to keep. That and your face, carries me to sleep. We can't see forever, tomorrow's so uncertain; the world may end, the portal close, but I will keep my promise. I will love you always."

He set the guitar down. It had been ten days since Silas arrived in Maine. Ten experience-packed days. Ten, confusing, enlightening and exhausting days. Ten days to develop a routine that would help him begin to cope with living here in Briana's world. He woke up each morning wondering what shocking new thing he'd learn and went to bed at night processing his feelings through songwriting, which became mostly songs about missing Briana. He spent hours on the internet studying modern military tactics, which he felt would be useful to Brath's army. He made a purchase at the local market with a debit card, learned to use an iPhone and washed a load of laundry.

They made another shopping trip to Portland and Katrina took him to Cabela's in Scarborough, where he saw a demonstration of modern archery. He was fascinated by the accuracy and power of the compound and recurve bows, and especially of the crossbow. He'd protested when Katrina purchased a crossbow and compound bow and some arrows.

"Consider it my first contribution to the war in Uisneach. If you can use these or figure out how to make something similar for the Taranian troops, then it's a great investment for the cause. When we get home, you should set up a target in the backyard."

The next day, he built a target and started practicing with the new equipment.

"Holy shit," he swore as a second arrow struck practically on top of the first arrow in the bull's eye.

"I see you're getting comfortable with modern vernacular," Katrina commented drily as she set a cup of tea on the deck table, then sat down.

"Sorry. I didn't know you were there. This crossbow is bloody amazin'!" She waved off his apology.

"The swearin' here isn't so different from home." He gathered the arrows and sat down beside her, trading the weapons for a cup.

"Have you thought about a last name?" she asked, reintroducing a topic she'd mentioned a few days ago.

"I've been thinkin'. Would Cedarmara work?"

"That was my first thought, too, but it would be a very unusual name, one that might prompt unwanted curiosity. I thought of giving you my last name, but that wouldn't work if Briana came back—don't want any raised eyebrows on that one. Why not use part of Cedarmara, and go with Mara or O'Mara? That's a common enough Irish name."

"Silas O'Mara," he murmured. "Briana O'Mara," he tried out, with a shy look at Katrina. "Do you think she'd like it?"

"She'd love it."

"Well, then." He stood and bowed to her. "Silas O'Mara, at your service, madam."

She chuckled. "I'm heading down to Robert's office to remind him that he's Irish. Hopefully, he'll be able to help us."

"Another man of Ireland? Perhaps that will make him sympathetic."

"Do you think so? I intend to remind him of his duty to the mother country and to faeries everywhere. Oh, and I'm going to Rockland to meet a friend for dinner. I won't be home until late, so do you think you can heat up the pork roast in the microwave?"

"Do I look helpless?" he joked. "You go and have a grand time. I'll see you in the mornin'."

An hour later, a knock at the door drew Silas' attention away from the television and the woman sliding her body across a sleek, red car on a rotating disc. *Lovely lass.* He wondered what prevented her from getting dizzy on that thing.

He opened the door to find Briana's friend standing on the step. "Hello, Debbie. Katrina's not here."

"I know. I just saw her down the street. I wanted to talk to you. She said to tell you I might be an ally." Her brows knit together. "Whatever that means."

"Come in, then." He stood aside and ushered her into the living room. "How's marriage treatin' you?" he asked, as he mentally ran through what he could and could not tell her.

"Fine. Katrina must have told you I was a newlywed."

Oops! Maybe that was the wrong thing to say. It was Briana who'd told him. "What can I do for you?"

"I haven't slept well since we were introduced last week."

He raised one eyebrow. "I'm sorry to hear that, but I don't…"

"I can't sleep because I can't convince myself that the story you and Katrina told us was the truth."

Silas didn't move and didn't reply.

She walked to the mantle and stared at a picture of Briana and her father. "Briana and I have been best friends since kindergarten. I know she wouldn't leave without saying good bye to me. And I know there's more to this story than you told us. That's good as far as Samira's concerned. She shouldn't know the details unless you want it reported on CNN. But I need to know, Silas. I really need to know what happened to her. You have something to do with this. It might sound crazy, and trust me, I'm no woo-woo type, but standing next to you, I can almost feel her."

Not so crazy, Silas thought, but he still had no idea what to say to this woman.

When he didn't respond, she sighed. "Just tell me, is she alive? Scratch that question. If she was dead, I'd know it. Did she find her King Arthur or Lancelot or whomever?"

He shuddered. "She found both."

Debbie made a sound in her throat. "Figures. The woman waits twenty-five years to date and gets two men at her first ball. Which one are you?"

"What makes you think I'm either?"

"Silas—oh, and do you really have no last name? That's odd, unless you're a famous musician I've never heard of. Listen, if Briana ever had a type, believe me, you're it."

Small consolation with her living in another world, married to another man. He studied Debbie and agreed with Katrina's hint that she might be a trustworthy person. But she also seemed a little too sensible to believe the truth. "What does woo-woo mean?"

"See, that's what I mean. That's a pretty common phrase and you don't get it. No disrespect, but there's something odd about you, Silas, whomever."

"O'Mara. That's me last name." It wasn't strictly true but would be soon enough.

"Okay, then. One mystery solved. Woo-woo is magic and mysterious stuff like chakra energy, angels, time travel, that sort of thing. Briana believed some pretty strange shit, so nothing you tell me will surprise me."

I'm pretty sure it will.

"Please, Silas. It's been horrible, not knowing. I asked Katrina and she sticks to her story. I spent the day before her disappearance with Mouse. If something had happened or she was going away, she would've told me. Plus, she wouldn't have left her mother so soon after Edwin's death. She just wouldn't have done that. What happened?"

He ran a hand through his hair. "If I told you, Debbie, you wouldn't believe it."

"Try me. As I said, if anyone could get involved with something weird, it would be Briana."

He nodded. "You might want a drink for this," he said. "It's as you called it, some strange shit. Wine, whiskey, ale?"

She shook her head. "I've just found out I'm pregnant."

"Congratulations!" he said, smiling widely. "Briana will be delighted. When are you due?"

Debbie cocked one eyebrow up. "Okay, that's a start. She'll get to know. I'm only a couple of months along. Due date is in December. I think Katrina keeps ginger ale in the refrigerator. Briana and I drank it by the gallons. That should help ease any gastric upset this story causes."

She came back with a full glass of effervescent golden liquid and curled up on the sofa. "I'm ready. Hit me."

"Well, it's like this. The day after your trip to Portland, yeah, she told me about that," he said, seeing Debbie's surprised look and knowing it would soon turn to a shock. "The day after Portland, she was gardenin' in the yard and heard a noise in the woods that she followed. She walked through a tree to a kingdom called Uisneach, which is where I live." He reached out to steady the glass of ginger ale that shook in Debbie's hand. She set it down on the table beside her.

"Okay, here we go," she said, and nodded for him to continue.

He plunged ahead. When the story was done, the room was draped in purple shadows of late afternoon. The ticking grandfather clock in the hall was the only sound in the room until Debbie picked up her cell phone and punched in some numbers.

"Hi sweetie. I'm going to be late. Yeah, I'm helping Briana's friend with something. Can you heat up the pot roast and have that? Thanks, Rob... love you too... yup, bye."

She punched in a new set of numbers. "Yes, I'd like to order a large," she looked appraisingly at Silas, "meat-lovers pizza."

After she'd given the address and set down the phone, she stood up. "Come with me," she ordered Silas, heading to Briana's bedroom without waiting for an answer. He followed, wondering what she was thinking.

She walked to the bookcase and swept her hand over the figurines. Moving down the shelves she tapped a few book spines. "This was her world. She lived, ate, breathed and probably dreamt myth and legend. This is why I believe you." She picked up the red archer and held it out to him. "And this is you. I know this was her favorite because often when we sat in here talking, she would reach for this guy and hold him. I'm not even sure she was conscious of it, but I noticed. She was embarrassed when I asked about it once, and said that it was just a habit, but I could tell that he meant something to her.

"I'm sorry she had to marry the king, though. Based on the Briana I know, he wouldn't be her preference."

"She had no choice. Our kingdom would eventually die if she didn't honor the prophecy. He's a good man and I think she'll be happy." He accepted the figurine when she handed it to him and studied it before replacing it and hiding his regret with a cocky grin. "He looks a brave sort of lad, doesn't he?"

Debbie smiled. "Handsome too. I told her in Portland that when she found her forever love, Samira and I would be jealous. I had no idea. Samira is falling all over herself about you. Don't be surprised if she shows up here."

"Briana warned me."

"Silas, if I give you a letter for her, will you take it back with you when you go?"

"Of course, but I have no idea when that will be."

"Whenever. Next question. What can I do to help?"

"I don't know of anythin' you can do, unless you happen to know the exact location of the runes. That's me quest."

"I could do some research. You say they're on the Hill of Uisneach in Ireland?"

"I think so, yes, but where exactly remains a mystery. The plan is for me to stay with Briana's grandparents, who don't live far from there, while I try to find them."

The doorbell interrupted the conversation. As Debbie answered the door to accept their dinner, he went into the kitchen for some plates.

After they ate, Debbie taught him how to text and instant-message on the iPhone. "We need to stay in touch and share information. Hmm... I'll have to remember to message you if I'm with Samira, so you don't text me or do something that clues her in on this." She flopped against the back of the couch. "This is so crazy."

"Havin' second thoughts about believin' it?"

"Oh, no. You can't make this stuff up." She glanced at her wristwatch. "It's late. I should go. Thanks for trusting me, Silas. I love Briana and I will do whatever I can to help her." She grabbed her cell phone and headed for the door. She was about to open it when she turned back around. "What do you think Briana is doing right now?"

He took a few moments to answer. "She's learnin' how to be a great queen."

❦

Two days later, Silas again answered the front door to admit Robert O'Shaughnessy, attorney-at-law. The garrulous older man grasped Silas' hand right away.

"Hello, boyo. Pleased to meet you. Katrina told me quite a story and I must say, I'm eager to hear your tellin' of t'ings."

"Glad to meet you, too, sir," Silas responded, smiling at the man's friendly and direct approach.

Robert explained that he'd been skeptical at first during his meeting with Katrina, but his granny always believed in the sídhe and the faerie folk. He'd promised to bring an open mind and a good appetite to this dinner.

Katrina came into the living room and gave her attorney a hug. "Thank you for coming, Robert. Dinner will be ready shortly. Why don't we sit down and have a drink first." She ushered him to a chair in the living room and asked Silas to pour them all a whiskey.

"Well, lad, I know t'e basics of how you arrived here, but tell me, you've been here a few weeks now. Are you certain you wish to stay? It has to be very different from your home."

"Aye, it is different, and I'm not all that sure I want to stay, but I also don't have a choice. I can't go back without the runes."

"I see. Well, boyo, tell me everyt'ing, t'en."

Silas told the lawyer all he wanted to know and then some, in colorful and magical detail. It was some time later that Katrina announced, "We'd better eat before this meatloaf gets cold."

"Aw, darlin', you made me favorite." He looked at Silas. "She makes t'e best meatloaf on the planet. Has she made it for you yet?"

He nodded. "Aye, she has, and it is good. Her daughter also makes a grand meatloaf. It's one of the dishes she taught the cooks at Ard Darach to make."

Robert shook his head as he settled himself at the dining table. "I can see her t'ere. We called her a wee mouse, but I always felt t'ere was more to her t'an what met me eye."

As they ate, Robert outlined a general plan for getting Silas to Ireland. "We'll have to come up wit' documentation to prove your existence. It's not so unusual for someone to find t'emselves with no birt' certificate and no identity, and twenty years ago it would've been easy to remedy. However, t'ese are dangerous times in t'is world, Silas, and identification, especially at an international level, is scrutinized very carefully. However, I believe we can get you somet'ing called citizenship by investment. I have connections in the Caribbean who will get us what we need—for a price. And a lot of time and paperwork. I hope you are a patient man."

"Patience is me middle name," Silas joked, having heard the phrase somewhere in these last few weeks. "I am concerned about the risk to you, though, and the cost to Katrina."

He saw Robert and Katrina exchange a look and Katrina shake her head slightly.

"Never mind about t'at, boyo."

By the end of the evening, nearly a full bottle of Jameson's had been emptied, and Silas was singing songs from Uisneach to the attorney's delight.

"Oh, lad, Uisneach sounds a lovely place. Perhaps you can get me t'ere someday!" They laughed and Robert declared it a good place to end the evening. "T'ank you, Katrina, for a wonderful supper and for including me in such a grand adventure. I don't know when I've been so excited about anyt'ing in me life."

"Let's hope you don't regret it," Silas said, shaking the man's hand again. "And thank you for everything, sir."

"You can cease with t'e sir, Silas. Call me Robert, it's me given name. Good night to you bot' now, and may you sleep peacefully in the arms of Michael and all his angels."

O'Shaughnessy was stepping out the door when Silas remembered the proper way of saying good bye to people here. "Toodles, Robert."

The man stared at him, then at Katrina and said, "And are you t'e one responsible for teachin' him t'at?"

Katrina smiled. "I think he picked it up from Briana."

Shaking his head and laughing hysterically, Robert O'Shaughnessy left, shutting the door behind him.

"Why did he laugh?"

"Never mind, Silas. It doesn't matter tonight," she replied, patting his shoulder before heading to the kitchen to clean up from dinner.

Silas followed her. Taking the dish towel in hand he went through the motions of helping her. "Katrina, I had the feelin' this was going to cost a bloody fortune. How badly is this is going to affect you?"

She sighed. "You may as well know. The other person I met after my meeting with Robert was a realtor friend. I'm putting the house on the market. I'm selling it."

"What!" He set down the glass he was drying and stared at her. "You can't do that! This is your home. It's Briana's home."

"Briana's home is in Uisneach and I will do whatever it takes to make sure she is safe and happy there."

"But where would you live?"

"I wanted to ask you about that. Do you think it's possible for me to go to Uisneach?"

Silas fell back against the counter, now gaping at her.

"Say something, please."

"I don't know what to say, Katrina. I have no assurance that *I'll* be able to get back through."

"Well, if I can't, then I will either rent a small apartment or go live with my parents in Ireland. With Briana gone, I really have no need of this huge house and I could easily transplant somewhere else."

"What about your work? You love being a midwife. And you've the herbal remedies to look after."

"I've only one mother to care for at the moment and I won't be accepting new patients. Wild Meadows can easily be closed after all the other orders are filled."

Silas ran a hand through his hair. "I wonder if anyone understood the cost of findin' the runes. Briana would be horrified to know what this is costin' you."

"Letting go of this house is nothing compared to the cost of losing my daughter. I am serious when I say I will do whatever it takes to help her. You need guns, we'll get guns. You need a passport, we'll get that too. And if you need those runes, we will bloody well find them!"

⋙

On July Fourth, Silas and Katrina arrived home from the parade on Main

Street ready to slap steaks on the grill and boil corn on the cob, when the doorbell rang. Silas answered to find Robert O'Shaughnessy standing there with a huge grin spread across his face and a manila envelope in his hand. He gave it to Silas.

"Congratulations, Silas O'Mara. You are officially a citizen of St. Kitts! Now, let's get you to Ireland."

CHAPTER SEVEN

DOUBLE CROSS

Briana, Ard Darach great hall, Dromdara, Uisneach

She was alone in the great hall; the sun hadn't even considered rising yet. She wouldn't have considered rising either, had she not been woken by cramps and wetness between her legs. *No baby this month*, she thought with an unexpected twinge of ambivalence. Knowing she wouldn't get back to sleep, she'd padded downstairs and settled at the hearth in front of a fire already crackling and snapping thanks be to the nighttime servants. A monarch never had to worry about coming downstairs in the wee hours of the morning to a cold hearth. She looked around for something to practice magic with. A kettle of water stood near the fire, waiting to be heated for tea. *Perhaps, I'll just give it a head start.* She wrapped her shawl around her shoulders, sat back in the chair and took centering breaths. *Focus. Toil, toil, bubble and boil.* She shook her head. *Focus. Water, hot... hotter... boil-ing.* She was rewarded with a slight movement of the kettle nearer the fire and the eventual burble and gurgle of water hitting the boiling point.

"Well done, Your Majesty."

Gray fur in her peripheral vision and Dara's whine confirmed the arrival of the mouse she'd spoken with before, she assumed. Distracted from her ritual, she turned to the creature with a long glance.

"You sure know how to sneak up on a person."

"Stealth is key to staying out of reach of O'Brien's broom. So, you're meeting with success in your magic craft," he observed, with a wiggle of whiskers and blink of his round, dark eyes.

"Trying. I need to prove myself for Brath to persuade him to let me go on the campaign."

One tiny foot scratched behind his ear. "Proving yourself. Hmm. Well, I don't agree that you have anything to prove, but having magic would certainly be advantageous in many ways. However, in magic and in life, fear will hold you back."

"Yes, Obi Wan. And what would you know about my fear?"

"You reek of it."

Briana frowned, automatically sniffing, but not smelling anything.

"Trust me. I have a marvelous nose for these things," he said. "What are you afraid of?"

She turned her gaze to the fire, not one bit sure she wanted to discuss this with the mouse. However, the flames mesmerized her into a soulful search of her own fears, and she heard herself admitting her worries of being left behind when Brath went to capture Shamwa, her anxiety about becoming a good queen, and her concerns about Silas' well-being and ability to find the runes.

"There's something else," the mouse insisted.

She stared hard at him.

He waited, nose and whiskers twitching patiently.

"You're becoming a pest, do you know that? Okay, I'll tell you what I'm afraid of; I'm afraid I'll get pregnant. Pregnancy and childbirth are dangerous here. I couldn't handle watching my child die and I'm too young to die."

"Die? You worry about death in childbirth, but not going into battle where it is nearly certain you could die? That's irrational."

"So you're a psychology expert?" Briana said, a little sharper than she'd intended.

"I know that everything in life carries risk. You can't just crawl in a hole to avoid it. If that were the case, I'd stay in my nest and never come out to avoid O'Brien's broom!"

They sat staring at each other. Briana couldn't come up with a sensible argument, so she changed the subject.

"If we're going to chat like this, should I give you a name?"

"I have one. Mouse."

"Wouldn't you like something more interesting?"

Pale gray whiskers twitched. "Your Majesty," he said haughtily, "just because you didn't like the name, doesn't mean some of us don't."

"My apologies. I didn't mean to offend."

Mouse squeaked dismissively.

"Briana, who are you talking to?" Brath asked, laying a hand on her shoulder and nuzzling his morning beard into her neck.

Mouse scurried away through a chink in the stone. "Oh, yeah, big risk-taker," she called after the creature before leaning into Brath. "No one, I guess."

Jonathan and Rippa entered the great hall almost at the same time and bee-lined to the sideboard. Grumbling seemed to cue the kitchen staff, who entered with platters of bread, gruel and boiled eggs.

"I'm sorry, lads," Brigit the house maid said, looking flustered at the group of people waiting for breakfast, "but the water's not yet—" she turned to see the pot of water bubbling away in the fire, "—boiled. Oh my." She turned to Briana. "Your doing, Your Majesty?"

"Just practicing a little magic."

The boys dove into the food as Brigit returned to the kitchen.

"Couldn't sleep?" Brath asked, still standing behind her, his hand on her shoulder.

She shook her head. "I woke with cramps." She twisted to meet his eyes. "Sorry." *Not sorry, not really.*

His lips formed a half-smile, but his eyes didn't match the sentiment. "Well, I'll just have to try harder," he whispered, sliding a hand covertly under her shawl to the soft, warm, swell underneath.

They stayed in the cuddle for a moment until the boys' noisy appetites stimulated her own. "Hungry?" she asked, and received two raised eyebrows.

"That's a loaded question, but unless you mean to take me back upstairs, I guess we best join the lads."

Sitting down at the table with her food, Briana was immediately assaulted by Jonathan.

"Your Majesty," he said, through a mouthful of egg, pointing a chunk of bread in her direction, "Tell me, how am I to protect you? You slip around here at all hours of the night. You're never where you're supposed to be. You need to tell me when you're about so I can do my job."

How could a boy of twelve seem both mature and boyish in the same instant? "Being my squire doesn't mean you need to be my shadow, Mr. Stark."

"Yes, it does," Brath disagreed, just before filling his own mouth with cereal. He waved a finger in the air as he swallowed. "Unless, of course, I'm shadowing you. Thank you, Jonathan, for taking your position so seriously."

Briana made a sour face. Neither looked the least bit disturbed by it.

Knights filed in for breakfast and Briana watched in fascination as Jonathan practically ignored the other pages, directing his conversation instead to Sir Fergal and Sir Cavanaugh. She wondered at his hubris.

"Do you think he thinks more highly of himself than he should?" she asked Brath quietly.

He shrugged. "He's a little arrogant at times, but I think he's a bit more mature than the other boys and will likely be their leader someday, so I'm not concerned."

Artanin slipped into the hall, seemingly unnoticed by anyone except Briana. He helped himself to breakfast and took a seat away from the rest of them.

"He's an odd man," Briana whispered to Brath.

"Regretting your decision to let him live?"

"Of course not. I'm just saying, he's weird. I need to work with him and learn magic, but he's a bit intimidating and he hasn't even approached me yet."

"Probably waiting for your invitation," Brath said, returning to his breakfast with fervor.

"Have you seen Dara?" she asked. She'd left the dog in the kitchen with his breakfast and just realized he hadn't returned.

Brath shook his head, chewing his bread.

"He keeps disappearing on me. He's up to something."

Brath shrugged again and swallowed his food. "Dogs usually are. Who knows what he's found to get into? A bitch he fancies at one of the cottages, maybe."

"Eat up, men! Practice in the yard in a quarter of an hour," Sigel boomed as he entered the room, stopping by the side board for a boiled egg that went directly into his mouth. The cup of tea he poured himself was empty before he reached the dais. "Swordsmen first and archers up second. You too, Jonathan," he said to the young man on his way past him.

Jonathan glanced at Briana.

"I'm coming out to watch," she told him, rolling her eyes.

He wasted no time dashing out of the great hall, Rippa hot on his heels.

"Rippa, put your shoes on!" Briana called to his back. While Rippa was settling in to court life for the most part, his penchant for running around barefoot remained Briana's mission to change. The last thing she wanted was for him to cut a foot and develop an infection she'd need to treat.

After a brief meeting, the king, queen and lord marshall met the gathered warriors on the practice field. Steel flashed and clanked, the air peppered with curses and guffaws.

Briana paid attention to the technique and style of the combatants to learn a few tips to improve her own skill, until she remembered that her new weapon of choice was magic. She began to see the skirmish in a different light and started the slow breathing and visioning that might influence the outcome.

Nothing's happening, she thought after several minutes passed with no evidence that she was having any effect. She bit her lip and considered why.

Before she could make another attempt, Sigel called archers up. The senior men shot at targets and though adequate, fell short of Silas' standard. It was an accepted fact that the bard was the greatest archer in all Uisneach. Sigel called Jonathan Stark up and Briana saw Sir Jameson put down the sword he was polishing to watch his young son. It was clear at the start that the lad had more natural talent any of the older archers. He lifted the longbow and pulled back the string with the ease of a professional. His concentration was fixed, and she was reminded again of Silas. The lad made two perfect shots in succession.

On his third shot, Briana, now in the zone herself and feeling some heat in her hand, directed her energy toward the arrow and urged it to follow a different trajectory. It worked; the arrow suddenly veered off wildly. Twice more Jonathan's arrows left the bow and took an unbelievable path away from the target. Still focused on magic, Briana heard Brath order two other archers to join the young man. As though in a dream, she watched them line up next to Jonathan, heard Brath give the order to shoot and saw the bowmen release arrows simultaneously. Briana mentally pushed them up and away. The arrows jetted into the air and then fell hopelessly to the ground.

She took a breath and pushed a bead of sweat from between her eyebrows. Returning to the present moment, she turned to find Sigel and Brath staring at her, thoughtful expressions on their faces.

Take that, she thought, smiling mysteriously.

A scree overhead broke the moment and Briana looked up, shielding her eyes from the sun to see the hawk Merlin streak overhead.

"Cailleach's here!" Briana exclaimed. Finally, she would find out how it went with Silas getting through the tree. Brath followed her back to the inner courtyard where Cailleach was just dismounting, clutching a leather satchel. The giant hawk returned to his normal size and perched on her shoulder. Dara bounded between her and Brath to sniff Cailleach and the hawk.

"There you are, Dara. Where have you been?" asked Briana. "Hi, Cailleach." Briana swiped her hand across Dara's back haphazardly before wrapping both arms around the witch in a warm welcome.

"Did the tree open for Silas?" Brath asked.

Cailleach nodded, glancing at Briana. "I did a rune reading and believe it confirmed that he is safely through."

"Good," Briana said, with a calm that belied her deep sense of relief.

Brath took the bag from Cailleach, his arm dropping slightly from its weight. "Maker, Cailleach, this is heavy. Did you bring the entire contents of your cabin with you?"

Cailleach's sweet laugh was music to Briana's ears, settling her instantly.

"Books for Briana. And a surprise, but that doesn't weigh anything. Let's get inside and I'll show you. I'll be looking for a nice cup of tea."

Briana surveyed the witch, who wore her usual long woolen skirt, tunic and leather boots, her amulet of amethysts and wren feathers lying over her long, gray braid.

"What is it, lass?" Cailleach asked.

"Nothing. I'm just glad to see you looking more like yourself. The trousers you were dressed in last time I saw you kind of freaked me out."

Cailleach chuckled. "Perhaps I should change my attire more often. Clearly, I'm too predictable."

Within minutes, Cailleach had a steaming cup of herbal tea and Briana was pulling the contents of the bag onto the table. Books of different shapes and sizes appeared. *Magical Craft in Uisneach* was a long, thin book with flourishes of gold letters across its red velvet cover. The pages of *The Art of Faerie Magic* glittered with remnants of enchantment. It promised instruction in such things as "Grounding and Centering in Faerie Fashion," "Holding Time," "Animal Speak," "Beguiling Humans" and "Rules for Inviting Gnomes or Other Sorts of Beings to a Party." *Oh, this is going to be good.* The largest and thickest tome came out last. *Complete Grimoire of Evalonian Faerie Magic* was emblazoned across the ancient cover in gothic lettering. A lock bound it shut.

"Oh, here you go," Cailleach said, reaching into a pocket for the key. "You'll need this."

Eagerly, Briana unlocked the heavy volume. She ran her fingers down what amounted to a table of contents. Spells and rituals were organized by elements. Scanning the titles, she found one in the air section that intrigued her, "Riding Air." Briana drew in her breath excitedly.

"That's an advanced spell, girl. You best start with something a wee bit less complicated. There's something else in the satchel, keep going."

Next was a blank book decorated with whimsical swirls and leafy patterns. She turned it every which way until Cailleach looked up from her tea.

"You'll undoubtedly come up with your own spells and rituals, or at least have thoughts about your magic that you want to write down. I thought you'd like a journal to keep them in."

"Thank you, Cailleach. It's beautiful." She kept pulling things out of what was beginning to seem like a bottomless satchel: more books on traditional Uisneachan witchcraft, quill pens, an ancient deck of divination cards, a special candle that Cailleach said was made with herbs keyed to Briana's energy, and a carved wooden mouse.

"A reminder of who you are," the witch said quietly.

Briana thought of the wee mouse that had counseled her this morning. "Thank you, Cailleach. I won't forget."

"It's time to get serious about your magic, lass. I've given you the tools and now you must get busy. Oh! There's one last thing in there."

Reaching in, Briana felt nothing at first and then something gossamer-light. She pulled out a nearly transparent piece of fabric. It was like holding a spider web in her hand.

"Put it on, over your head."

Obeying, Briana realized at once what it was. "An invisibility cloak! Just like Harry Potter's!" she exclaimed.

Brath choked at her sudden disappearance. She grinned and tiptoed around to his other side. Leaning in, she blew lightly into his ear. He twitched. She moved closer and pressed a kiss to the side of his cheek.

"Hmm… this could be interesting," he said, sitting very still and letting her run her fingers down his neck, across his chest and a bit lower, knowing the invisibility cloak gave her license to torment him without Cailleach's knowledge.

"Stop that, Briana," Cailleach warned sternly.

Briana threw off the cloak and gawped at the crone. "You could see me?"

"No, I could not. But I know you and I could imagine what was going on under there. I don't want to see your husband squirm as you irritate him."

"Oh, I wasn't irritated," Brath said, patting Briana's now visible hand.

"Brath, I could use this to hide while I'm with you on the road! I'd be with you, but safe." Her eyes pleaded with him.

His smile faded. "I was thinking of something much bigger. Cailleach, is it possible to mass-produce this?"

She considered the idea. "The inspiration for the cloak came from that tent the gnomes gave Briana, so I imagine they might be able to make more. Shall I go to Wellsland and enquire?"

Briana frowned. "I know we could use these, but I need you here to help me get better at using magic."

Brath turned to Cailleach. "Let's send a message by crow. It's more efficient and you can stay with Briana and work on her skills while we go after Shamwa. I'll have the message sent before I head to the stables." He kissed Briana quickly, returning her disappointed glare with one of affection and regret, and left the two women to their devices.

"I take it there's some disagreement about you joining the men in battle," Cailleach commented.

"He's all worried that I might be a distraction or get hurt."

"He's right to be so. There is much you can do here, Briana, without needing to put yourself or the men at greater risk."

"I'm sure there is, but I don't want to stay behind."

"I see your petulance remains. Come now, let's get to work. I want to see what you can do near the faerie tree in the garden, and then try and retain some of that energy away from it. And you've yet to tell me about this new design on your hand."

"Oh, geez, I forgot all about telling you what happened in Evalon!"

❦

By lunchtime, Briana had learned how to tap into the tree's energy and store it in her body. She took Cailleach to the turret room Brath had given her, and they set to making the place a workshop where she could make herbal remedies and practice magic.

Patting the edges of the cloth cover on the table, Briana turned to Cailleach with a smile, pleased with what they'd accomplished. Cailleach was staring intently at her.

"What?"

"I wonder if you'd care to share a memory?"

Briana wasn't sure what this was about, but she wasn't about to turn down whatever opportunity the witch was offering her. "Sure."

Cailleach moved two chairs to face each other and sat in one, nodding at Briana to sit in the other.

"Ground yourself and concentrate on seeing what I'm holding in my mind."

Briana focused on her breath and felt the tingling begin in her hand. Sandalwood scented the air as she began to drift into a world that only she and Cailleach were aware of.

She saw Silas step nervously toward the green door and reach for the silver handle. He looked back toward the witch and the Wellses, though it seemed he was looking directly at her. She felt his curiosity and excitement mix with fear and grief. He looked around, wondering if this was the last time he'd see his homeland and if he'd ever see Briana again. He said, "Tell Briana..." and Cailleach interrupted, "I'll tell her that you made it through safe. Go on, the tree won't wait forever. Makerspeed, Silas of Cedarmara." He nodded, turned back and stepped inside the tree. The door closed and disappeared.

Releasing the image, she said quietly, "I must say, Cailleach, I'm surprised you allowed me that vision."

"I'm not totally heartless, Briana. I wanted you to see for yourself that he did get through."

"And you're sure he made it to the other side?"

"Don't take my word for it. Read your own cards."

Briana quickly centered and laid out a past, present and future reading. The first card was an oak tree. Briana started when a door suddenly appeared in the trunk and opened. A ghostlike presence entered, and the door closed. She nodded to herself. *He made it in.* The next card depicted a tall-masted ship bobbing gently in the harbor at Cedarmara. *That could also be Penobscot Bay,* she thought with relief. Not at all sure she wanted to see the future, she paused. What if she saw something awful? What if she saw something wonderful? What if the power came on her and she actually connected with Silas? But there was no aura at this moment. Drawing inward, she breathed out and turned the card over. The Uisneach Tree glowed green in the center of the card. Before Briana could read anything into it, two featureless light energies materialized from the stones to wrap themselves around the tree and each other, separated only by the dryad, now fully emerged from the bark of the tree. Lovers? Briana held her breath, waiting for more revelation, only to be left wanting.

She glanced up at Cailleach but said nothing. The witch's face remained blank as she watched her student. Briana swiped the cards up and slid them to the corner of the table. Obviously, she was not going to be able to identify the energies or understand their connection to the Uisneach Tree.

"Satisfied?"

"Hardly, but at least I know he's in Maine." She sucked in a huge, cleansing breath. "It must be time for lunch," Briana said, rising from the table.

The two made their way down to the great hall where the men were already eating. Brath smiled and patted the seat beside him. "I wondered if you planned on working through lunch."

Reilly served her meal and she tucked in with gusto. "This magic business makes me hungry."

"Everything makes you hungry," he said, patting her thigh.

"True." She bit down on a piece of freshly baked caraway bread. "Maker, this is good."

"Didn't your mother teach you never to talk with your mouth full?"

"Um hmmm," she mumbled, her mouth now closed. She chewed with enthusiasm.

Lunch was loud and exuberant. Briana learned that one of the mares was foaling. Brath was concerned because it was her first, and the horse seemed a bit anxious.

"Well, if anyone can get her through it, it's Riordan," she said, referring to the Master of Hunt whom she found both fascinating and intimidating.

As though summoned by her comment, Riordan made a rare appearance in the great hall. "Your Highness," he said, addressing Brath. "The mare's having more difficulty than I expected."

Brath was already on his feet. He turned to Briana and Cailleach. "I'd like you both to come as well, in case there's anything you can do to help."

Nausea gripped Briana. *No way am I going through this again,* she thought as her feet followed traitorously behind her husband, Cailleach's presence behind her preventing a bolt.

The dun-colored mare lay writhing in the most well-lit stall in the barn. Briana cringed at her agonizing whinnies. She hated seeing the poor creature turn and twist with each contraction, her eyes wild and unfocused. Riordan and Brath were in the stall beside her. Birthing fluids gushed from the mare, but no sign of hoof nor head.

Cailleach took Briana's hand and started through the door, but Briana yanked back. The witch canted her head and raised one brow. "What's this about? The mare needs us."

Briana shook her head mutely.

Cailleach entered the stall alone and kneeled beside the laboring mother, sliding her hands along the mare's ribs and whispering words of comfort that Briana did not understand but felt in her core. Somehow, Briana felt comforted as well, and joined Cailleach near the mare's backside.

"I'm no vet, but I have some experience with this in humans," she said, almost grudgingly. She rolled up her sleeves. Uttering words that were more prayer than incantation, Briana slipped a hand inside the warm, moist cavern of the birth canal to find the presentation of the foal. Relying on her sense of touch, she closed her eyes and imagined the necessary adjustment, which she followed with a few gentle manipulations. The mother gave a heave and groan as another contraction hit. Briana felt pressure crush down on her hand, keeping her gripped inside the mare. She breathed through the spasm as she felt the foal slide. As the contraction eased, Briana removed her arm and allowed the next few contractions to bring the foal into the hazy light of life. The mare was weak from her ordeal, but steadfastly began to lick the filmy wrap from her baby, who nickered softly and began to thrash around in the bedding. Briana sat back on her heels and breathed a sigh of relief.

"Well done, Bri," Brath said in her ear.

Briana looked at him and the tears fell. She didn't wait for his comfort, but stood and left the stall, desperately needing air and privacy. Outside, she found a barrel of water to wash in.

"Want to tell me what that was all about?" Cailleach asked softly behind her.

When Briana finished her story of the mother in Inis Fáil, Cailleach gave her a sympathetic look.

"'Twas an awful thing, to be sure, but it's not the usual outcome for births in Uisneach. Most babies are born just fine, without so much as a midwife."

"Maybe so, Cailleach, but it only takes once to be tragic if you're the once."

The witch studied her thoughtfully. "Well, thankfully, this birth was not a tragedy. Time will take care of your fears, Briana. I'm sure of it."

◈

Later that afternoon, in a section of the garden secluded by junipers, Cailleach taught Briana how to use magic to replace weeding by hand.

"I'm not sure if I like this method of weeding or not," Briana commented, staring at the pile of magically collected drooping weeds and blades of grass. The two of them had been gardening for the last couple of hours, mostly silent, serenaded by birds and the ocean just beyond the castle. "I've always found weeding a Zen sort of activity."

"What's Zen?" Cailleach asked, her finger twitching away her small pile of weeds into Briana's larger mound.

"Well, it's a type of spirituality marked by the practice of being still and quiet, of focusing on the moment."

Cailleach looked at her through one eye. "How is that different from anything you're learning to do with magic?"

Briana placed a hand on her hip and stared at the pile. "I don't know that it is, except that when I'm Zenlike I'm usually not thinking about anything, and when I'm working magic, I'm focusing intently on something."

"I see."

They went back to gardening and didn't speak for some time.

"Closer than a heartbeat... humm, nnee aaala... further than the sun..."

What's that you're humming?" asked Cailleach.

"What? Oh... I was humming, wasn't I? Zen thing, I guess. I don't know what it was, but I kind of like it."

"Pretty, though a wee bit sad."

A muffled voice caught their attention. Cailleach's eyes glinted and she put a finger to her lips. Easing closer to the voice, Briana heard Artanin speaking in some ancient language. After several minutes, Cailleach motioned Briana to follow her.

They walked through the great hall upstairs to her private quarters. Cailleach gave a loud bang on the door and pushed it open without waiting for an invitation.

Brath and Sigel were standing next to a table, maps spread out around them.

"We've been duped!" Cailleach exclaimed. "I just overheard Artanin communicating your plans, presumably to Ealga, who will presumably communicate them to Lord Shamwa!"

Briana gasped. *Artanin's a spy?*

"I told you we should have killed the bastard!" Sigel pointed a finger at Briana. "Now, I am going to kill him." He took a step toward the door.

"Wait a second, Sigel." Brath put a hand on his arm. "Let's think this through. Cailleach, tell us exactly what you heard."

When she finished, Brath told Sigel to have Artanin put under guard again, and to gather the knights. If Shamwa knew the plan, they'd have to change it. Watching Sigel's barely controlled anger, Briana knew she had to be the one to fix this. It was her naïveté that gave the druid access to their military plans. It was she who had to deal with the consequences.

CHAPTER EIGHT

CLASH OF WITCHES

Artanin stood before his king, head held high, gaze boring straight through Brath. Briana wasn't sure if she should be impressed or disturbed by his composure in the face of probable death.

"You were overheard sending information to someone about our plans to defeat Shamwa. Do you deny this?"

Artanin stared at him in silence.

"Your silence could be construed as an admission of guilt," Brath told him calmly. "Your actions constitute treason and carry a penalty of death. Care to end your silence?"

Nothing.

Briana stepped forward. "Artanin, why did you save my life if you weren't on our side?"

She thought his glare was tinged with regret.

"I thought we could use you. I thought you could be convinced by Lord Shamwa to see things more clearly. When I realized you held the potential for powerful magic, I knew we had to use that to our advantage. Deception seemed more advantageous in the long run."

"So, you let me escape as a means to save me and make us believe in your loyalty to Uisneach?"

"Right. Only make no mistake, my loyalty *is* to Uisneach, just not to *him*," he spat out in Brath's direction. "Lord Shamwa sees the future of Uisneach in the right light."

"Artanin, you just signed your death warrant." Brath said, his voice devoid of emotion.

There must be a way to resolve this without Artanin's death, Briana thought. The druid's execution could backfire, provoking Shamwa to action sooner than they wished. She pulled Brath aside and said as much.

"Briana, he's a traitor. He can still communicate with Ealga and Shamwa and bring them right to our doorstep. I cannot risk that."

"I see your point, but still, he might provide valuable information."

He looked at her thoughtfully. "I will concede you one opportunity for diplomacy. But I reserve the right to decide whether we employ clemency or the death penalty. Understood?"

She nodded and turned back to Artanin. "You have much to offer Uisneach, Artanin, and I would encourage the king's mercy if you were to give me any reason to do so. Would it not be better to transfer your alliance to us and save your life than to end it here and now? Either way, Shamwa will not live to become ruler of Uisneach. Helping us defeat him quickly would boost your standing in the king's army and ensure you a place at the table."

The druid shook his head slowly and focused his stare not on the queen, but King Brath. "If it means my life, I would not support your hopeless plan that will weaken what once was strong."

Briana's heart sank.

Brath gave his queen a look of regret before pulling out his broadsword.

After only a split second's hesitation, Briana stepped forward, pulling Nua out of her sheath. "Brath, this is mine to carry out."

She heard Sigel mutter in the background, "Oh, Maker, she's still going to grant mercy."

Her look to Brath conveyed quite a different intention. He nodded gravely.

She stepped toward Artanin, heart pounding harder with each step. It was one thing to kill a man in the heat of battle, quite another to do it with calculation and precision. She was about to commit murder under the guise of justice. Her mind was divided. Half of it understood the necessity of it while the other half recoiled in horror.

Her guts shook as she met the druid's eyes. She swallowed the rising ball of bile. "You've brought this upon yourself."

"Keep telling yourself that if it helps, Mouse."

His calling her by that name shifted something inside. She *was* the Mouse of Prophecy. The protection of Uisneach was her primary objective. This man shamelessly threatened her country and for that, he could not live.

Without being asked, Artanin knelt before her, eyes intent on hers in fearless acceptance of his fate.

Silence hung heavy over the courtyard as Briana planted her feet in a sturdy stance. *What a waste.* Without warning, she smelled sandalwood, her consciousness shifted, and she felt separated from her body as she lifted Nua high above her head. She felt the heat and saw the scar on her hand pulse with power. Gripping hard with both hands, she swung out to the side. *Nua, strike true and strong. Do not let him suffer.* Conviction welled up to strengthen her resolve when Artanin smiled deviously. *He thinks I won't do it,* she thought, just before she forced every ounce of strength she had into the swing. Silver sliced through the air and disappeared in a fountain of red as it severed Artanin's head from his body.

Rolling to a stop in front of her, Artanin's soulless eyes stared up at Queen Briana with shocked realization. Real time returned to Briana. She returned the filmy stare of the druid with a shudder. It was done. "Have his head mounted on a spike and placed at the doorstep of Aurum Castle," she said. "Let Shamwa be put on notice. He's next." With that, she walked past Brath, and then past Sigel, who nodded his approval. When she passed in front of the knights, they took a knee in a sign of respect. Only Cailleach seemed to understand the real battle that had been waged. Her expression conveyed equal measures of validation and sorrow.

"We'll bury him," Brath said later, in their quarters. "Better if Shamwa doesn't know we're coming."

She nodded absently, staring tearless out the window, seeking something from the ocean view that her soul desperately needed in this moment.

"For what it's worth, I'm proud of you. I know that had to be agonizing for you."

"I'm more concerned now about whether or not Sigel or the men will ever trust me again. Sigel was so angry. I guess he was right after all, I should've let him kill Artanin the day we arrived at Ard Darach."

"Mercy and diplomacy are not signs of weakness in a monarch. As to the men being angry or mistrusting of you, you saw them take a knee. You just proved yourself a queen to them. Personally, I'm relieved to know you can make hard decisions and that should anything ever happen to me, you could carry on and the men would follow you."

"And anyway, it wasn't totally idiotic to believe Artanin. He told a logical story that I believed, too."

She pressed a fist to her mouth and Brath came to her side immediately, pulling her into his arms. "It'll be okay, Bri. But we need to go down and devise a new strategy before Shamwa gets wind of this."

She allowed herself only a few moments of comfort in his embrace before taking a deep breath and pulling away.

"Ready?" he asked, searching her face.

She nodded and led the way down to the great hall, where the others were waiting. Discussion was already underway.

Briana considered the tools they had in Uisneach. "Do we have time to build some weapons, like a catapult? We could assault the castle and draw him out."

"No," replied Brath. "That would be a fine idea if our army was big enough and ready to make one great surge. It's not. In the meantime, Shamwa has multiple troops bullying the villages and destroying faerie trees.

"I propose that we release false information suggesting the entire army is staying at Ard Darach to build up our battalions. Hopefully, that will convince Shamwa to continue his current strategy instead of pulling all his troops together, which would give him the advantage of numbers. We'll send most of our forces out after him, leaving behind a small group to build weapons and guard the queen."

"What about the faerie army?" Briana gave Brath a pointed look. They were, after all, her army, and if she wasn't going, what would they do?

"I propose that Aya'emrys stay here with you, and his warriors travel with us under my command." He looked at the Evalonian captain, who nodded agreeably.

Briana *harrumphed* and was largely ignored. His plan was met with enthusiasm by most.

Cailleach said, "I would remind you, Sire, that my sister Ealga is still a threat. I'm certain she was Artanin's contact. We need to remove her from having any further opportunity to aid Shamwa."

Briana opened her mouth to speak, but Brath's response stopped her.

"Right. I'll send a small contingent to arrest her and bring her here."

"They wouldn't be able to handle her magic. She'd only have more information to share with Shamwa. I need to go."

Briana knew she could help Cailleach capture Ealga, her sister, head of the abbey and a powerful witch in her own right. She started to say so, but Brath stopped her with a look and slight shake of his head. She ground her teeth together and glared at him.

"It's too late to head out now, but let's plan midday tomorrow. Arriving at Shannon Abbey at night will give us the advantage of surprise."

∽

Watching Brath rally the men, Briana waffled between being sulky that he refused to take her and contrite that she was angry, when the truth was, she was going to miss him. She tried to put on a brave and supportive face, but it was a matter of opinion as to how well she managed it. She ended up going to their chambers, close to tears.

She heard their door open and shut quietly, but kept her eyes cast down at hands that lay docile in her lap. It wasn't until she saw his boots in front of her that she forced herself to look up.

"What is this?" she said, surprised to see him standing in front of her, holding Nua and her shield.

"You better hurry. We're leaving in five minutes." He sighed. "Briana, I can't leave you here, as much I want to. I'll probably live to regret it, but you'll ride with us."

She wondered at the change of heart, but before he could change his mind, she squealed in delight, threw herself into his arms and rained kisses on his face. "Thank you, Brath. You *won't* regret it. I promise."

"Mmm… I hope not. Five minutes, Bri." With that he left the room and Briana yelled for Gael to come and help her change.

She entered the courtyard with one minute to spare and found Jonathan holding Banrion's reins, a grin splitting his face.

"What are you so jazzed about?" she asked, taking her reins and mounting.

"You get to go means I get to go."

Captain Aya'emrys rode a horse whose golden color was a near perfect match for his own. When Briana rode by, he tipped his head to her. "I assume this arrangement meets with your approval, Tuathla?"

"It does, Captain." She offered him a genuine smile and was rewarded with a quite human wink.

Rippa, on his new pony, a strawberry roan named Starlight, offered a rallying song, less stunning than Silas would've prepared, but not bad for his first attempt. He ended with, "Maker, watch over us," and they were underway.

When they settled into a solid rhythm, Briana moved up next to Brath. "So, what brought about your change of heart?"

"Do you mean other than your sulkiness?" he said, looking sideways at her.

"I wasn't that bad."

"That's debatable." He turned serious. "You're going for three reasons. One, it has occurred to me that if Shamwa knows you're at Ard Darach, you might be more vulnerable. He might decide to send troops there. Two, your magic is becoming impressive. Being able to divert arrows away from our army would be handy."

He stopped talking and looked away.

"You said there were three things."

He looked her way again and his eyes had taken on a mossy warmth, his voice a quiet, husky tone. "The third reason is that I can't stand the idea of going to bed at night without you beside me."

She mentally ordered the butterflies in her stomach to stand down. "Wow, you sure know how to take a girl's breath away," she said, hoping her eyes conveyed what she couldn't say with words. What her heart was slow to accept. What she felt would make her a traitor to Silas and their love.

He held her gaze for a long moment before smiling gently and squeezing her hand.

"Do you think people will say I'm spoiled?"

"I hope so, my lady. It would be my honor to spoil you shamelessly for the rest of our lives."

"Maker, Brath, you need to stop right now, or I'll have to give the order to strike camp."

He laughed out loud. "Now who's shameless?"

⁂

Purple twilight wrapped a soft cloak over the standing stones of Shannon Abbey, a white ghost below the hill.

I would marry you, Briana, here in the stones, witnessed by the ancestors and Maker.

She shook her head, trying to dispel the memory of Silas at the stones, forcing the longing to retreat into its usual corner of her heart. *In another lifetime, perhaps we can be together, Silas. In this life, my place is with Brath and my responsibility to Uisneach.*

"Are you all right?" Brath asked quietly.

Gone was the image and voice of Silas in her mind. She nodded, and they slipped through the stones into the forest. Brath wanted to wait until they were certain the household was asleep and unprepared for their attack.

Silence saturated the forest, with not so much as an owl or a tree frog breaking the heaviness in the air. Distant thunder rumbled, sending a chill up Briana's spine. Could the night be any eerier to arrest a witch? A flash of light in the distance elicited a squeak from Briana and a chuckle from her husband. Dara growled under his breath.

"Scared?"

"Of course not. It's just spooky."

"It is," he agreed calmly. "Perfect night to seize a witch."

One by one the candles in the abbey were snuffed out. Except for one in the window of the room Briana knew was the chapel, where Ealga had pretended to bless her and Silas when she was really trying to put a curse on them.

Cailleach rode up next to them. "She's in there working a spell. I can feel it." Briana could feel tension rolling off Cailleach. It was disconcerting, to say the least, that this usually calm and steady woman was anxious. "I need to get in there now," Cailleach continued, "before she casts an evil spell on us or sends information to Shamwa. There's no time to wait for all the troops."

"Take the cloak, Cailleach," Brath said. "Briana, Jonathan and I will be right behind you. Sigel," he called, "position the troops so that no one escapes the abbey, and then join us inside."

Sigel whirled Orion around to carry out the order. Cailleach took the cloak Briana handed her and in a split second, disappeared. *Freaky.* "Cailleach? Cailleach? Cailleach!"

No answer. Seconds later, the front door of the abbey opened and then closed.

Brath grumbled beneath his breath. "Jonathan, Bri, come on!"

Four figures, including Dara, raced down the hill through the waning moonlight. Shadowy figures danced in the chapel window. *Geez, Cailleach, you sure didn't waste any time*, Briana thought as she pulled Banrion up behind Ruark at the abbey door.

Brath was already off Ruark and attempting to open the door. It didn't budge, despite a mighty shove. "Briana, can you sense anything inside?"

Sigel and Jonathan silently joined them. Shutting out every other noise or sensation, she reached inside the abbey with her mind. Scurrying. That was the sisters hiding from Mother Ealga. A dark wind swept through Briana's mind, leaving behind a blank, black slate. A flash, and then she saw two women, near mirror images of each other and equal in power, facing each other.

"Brath, get that door open! They're already fighting!"

Brath and Sigel forced the door open a crack, but it immediately slammed shut in their faces.

Anger overtook Briana. She drew in every ounce of magic she could muster and hurled it at the door, which flew open, splintering and falling in a heap at her feet. She stepped past Brath and Sigel's shocked faces and over the broken boards.

It took her a second to get her bearings, but she led the way through the abbey to the chapel.

Thumps and grunts could be heard from the room. As she rushed in, Briana saw Ealga standing on the stone altar—candles scattered and toppled around her and across the floor, pools of melted wax streaming everywhere and the scent of lavender filling the chapel. Briana's eyes followed the trajectory of Ealga's extended hand to a spot in the corner, near the ceiling. Her eyes widened at the sight of Cailleach levitating feet above the ground! Waves of hot energy passed between the two witches, as Cailleach struggled to break free of her hanging confinement. "How could you even think of harming your own sister?" Mother Ealga asked.

"I would kill myself to protect Uisneach. You, Ealga, I will kill with regret, but not with guilt. I will do what must be done to prevent your evil from harming this kingdom!"

"You force me to kill you first, dear sister," Ealga said with mock sweetness.

Briana pointed her finger at Ealga. "By the power—"

Before she could get the words out, her hand was invisibly forced down. Simultaneously, she and Brath were magically bound by thick ropes of grapevine.

Briana tried futilely to break their bindings. "Cailleach, let us go this instant!"

"Not Cailleach." Ealga laughed while hurling a ball of fire at her sister, who managed to twist out of its path by a hair's breadth. "Me!" Her laughter was almost giddy.

Cailleach, in contrast, was focused and serious as she deflected the elements Ealga forced in her direction. Fireballs fizzled, ice bolts melted and the stones that were loosed from the chapel walls were pushed back—except one that connected with Cailleach's temple, knocking her to the ground. Ealga was on her immediately.

"Nordosa, emmeretium." A purple cloud began to form around Cailleach, who appeared dazed. "Eternio son magor mo cardo infernium."

Briana went wild against the bindings around her shoulders and legs. Where was all this magic coming from? And why was she not able to make hers work? "Damn you, Ealga. I know what that means. It's a curse! You won't get away with this!"

Yet she seemed to be getting away with it just fine. Cailleach, eyes unfocused, hands limp against her side, appeared completely paralyzed by the spell and the mist.

Ealga lips curled cruelly as she stood above her sister. "Borrum is avenged," she said triumphantly before turning toward her other captives.

"I wonder what you have done with Artanin? Obviously, he has compromised the plan. Tell me where he is, and I will deal with him."

Briana started to tell her it was too late, but an elbow from Brath made her stay silent. With good reason. If Ealga didn't know about Artanin's death, then she probably didn't know that they knew all about her pact with Shamwa, or if she did, didn't know the extent of their information.

The nun leaned down and grabbed Briana's chin, twisting it painfully. "You, Miss High and Mighty Queen of Uisneach, I haven't liked since I first laid eyes on you."

Briana ignored the taunt and let herself totally relax. Let Ealga believe she was surrendering.

"Where's your lover?" Ealga asked Briana. She turned to Brath with a sly expression. "Oh, did you find out and have him killed?"

Briana saw movement behind Ealga as Cailleach, free of the magic that had bound her, silently approached.

Intent on disparaging Briana, Ealga was unaware of Cailleach's approach. Briana watched Cailleach silently mouth words while making hand gestures in the air. At the same time, Briana felt the heat burning the cords that imprisoned her and her companions. The vines snapped free. Suddenly, Ealga jerked back, her hand clutching her throat. She whirled around clumsily to see her sister in the middle of an enchantment. Ealga fell to her knees, eyes wild, spittle forming at the corners of her mouth.

Ealga fell haphazardly on the floor, but even as her eyes closed in death, her lips moved in an incantation that gave Briana goosebumps. As her mouth stopped working, a light mist rose out from her body and dissipated in a thin curl into the air.

"Dear Maker, no!" Cailleach said.

"What was that, Cailleach?" Briana asked as Brath removed the last vines from their legs.

"I'm afraid she cast a spell to allow her spirit to move into someone else's body."

"How will we know if she has?" Briana rubbed at the red marks on her arms from the binding.

"We won't."

Briana heard the fatigue in her mentor's voice and saw the grief in her eyes. She also saw an ugly red swelling on her temple. Briana moved toward Cailleach and was surprised when the older woman allowed her to place a healing touch on the injury.

"I'm sorry, Cailleach."

Rare tears touched the corners of Cailleach's eyes. "Aye, me too. I wish it could have turned out differently. She was a loving, talented young woman who was changed terribly by grief and hatred."

"Cailleach, come away from here." Briana gently turned her away from the sight of her sister, crumpled lifeless on the ground.

The anchorites had been rounded up and brought outside, where they were surrounded by Brath's army. Most of them shivered in fright, except Sister Enda, who looked defiant. *She always was a cheeky one.*

They admitted they'd known Lord Shamwa's visits to the abbey, but they'd been threatened with their lives if they whispered a word to anyone. They knew nothing beyond that.

When one of the sisters asked about what to do with Ealga's body, Cailleach said matter of factly, "We'll give her a proper burial and hope that Maker will have mercy on her soul."

The ritual was conducted hastily, with a few prayers offered on her behalf. Cailleach seemed ready to leave behind whatever sorrow and regrets were stored in her heart.

As the Taranian army was about to leave, Sister Clare stepped forward. "Wait!"

Brath remained seated on Ruark, but gave the young woman his full attention.

"I do remember something. I overheard Mother Ealga talking with Lord Shamwa. They agreed to meet at Dun Lura. She was preparing to journey there. They were supposed to meet the day after tomorrow."

"Thank you, Sister. That's helpful. Now, could you do us one favor and bring whichever horse Ealga usually rides."

"Two days!" Sigel said, his eyebrows coming together. "It's at least a three-day ride from here, four if we stop at all!"

"I know," Brath said, pinching swiping a hand across his chin. He turned to Briana and Cailleach. "Any chance magic can speed up time?"

Briana whipped her head in the witch's direction, her eyes rounded in question.

"Maybe. 'Twas a lot of magic thrown around in that abbey. I'll try, but I make no promises."

Brath turned to Sigel and shrugged. "And in the event that magic fails—we ride like banshees are after us!"

Cailleach barely finished an ancient time distortion ritual when the young nun returned with a handsome bay stallion with a perfect head and high energy.

"My goodness," Briana exclaimed. "He's gorgeous. I wouldn't have thought a religious person would own such an extravagant animal."

"Ealga always did have an eye for fine things, especially horses."

At Brath's order, the animal was tied to Rippa's horse and the group prepared to leave.

Brath turned to Cailleach and Briana. "Lord Shamwa will not meet Ealga there, but he will be well met!"

CHAPTER NINE

ART ARON

Briana wasn't sure if it was magic or the threat of banshees that made it seem as though time really were speeding up, but miles had been covered when they stopped to water the horses at dawn the next morning.

"I don't see why the faerie always has to be around," Jonathan grumbled to Briana as they let the animals drink. "You'd think *he* was your protector."

Briana hid a smile. Jonathan's indignation was sweet but needed a reality check. "He *is* my protector. Just like you."

He glared at her and pursed his lips.

"Well, maybe not just like you. You're very different, but his responsibility to keep his tuathla safe is as great as yours to your queen. I feel fortunate to have such strong, brave men at my side."

His shoulders rose a bit and the look of defeat faded.

"Briana, I'm having some of the faerie and crow troops sent ahead to Dun Lura to reconnoiter." Brath slid off Ruark and let the stallion sidle next to Banrion for water.

"Is Aya'emrys going with them?" Jonathan asked hopefully.

"Mr. Stark, you really need to stop worrying about the captain," Briana admonished him. "You both have jobs to do and I suggest you focus on your own."

Rippa chose that moment to ask Jonathan for help with Starlight. Briana heaved a sigh of relief at the boy's departure.

"What's that about?" Brath asked, moving closer to Briana and sneaking a hand between her backside and Banrion.

"Men," she huffed, easing his hand out in the open. "He's feeling a bit jealous of Aya'emrys."

"Oh? Attracted to older women, is he?"

"It's not that, Brath. He thinks he should be my *only* protector. It's a macho thing, I think. And for future reference, I don't exactly consider myself an older woman. That would be my mother."

He leaned over to kiss her cheek. "I'll keep that in mind. So, you're okay with me borrowing your army?"

"Of course. But, thanks for asking, not that you actually did," she said, scrunching her nose.

He grinned and walked to the center of the troops, delivering orders as he went. Faeries and crows were split. Half would go ahead to Dun Lura and half would travel with the Taranian army. "Since we can't fly the direct route like the crows, we'll head north toward Poet's Gap. The path through the mountains is shorter and would allow us to stay hidden, but as you know, it's treacherous. If we go over the top, it'll take longer, but we'll see what's going on down below.

What he didn't say, but Briana understood, was that the trail between the mountains wound through steep sections that would make Sigel's hair stand on end.

"Send crows up to scout the faster route," said Sigel. "If the way through is clear, we take it."

Brath nodded. "Then let's wait here for their return."

After what seemed like minutes, but was more likely a couple of hours, the crow messengers returned with a report that the pass was clear.

Briana noticed Sigel looking grim but resolute. He hated heights and probably had PTSD from watching his bride fall from a cliff into the ocean, as well as from his own childhood fall off the castle ramparts, an accident that left him physically scarred too. She'd seen his fear firsthand. However, she said nothing while she placed the saddle blanket across Banrion's back.

"Sir," Rippa said in his child-trying-to-be-an-adult voice, "the men are waiting for us. Shall I begin the rally song?"

"Yes, Rippa," Brath said, turning to his own horse.

They rode hard the entire day, stopping only to water the horses and refill their water bags. The sun was only a suggestion away from setting when Brath decided they had to stop and rest themselves and the horses for the night.

✦

The following day dawned under an azure blue sky dotted by white, wispy clouds. They rode two abreast through a meadow of wildflowers. Even at the pace they maintained, the colors and scents relaxed Briana enough to think of a bouquet. Flowers picked themselves and flew into her hand.

"Clever," Brath commented. "I won't have to worry about bringing you any flowers."

"You may still do so. I wouldn't throw them away."

Her peaceful state deteriorated when they came to the bridge over a fast flowing tributary of Long River, dotted with boulders. She looked beyond to the two mountains that stood as guardians to the Dromdara Mountains here on the southern end of the chain. Pewter clouds gathered and swirled above the summits, at war with the blue sky. Spiked, jagged peaks stared each other down across a trail between them and the robust river that ran beside it through the pass. The path was straight, but narrow. One misstep…

Sigel sat stiffly on Orion staring at the path ahead. She felt his angst and called upon her own energy to fortify him. Brath wisely waited for Sigel to gather his wits. Jonathan, on Briana's other side, gave her a questioning look, which she dismissed with a slight wave of her head. Crows continued to fly overhead, searching for traps or ambushes.

"A protection spell, High Lady?" Captain Aya'emrys suggested.

She nodded. He could've done it easily, but gave her the opportunity. "Cloak us with power and strength," said Briana, using hand gestures to encompass the whole army. "Harm come to none, safe passage through this mountain. Rivers flow below, path above wide, wider, widest yet. Protection to those who protect Uisneach." She imagined a golden light surrounding all of them.

Finally, Sigel sucked in a reservoir of breath and urged Orion forward.

There was barely enough room for her horse. Glancing behind at Aya'emrys, she asked, "Do the protection spells always work?"

"They are subject to the same variables as anything in this world, High Lady."

She frowned. *I guess that's a no.*

As the trail rose up between the mountains, the river dropped away to the valley floor. The clouds, which at first seemed isolated, had morphed and now encompassed the tops of both peaks and slid downward toward the army. Briana felt a chill travel from her toes to the top of her head. Standing slightly in the stirrups, she twisted around to find Cailleach and was disturbed by the tense expression on the witch's face. The trail behind the army seemed to be shrinking. Something was wrong. The mountain seemed an almost malevolent force, threatening and dangerous. Forcing fear aside, she reached inside herself for more of the magical energy needed to protect them. She felt suddenly blocked. Stones skittered beneath the horses' hooves and clattered down the side of the mountain. She wanted to call a halt, but didn't dare interrupt Sigel's intense concentration. Anxiety became horror when the trail underneath Sigel narrowed, and Orion slipped.

"Sigel!" she yelled as his horse's haunches slid backward, unseating him. Orion scrambled forward to safety, but Sigel slid over the cliff, barely hanging on to the edge. Brath was off Ruark instantly and grasped Sigel's hand, trying to pull him up. They struggled. Brath's grip slipped and Sigel slid lower. Briana cried out, sickened by the look of terror on his face. Sheer willpower seemed all that was keeping them connected.

"Aya'emrys, do something!" she yelled, jumping off Banrion. There was no room on the narrowing trail for anyone other than her husband and Sigel, and it seemed the sliver of land was shrinking even more! Even so, Brath was not about to let his best friend and lord marshall fall to his death.

Aya'emrys' attempted to conjure something. Milliseconds seemed hours.

"I'm not able to help, High Lady. You must do something."

"Me! What can I . . ." *Relax*, she told herself, searching for her aura. It didn't come. *Fake it till you make it, queenie.* In a flash of inspiration, she reached into the mist with her ringed finger and drew a single nebulous tendril toward the two men fighting for their lives. Using every ounce of magic she could find, she guided the stream of white to bind around their wrists. When their arms were held fast in the mist, she imagined the vapor hardening to steel. Sweat rolled down her neck and back as she dug deep for the power to save two men she loved.

With a heave, Brath pulled Sigel over the edge of the precipice. The two men crouched against the skinny bit of remaining ledge. Briana maintained her focus long enough to rebuild a solid trail, using dirt and stone from the mountain wall.

Relief mixed with mental and emotional exhaustion overwhelmed her. She leaned into Banrion, shaking from head to toe, tears dampening her cheeks. Not wanting anyone to see her breakdown, she turned her face into Banrion's side, pretending to tighten her girth. An arm slid around her shoulder. Expecting Brath, she turned into it. Sigel held her firmly. "I'm okay, little warrior," he said, his voice husky and more than a little shaky.

She looked up through glistening eyes. "I was so scared, Sigel."

"Me too," he said, forcing a weak laugh. "I'm glad Brath decided to bring you along. I think you just saved my life."

Calming, they separated, and Briana turned to Aya'emrys. "What happened? Why didn't your magic work and mine did?"

"I didn't actually try, High Lady. This was something you needed to do."

It took Briana a moment to process what she heard. "One of my dearest friends and my husband nearly died because you wanted me to learn a lesson? Are you insane?"

Captain Aya'emrys stood silent.

"The next time you do something like that, Captain, I will consider it an act of insubordination."

He nodded, unfazed.

She went to Brath to assure herself that he was, in fact, okay.

"I'm fine, Briana. You did save us, you know."

"Whatever. It's not like I had a choice. Someone had to," she added stealing a bitter glance at the faerie captain.

"You were a bit harsh with him."

"Yeah, well, this was no time..."

"I think it was exactly the time. You needed to know you could do this. Perhaps the urgency of the situation allowed you to access your power without the filter of self-doubt."

She shook her head. "You people are crazy. This is no time for Briana life lessons or self-analysis. Let's just go."

He gave the order to remount and ride. Pushing through the pass, along a wider and less hazardous section. All seemed quiet. Nerves eventually settled. Perhaps the faerie captain was right. In that do-or-die moment, she'd had no option other than success. Magic, it seemed, was more a matter of trusting what was within than it was of learning words and rituals. Tapping into her power was easier than she thought. *Or maybe I'm just feeling a little cocky after a spectacular success.*

Brath's voice cut into her reverie. "I made a tactical error, Sigel."

"Which was?"

"Allowing myself to get distracted by chasing after Shamwa. He's got us on the move and can bend us to his whim at this rate. I also wonder how much magic he has. Someone powerful caused that incident in the pass."

"Aye, that was no accident. You think he knows where we are?"

"Someone does."

"Well, I think we stay the course and hope it isn't him. If he arrives at Dun Lura unsuspecting, then this could be the easiest way to end this with the least loss of life."

Briana was toying with ideas of how to use magic to ensure Shamwa didn't know they were on their way to meet him when they heard voices and chopping nearby.

Brath raised a hand to stop the troops. Sigel dismounted and moved ahead to where the trail curved slightly. After a few moments, he returned with an alarming report. A boulder narrowed the exit from the pass to the Leanach plains and a small group of Gray Military were cutting down trees, apparently trying to block their passage with a barricade.

Brath ordered the faerie's to move to the plains side of the mountains to prevent any of Shamwa's troops from escaping as the Taranian army charged the Grays from this side. As they waited few moments for the faeries to reposition, Briana and Cailleach cast protection around the army. Briana felt certain of their combined effort. After about a quarter of an hour, Brath gave the command and the Taranian army surged.

"Catchachurra!" Sigel's yell never failed to make her shiver.

Brath shot her one quick glance. She read his concern for her safety. In response, she flashed an overconfident smile.

Game on! She followed him around the curve into a melee of soldiers. The faerie warriors attacked from one side while Brath's forces dove in from the mountainside. The wooden barricade splintered apart at the force of the Taranians' horses and troops. Banrion gave a small leap over part of it onto flat, open land of the Plains of Leannach. Nua slid eagerly out of her sheath and Briana, shield raised, immediately deflected an attack with a determined swing of the sword. Dara jumped between her and the Gray, ending his assault with a crushing bite to his neck.

Three men tried to overwhelm Brath only to be invisibly pushed back. *The protection spell must be working, thank Maker.* He, on the other hand, sent two others to the Underworld with brutal grace.

"Cailleach, get to the trees!" Briana shouted.

The witch followed Briana's orders, but not before flashing a bolt of light through the chest of one enemy in her way.

Briana was pulled backward on Banrion, but before she could be unseated, she whipped Nua backward and heard a dull thud. Turning, she shrugged as the surprised warrior fell back, Nua protruding out of his forehead. She pulled back to retrieve the sword as the man fell dead in the field. For such a small force, these soldiers put up a fierce fight. Briana worried about how long the protection spell would hold, as well as her own physical strength.

"Sigel! Watch out!" she heard Brath yell, and turned in time to see gray and black fletching whiz through the air, on target to strike the lord marshall. She automatically sent a deflection spell to stop the arrow. She was too late. Sigel fell face forward as the arrow lodged in his spine, midway down his back.

"Sigel! No!" she screamed, racing to his side. Dara beat her to him and stood in front of Sigel to prevent anyone else from attacking the lord marshall. Briana was off Banrion before the horse even stopped. Swirling her finger in the air, she drew a drape of protection around them.

Seeing their general down, the Taranian army responded with heart-stopping fury. In seconds, the only Gray Military standing were drenched in blood. A single Moherian soldier stood as witness to the decimation of his unit, bound tightly by leather, guarded by two faerie warriors.

"Maker, damn them," Brath cursed the dead soldiers before turning to one of the crow generals. "Where did they come from? You said the pass was clear."

"It was, Sire. They had to have been hiding in the forest underneath our sight."

Brath dismissed him and turned to Sigel, who lay still on the ground, moaning in response to Briana's physical assessment.

"We need to stabilize the arrow and cut the end off," she advised.

"Take... it... out," Sigel groaned.

It seemed Brath was going to comply, but Briana put a hand on his arm. "No, it could make things worse. Is there a surgeon in any town nearby?"

"Maybe Ratskillen, but at the moment, you are his best chance."

She didn't bother saying she hadn't a clue how to properly remove the arrow.

"Sigel, I can't take it out safely, but we'll cut this off and get you on a horse and to a surgeon," she said, with more assurance then she felt.

After Briana used cloth wrapping to prevent the arrow from movement, Brath, with nothing more than a hunting knife, cut the arrow down to an inch of his body. Together they rolled him on his side. Sigel was barely conscious through the procedure.

"Sigel, can you bend your knees?" Briana asked him, hoping to get him upright.

While his upper body attempted to shift, absolutely nothing happened from the waist down.

"Sigel, can you wiggle your toes or feet?" She held her breath.

Nothing.

Sigel looked not at his feet but at her, his eyes glassy and unfocused. "How's that?" With those words, his head fell back, and he lost consciousness totally.

Briana looked dismally at his flaccid lower body. "I think he's paralyzed."

CHAPTER TEN

DUN LURA

Their hope for a surgeon was dashed when they arrived in Ratskillen near midday and discovered that the surgeon was taken by some of Shamwa's soldiers to treat their own injured. She and Cailleach worked together to remove the arrowhead and treat the wound with a thick dressing of willow and comfrey, and a healthy dose of healing intention. Briana stared at the dark hair of Sigel's chest that lay in stark contrast to the ghostly pale skin underneath, which was better than staring at the violent weaving of old scars across his back that she'd been focused on for the past two hours. The wound would heal. What remained uncertain was whether he'd regain use of his lower body, or if he'd even become conscious again. She'd been glad of his semi-comatose state during the trip, since the pain would've been excruciating and he probably would've resisted travelling in a litter. Now she desperately wanted him to wake up.

"We've done all we can for now, Briana. Time will tell the rest of the story," Cailleach said, her hand patting Briana's lower back.

"It's just wrong," she said, wiping a tear from her eye. "He's the strongest man I know. What if..."

"Now, now, Your Majesty," Mrs. Thacker interjected with a cluck of her tongue, her wild, variegated hair waving about. The owner of the Seven Hearths Inn had provided everything they needed to care for Sigel. "No what ifs," Mrs. Thacker continued. "The lord marshall will be right as rain in no time. Not to worry, not to worry."

Briana couldn't help but stare at her odd eyes, one light blue, the other a melding of amber and emerald.

"Thank you, Mrs. Thacker, for everything. You've been a gift from Maker. You're sure it's okay for Sigel to stay here?"

"Of course, of course," she said, sniffing through her bent and misshapen nose, while at the same time smiling widely through two rows of perfect, brilliant white teeth. "I'm happy to do my part to support the king. Besides, Lord Marshall Sigel has been a friend for a long time. We'll see him through this."

Brath entered the room and stood beside Briana, his arm around her waist. He joined her in staring down at the stalwart general.

"Armor would have prevented this injury."

"I know. I've got the smith working on it, Briana." He let out a long sigh. "Bri—we have to get going if we're going to beat Shamwa. The horses are waiting. Cailleach, stay here with Sigel and send a crow if anything changes."

Leaning down, Briana placed a kiss on Sigel's pale cheek. She thought he stirred, but maybe it was her imagination.

Horses stood in the yard, packs loaded with supplies. Captain O'Rourke and a few of the local militia stood nearby.

"Your Majesty," the captain addressed his king, "I and a group of my men are prepared to ride with you."

"Thank you, Captain, but I need you here to protect Ratskillen and Lord Marshall Sigel."

"Aye, Sire, as you wish. What about the prisoner?"

"Keep him under close guard. When we finish at Dun Lura, I will send Sir Cruahan back to try to turn him to our side. He'd be a useful spy. For now, keep him fed, watered and bound tight!"

Brath mounted Ruark and without so much as a tally-ho, they were off.

⤸

Dry weather continued to bless their journey and they halted in the forest around Dun Lura in afternoon. Whether it was Cailleach's spell or the furious speed they'd kept, they arrived on time. The old, abandoned fortress, once part of a small village, lay eerily silent, except for the distant sound of birds in the surrounding forest. Brath had a troop of faeries investigate the inside of the ruins for any sign of unwanted guests. In moments they returned with the information that only members of the Winge army were inside. Brath led his party out of the forest to the fort.

"Your Majesties," said Sir Thomas in his smooth voice, from the remnants of the fort's front doorway.

Despite the situation, Briana couldn't help but smile, happy to see the elegant clan chief of the Winges. Dressed head to toe in black silk and black leather boots, his shoulder-length black hair winged back to perfection, he appeared more appropriate for GQ than for a battle with an evildoer, although the sharp focus in his black eyes suggested otherwise. At his side was an equally elegant Epona, decked out in her own battle gear, the black trousers hugging her long legs tucked into boots, swords flashing on both hips.

Brath dismounted and Briana slid off Banrion as well, heading to Sir Thomas for a hug.

He embraced her quickly. "Lady Isabella sends her love. Now, we must get you inside. Messengers report that Lord Shamwa is not far off."

Epona and Briana hugged quickly. "We've lots of catching up to do," the Mistress of Horses said. "*After* we kick Shamwa's arse."

Brath delivered the news about Sigel before giving everyone their orders. Everyone, including horses, was to be hidden inside the fort. Jonathan was instructed to tie Ealga's horse to a stone post near the front of the ruins.

"If he sees her horse, he'll believe she's inside. I hope," Brath said.

Faerie warriors joined the crows as tiny points of light in the forest. Aya'emrys remained with the group in the fort.

"If it pleases Your Majesties, I would prefer to stay with my tuathla," he said, and was granted permission by both monarchs.

Epona and Aya'emrys led Briana, Jonathan, Rippa and Dara to the back of the fort and up an intact stone staircase to a massive room with a partial roof and the remnants of a fireplace. One wall had crumbled, but three stood, still boasting a few windows. Epona placed herself at one after urging Briana to crouch in the corner.

"Really, Epona, do you think I'm going to sit back and do nothing?"

Epona flashed her a serious look. "Today, you are not my friend, but my queen. My main priority is to keep you safe."

"The mistress is correct, High Lady, we must keep you safe," the faerie captain concurred from her other side.

Briana stepped back but did not crouch. "I…" The ear-splitting whinny of a horse ended whatever argument she meant to make. Dara stepped in front of her, growling low in his throat, the hair straight up on his back.

"Party time," Epona whispered, raising one of her swords.

Briana moved closer to the window despite her guardians' warnings. Her heart went straight to her throat. The horse of the Dar Morch reared up, his legs pawing at the sky, steam curling from his nostrils under red eyes that glowed violently. Holding his seat without the least difficulty was Lord Shamwa, his own eyes still filmed with a glassy red sheen from the spirit who currently inhabited him.

"Sweet Maker, that is some horse!" Epona murmured, awestruck.

"Where's Brath?" Briana asked, hoping he and his men had hidden themselves before Shamwa's arrival.

Epona gave her an odd, sidelong glance. "He and the men are beneath us. Don't worry, Briana—Your Majesty—he's hidden. Our armies have Shamwa surrounded. He isn't getting out of this alive."

Knowing Shamwa and his men were surrounded by crows and faeries didn't make Briana feel any more secure. This horse, and Shamwa by extension, held strong magic. She was quite sure that only magic would win the day. The question was whether her magic was stronger than Shamwa's, and how best to use it to their advantage. The beast threw his head about wildly, stamping the dirt. Briana forced herself to center and allow the magic inside her to build. As the colors in her mind surfaced, she mentally reached in for red and black and sent the ribbon through the air, whispering, "Dar Morch, you belong to me. You will obey your tuathla."

With a great snort, the stallion whipped his head in her direction and stopped stomping and blowing smoke. Briana watched his gaze travel directly to the upper floor of the ruins, where she remained out of sight. A brief, fiery blast from his mouth torched a round spot on the ground in front of him.

Briana considered possible scenarios. Ideally, the horse would totally recognize her power as the tuathla of Evalon and unseat his current rider. Or, would he remain under the influence of whomever had called him up? Surely, Shamwa hadn't been able to do that. Who then?"

As another shot of fire burst from the beast, Briana realized he might burn everything to the ground. Could she fight fire with fire? *Yeah, I can,* she thought, *but a fiery blaze in a heavily forested area doesn't necessarily ensure anyone's victory.* Instead, she held her breath and waited.

Shamwa was surrounded by several dozen Gray Military. He scanned the area and seemed to take note of Ealga's horse. He looked at the fort's entrance, clearly suspicious. "Search the fort," he ordered. Three men left his circle of protection and went into the building.

Although all was silent around the fort, the fact that the men did not immediately return must've alerted Shamwa. Snapping the reins on the faerie horse, he shouted, "Back! Back to the forest!"

The instant he moved, the crow and faerie armies materialized in a line around them to block their escape. Two lines of Gray Military soldiers encircled Lord Shamwa.

"Shields up!" he yelled. The stallion was in a frenzy, stomping and pawing, smoke and fire blasting from his nose, starting tiny blazes in the dry grass near the fort. The Grays raised their shields, leaving a large gap at the apex of the circle.

"Mr. Stark, I do believe you are in the best position to attack," Briana said, encouraging the young man to raise his bow.

Jonathan nocked an arrow, moved to the window and let one fly into the center of the circle. He missed Shamwa but impaled a soldier. He let loose a second arrow before the man dropped. It took Shamwa's men seconds to locate the archer. By the time they did, several more Grays were dead. Shamwa, however, managed to push his shield warriors back inside the tree line.

The acrid smell of smoke reached inside the fort. Briana ran to the other side of their room and looked out the window to find one whole side of the fort ablaze, flames growing and crawling through window openings and cracks in the stones.

"Hey, guys, we have a wee problem here," she called out to her companions, who were lobbing whatever they could find in the direction of Shamwa. She was trying to garner enough magic to pull water from somewhere to douse the threat, but her concentration was impaired by the chaos around her. "Arr," she growled.

Brath burst into the room. "Get out! We're on fire!" He glanced at Briana with a shake of his head. "I really didn't want to do this, but we're all going to have to fight." He grabbed her hand and pulled her down the stairs, Dara and Rippa on their heels. Epona and Captain Aya'emrys were right behind them with Jonathan pulling up the rear. Briana hopped neatly over one of the three dead bodies. By the time they made it outside, Briana had her shield in front of her and Nua raised high as she charged the nearest man. Nua did most of the work, finding the sweet spot on the soldier's chest, resulting in a flowery bloom of red across his tunic.

"You would be at less risk and perhaps more able to help by seeking a hiding place and using your magic," Captain Aya'emrys informed her, sounding as though he were suggesting she walk by the garden instead of the seashore.

"I tried. Can't think in all this madness," she answered, banging her shield against the head of a Gray. He did a little crabwalk before falling against one of his comrades. The next thing she knew, she was plumped down on her backside next to a large oak. Dara joined her and took up a guarding position. She felt a protective force surround her. Compliments of Aya'emrys? Not sure if she should be angry or grateful, she decided to take advantage of the situation and do as the captain suggested. She forced herself to calm as she viewed the scene around her. Brath was in sword-to-sword combat with a large Moherian. When the tip of the gargantuan's sword swiped across the king's shoulder, she issued a prayer of gratitude for the thicker leather vest he had worn.

Where was Shamwa? What started out as organized troops had become a melee with the faerie horse and prime minister seemingly absent. At least until she heard a chilling whinny. She spotted them, lightly surrounded and about to escape.

"Oh, no you don't." She pointed her finger and spoke the words of power. The birch and cherry trees nearest Shamwa bent and wrapped around each other, creating a living cage that stopped him in his tracks. She grinned when the trees seemed impervious to the flames from the horse. "Thanks, guys."

As Shamwa scrambled to get through the fence, Epona was almost upon him, her sword raised to strike. A split second before Epona struck, the flat of a sword came across the side of her head, dropping her in a heap on the ground. She didn't move. The Gray soldier was about to run his sword through her back. Briana's heart stopped. A dark blur whooshed past Briana. Sir Cruahan barreled into the man, his sword sinking into his gut. With his free hand he pulled the soldier to the ground and held him, slitting his throat with a smaller knife. None of the sounds she heard came from Epona. Was she dead? She needed to get her out of there, but she might be killed herself in the attempt. On cue, she felt the aura come over her. She forced herself to relax and use the altered state of consciousness more effectively. Heat suffused her hand; indeed, her whole body felt like a fireball. She had to release that energy. Pointing she ran her hand over and around Epona's body and then drew her finger in. The unconscious woman slid toward her effortlessly. When she lay motionless in front of her, Briana let out her breath. *It worked! If I can do that...* she turned her attention to Shamwa. The Dar Morch's horse, carrying Lord Shamwa, soared into the air and landed beyond the tree fence. *Dammit, he's escaped!* She took three steps to go after him but checked the impulse. Brath would throttle her and besides, she needed to stay and watch over Epona. She checked the woman's carotid pulse. Her heart beat strong, but fast. Briana guarded over her as men fell left and right all around. Except for Epona, the good guys all seemed to be still in the fight. Sir Thomas glanced once at her and nodded before dancing again with his foe. Silver sword and black silk whirled and dipped among the soldiers, making war an art form for the leader of the Winge clan.

Time lapsed into a sequence of deathly images and heart-clenching moments. Briana maintained her vigil over Epona, making mildly effective, magical jabs at Shamwa's soldiers from her protected position.

She jumped up and did a fist pump when the last of the enemy was captured and bound, joining a handful of Gray hostages.

"Yes, well, that's all well and good, but it seems our real target escaped," Brath said, startling her. She hadn't heard or seen him come near.

"I almost went after him."

He narrowed his eyes. "Thank you for rethinking that." He knelt beside Epona. "Will she be okay?"

"I hope so, but we need to get her somewhere a little more conducive to healing."

While the men were gathering booty that would be useful to the cause, and crows were scouting for Shamwa, Epona came to life.

"My head hurts," she said suddenly, rubbing at the swelling on her temple.

"Yeah, I bet. The bastard whacked you a good one," Briana replied, assisting her friend to a sitting position. "Anything else hurt?"

The Mistress of the Hunt stretched her limbs and shook her head. Standing, she seemed to shake off the effects of the injury with ease. She brushed away Briana's attempt to check her pupils. "I'm fine. What happened to Shamwa?"

Briana explained. The crows returned with the news that Shamwa had disappeared. Brath rubbed his temples. Sir Thomas asked about the disposition of the prisoners.

"Do you have room at Winge Mansion? That would be the closest place to deal with them."

"We can detain them in the dungeon and begin interrogation."

Briana remembered the room where she had interrogated Jonathan Stark; apparently he did, as well. "It's too small to hold five men," she said.

"There is a real dungeon, below Winge Mansion, that is more than large enough," Sir Thomas said, winking at her.

"Is it secure? If these guys escape, your whole family is at risk."

"It is *very* secure, my queen." He turned to the young man who had once graced his other interrogation room. "You, young man, were brilliant. I dare say, I never expected you to master archery skills so quickly. You may just give Silas a proper challenge when he returns."

A tiny bird fluttered through Briana's heart, but was gone with Brath's next words.

"Sir Thomas, would you see Briana and the others safely to Winge Mansion? I'll return to Ratskillen and see what can be done to get Sigel to your home to recuperate. Briana's faerie warriors will accompany you. I'll take my knights, except you, Cruahan. You might be the most helpful in persuading the Grays to our side. I'll bring the prisoner at Ratskillen back with me to join his friends."

Briana frowned. She hated the thought of them going in opposite directions. Apparently, he had the same misgiving. "I'd have a moment with my wife," he said, taking her hand and leading her away from the others. "I wish we didn't have to separate. I wish you weren't here at all. I should've left you at Ard Darach."

"Don't start." She jabbed her shoulder into his side. His angst turned her own worry into a reason to be strong. "We'll be fine. Besides having plenty of security," she gave a nod toward the group of faeries and crows waiting for her, "I have courage." She growled like the cowardly lion and then added playfully, "and if that fails, I'll try magic. Now, why don't you give your wife a kiss and go get Sigel. I miss having him around, barking orders and giving me a hard time."

He complied, holding her as though he might never see her again. When they finally drew apart, he searched her face.

She stared back, feeling like something else needed to be said.

Neither spoke.

He turned and walked toward his knights.

"Brath!" she called out suddenly, loath to let him go just yet.

He whipped his head around. "Yes?"

She opened her mouth to speak, but nothing came out. When it did, it was not at all what she thought she meant to say. "Be safe. Hurry back."

His shoulders drooped slightly as he nodded and mounted Ruark. One last look, and then he disappeared with his men through the trees toward Ratskillen.

Night was falling two days later when they rode onto the oak-lined avenue leading up to Winge Mansion. The black-and-white marble estate appeared spectral in the fading light. Crow warriors transformed into their avian form and perched along the avenue and atop the towers of the mansion. Ballynickle, the butler, met them at the entrance.

"Captain Aya'emrys, I'd like you to stay inside. Brath will have a fit if I don't post a guard outside my room. Between you and Jonathan…"

"Begging your pardon, High Lady, but let the lad sleep. I do not require sleep and will look after you tonight."

As instructed, Cruahan led the prisoners away from the mansion to the mysterious dungeon. Briana shuddered to think of it just below them, but trusted Sir Thomas' judgment.

Ballynickle's attempt to speak with Sir Thomas was thwarted by the sound of voices in the library nearby. Epona sucked in a breath. Sir Thomas made a strangled sound.

Alarm rang through Briana. She placed one hand on Dara's back as she followed her host into the library.

"Sweet Maker." Epona gasped and raced to the man standing in front of the fireplace, dressed in dark leather, with a hand on his sword.

Sir Thomas stood rooted to the floor, his lips pressed firmly together, jaw clenching and unclenching. A curious mix of anger and pain burned from his dark eyes.

When Briana looked back at Epona, it was to find her in front of the fire, wrapped in the arms of the devilishly handsome man, tears streaming down her face. *This must be*, Briana thought, *the errant son, Kieran Winge.*

CHAPTER ELEVEN

IRELAND

Silas, Dublin airport, Dublin, Ireland

The people exiting the Aer Lingus plane probably thought Silas was gallantly holding Katrina's arm to assist her down the ramp. The truth was quite the opposite. Silas was so sick to his stomach and weak-kneed that she was holding *him* up.

It had been the wildest, most daunting twelve hours of his life. Boston Logan Airport was enough to make him want to run back through the tree to Uisneach. Bright, artificial light blinded him. His ears were assaulted with the sound of crying babies, arguments, emotional greetings and departures, and the intermittent roar of jet engines as massive airplanes taxied down a long road and impossibly left the earth to presumably fly thousands of miles over the ocean. Even the smells bombarded him, of people, unwashed or heavily perfumed, of jet fuel and a thousand new foods that nauseated him. The airport was even busier than usual because people were returning home after the Fourth of July holiday, Katrina told him. Constant noise from the overhead communication system in several different languages, the push and bump of humanity through security and the added indignity of a body search made him a nervous wreck. Oh, how he'd like to have a few of these TSA agents in his arrow sights. He wondered why Katrina didn't seem affected.

Dublin Airport was only slightly less overwhelming. Colored light from the arrival and departure screens reflected against glass storefronts, instruction and information were given in both English and what Katrina said was Irish Gaelic, new smells challenged him and the ever-moving metal stairs going up and down to the different levels of the concourse made his stomach wobbly. By the time they found the baggage claim area, Silas' head was throbbing.

"Are you going to make it, Silas?" Katrina asked sympathetically.

"Aye, I suppose. Will we really have to do this all again?"

"We will when you find the runes. Could be next week or next year. God knows."

"Katrina! Katrina, dear!" a sweet Irish voice broke over the hum of conversation around them and the cacophony of the spinning luggage delivery system. "Mum!"

Katrina ran into the outstretched arms of a woman who appeared not much older than herself. The two women talked a mile a minute. Silas stood by patiently, knowing he would be introduced at some point. Caitlin O'Brien was faerie, all right. Petite, quick moving, yet graceful in a flowery blouse and flowing rose-colored skirt. Silver hair, cut short and wispy around her face, reminded him of Teaguen, Briana's faerie mentor. Her eyes, gray like Briana's and Katrina's, shimmered with happy tears, but he could imagine them just as easily twinkling with mischief. Her voice sounded like summer. She may have seen more than seventy seasons but there was a youthfulness about her. A playfulness. She was faerie.

"They'll get to ye eventually," said a man with a warm, deep voice. Silas turned to him. The wiry man rose only to his shoulders but had an unmistakable strength of presence. His bright blue eyes twinkled under gray winged eyebrows. matched by a wide grin. His face was solid, gently lined, with a long, hawkish nose under dark gray hair that was neatly combed back, showing a dusting of white at the temples. The total picture was one of an old and kind soul, a man who had befriended both happiness and sorrow in equal measure.

"Finnegan O'Brien," he said, holding out his hand.

Silas took it. "Silas O'Mara."

"Aye, I'd have known ye from Katrina's description. Welcome to Ireland."

"Thank you, sir."

"Och, no sir. Call me Finnegan."

"Thank you, Finnegan."

Caitlin finally addressed him. "All right, then, let me get a good look at you, lad. Katrina has told us so much about you." Her eyes assessed him from head to toe. "Ah, you're a handsome one, you are. I can see why Briana's so fond of you."

"Caitlin, hush," said Finnegan. "That's no way to greet the lad."

She peered up into Silas' face. "Hush yourself, auld man. I think Silas and I will understand each other just fine."

He smiled, despite feeling mildly embarrassed. He knew they knew everything about him and why he was here, but it felt odd just the same.

Katrina stepped in. "I was thinking we could take Silas on a quick tour of Dublin while we're here. Can you do one more city, Silas?"

"Does it involve food?" he asked, his stomach, now settled, reminding him that he hadn't eaten all day."

Finnegan clapped his shoulder. "A man after me own heart! We'll take ye to O'Neill's. It's close to the castle and to Trinity, a good place to start the tour. Just tell us when ye get tired. Jet lag is sure to knacker you at some point."

Luggage collected, they headed out of the airport and into the city. Silas asked a few questions as they drove, but mostly alternated his time between studying the amazing architecture of the city, a blending of old and new, and studying a different method of driving, on the opposite side of the car and the road. After a while, he thought he could get the hang of it.

"I can't believe you found space at Trinity Street parking," Katrina exclaimed as they entered O'Neill's, a popular pub in the Temple Bar district of Dublin.

"Perhaps the faeries are with us." Caitlin giggled, stealing a look at Silas, who winked back at her.

"Or perhaps Molly Malone," Finnegan whispered in his ear, referring to the statue of the buxom fishmonger they'd walked by that had Silas' eyes bugging out.

They were led through a maze of rooms that would excite any nest-seeking mouse. Rich, warm wood floors, walls covered with endless portraits, framed posters, and mirrors with advertising like Powers Whiskey and

Shamrock Rovers, along with gobs of antiques. Silas ran his hand across the banister of a magnificent curved staircase. A young couple sat tucked at a small table in a snug under the staircase. Traditional Irish music played in the background.

He sat between Caitlin and Finnegan. They ordered tea and full Irish breakfast all around.

"Silas, do ye have a plan for how to begin the search for these runes?" Caitlin asked.

"I think I should start at the Hill of Uisneach, but beyond that, I've no idea. Clues are in short supply. Since I don't know how long it will take, I think I should also get a job doin' somethin' to earn my keep."

"Ah, well, ye see, we've taken care of that," Finnegan said. "Cait's brother, Seamus, he owns a pub in town. When we told him a friend of Briana's was comin' for an extended visit and was a musician, he thought it would be craic for ye to play on the weekends. With the tourists pourin' in, he could use ye."

The server arrived with plates heaped with eggs, sausage, bacon, black and white pudding, grilled tomatoes and mushrooms, baked beans, potato cakes, toast and an assortment of jams. Silas eyed the food with enthusiasm.

"I can't eat all this," Katrina moaned, gawking at her plate.

"Aye, but I see a lad before me eyes that will finish what's left," Caitlin said, grinning as Silas tucked into his food with gusto.

After he swallowed a mouthful of pudding, he asked, "What kind of music would he be expectin'?"

"He'd want some of the traditional tunes, of course, but anythin' you can sing, he'd welcome."

Silas had mastered Briana's guitar and with Katrina's blessing, brought it along. He also found a bodhran, but Katrina advised purchasing one in Ireland. With those two instruments and his voice, he could manage well enough as the local bard of Tullamore.

"I've been learnin' Irish songs from YouTube and some of Katrina's CDs. I'm ready to start whenever he needs me."

His eagerness prompted Caitlin to insist he take the time to get acclimated and learn to drive before taking on a job. Finnegan promised to start driving lessons tomorrow.

Talk turned to Briana and faeries. Silas answered all their questions about their granddaughter, now the queen of a faraway kingdom. Caitlin gazed at him pensively as he quietly described her life and how committed she was to bringing harmony between all factions of the kingdoms, including the faeries of Evalon.

"It's hard to believe that me mother was a druidess and me father is a real faerie," Caitlin whispered, almost to herself. "And the faerie king?"

"I knew there was a reason I always called ye princess."

"Ye never called me princess, auld man. Many other things, but not that." She giggled and patted his hand. "What's he like?" she asked Silas. "Me father, I mean."

"I only met him once, but he's impressive." Trying to describe a golden, majestic and magical being was not easy, but watching her eyes light up and wander into some romantic notion of Evalon, Silas was happy he could give her something.

"Why do you suppose your mum never told you about your history or the runes?" Silas asked.

Caitlin sighed. "I've no idea. I can only think she felt we would be safer if no one knew about us or the runes."

That didn't make sense to Silas. If Catriona knew the runes would be needed for magic to flourish in Uisneach, why would she make it impossible for anyone to find them?

When breakfast was over they walked across the street to Trinity College, entering through the front gate into Parliament Square. While none of the buildings remotely resembled anything in Uisneach, Silas found himself feeling more at ease here than anywhere he'd been so far. These buildings were old and comforting. Students sat under the hardy old maple trees on the square. Walking by one grand old soul, he laid a hand on its rough old bark. Disappointment fluttered through him. He pushed and frowned when nothing happened. When he turned away from the tree, he caught Caitlin's curious and sympathetic gaze.

He entered the Old Library silently. *This is a sacred place*, he thought as he stood at one end of the long room and stared mesmerized by the dusty light filtered through high windows into a two-story room filled from floor to ceiling with millions of bound books, some likely as ancient as Ireland.

"Has Briana seen this?" he whispered to Katrina. To speak louder than a whisper felt sacrilegious.

"This is her favorite place in Dublin."

"Aye, I believe that." He paused, staring at one of the busts of someone identified as Shakefpear. "Is this the same *Shakespeare* that you told me about, the poet?"

"It is."

He marveled at the beautiful artwork of the *Book of Kells* displayed in another room and wondered why the sight of it brought a tear to Caitlin's eye.

"I'm a silly auld woman," she said, covering her emotion with a small laugh. "It's just that something so ancient reminds me of how very far away Briana is."

Silas put a hand on her shoulder, fearing that if he spoke he, too, would shed embarrassing tears.

They left the library and headed back to the chapel, where a group of students was rehearsing a scene from Shakespeare's *Romeo and Juliet*. Silas paused at the Campanile, a one-hundred-foot bell tower that seemed to him a portal of sorts. His companions, not realizing he'd stopped, continued around the side toward the chapel. Silas took a breath and walked through the archway in the base of the tower into the center. Looking up and around, he again felt mildy disappointed that nothing magical happened. He was still looking skyward as he came out of the tower, when he bumped hard into a woman with a briefcase in one hand and a book in the other.

"I'm so sorry, miss," he said, picking up her book and handing it to her.

"No worry, lad. I'll not batter you for it."

She smiled brightly, and the hair raised on his neck. She was a pretty lass, hair as black as a raven's wing and eyes the color of bluebells. And then she was gone, taking the shiver with her.

Katrina was waving him over, so he rejoined Briana's family to suffer the grievous reenactment of two star-crossed lovers.

"Silas, can you come up here a minute, please?" Katrina called to him from the back bedroom in the cottage behind the O'Brien home.

He was helping Finnegan open a stuck window in the kitchen. The bright and cheery cottage hadn't been used since the last time Katrina, Edwin and Briana visited, a couple of years ago. Efficient and tidy, with a kitchen and living area in shades of green and yellow, one small bedroom and a larger bedroom with its own bathroom. Silas felt his doubts about being in Dublin begin to melt away. The woodstove in the corner would be a welcome companion this winter, should he be here that long. Bookcases, a small television and a laptop on a desk would provide him more than enough to do in his spare time. Briana's guitar now sat beside the sofa, along with the notebook Katrina had given him. He planned on spending most of his time searching for the runes, but he would have a job, and part of that job included learning current and traditional tunes and writing new music of his own. Yes, he'd be busy; hopefully busy enough not to dwell on missing Briana.

"Be right there," he answered Katrina, giving the window frame a hefty heave. It jerked open, nearly knocking him off balance.

"Och—nice to have some young, strong muscles handy. I'll see if I can find a few other things in need of a good arm," Finnegan teased him.

"Make me a list," Silas replied before going to the small bedroom where Katrina was halfway in a closet.

Caitlin sat on the small bed nearby. "Can you help her get that chest out, then?"

"Stand aside, milady, and I shall retrieve it for you," he said in his most gallant tone.

When Katrina moved out of the way, he stepped inside the closet and grasped the trunk handle with both hands and pulled. It was heavier than it looked. "What have you in here?" he asked with a grunt. "Stones?" He put his whole body into it and pulled out a white, humpbacked trunk with mauve colored straps and ornate corners and silver handles, latch and lock. Across the top of the trunk was a carved and stained image of what appeared to be the Tree of Uisneach.

"It's all me mum's things," Caitlin murmured, laying a hand on Silas' shoulder and peering around him as he wiggled the clasp open.

He felt something coming from the hand on his shoulder, something tenuous but energetic. He heard a swift intake of breath. A second sharp inhalation came from Katrina. He glanced up to see them both pale and round-eyed.

"What's wrong?" he asked.

Katrina shook her head.

"I don't know," Caitlin said. "I feel odd."

"Have you never looked inside the chest?"

"Never," Caitlin replied. "I tried a few times, but it never seemed right, almost like even if I had tried, it would have refused to open."

Silas grinned. "Says the woman who doubts herself a faerie. I don't suppose you have a key to this lock."

She handed him an ornate silver key which he fit in the lock with a *click*. It opened effortlessly, and he lifted the lid with ease. He stood and moved aside, giving the women room to kneel beside the trunk and sift through the items inside.

Oohs and *ahhs* accompanied the removal of colorful shawls, glittering jewelry and a pair of handsewn and brightly embroidered slippers. Nothing accounted for the heaviness of the trunk. A picture of a woman and a child caught Silas's attention. The mother sat demurely in a high back chair while her small daughter stood beside her mum, one hand resting politely on her lap.

"She was beautiful," Caitlin said wistfully, "and so much fun. I don't remember where this was taken and it's curious that me father wasn't there. Or at least the father I knew." She set the photo aside when Katrina removed a plaid wool cape from the trunk and nearly dropped it.

"That's one heavy cloak," she said, turning back the edge. She gasped in shock.

Wrapped inside the cloak was a dagger, jeweled and carved with runes that Silas knew could only have come from Evalon.

"That doesn't look like any metal I've seen," Finnegan interjected, having joined the group around the trunk.

"It's Evalonian steel," Silas said. "Faerie steel." If he'd had any doubts about the veracity of all this, the dagger murdered them. Catriona was a faerie from Evalon and somewhere, perhaps even in this trunk, were the runes that would get him home and restore magic in the kingdom! His heart pounded as he searched the rest of the trunk, but the search came up empty. No maps, journals or anything that included the prophecy or clues to where the runes might be hidden.

Caitlin picked up the dagger and turned it over and over in her hands. "Uh, Silas, I feel kind of funny," she said, her voice weak and her eyes drooping.

"Hand it to Katrina," he said, curious.

She passed the knife to her daughter and instantly Katrina fell back on her hands, face gone ghost-white, eyes rolling backward. Silas grabbed the knife, without any ill effects.

Katrina's color returned and her eyes refocused, but she put a fist to her mouth, attempting to stifle a cry. "I saw her! I saw Briana. It was only a flash, but I saw her."

"What did you see?" Silas asked eagerly.

Katrina bent her head and closed her eyes as though trying to see it again. "She really is a queen. She has power, equal to her husband's. Oh, sorry, Silas. It's just that I feel a man beside her. But, she's worried, or scared or… something is bothering her." Katrina pounded her fist on her forehead. "No details. We've got to get these runes, Silas."

"I know," he said, wishing for more information but knowing it didn't matter. Whatever was going on in Uisneach, his job was here for now, and she was right. They needed to find the runes.

"Oh, heavens, a memory came to me," Caitlin said excitedly, picking up the photograph of her mother once again. She began humming. "She had a lullaby she used to sing to us children. I can't remember it all, but I loved these words:

"Faeries sing and place a ring upon their own,
Druid, crown and faerie, three become the one,
Cheerful celebration."

"I know this is written down somewhere and I will tear this cottage and our house apart looking for it."

"In the meantime, the dagger needs to stay in the trunk." He and Katrina exchanged a knowing look. Having seen her daughter once, she'd risk the physical effect to get another glimpse of her. The last thing they needed was her slipping through some sort of portal or otherwise coming to harm.

⟡

"Och, man, did ye drive in Maine?" Finnegan asked as Silas attempted to back out of the driveway and nearly hit the shrub at the end of the drive.

"Mostly watched. Katrina didn't want to confuse me with learnin' to drive two different ways."

Finnegan groaned. "Well, lad, then our first stop best be at Seamus' Pub for a drink. Not sure I'll survive this without a pint."

"I'm certain Katrina said I must never drink and drive."

"Aye, well…" He winked at Silas, but said no more.

They made it to the pub in one piece.

"A ball of malt and a pint of plain!" Finnegan told the barman, who happened to be his brother-in-law, Seamus Kelly.

Seamus Kelly was barely tall enough to see over the bar. His bright red hair stood on end every which way and his sharp blue eyes assessed Silas with one quick sweep from head to toe. He gave a friendly nod and pushed a couple of pints in front of the men.

"Seamus, meet yer new minstrel, Silas O'Mara. Silas, yer new boss, Seamus."

The men shook hands. Silas was introduced to Rebecca, his very tall and very thin daughter and second barkeep.

Seamus caught Silas' surprised glance.

"Her mother's tall," Seamus said, not the least offended.

The nutty spice of Tullamore's finest whiskey burned the back of Silas' throat and within minutes he knew he would not be driving home.

"Up to playin' somethin' for us, Silas? So's I can see what I'm payin' for."

"You have a guitar handy?"

Seamus nodded toward the tiny stage in the corner where a guitar stood lonely against the blackened wall.

"That so-called stage is mostly storage or sometimes serves as a dance floor for the lovebirds who need to get a bit close, if ye take me meanin'. Usually the entertainment sits at the table yonder, and whoever comes with an instrument joins in. Supper and drinks are free, and I'll give you a stipend as well. Most of yer earnin's are from tips."

Silas fetched the instrument and came back to the bar. "Any requests?"

"I'll make it easy. You know 'Danny Boy'?"

Silas strummed the opening chords. "Oh, Danny boy, the pipes, the pipes are callin'."

Seamus wiped more than one tear from his eye during the song and when Silas finished, he cleared his throat. "Yeah, man, yer hired."

Silas was grateful that Finnegan didn't even ask if he wanted to drive home. The older man slid behind the wheel and drove through town as though he hadn't had one drink, never mind the three!

They curved through a roundabout and Silas' eyes swerved to a woman walking down the street. He recognized the briefcase, the raven hair and the curves of the woman he'd bumped into at Trinity College. *How odd*, he thought, to run into her twice in as many days.

Chapter Twelve

Hill of Uisneach

IT TOOK NO time for Silas to get a learner permit to drive. Finnegan spent two solid days on the road with him, teaching him to drive him before he took and passed his driving test with the instructor. He hadn't thought any of it would be so easy, but here he was driving himself to the Hill of Uisneach for the first time.

The sun had long passed the midday point when he arrived. The woman at the visitor center took his donation.

"If you hurry up the ancient road," she pointed to a path away from the visitor center, "you'll catch up with the tour and not miss much."

He thanked her and followed the shrub-lined track across a field. Cows grazed nearby. To think that thousands of years ago, druids had made their way up this same path to carry out a fire festival that worshiped the ancient gods and goddesses.

He caught up with the tour as they neared the Royal Palace and was stunned to find the tour guide was the very same raven-haired woman he'd come across twice since his arrival in Ireland! Hair stood straight up on his arms. What were the chances he'd run across this same woman three times in one week?

"Not only was this the palace of King Tuathal Techtmar," she said, "but it was the palace of Dagda, the Irish god of the earth, the high king of the magical race, the Tuatha De' Danann. It is believed the high king's horses were stabled over there, on the north side of the hill. Given the rich royal and magical history of the site, I want you to be very careful what you say. You never know when the *auld ones* will be listenin'."

All chatter stopped, and he watched her bite back a grin. This had probably happened hundreds of times before. Believers in the old ways or not, people naturally responded to such a subliminal message. That was the magic of storytelling, after all. He jerked when she suddenly turned her bluebell eyes in his direction and winked!

She turned her attention back to the Royal Palace and her visitors. There wasn't much to see if you weren't truly interested in the palace. The site was mostly a green mound of grass-covered rocks with an old stone wall and trees.

Silas was more interested in the tour guide. He took advantage of her diverted attention to study her fully. She was lovely, however different from Briana. In contrast to Briana's lean, warrior build, this girl was full and curvy in all the right places. Her summery blue eyes were set into a soft face with a creamy complexion. He noticed the edge of a tattoo peeking above the neckline of her blouse but couldn't tell what it was.

His attention was properly brought back to the hill when she showed the group the remains of two souterrains, hidden caves that might have been used to hide important artifacts in the event of a conflict in the area.

It was a lengthy tour and Silas eventually found himself interested in the archaeological and mystical history of the land. He thought it a shame that a sun god who owned a sword of light was drowned in the swampy lake before him. A god as important as Lugh should've had a more noble end. But then, as the guide pointed out, "we Irish do love sorrowful endin's." Nearby stood a tall wood sculpture of the god himself, with a long beard, haunted eyes and a pronounced frown.

Aye, I'd be frownin' too, were I you, Silas thought, ready to move on. Nothing here seemed a likely place for Catriona to hide runes.

He listened to the story of the druid's worshiping at the hill on Beltane, the first day of summer. While all the households extinguished their hearth fires, the two Beltane fires were lit. Cattle were herded between the fires to receive special blessing, and then the householders took an ember from the Uisneach fire to re-light their own fires at home.

"Even Julius Caesar wrote about the festivals that were held at the sacred place in the center of Gaul. Of course, then the eejit wiped out the druids who led the sacred festivals."

"Orla, is that St. Patrick's Bed?" a young man with short cropped hair and round glasses asked, sounding excited.

Orla. Pretty name. It suits her, he thought.

"Aye sir, it is. Good eye."

"He's my patron saint. I'm trying to visit all the places named for him."

"Well now, that's class!"

They were on the highest point of the hill, a spot that commanded impressive views of Westmeath. A lone, gangly tree and a littering of old stone relics stood on the summit. Marking the spot where St. Patrick may have added his name to those of the high kings, stood a stone monolith not much taller than the tour guide.

"St. Patrick was not Irish, did you know that? He came from England as a young lad, practically a slave, but he felt for the poor Irish, not havin' the love of Christ in them, and made it his mission to convert them. The name Patrick, if you're interested, is Latin and means regal or noble.

"On the handful of clear days in Ireland, you can see twenty counties," Orla said. "St. Patrick, himself, stood on this very hill in the fifth century. You can imagine why he thought it a good site to build a church. Some would say he wanted to put a church on every sacred site on the island. Alas, we cannot know what he was thinkin' but we do know that the O'Neills opposed the church. It is said that in response to their disapproval, St. Patrick cursed the very stones of the well down below, and to this day they are useless for any sort of practical purpose. I suppose it must be some consolation that he got a well named for him." A murmur of giggles ensued as she shut the gate. "I'll be showin' you the well a bit later that has Patrick's name on it."

She led the tour down the hill, never looking back, leaving Silas the freedom to consider her jean-clad backside. On the downward slope of the hill, somewhat protected by yellow gorse shrubs and wind shaped trees, sat a roundish mash of stone more than twice his height.

"And now, lads and lassies, here we are at the legendary capstone—oops, I mean the legendary Catstone—the *Ail na Mireann!* Gather round and look carefully to see the obvious cat about to pounce on the wee mouse."

Her use of wee mouse jolted Silas. He grew hot, feeling Briana's presence beside him, calling him, as she had many times, her great cat.

"I see it!" said a woman with an American accent who looked very much like the mouse about to be pounced upon.

"Well done!" the tour guide clapped her hands enthusiastically, as though the American was the first to have ever seen the image.

Silas had to walk about to find the angle that made the cat and mouse appear. Briana, the Mouse of Prophecy, and her great cat. He blinked away the moistness at the corner of his eye.

"The *Ail na Mireann* is the Irish Gaelic for the Stone of Divisions. Does anyone know why it is called that?"

Heads shook unanimously.

"You're in luck then, because I do!"

There was tittering, and Silas couldn't help but smile. Her outgoing nature and good humor made her perfect for this work.

"This stone, dear ones, is the true center of Ireland. Geographically it's the place where all the provinces of Ireland—Leinster, Munster, Connacht, Ulster and, up until the 17th century, Meath, come together. Spiritually, it's said to be the *Axis Mundi*, or the navel of Ireland, connectin' this world and…" she lowered her voice to barely above a whisper and gave the audience a mysterious gaze, "the other. The goddess for whom Ireland is named, Éiru, is said to be buried under that stone. It is an extremely sacred and magical place."

What it sounded like to Silas was a portal. A very good place to hide magical runes, he thought, studying every inch of the stone while trying to be discreet.

"Speaking of Éiru, myth tells the story of how the ancient druid, Amergin, met the goddess on this very hill and vowed to name the country after her; thus Éiru became Eire, or Erin, and finally, Ireland." She looked wistfully to the heavens. "Oh, how I'd love a man to name a country after me." When she looked back at the group, it seemed no coincidence to Silas that her eyes landed on him. She smiled a little flirtatiously before giving her full attention back to the tour group.

"It's said that there are places where the faeries can come and go as they wish. Places like the dolmens, ring forts and certain trees."

Silas jerked involuntarily.

"Can you feel the presence of faeries here?" Her twinkling gaze scanned the circle of tourists. "Do you see the sparklin' of the trees? It's said that the places where faeries have had their hearts broken are very powerful and quite spiritual."

The hill was cluttered with wells, souterrains and stone relics from the ring forts. There were potentially hundreds of places Catriona could hide magical runes. While he investigated the rocks around the ring fort, the group moved on, and he had to hurry to catch up with them at St. Patrick's Well, a rectangular, moss-dappled hole lined with stones. A vine that looked like ivy grew up around the edges, climbing the metal gate and post. Opening the gate, Orla moved aside so the tourists could get a better look. Silas took a turn leaning in, accidentally brushing against her as he did.

"Sorry," he mumbled.

"No worries, lad. No worries at all."

Something in her tone made him shiver. He turned his attention to the well. Intent on his examination, he didn't realize he was taking a lot longer than most did.

"Are you thinkin' of movin' in, then?" Orla asked from behind him, "or do you also have a love for the departed saint?"

He chuckled. "I suppose I'm just wonderin' what makes one hole in the ground more special than another."

The rest of the tour consisted of chitchat about the flora and fauna of the hill, examination of a few more archaeological sites and relics, and a short historical lesson on the modern-day Irish giants who had visited the hill, men who made the tourists sigh with nostalgia, like Pádraic Pearce and Éamon de Valera, leaders of the Easter Rising. Daniel O'Connell and poet James Joyce. Orla quoted from one of his poems and Silas made a mental note to look that fellow up.

Silas was disappointed when the end of the tour came and he hadn't discovered anything to help guide him in his search. The tourists were all saying good bye, some hugging Orla, others asking for a picture with her. Silas couldn't think of a reason to stay longer, so turned to leave. He felt a hand on his arm.

"Could you hold up a minute, lad?" Orla asked, her eyes less confident and tinged with a touch of shyness.

He nodded and walked over to the fire pit centered among risers in front of the visitor center. Feigning interest in the design of the primitive design, he waited.

"There, then, that's the last of them," she said at his shoulder, in a musical voice.

Again, the damn hackles rose on his neck. "Thank you for the tour, Orla. You're incredibly knowledgeable about the history of this place."

"Been doin' the tours for a few years now. It keeps me flush while I go to Trinners."

He knew she meant Trinity College. "I saw you there."

"You nearly banjaxed me there."

They laughed at the same time.

"So are you a ghost warrior or a faerie?"

"Beggin' your pardon?"

"Well, if you were wearing a kilt and wielding a sword, you'd pass for one of Boru's warriors. But there's an otherworldly presence about ye that makes me wonder if you're one of the Dé Danann come to life."

He pushed off from the tree and looked around, uncomfortable with her reference to otherworlds and faeries.

"What's your name?"

"Silas."

"Man of the stream," she replied immediately, tapping her lip. "Not an Irish name. Last name?"

"O'Mara," he said, after the smallest hesitation.

"Of the sea. Hmm… a man of the stream and the sea. Water's big to you, then."

It wasn't a question and he watched her play with the information in her mind.

"I'm Orla Kennedy. Orla comes from the old Irish name which means golden princess, and Kennedy is from the old Ceim'eidigh which is son of Lorcan, the king of Thomond, whose wife, Bebinn, was Brian Boru's mother."

He'd learned enough of Irish history to know that this made her and Briana clan kin. Brian Boru was the ancestral head of the O'Brien clan. *Interestin'.*

"Really," she went on, "look at me, why on earth would they have named me somethin' that means golden? That was certainly actin' the maggot. They should have named me Brenna. After all, I do have black hair. I have a thing for names," she said. "Our names, the names of places, it's what connects us to our history. I love history. I'm studyin' to complete my M. Phil. in Public History and Cultural Heritage." She glanced around the amphitheater. "This is the perfect place to combine work and education."

Just as Silas started to wonder if she was going to take a breath, she stopped talking. She kicked at a stone on the ground. "Well, you must think me dope, rattlin' on so."

"You have a nice voice, but I'll admit, I'm workin' to keep up with you."

"Sorry."

"No need."

"So, what are *you* doin' here?"

He fell to the cover story he and Katrina had created. "I'm writin' a book about faeries and this is part of me research."

"Faeries, is it?" She frowned. "We didn't talk much about the faerie lore."

"Not much, but what you did say was quite movin'. I could almost feel their wee broken hearts."

She looked up at him, all pretense dropping away. "I don't think it's an accident that we've met, Silas. I believe everythin' happens for a reason."

He nodded his agreement. "I'll have to come again and finish me research."

"Aye, do that, man of the stream. Maybe I'll give you a private tour."

This was where he was supposed to mention the other part of his cover story, that he was married. But he didn't.

He turned and walked toward the gate.

"Mr. O'Mara?" He turned to find her grinning. "Not a sword. Bow and arrow."

He stumbled sideways. "Beggin' your pardon?"

"That's what I see you with."

"Have you the sight, then?" He attempted to cover his shock with a joke.

She pushed a curl behind her ear and winked. "No, but they say my granny did. She's passed on now, joinin' the saints in heaven. I hope I see you around."

She turned and walked away, lifting her hand behind her in a backward wave that intrigued him. Who was he kidding? Everything about her intrigued him.

～

"Mother took me to the hill once," Caitlin said at dinner. "When I neared the Catstone, I became quite dizzy and ill. Mother was upset and forbid me to ever go to the hill again. I wonder if she knew that it was a portal back to Uisneach. I caught her cryin' that night in her room. When I was older and had suffered me first broken heart, she told me that she'd had her heart broken when she came to Ireland and left the man she loved and had longed for him every day of her life. Her eyes always carried a hint of that lingerin' sorrow."

Silas wondered if Briana's eyes carried a hint of sorrow or whether she was settled into her marriage and had forgotten about him. No, she couldn't. Could she? He accepted a second helping of potatoes, trying to shake off his own lingering sorrow. "Would you ever want to go there, Caitlin? Perhaps your faerie blood would allow you to get through. Maybe that's what made you ill."

While there was a wistful look in her eye, she shook her head. "No, lad, me life is here. Everythin' I know and love is here. It would be grand to help Briana and see such a magical place. However, I have too much to lose should I be sucked into a gateway to another world and not be able to get home." She reached for Finnegan's hand and kissed his weathered knuckles. He looked relieved.

"Do you think I could get to Uisneach?" Katrina asked, her voice a little wavery.

"Given that you have the same faerie blood as your mum and daughter, I would think it likely," Silas said.

Katrina looked at her mother and both women's eyes glistened. "How would you feel, Mum, if I went?"

The ticking of the grandfather clock in the living room seemed to fill the space while Caitlin regarded her daughter. "As much I might wish to be immortal, I am not, and I have only a handful of years left, Katrina. If you have the chance to be with your daughter and," she glanced briefly at Silas, "whatever grandchildren you might have, you should go. Are you considerin' it, then?"

Nodding, Katrina reached for the bottle of wine. She refilled her glass and tipped it toward Silas, who shook his head. "I've given the idea considerable thought. I've already put the house on the market. I don't know for sure that I would or could go, but knowing that Briana is out there somewhere…"

"Katrina, I'd remind you of the uncertainty of findin' the runes. What if you sold the house, gave everythin' away and couldn't go?"

"You'll find them, Silas, and I want to be ready when you do. The burden of this quest is on you and you must work hard and fast to find the runes. We'll do what we can to help."

"I swear to you all that I will move mountains, divert rivers and dry up sacred wells to find the runes. I will not fail Briana or Uisneach!"

Following that little speech, he collected his hat and a light coat, as the forecast was for rain, and the keys to the car he was using and headed back to the Hill of Uisneach.

He parked down the road and walked to the gated entrance to the hill, hoping to avoid attracting attention. Twilight bathed the landscape in blue and purple hews. Early stars twinkled teasingly through dark, passing clouds. He stopped at the entrance and leaned against the gate, reminded of the wee prayer Briana had shared with him. "Star light, star bright, first star I see tonight; wish I may, wish I might, wish I'd get my wish tonight," he whispered to whatever gods were listening. "Maker, please don't let me fail in this quest for the runes."

Cutting across the hill, he went straight to the Catstone. Darkness was not far away, but he really did want to see what happened in the time when twilight turns from amethyst to deeper blue, as Orla had quoted from the Irish poet. He hoped to see faeries.

Chapter Thirteen

Arthur Guinness

"Well, it could be worse," said the man, thumping the bar at Seamus' Pub. "We could be debating the choices America faces." There was a smattering of laughter at that and a few groans.

"Are ye daft, man. At least in America, the people know which side they're on. You're either a conservative or a liberal and ye hate each other. We don't even know what the difference is between the Fianna Fáil and the Fine Gael!"

"Stall the ball, Jack. Are ye, tellin' us ye don't feckin know which party ye belong to?"

"How long did it take to elect a taoisech, I ask ye?"

"Well, I'll give ye, the elections were brutal. But, Kenny is the taoisech and he'll bring order to the Dáil."

"Yer mad as a box of frogs, Liam," Jack said. "Go on with ye, then. Just order up another round."

Silas sat on the corner of the bar listening to the local debate on recent elections, the strangest that Finnegan could remember. For a bit, they weren't even sure who was running the country.

"What's the story?"

The familiar feminine voice brought a smile to his lips.

"Not familiar with that phrase. A way of sayin' hello?"

Orla punched his shoulder lightly. "Am I lucky enough that we live in the same town?"

"I'm here temporarily, but aye, I'm currently livin' in Tullamore."

"That's craic! So, out enjoyin' a pint of Arthur Guinness?"

"Workin'."

"Research? Here?"

"Silas, man, you ready?" asked Seamus.

He nodded and grabbed the guitar leaning next to him, giving Orla a sly smile and a wink. "No, singin'."

Her jaw went slack for a moment and then she smiled broadly. "That's savage."

The pub was a hive of local news and social connection and Silas' first set was barely audible. He sang traditional songs such as "Galway Girl," "The Ferryman," "Wild Mountain Thyme" and "Back Home in Derry."

He took a break and Orla had a Guinness waiting for him.

"Silas, let me introduce you to some of my friends." She pulled him to a table where he met Grady, Eileen, Tommy-boy and Jinx.

"Not my real name," Jinx said, "but that one is so horrid, I don't tell anyone I'm not sleepin' with."

Silas laughed out loud.

"Nice to meet ye, Silas," Grady, said, his bright blue eyes echoing a cheerful greeting. "You want to be careful with Orla. She's not the full shillin', if you know what I mean. Way too serious about her studies. In fact, it's bloody amazin' she's come out of her room to have some craic with us."

"Feck off, Grady."

Tommy-boy reached out a beefy hand to shake. "Hi, Silas. Seamus' could use some good music."

Eileen nodded at him and offered a shy hello.

They chatted amicably for a few minutes and Silas finished his beer. "Better get back up there and earn me pay," he joked.

Orla leaned over. "Do you write any of your own songs, Silas? The traditional tunes are all well and good as far as that goes, but we don't listen to it *all* the time."

"I'll see what I can do." He headed for the table where he had been the only musician so far. He strummed a few lines of a song he and Briana wrote about an enchanted sea. He sang of chasing unicorns and great warriors and epic battles. The room grew quiet, the eyes of quite a few patrons misted over with longing. A young man with a tin whistle joined him, as did a fiddler. They found a melody that accompanied him perfectly. He encouraged them to play some instrumentals and he joined in with his guitar.

Finally, the set, and his work for the evening, came to an end. "This song is rather sad, but as I was told recently, 'the Irish love their sorrow.'" He threw Orla a smile and started strumming an opening. The other musicians found the melody. When they had things going, Silas began the words:

"Your heartbeat and mine, solace we find,
next to the firelight.
Feathers and ivy, the ties that bind,
shine in the moonlight.
Your arms, they hold me, while holdin' a line,
in ruins at twilight.
Stay here, my heart, don't leave me lonely,
forever in midnight.

Unbroken, one soul, given forever
Unbroken, one life, livin' together
You ask will I wait, I promise I will
If you'll only remember.

You rode away, slippin' through time,
Leavin' me broken
No word from you, from lips or from mind,
Nothin' is spoken.
Alone in a crowd, livin' a lie,
I keep on hopin'.
One day you'll come home, our warrior's hearts,
forever unbroken.

Unbroken, one soul, given forever
Unbroken, one life, livin' together
You ask will I wait, I promise I will
If you'll only remember.

Separate lives in different lands,
Starless and lost, reachin' out our hands. Against the
odds, we take our stand,
To make whole what was broken.
To make whole once again, our souls which
were broken."

A moment's silence was followed by claps and cheers. He made his
way back to the bar through a gauntlet of back slaps and congratulations.

"T'anks be to God, I did a grand thing, hirin' you, Silas O'Mara. You're
bloody brilliant!"

"That was massive, Silas," Orla agreed sitting on the bar stool next to
him. "Hey, can you hang out with us for a bit. It's still early."

Smiling, he grabbed his Guinness and followed her to the table. Orla
sat down next to Grady and patted the chair next to her for Silas. The group
celebrated his first night at the pub with enthusiasm. Jinx raised her glass.

"Long may ye grace the stage of Seamus' pub. *Slàinte!*"

"*Slàinte mhaith!*"

Conversation swirled around many topics. When it touched on magic,
Silas jumped on it.

"Has anyone ever seen faeries or found portals to other worlds?"

Silence and covert glances around the table met his query. Orla broke
the hush. "Silas is writin' a book about faeries."

"Oh," Tommy-boy said, as though that explained everything.

"Well, here's the thing, Silas," said Eileen. "Most Irish people believe in
faeries and such, even if they won't admit it. For example, you'll not hear a
construction worker openly admit to believin' in the Good Folk, but you
will also not get a construction worker to tear down anythin' that remotely
resembles a fairie ring or mound. Aye? No one, and I mean no one, wishes
to bring the wrath of faeries upon themselves." Eileen punctuated her statement with a swig of stout.

Murmurs of assent followed before Jinx spoke up. "Me granny says
she saw a faerie once, out at Moher. Said she'd gone down near sunset and
a charmin' fellow no taller than her knees was sittin' beside the cliffs. He

was startled when she arrived but tipped his cap to her and disappeared like the mornin' mist."

Silas listened as a man he didn't know, having overheard the conversation, slid over to tell them that he had a friend who disappeared at the ringfort near Ballyvaughan in Clare.

"He was taking photographs of Irish ringforts for an archaeology magazine and was seen walkin' along the stone ridge of the old fort between two trees and poof! He was gone! That was about eight years ago, and he's not been seen since."

Several more pints and a dozen more stories were shared until Seamus came over to shoo them out. Orla's friends split up and headed home, which left him awkwardly with Orla. Making matters more complicated, he was feeling the effects of several pints of beer. The black stuff, as they called it, was much more potent than what he was accustomed to drinking in Uisneach. He was having to work to think clearly about what to do next.

"Where do you live, Silas? Did you drive here?" Orla asked.

"I just live with friends on Clontarf Road. Across from the distillery. It's only a short walk."

She grinned. "That's class. I live on Convent View, the next street over. Ha! I'm tellin' you, Silas, our meetin' is no accident."

He was beginning to believe her. "Can I walk you home, then?"

"That'd be grand."

The night was warm with a light breeze. No rain was mentioned in the forecast so neither had a coat. As they walked the few blocks from Market Square up Columcille Street, they talked about the hill and what everyone said about faeries.

"Do you believe in them then, the faeries?" asked Silas.

"As a scholar, I find it a bit hard to swallow. As an Irish woman, I wouldn't be messin' with anythin' smackin' of faeries. I like the possibility that they exist. It's a bit chilly, isn't it," she said, moving in closer to him.

He didn't think it was, but it seemed the right thing to do to put his arm around her shoulder. Queasiness stirred in his belly. *For Maker's sake, man, it's not the first time you've been with a girl.* It was however, the first time he felt as though he were cheating on another girl. *Aye, the one who is at this very moment probably makin' love with her husband?* He shoved the thought out of his mind and tried to relax.

They stopped on the bridge over the Grand Canal. Her street was on the other side of the bridge, while his was half a block up and to the left. Streetlights cast a yellowy sheen over the dark water flowing beneath them.

"Darkness flows beneath the bridge," he murmured. "Beyond the world of light."

"Hmmm?"

"Just words. Maybe part of a song." He shrugged.

"I liked your songs tonight. The last was a bit sad, but you're a class songwriter. Did you write that for someone special?"

He glanced down at her but didn't reply.

"I'm sorry, I shouldn't have asked."

His tongue seemed to be locked, so he simply shook his head, which gave nothing away.

"Well, Silas O'Mara. I'm happy to meet you and thank you for walkin' me home. I just live right there," she said, pointing to a modest building. "Let me know if I can help you with your research. It is, after all, what I do. I'll see you around."

"Hope so, Orla." Before things could get awkward, he moved away toward his street, though he kept an eye on her until she got to the door of her home. She turned and waved. He waved back and walked on, attempting to sort out the uncomfortable feelings in his head, belly and heart.

⇜

"In the dark pine wood, I would we lay."

The musical adaptation that Silas had chosen for his iPhone ring woke him out of his Guinness-induced coma. His first attempt at sitting up failed. He grabbed the phone and fell back against the pillow.

"Good mornin' Silas," Orla greeted him, her voice chipper. "How you feelin'?"

"Orla? How did you get me number?"

She laughed, a sound like wind chimes. "You gave it to me last night. Don't you remember?"

"No, I don't. Maker, me head hurts. I swear beer is stronger here."

"Huh? Stronger here than where?"

Realizing his mistake, he changed the subject. "Did you call me for a reason, Orla?"

"Well, I had a feelin' you'd have a big head this morning, and I thought maybe you'd appreciate a hand-delivered breakfast. There's a place nearby that makes lovely take away. I'm standin' in the doorway at this very moment. I would be happy to be your very own delivery girl."

He paused and closed his eyes, rubbing a hand through his head. He didn't feel well enough to think this through. How close did he want to let her get? He needed her help, but he didn't feel right about how he seemed to be responding to her. *Sweet Maker, what do I do?"*

"Silas?"

"I'm here. Just tryin' to wake up. Sure, Orla, you could bring breakfast." Did he really say that? "My address is…"

"I know where you live. You told me that too, last night. You live in the cottage behind the house, right?"

He'd told her that too? Did he also tell her about Uisneach and everything else about himself? He'd best give up the beer.

"Right," he replied weakly. "Give me ten minutes."

"I'll give you twenty. It'll take that long for the food to be ready. See you soon!"

He hung up the phone, and holding one hand to his head, started moving to the bathroom.

When she knocked on the door he had on a pair of jeans and a tee shirt with his hair combed and teeth brushed. He was working on tea.

"Good mornin', Silas. Feelin' rough? Ah, *carpe diem.* Seize the day." She nodded at the saying on his shirt. "That sounds promisin'. Where's your plates?"

She was cheery and energetic, though she hadn't had any more sleep than he, and he was certain she'd had at least as many stouts as he did last night. Yet she was up, looking lovely and had brought him breakfast. He reached into a cupboard for plates.

"Orla, I don't know what to think of you."

He turned and she was standing next to him. She looked up, her eyes twinkling. "That's promisin' too. At least you are thinkin' of me." She took the plates and began to spoon eggs, bacon and potatoes onto each.

The food went miles to easing his sour stomach.

"I did a bit of research last night on faerie portals and…"

"Did you sleep at all?" he interrupted, shocked.

She shrugged. "A little. I'm excited about your research. Anyway, there are tons of places in Ireland where faeries are believed to come and go. The Shannon Pot, for example. Not only is that where the River Shannon begins, it is believed to be an openin' to the faerie world."

As she rattled off several other locations around the country, he sighed. He could spend years searching for the runes. It was a daunting task. He watched Orla, who was still talking. Normally, he would be irritated by someone who talked as much as she did, but something about her nonstop chatter was charming. She was also knowledgeable and eager to help. He needed her. Warning bells went off in his head. She posed a threat he didn't even care to think about.

"Orla, I *think* last night you offered to help me with research. Were you serious?" What had possessed him? He was losing all control.

She raised an eyebrow. "It's temptin', Silas, but here's the thing. I don't know much about you and I've been raised to be wary of strange men. Given what I do know, I suspect you might fall into that category."

"You brought me breakfast. I doubt you're too afraid of me."

She took another bite of egg and chewed. After a minute she said, "I'll make you a deal. I'll take you to Ardara Bridge, where it's said faeries have been seen, if you tell me who inspires your songs and what the necklace you wear means to you. That should be a simple trade, aye?"

No, he thought, *nothin' simple at all about it*. But Ardara Bridge sounded so close to Ard Darach that he would've agreed to anything to get there. He was saved from answering by a quick rap at the door and Katrina's voice.

"Silas, you up? Oh," she said coming in to find him having breakfast with Orla. "Oh," she repeated.

Before Silas could get over what this must look like, Orla was on her feet and her hand out to Katrina.

"Hi. I'm Orla Kennedy. A friend of Silas'."

Katrina shook the young woman's hand, while her eyes questioned Silas, who appeared to have gone mute.

"I'm Katrina Brennan, Silas'…" she looked to Silas who offered no assistance. "Mother-in-law."

Silas' shock was only exceeded by Orla's, who turned to Silas, her eyes wide with confusion.

"You're married?"

"Uh, not exactly." He cringed at the disappointment he saw in Orla's eyes.

Katrina caught on quick. "Well, I consider myself his mother-in-law, even though my daughter has been lost to us."

Silas silently thanked the woman he truly wished was his mother-in-law. Without outright lying, she gave him cover, explaining his desire to evade any complicated relationship issues.

"Oh, Silas, I am so sorry. Sorry to you as well, Mrs. Brennan. You should have said so, Silas. It would have explained a lot."

"Orla is the interpreter at the hill I told you about," Silas finally spoke up. "She's offered to help me with researchin' the faeries. We'll start at the Ardara Bridge."

"Terrific. Thank you, Orla, for wanting to help. It will mean a lot to us. Silas, I only came to say that I've booked a flight back to Maine. I have things to take care of there. I hope to be back in a few weeks. Mum and Dad will drive me to Dublin. My flight's at nine thirty."

"I've got to work tonight, so I won't be able to go with you. I'll try and be home for supper to tell you how we made out today."

"You're on your own for supper. We're going into the city early and will get supper there. You can text me. Well, I'll leave you two to your plans." She gave Silas a hug. "Good luck with your research. See you in a few weeks. Orla, nice to meet you."

"You, as well, Mrs. Brennan. Have a safe flight. Oh, Mrs. Brennan, is your name a variation of the Greek, Dutch or Gaelic Catriona?"

"My grandmother's name was Catriona. She was… Irish."

"Ah. Well, either way, it means pure one. Did you know that?"

Katrina smiled. "I did not, but thank you. Interesting fact." She headed for the door, giving Silas an odd look before leaving.

"Lovely woman," Orla said quietly when she was gone. "You should have told me about your wife, Silas. That was a wee bit awkward."

"We should get going," he replied, not yet willing to discuss Briana with her. He wondered about the wisdom of ever discussing Briana with her, or getting in a car with her.

She sighed and asked to use his bathroom or jacks, as she called it. He directed her back through his bedroom and picked up their plates to put in the dishwasher. It wasn't until she was already in there, that he paused, wishing he had put away the picture of Briana that sat on the nightstand beside his bed. *Maker, this is messy.*

⤙

"Hello. I'm Orla Kennedy, an interpreter at the Hill of Uisneach. This is my friend, Silas O'Mara, a writer. We're doin' research on ancient sites that might attract faeries. Would it be okay for us to explore the bridge and surroundin' areas?"

"Oh, aye, just mind the cows and the mud. Got your wellies, I hope?"

Orla and Silas both lifted a foot for his assessment of their boots.

"Aye, that's fine. Go on then, enjoy your walk."

They made their way through the garden to the start of the leaf-strewn trail. It was a good half mile to the bridge, but they took their time. The muddy river rolled and curved over mossy stones and past a few recent blowdowns. Silas took Orla's hand to assist her over one fallen tree, his gut clenching as images of helping Briana across rivers and downed trees flew into his mind. Thankfully, Orla was so strikingly different from Briana that the memories wafted into the air, replaced by new images of a vivacious raven-haired woman who talked incessantly and was frighteningly bright and outgoing.

She turned to him. "You've said not a word, Silas. Are you all right, then?"

"I'm fine. Just tryin' to focus and get a feel for the place. I suspect that findin' faeries is as much about intuition as it is history."

"I should be quiet then and let you intuit."

A kingfisher rattled, diving across the path to the river.

"Wow! That was incredible, though I don't know why the Greeks considered them a bird of peace. They aren't very quiet and the full-speed dive is a bit joltin'. Oh, okay, now I'll stop talking. I do talk a lot, sorry."

The bridge itself seemed ancient. One side was cloaked with moss, and on the other, an old stump perched precariously like a crown on a drunken king. Arching over the water, the stones of the bridge seemed determined to stick together despite centuries of weather working to break them apart. Here and there a stone lurched out of the wall and the occasional chink in the bridge did indeed, seem a good place for a faerie portal. Yet Silas thought the place a bit gloomy and not at all an ideal spot for Teaguen to come floating out. If intuiting was the path to finding the runes, he wouldn't find them here.

However, what he was finding here was time pleasantly spent with a pretty woman, who he now realized was gazing thoughtfully into the water and was uncharacteristically quiet.

"Orla? Is somethin' wrong?"

She cocked her head toward him and smiled. "No, nothin's wrong. It's just peaceful and I'm tryin' to join you in intuitin'."

"I see. And what are you intuitin'?"

"I don't believe you'll find your faeries here."

He looked down at the busy river and up at the drunken crown of stump. "No, I don't think so, but it's a nice spot."

She tapped her lip. "I held up my part of the bargain."

His hand automatically went to his heart necklace made of warrior's bones. "Aye, you did. I suppose it's me turn to grant your request."

What should he tell her? So much of his life was untellable, and he didn't want to get into the complicated story of Briana because he would have to lie. The truth was something out of one of Briana's romantic fairytales.

Two otters swam into view, tumbling each other in the pools along the bank. It bought him time to think as Orla's attention was diverted to the cavorting creatures below. Her laugh was pleasing to his ear and her smile made him wish he were free—emotionally and physically. He was neither. He belonged in another time and place and his heart was owned by another woman.

Orla straightened suddenly and broke his train of thought.

"I'm *intuitin'* that you are not ready to talk, so I release you from your side of the deal."

"I'm not tryin' to be mysterious. It's just…"

She hushed him with a soft fingertip to his lips that he had to fight the urge to kiss. "It's okay, Silas. When you're ready to share a bit of yourself with me, I'll be ready." She glanced at her watch. "We need to get home anyway, if you're goin' to take me for supper before you play."

"Thank you, Orla. You're a kind lass."

"I'm a bloody patient lass."

By the time they got back to the car, he'd learned she was committed to her studies and wanted nothing more than to be a professor at Trinity College someday. She claimed not to want any complicated relationship that would alter the trajectory she was on. That was a relief. Or was it? He couldn't help a twinge of regret and was fairly certain he saw the same conflict shadow her face. Buckling up, he realized there was just enough time for a bite to eat before his first set, which meant it would be best to eat at Seamus'.

They sat at the bar, eating fish and chips, which Orla insisted he pay for. He agreed, though he only paid for hers, his being part of his compensation.

"Silas, you haven't told me about your family."

"You've met what family I have."

She frowned. "Katrina and her parents are your only family?"

"Umhm…" he nodded, chewing a bit of fish.

"What happened to your birth family?"

"Only child, and me father and mum died at sea."

She put a hand on his arm. "Oh, Silas, I'm so sorry. You must have been lonely."

Oh, no, he thought, *the king and queen of that kingdom took me in and I became the Royal Bard for a man, like a brother to me, who just married the woman I love.* "A family took me in, and I feel blessed to have had them as surrogate parents. They've since died as well. And you? Siblings?"

"My parents, William and Janet Kennedy, had three darlin' children. Brian, which means high noble, or strength. True enough in his case. He's a banker and solid as they come. Sean, the middle child, was definitely named right. God was gracious all right and took the lad from a tender age. He's always been super religious and a bit of a dreamer. He's a priest here in town. Everyone loves Father Sean, may God continue to bless him," she ended by touching her forehead, chest and both shoulders, a ritual Silas had learned was unique to the Catholic faith.

She rose suddenly. "I'll be right back. Need to visit the jacks."

He watched her walk away, marveling at the combination of sauciness and grace that made her such an attractive woman.

"She's a wee cracker, our Orla," Seamus said, taking their plates away and replacing them with another pint.

Silas knew a wee cracker meant something like a beautiful girl. He nodded.

"You've chosen well. But she and James haven't been broken up very long. Go gentle with her. Ah, she hasn't told ye yet." Seamus grimaced at the look of surprise on Silas' face.

"Aye, well, it's not like that anyway," Silas said. "She's helpin' me with research."

"Oh, I'm sure she is," the barkeep replied as though Silas had just said faeries were at the front door.

"Silas, I just realized that Ireland is filled with nooks and crannies that could house faeries," Orla said, returning to her seat. She had removed her long-sleeved shirt, revealing a scoop-neck tank top. He wondered again about the tattoo that rose above the neckline but didn't dare lower his eyes enough to get a good look. "How are we ever goin' to find what you're lookin' for?"

Silas turned suddenly to Orla, a brilliant idea having just formed in his head. "Orla, do you think you could find me a witch?"

Chapter Fourteen

Return of the Prodigal

Briana, Winge Mansion, Tynan Ibor, Uisneach

It was instantly clear to Briana that the Winge family had issues to work on, but everyone still needed to eat. Perhaps the normalcy of taking dinner together would reduce the tension. *Or, maybe not,* she thought looking again at the glare in Sir Thomas' eyes.

"Lady Isabella, should I make arrangements for dinner?" she asked.

The mistress of the house stood next to her husband, her eyes darting anxiously between him and her son. She turned to Briana with a grateful smile.

"Well, then, have you managed to become comfortable with ordering servants about," she quipped, referring to a comment Briana had made months before as she came to accept the idea of becoming a queen.

Briana gave an exaggerated toss of her head. "Oh, quite," she said effecting a fake British accent.

"Thank you, Your Majesty, that would be helpful, indeed."

Briana signaled Aya'emrys, Jonathan and Rippa to follow her out of the library. Dara led the way to the kitchen, having learned it was a food source during his last stay here.

Briana was greeted in the kitchen with an enthusiastic hug from Mrs. Churchill, the head cook, and her daughter, Nieve, assistant cook. The scullery maids stood tensely nearby. It was unnervingly quiet in the usually bustling kitchen. No one seemed sure what to do.

"Will they be having a usual dinner, Your Majesty?" Mrs. Churchill asked. "I've a turkey roasting, but I wasn't sure what would happen when I heard Sir Thomas was home. I still recall the day Master Kieran left. It…"

Despite her own curiosity about the situation between Sir Thomas and his son, Briana didn't want to encourage the staff to gossip, so she interrupted Mrs. Churchill.

"Dinner will be as usual, but you have a few more to plan for, Mrs. Churchill. I know it's late notice, but can you have a meal served in an hour?"

"Of course, Your Majesty," the woman said, already swinging a finger around the kitchen with unspoken orders that the staff understood. "Don't you worry, dinner will be ready. Just you see to it that there are bodies left living to sit at the table and eat."

Briana laughed at that. "I'm sure no one will be killed this evening, Mrs. Churchill." She left as maids scurried around with extra vegetables to be chopped and extra loaves of bread to be sliced.

Eugenia Ellsmore waited outside the kitchen door. "Your room is ready, Your Majesty. The same as you were in last time. Will the king be joining you?"

"At some point, yes. Probably not until tomorrow. We'll need rooms also for the boys." She nodded at Jonathan, who clearly resented being called a boy, and Rippa, who was still examining his surroundings with round eyes and a slack jaw.

"The boys' rooms are ready, ma'am." Mrs. Ellsmore's eyes travelled to the giant faerie warrior standing quietly beside Briana.

"Captain Aya'emrys will also need a room, near mine, if possible."

The head housekeeper curtsied and went to carry out this final instruction. Briana headed for her room, wanting nothing more than to wash the dust and grime from her body and have a moment to gather herself before what could be a dramatic dinner.

"Mr. Stark. Rippa. You two get cleaned up and come back for me in an hour. We'll go down to dinner together." *My*, she thought, *I am getting good at ordering people about.*

"I will wait outside your door, Tuathla," Aya'emrys announced, already moving into position.

Briana nodded and went into her room and was immediately enveloped in a hearty embrace.

"Your Majesty, it's so good to see you." Claire McClune, the lady's maid assigned to her during her last visit, greeted her warmly. The two of them had grown close when Briana was here as a single woman.

Briana hugged her. "Nice to see you, too, Claire."

A bath had already been drawn for the queen. Briana wasted no time in stripping off her filthy tunic and breeches and sliding into the warm water. She laid her head back against the back of the tub and took a deep breath, letting go of the myriad thoughts of the last two days and focusing on the crackle of a comforting fire and the sound of Claire puttering about. It wasn't long before the empty space in her head was filled with memories of this room, specifically, memories of Silas. Silas coming in to check on her when she woke from an infectious delirium after sustaining a life-threatening gash on her inner leg. Silas outside her door, guarding her as they communicated telepathically and wrote a song together. Climbing out the window and down the tree to where Silas waited beside the ocean cliffs. The one and only kiss they'd shared. She could almost smell the salt of the ocean, feel the wind in her hair and feel him touching her, kissing her lips with passion kept in check only by destinies determined to keep them apart. Was it cheating on your spouse to remember such a thing with another man?

Almost exactly an hour later, Briana was refreshed and dressed in a gold and forest-green gown. She opened her bedroom door to find two boys and a faerie guard standing at attention in the hallway. "Okay, guess we're ready to go down and see if there are," she recalled Mrs. Churchill's words, "any bodies left alive."

The household arrived at the dining room at the same time, and everyone took their seats. Only the sputter of candles and the clink of glass on glass, as Ballynickle and the under-butler served wine, was heard in the room. Briana noticed Kieran put a hand over his glass, declining the spirit. A cup of tea was poured for him instead.

The heavy silence was beyond uncomfortable. While dinner was served, Briana looked around at her dining companions. Her guards on either side, Jonathan and Rippa, seemed oblivious to the tension and were more focused on the food, sending her questioning looks about when it was okay to eat. Aya'emrys was next to Sir Thomas, who sat pillar-like, his eyes staring down at his plate. Briana watched his eyebrows and jaw flex. She caught the small movement of Lady Isabella's hand under the table, taking his, and saw the pleading look in her eyes.

Across the table, Epona and Kieran sat side by side. Epona looked hauntingly beautiful in a floor-length black gown with burgundy tulle at the neck and matching burgundy slippers. She stared at Kieran like he was the first sun ever to rise in the morning sky. This was a side of Epona Briana had never seen. Her usual flamboyant irreverence was replaced by a demure vulnerability. It was a little disconcerting.

Kieran had also changed into an evening suit, an edgier version of Sir Thomas' elegant attire. He sat as stonily as his father but responded to Epona's adoring gaze with a tender smile.

Briana studied him. He was, as Samira might have said, totally hot, in a bad-boy sort of way. His shoulder-length hair, though not as coiffed as his father's, was the same ebony black as the rest of the family. He was the only member of the clan with a beard and mustache, neatly groomed. His eyes, also familial, were black, but uniquely ringed and flecked with shades of umber that made them seem like cavernous pools, and his lips were fuller than his father's and almost a burgundy color. She couldn't decide if he was sexier in the black leather he'd been wearing when she arrived, or the sleek slacks, white shirt and black coat he now wore.

The silence was deafening. Briana ran through a list of possible subjects to raise that wouldn't ignite any powder kegs.

"I hope Brath will be able to get Sigel here tomorrow," she ventured. "Do you think he'll be okay, Sir Thomas? Sigel, I mean."

Sir Thomas slowly raised unfocused eyes to her. His entire expression was blank, as if he hadn't understood her. She started to speak again, but he answered. "I hope so, Your Majesty." He went silent again.

Not only did she hate it when he called her by the honorific, but his withdrawal freaked her out. This was not the Sir Thomas she'd known since coming to Uisneach. She looked to Aya'emrys for help. He glanced pointedly at her ringed hand. She looked down and noticed the stones on her tuathla ring were gleaming. Could magic help here?

Discretion wasn't necessary. No one was paying attention to her except Aya'emrys. She drew in a breath and held it momentarily as she scanned the table. She let her eyes fall closed. *I call on the wisdom and power of the tuathlas*, she invoked in her mind. Sandalwood filled her senses and she felt the split in her consciousness. Looking down she saw the familiar glowing of the ring and pulsing scar. *So, that's how it's done. All you do is ask nicely.* In her mind's eye, a tower of golden energy arose, filling her head. She invited the image to travel to her heart and fill it as well. When the energy seemed to be at a peak, she casually pointed her finger toward every person at the table. Visualizing the glow wrapping itself around each person, she held the power until it made the circuit around the table and back into her own heart, feeling a definite change in the tension and mood at the table.

Sir Thomas turned to her, the blankness erased from his face. "Briana, you asked something about Lord Marshall Sigel."

"I just wondered if you thought he would be okay?"

"You said Cailleach was with him?" Kieran asked.

Briana nodded, but was watching Sir Thomas. He stared at his son, the anger and dismissal she'd seen in his eyes earlier gone, replaced by a sadness and tenderness that he'd been trying to keep hidden. He loved his son, but whatever broke them apart was traumatic and had resulted in a heartache so great that only burying the pain and rejecting his son could help him bear it. *What the hell happened here?*

"If he can be helped, Cailleach is certainly equal to the task," Kieran said, and took a sip of his tea. "Quite honestly, I can't believe he was that seriously injured. I thought the fellow was indestructible."

Briana had thought so too, and her heart tripped at the thought he might die.

Briana's magic lasted throughout dinner and conversation resumed in as normal a manner as it could, given that all the things that really needed to be talked about were completely ignored. Briana hoped that much of tonight's angst would be resolved tomorrow when everyone had a clear head.

Captain Aya'emrys had already left, wanting to check on his troops. Jonathan and Rippa rose when Briana did to go upstairs. As they were leaving, a hand on her arm stopped Briana. It was Epona.

"We need to talk," she said.

Briana nodded and gave her a tired, but reassuring smile. "We do, but not tonight. Get some rest, Epona."

The Mistress of the Hunt nodded, looking relieved.

Briana continued upstairs, Dara at her side, looking pretty fagged out himself. She stopped to drop Rippa off at his room and tried to talk Jonathan into getting some sleep. "I have Dara with me. He'll let me know if anyone's about and I'll give you a holler."

He would have none of it. "I don't need to sleep, and your husband would kill me if he knew you'd been left unprotected. Don't you worry. Just go to sleep and I'll watch over you."

She swallowed the lump this young man so frequently caused in her. Although she was way too young to be his mother, she wanted to wrap him in her arms and protect *him*. However, what he needed was her confidence in him. And she knew Aya'emrys would not let her remain unprotected.

"Well, then, I shall sleep like a baby, Mr. Stark, knowing you're out here."

She might have, except for two things. One, she realized she missed having Brath next to her and two, a low chatter outside her door forced her up to see what was going on.

It was no surprise to her that when she opened the door, both Jonathan and Rippa were sitting on the floor in front of her door.

"What are you doing?" she asked.

"I'm keepin' Jon comp'ny," Rippa said, looking up at her with round, blue eyes that looked tired but determined.

"I told him I could manage alone, but he insisted on staying."

Briana bit down the smile wanting to escape. "Well, my suggestion, then, is that you take turns sleeping. Whatever you do, just keep it down to a dull roar. I'd like a little sleep."

"Yes, ma'am," they said in unison.

She returned to bed and futzed around trying to get comfortable until exhaustion drove her into dreams.

Rain hammering the balcony woke her. *Oh, no. Brath won't make it home today*, was her first thought. She slid out of bed, waking Dara, and grabbed her dressing gown, but paused in the act of putting it on, aware of how heavy her heart felt at the idea that he'd be gone another day. "When did that happen?" she said to the empty room. Walking to the balcony doors, she looked at the steel gray skies and rain coming down in sheets and sighed. It was light enough to know she'd find breakfast downstairs.

Quietly opening the door, she was not surprised to see two heads leaned against each other on the floor. Captain Aya'emrys stood, wide awake, beside the door and gave her what amounted to a grin. "I will go and check on the faeries, then," he said, and left before the boys could know they'd failed at guard duty. Dara was not as willing to let them off the hook. He nuzzled the boys, bringing them instantly awake.

"Must have just dozed off," Jonathan said, yawning.

Rippa followed suit, rubbing his eyes, blinking away traces of sleep.

"Well, we best go find some breakfast, then." She led the boys and dog downstairs, her stomach growling at the meaty aroma wafting up from the dining room.

She marveled once again at the elegance of Winge Mansion as she followed the gleaming black marble staircase into the entryway, with its stone sculpted tree trunks holding up wall sconces that looked like nests, each one holding a black candle shaped like a crow. She nodded at the giant crystal crow in the center of the foyer and shivered when she could swear he nodded back. Muted gray light poured down on to the center of the entry hall through the massive skylight above.

Her favorite raspberry scones awaited her in the dining room. She smiled at Lady Isabella's thoughtfulness. Briana sat in front of the fireplace, sipping tea and eating the buttery bread when suddenly, the hairs on the back of her next raised. She turned her head, knowing who would be standing there.

"Hello, Kieran," she said, without turning.

"Ahhh," he murmured. "She has magic."

Briana turned around. "It doesn't take magic to feel you. Your energy is intense."

He didn't comment as he walked to the sideboard and poured a cup of tea.

"I suppose you've heard all about me by now."

"To the contrary, I've never heard of you before," she replied honestly, sorry that it made him wince. "I was just wondering if there are any more secrets around here, or any other family members I'm not aware of."

"I don't know if I could qualify as a secret, really. More like a sore subject." He sipped his tea. "I understand you and Epona are best friends."

"I thought we were," Briana replied with a slight humph. "And yet, I didn't know about you."

"She's not to blame, I'm sure. No doubt Himself gave strict orders never to speak my name again." There was no inflection of anger, sorrow or any other emotion in his words. He was merely stating a fact.

"Why?" Briana dared to ask, totally curious about this young man.

"Because they think I killed our baby and my sister."

Briana jerked and nearly lost her tea cup. He quickly reached out to steady it. There was nothing he could do to correct the mouth she left hanging open. After an awkward silence, she felt compelled to ask, "Well, did you?"

"Of course not," he continued, in the same unaffected voice, though she could see something spark painfully in his eyes. "But I did do a lot of other terrible things and it seemed logical to them that I would've been at fault for those two tragedies, as well." He put the cup to his lips.

Briana wasn't sure what to say next.

"Thank you for what you did for Epona," he said, breaking the awkward silence.

"I only did what I could for a friend."

"You have some good healing skills and more than a little magic, I'd say."

She shrugged. "Her injuries weren't so bad. She means a lot to me, Kieran, and I hate to see her in pain. In fact, I hate seeing anyone in this family in pain."

"I feel the same."

"Glad to hear it. Epona seems to care for you and she deserves to be happy."

"Another point of agreement. Shall I give you some history?"

"You would find me an eager listener."

The housemaids entered, with dishes of eggs, sausages, grilled tomatoes and the endless raspberry scones. Kiernan nodded a thank you to the girls. When they'd gone, he rose and began filling a plate. "Eggs?" he asked, casting a glance at Briana.

"I'm not…"

"You didn't eat much last night and this is a long story."

"Fine, whatever. I like eggs."

He heaped her plate, ignoring her protest, and handed it to her along with some silverware. Taking only a scone for himself and setting it beside the tea on the table next to him, he stared into the fire for some time before beginning his story.

"Epona and I grew up together, quite literally. We were born on the same day. I know, strange," he said, interpreting Briana's surprised expression. "We were inseparable as children, learning to ride together, taking our lessons together, everything. If one got a scrape, the other of us would find a way to get one, also. If one took ill, the other would soon be in bed with the same ailment. The only difference was Epona was good and I was not."

Briana cringed.

He shrugged. "It's the truth. I was always trying to figure out what made things tick and sometimes I wounded animals just to see what would happen. I'm not proud of that and I don't do it anymore, trust me. But I was a rough kid.

"One day I realized two things: first, that I'd grown up looking like something women liked and wanted, and secondly, that Epona had also grown up, looking like something I wanted. And she loved me. I suppose I loved her too, but I hadn't the least clue what that meant, and I chose to hurt her by giving other women what they wanted, making no secret of it to Epona. I was a philanderer. I had as many women as I liked, but the one I wanted and couldn't have was Epona.

"For the record, I also gambled, ran away from home a couple of times, got into trouble with a gang from Ratskillen and nearly did kill an old woman, although that was an accident. She got in the way of a horse I was racing through town. I also learned I had some shapeshifting power and I used those powers not only with the ladies, but to cause tremendous amounts of hardship to the locals. That is part of the reason people think I was responsible for my sister's death, but I'll speak to that later. I was a liar, a cheat, a drunk, probably, and a womanizer. But hey, what's not to love?

"Anyway, Epona loved me, but she did not approve of me and was smart enough to keep her distance. Being snubbed by any woman drove me insane and I kept after her, desperate to have the one thing I couldn't. I reckoned if she thought I was turning over a new leaf, she might come around, so I gave up on women, kept my head low for a while and everyone thought I was shaping up. One day, I shapeshifted into one of our horses, broke through the stall and headed for a secluded glen near Derryfeeny. Of course, Epona followed me, thinking she was retrieving a horse. When she found me in the glen, I shifted to myself. She was furious at first but accepted my explanation that I just wanted to get her alone to tell her how much I loved her.

"Long story short, she believed me, and the truth is I did love her. I just had a poor way of showing it and I certainly didn't think I was ready to settle down with one woman. We were barely sixteen. But, I had fallen in love, totally, and begged her to forgive everything from my past and promised I would turn my life around. She, being who she is, did, and we went home to share the news of our great love with our families.

"Hard to believe I could have been so naïve as to think they would be happy for us. They were furious and when a few months later we knew she was pregnant, her father bloody near killed me. I don't blame him, and I didn't resist. I felt terrible about putting her in that situation, but I was also happy about the idea of getting married and starting a family. I won't say that I was a completely new man. I still drank too much and went to Ratskillen to gamble every chance I got, but the meanness in my heart was gone.

"Marriage seemed logical to me, but our parents were dead set against us being together. We had to sneak to spend time with each other. One day, we met on horses near the glen where we had become lovers when suddenly she started having some pains and began bleeding like I have never seen. I brought her home as quickly as I could, but she lost the baby. Both families believed I had done something to her, to purposely cause the miscarriage. Although I can understand why they might think that, I cannot forgive the fact that they think I would have killed my own child, nor can I forgive them for not hearing the truth from both of us."

Briana didn't know what to say. She desperately wanted to believe him, but he started out by saying he was a liar. Luckily, she was spared having to say anything as he continued with his story.

"I was forbidden to have any contact with her, in fact, my father began preparations for sending me to away to Cedarmara. While this was all going on, my sister Leieria fell in love with a mysterious man. No one knew where he'd come from. Some say through the tree, but others say he was from someplace even more strange."

Briana grunted, wondering what could be stranger than coming from a parallel universe through a tree!

"Leieria was a powerful shapeshifter. When this man she had fallen for left without a word, she tried using magic to find him and then shapeshifted to follow him. It seems she found herself between worlds and couldn't get back. I shapeshifted into a dragonfly, thinking somehow being so small I could get to her and bring her back. Father also changed, into a unicorn, believing he could break through whatever barrier was preventing her from coming back. When I saw him come through, I panicked, thinking he would be stuck there, too, and I used magic to push him out. He assumed I was pushing him back to prevent Leieria from coming home.

"We both watched as my sister died in that in-between place. When I came back through you can imagine my father's fury. Without giving me the opportunity to explain, he mustered every ounce of magic he had to banish me on the spot. Again, I understand why he thought what he did, and did what he did, but it has taken me this long to get the nerve to come home and try again."

"Why now?" Briana asked bluntly.

"Because Uisneach is in trouble and I want to do what I can to help. Truthfully, I also think it's bloody well time to mend this fence and see if Epona still holds any love for me."

"Why, so you can break her heart again?" asked Sir Thomas, his voice stern.

Briana nearly jumped out of her skin. Sir Thomas stood in the doorway. His face was strained with shadows and lines of fatigue circled his eyes.

"Why would I do that, Father? I love her. I have always loved her and never did anything to hurt her, unless you count the fact that my love for her resulted in my exile which hurt us both. Maker, I couldn't even be here for her when her father died!"

Briana stared between the two men, wondering where this would go, when Epona changed the dynamic. "And I love him too. This must stop now. Too much time has passed with you two angry with each other. And way too much time has passed during which Kieran and I could've been building a life together. You must listen, Sir Thomas." The girl's eyes were shining with pain and pleading. "Please, listen to us."

Awkward, Briana thought. *I need to get out of here and let them sort it out.*

She stood to leave but Kieran's voice stopped her. "No, please stay, Your Majesty. Epona and I have things to discuss. We'll go to the garden so everyone else can eat." Neither he nor Epona waited for anyone's permission, but left the room in silent agreement.

"I know it's none of my business, but I do feel like I've been pulled in."

"It's okay, Briana. We've made it your business, so ask whatever you wish, and I'll answer."

She sat back in the chair next to the fire, folded her hands in her lap and thought for a moment. "Is it possible that he's telling the truth and that he's changed?"

"I don't know," he answered honestly, running a hand through his hair. "I just don't know, and the consequences of what I choose to believe could be potentially devastating to Epona."

"She does love him, that much I can see," Briana offered.

He nodded. "She does and likely always will. If I thought for a minute that he wouldn't abuse that love, I'd welcome him with open arms, but trust me, I've had years of being hurt by my son and I'm not anxious to repeat the experience."

"What does Lady Isabella think?"

"She's his mother," he replied simply.

Briana knew there was nothing she could or should say. She'd been called to be the vessel to receive this man's emotional problem-solving. She waited. After what seemed like an eternally long time, he sat down in the chair beside her.

"I see something in his eyes that I never saw before. There's maturity, and dare I say regret for his own past? And when he looks at Epona, I see love. But we're shapeshifters and it's hard to be certain if this is real or a mask."

"Maybe it's time to let them work it out. They're adults now, after all, not children. Epona may love him, but she isn't stupid. I think if he's insincere, she'll see it."

He studied her face for a moment. "Is it worth risking the fall?"

She knew he was asking about more than Epona and Kieran and without hesitation responded, "Yes, it is."

A crow messenger arrived, clearing his throat to announce his presence. To Briana's surprise and concern, he brought word from Brath that he expected to be at Winge Mansion by evening. They were en route with Sigel in a wagon.

"In this rain?" Briana questioned. "That's not going to be safe or healthy for any of them."

"They'll make do," Sir Thomas said wearily.

It rained all day. Briana spent most of her time in her room, reading from Sir Thomas' library, writing in her journal and playing a half-hearted game of ríocht with Jonathan that reminded her way too much of Sigel. A knock on the door interrupted them.

"Come in."

"Hey." Epona walked in, color in the cheeks that had been so pale this morning. "Can I talk to you?"

"Of course. Mr. Stark, please excuse us."

"I'll be right outside," he said, giving one last thoughtful glance at the ríocht board.

When the door closed behind him, Briana turned to Epona, nodding at the empty chair.

"I want to apologize for not telling you about Kieran."

"It's okay, Epona. I understand why you didn't."

"I want you to hear my side of the story."

She spent the next hour listening to Epona relate an almost identical story to Kieran's, except that she never really saw him as he thought she had.

"I only ever wanted him to see himself as I did. Anyway, Kieran went to my father and asked to marry me. I begged father to give his permission, if not his blessing, but both he and Sir Thomas refused. We continued to defy them and then the unthinkable happened. Kieran and I met in the glen, just to talk. I began to have terrible cramps and the bleeding started. We were both terrified, but he did the proper thing and carried me back home. I told them Kieran had done nothing wrong, but they wouldn't believe either of us. He had been in so much trouble for so long, and they thought I was protecting him. Sir Thomas sent him away and we grieved the loss of our baby separately and alone. I never saw him again until now."

Briana touched her friend's hand in sympathy. "You must've been shocked to see him in the library."

Epona nodded and then looked at Briana with determination in her eyes. "Things are going to be different this time. I love him and we are going to marry, whether Sir Thomas likes it or not."

After Epona was calm, she left. Briana walked to the balcony. It was still raining, and she was worried about Brath and Sigel. If they were on their way, she hoped Cailleach could conjure up something to keep them dry. She wished she could talk to the wee mouse from Ard Darach. Or Silas. She wished Brath was here.

Briana was practically biting her nails by dinnertime. The rain never let up and darkness came early. She was sure Brath would have stopped somewhere by now and felt a heavy weight of disappointment mixed with worry about Sigel's condition.

She was on her way downstairs when she caught Ballynickel racing toward the front door. Wind and rain carried Cailleach inside, followed by four of the knights carrying a litter with a covered body on it. Briana cried out, "Oh, Maker, he's died!" Before she could get to the litter, Brath was inside, drenching wet. He put an arm out to hold her back.

"He's not dead, Briana. We've only covered him from the rain."

She lifted the tarp from Sigel's face and was relieved to find he still had a little color and was breathing. He had not, however, regained consciousness and she knew the longer he remained in this state, the less likely he would recover from his injuries. She touched his face. "Oh, Sigel, please wake up."

Servants and family members arrived and Lady Isabella gave orders to take him to a room upstairs and bring supplies to tend to him. Briana hugged Cailleach quickly and urged her to go up and get into dry clothes. Then it was just her and Brath. She took the few steps that would bring her into his arms.

"Briana, I'm soaked."

"I don't give a damn," she said and wrapped her arms around him.

He chuckled, but only held her a moment. "Come, help me get into some dry clothes. I'd really wouldn't mind a quick, hot bath."

There wasn't much she could do with Sigel until they got him settled. She wanted to make sure Brath was okay, so she led the way to where a bath was already being prepared in their room.

"It's not hot, my lady," Claire informed her.

"I'll see to it, Claire, thank you," she said, dismissing the lady's maid so Brath could get out of his wet clothes.

Brath wasn't waiting for her to leave to undress, or wondering how his bath would get hot. Briana touched the water inside the tub with her ringed hand and closed her eyes. *By the power of the tuathla, make this water warm.* Removing her hand with a pleased smile, she turned to Brath and bowed. "Your wish is my command, my lord."

"Ah," he murmured as he lowered himself into the warm water. "I was smart to marry you, Bri. Who knew you had the power to make my world so perfect."

They both knew the world was anything but perfect at the moment, but it was nice to imagine that it was.

"I do what I can, husband. Tell me why you felt it necessary to bring Sigel through this horrific storm."

He met her eyes with total seriousness. "I missed my wife."

"That had better not be the reason."

"Well, I did, but no, when we left Ratskillen it wasn't raining. By the time it started, we were closer to Derryfeeny. I was most worried about Cailleach, but she took it like a warrior. We just put the tarp over Sigel to keep him dry."

She hadn't realized that while they were talking, her hand had dipped down into the water and was making lazy circles on his chest. He took her hand, and bringing it to his lips, kissed her fingers. "I would've come through any storm to get to you."

Words seemed unnecessary in that moment. She squeezed his hand. He leaned his head back and closed his eyes.

"I need to go check on Sigel, but I'm worried you'll fall asleep in the tub. You look exhausted, Brath."

"I am tired, but I won't fall asleep."

"Shall I send Claire in to check on you?" she teased.

He opened one eye and slanted it toward here. "Sure."

"What! That's not the right answer."

His voice lowered huskily. "I know you well enough to know you would never send another woman in to take care of what's yours to take care of."

Her mouth went dry as she stared at him. He was so right. Why couldn't she say what she felt? *Because you'd have to admit something you aren't ready to admit just yet.* Instead, she leaned over the tub and kissed his lips. Maybe she could say it without words.

His hand wound around the back of her head and held her gently. His lips responded to what she was saying with gentle acceptance. "Go on now, love," he said quietly. "Check on the lord marshall before I pull you into this tub with me. I'll come and get you for dinner."

Sigel had been settled into his old room. A valet puttered about. Cailleach sat by the fire, warming her hands.

"Shall I leave, Your Majesty?"

"No, Mr. Rimmerston, no need. I just want to see how he's doing." She touched his forehead to check for fever. He was cool. "I hadn't noticed this nasty bump," she uttered to herself, noticing the swollen and purple area on his forehead. He had fallen forward and hit his head, but apparently the swelling didn't show up until later.

"The back wound is nice and clean. I changed the dressing as soon as we got him in here," said Cailleach. "Are you okay?" Briana asked, giving her a once-over assessment. The witch had changed into a dry dress, combed and re-braided her hair. She looked no worse for wear.

"I'm fine." Can't say as much for our friend." She tipped her head toward Sigel.

"He's not regained consciousness at all?"

Cailleach shook her head. "As you said, these injuries take time to heal. We'll give him the benefit of the doubt."

Briana turned back to Sigel, raised the blanket over his foot and ran a fingernail up the bottom of his foot. No response. She sighed. Replacing the cover, she stared at him thoughtfully. "Oh, Cailleach, I can't even imagine what it will mean if he doesn't recover."

"Don't go borrowing trouble, lass. One day at a time, aye?"

Briana nodded and turned as she heard the door open. Brath entered, clean and dry, except for his hair, which had been combed back but was still wet.

"I didn't fall asleep," he said. Moving in close to her he whispered, "Claire wouldn't let me."

She nudged him with her shoulder.

It seemed pointless to stand around staring at Sigel. If he regained consciousness, it would not be because they all willed it into being.

"I saw Sir Thomas on his way down to dinner," Brath said. "Shall we join him?"

Dinner was a quiet affair. The new arrivals were clearly tired from a long day of travel in bad weather and although Brath tried to keep the mood light with tales of some of the more humorous moments along the road, such as a toad somehow getting into the cart and settling onto Sigel's chest for the ride, Briana could see the fatigue in his face and hear it in his voice.

The Winge family was less tense. Sir Thomas even directed some of his comments to Kieran. Kieran and Epona sat beside each other and Briana noticed the frequent glances, smiles and encouraging expressions between them.

Sir Thomas asked Brath if he would head back to Ard Darach soon.

"Probably. We can't leave Sigel here forever, and I need to think about how to move forward. I'd like some intelligence on Shamwa's whereabouts so I can plan a strategy to deal with him."

"Your Majesty," Kieran spoke up, "I suggest you look at what's going on in Cedarmara. I can tell you that's where Shamwa's focusing the Gray Military. He has quite a base of support there."

Brath gave him a keen look. "How much information are you privy too?"

"I've been living there for the last few years, working with a house-builder. The city is almost entirely supportive of Shamwa and they feel Ard Darach—you, Sire, are too distant and disconnected from the western coast."

"Too distant!" Briana exclaimed, outraged. "He's been imprisoned in the castle, thanks to Shamwa!"

Kieran shrugged.

Brath was rubbing his chin thoughtfully and said nothing.

"Please," Lady Isabella interrupted, "can we postpone this discussion until tomorrow. I don't think anyone at this table wishes to stay up all night making battle plans. The king has had a long day. Tomorrow is soon enough to make military decisions."

Brath tipped his head to her. "You're right, Your Ladyship. I doubt I could make a coherent thought tonight, in any case. We'll meet after breakfast tomorrow morning and take stock of the situation. Kieran, please join us. Your insight could be useful."

Kieran nodded. During a pause in which no one knew what to say, Lady Isabella asked Briana if there was anything she needed while at Winge Mansion.

"Cailleach and I will go into Derryfeeny before we leave for medicinal supplies. I fancy a visit with Hapgood Broomesly-Wells."

Conversation floated around the table. Cailleach and Lady Isabella discussed local midwife matters, something Briana had no desire to get involved with. Instead, she and Aya'emrys talked of assigning the faerie warriors to heal a faerie tree they'd found nearby.

"They can be called up in an instant," he reminded her, "but in the meantime, they might as well make themselves useful."

The usual evening sherry in the salon was nixed in favor of an early night.

"My lady, would you be so kind as to assist your tired, old husband to his rest. I'm not sure I can manage the stairs unassisted," Brath said, feigning a hobble.

"I'd be honored to, Your Majesty. Shall I fetch your cane?"

Laughter, the first she'd heard since her arrival at Winge Mansion, lifted Briana's spirits. Jonathan offered to take Dara out and bring him up when he was done. Brath had no difficulty managing the stairs and wasted no time in undressing and getting into bed. By the time Briana had gone through her nightly routine and gotten Dara settled, Brath's eyes were closed. She eased into the bed beside him.

"What do you think about Kieran?" he asked. His eyes remained shut but his arm reached under her shoulder to draw her to his side.

"I thought you were asleep."

"Just resting my eyes. Kieran? I know you've got an idea about him."

She did, but hadn't fully formulated it. "I'm not sure what I think.

Only that I believe he's sincere and I'd like to see him get a fresh start. Sir Thomas clearly can't trust him yet, but I think he might be useful somehow. He has a bad reputation and it's widely known that he's estranged from the Winges. Perhaps he might be spy material? I think we just need to listen see if there's a way to use him."

"Fair enough."

"There's something else I've been thinking about tonight."

His lips curved. "You sure think a lot for a woman."

Had she not known he was teasing, she would've taken offense. Instead, she elbowed him and replied, "Just a quirky thing about me. Seriously, as much as I hate to think about this, I do wonder what you'll do if Sigel doesn't recover from his injury. Would you try and replace him as lord marshall?"

"I have thought about that and although Sir Jameson is the obvious choice, I think I'd rather wait and see. We can do without a lord marshall for the time being. Sir Jameson can still act as commander, so I think I'll just leave things be for now. And now, my lady, if you are through with thinking me to sleep, might we possibly turn to more gentle pursuits than war plans?"

She turned on her side and leaned on her elbow to kiss him. "Something like this?" she murmured, then slid her hand under the covers. Her fingers found and stroked the silky skin that told her he wasn't so tired after all. "Or like this?"

"I'll take both," he whispered against her lips.

CHAPTER FIFTEEN

COVERT OPS

"Isabella, I know you think me heartless…" said Sir Thomas.

"No, I do not. What I think is that you are *heartbroken* and don't want to risk being hurt again, but I truly believe things are different now. *He's* different. Surely you can see that?"

Brath and Briana paused in the doorway to the dining room and exchanged glances, both clearly wondering if the other had a good idea about how to make their presence known. Dara provided the solution by pushing between them into the room. They only had to pause a minute to "catch up" to the hound. By the time they entered, trying to appear as though they hadn't heard anything, the Winges wore hospitable smiles and invited the king and queen to join them.

Ballynickle appeared instantly at their side with tea and breakfast. Brath wasted no time in tucking into coddled eggs and fried bacon. The smell of the meat alone would have stimulated Briana's appetite, had she not already been ravenous.

"Your Majesty, the men will be here any minute. How shall I best help?" Sir Thomas asked.

Brath put a hand on his shoulder. "By maintaining an open mind. Kieran seems to have information that might be useful and I want to hear what he knows. Briana thinks he might have a part to play in this war against Shamwa. We want to consider putting his knowledge and skills to good use."

Sir Thomas sighed. "Lady Isabella is of the same mind. Perhaps it's time I let go of the past and give him another chance."

"You must decide what's best for your family, but I need to take advantage of every opportunity that presents to build our defenses."

"Speaking of the army," Lady Isabella broke in, "have you seen Sigel this morning?"

"I looked in on him," Briana answered. "He remains unconscious but appears comfortable. Cailleach is with him now, but we'll need someone to stay with him when we go to Derryfeeny."

"I'll make sure a valet is with him at all times," she promised.

They heard the knights, Kieran and Captain Aya'emrys gathering in the library and turned their attention to the task at hand.

Brath, Briana and Sir Thomas left breakfast to join them in the library. When Briana eyed her half-eaten scone on the way out, Brath teased her.

"Would you like to bring it with you? I'd hate for you to starve before lunch."

She punched him lightly. "I'll survive."

After briefly summarizing where things stood, Brath invited Kieran to tell the group what he knew.

"I've been living in Cedarmara for a few years now." He glanced at Epona and took a breath. "As I indicated last night, most people there support Lord Shamwa. The man did an ingenious thing while you were… indisposed, Sire. He used the Gray Military to collect all of the taxes due.

"At the same time, he instituted tariffs on all trading between kingdoms. This placed a terrible financial burden on people. Groups of ruffians, who I believed were hired by Shamwa, went around the country destroying farmland, cutting faerie trees and attacking any traders along the road. It wasn't long before there was little to trade and no safe way to travel. The kingdoms became isolated."

Briana knew this to be the case from what Rippa's family had experienced and in fact, she noted Rippa's little head nodding briskly. He was a smart young boy, but then going through the years of Shamwa's terrorism would cause children to grow up fast.

"Shamwa bided his time. People forgot how things got to be so bad. That was the moment Shamwa started handing out money to the people, making sure they knew it came from him. And then he opened limited travel routes and encouraged some trade. All in his glorious name."

"So, he built up his own coffers and then gave some back," Brath said disgustedly.

"Exactly. I would bet my last coin that he has a huge amount of Uisneach's wealth sitting underneath Aurum Castle."

"This went on across Uisneach?" Briana asked.

"To some extent," Kieran replied. "He focused mostly on Cedarmara because it's the most populated and would provide him with the most return in resources, both in terms of money and men, should he ever need to augment the Moherians.

"Since your resurrection, some have returned their allegiance to you, but not all, and none in Colmer Harbor. They are staunch Shamwa supporters. He's convinced them that the policies of the Taranians are bad for Uisneach."

Brath leaned forward. "And what do you think, Kieran?"

This clearly took the young man by surprise. He sat back in his chair and narrowed his eyes. Briana saw a pained look come across Epona's face as well, but Brath was right to question Kieran's loyalty after everything that had happened.

"If that's our starting point, we have a long way to go," Kieran said.

"It must be our starting point. I cannot have a single man with me that I can't trust."

After a moment, Kieran nodded. "Fair enough. One of the reason's I came back was because I have heard much talk about an insurrection against you, Sire. That is *not* in the best interest of Uisneach. I will do whatever I can to make sure there is no such rebellion."

"Can they be turned back?"

"I don't know, but I do believe you must go there and rebuild a relationship with them. That won't be easy, and things may get worse before they get better, but if Shamwa remains in control, it won't be long before he spreads his nasty branches to Appleduir and Evalon. In fact, I suspect Evalon is high on his priority list, because of the faerie trees."

Brath turned to Captain Aya'emrys.

The golden warrior shook his head. "Focus on Cedarmara and Shamwa.

He is dividing his troops to increase confusion and make you uncertain about your best targets. Do not be distracted by his maneuvers. It will be easier to restore the faerie trees when Lord Shamwa has been stopped."

"Cut off the head of the snake," Briana muttered.

Brath glanced at her hip and raised an eyebrow. Following his gaze, Briana realized she had her hand on Nua's grip. She grinned and shrugged. "I would do it."

"I know you would, darling." He closed his eyes and rubbed the spot between his eyes. Minutes passed before he looked toward Kieran again. "You have good relationships in Cedarmara and in Colmer Harbor?"

"I did a lot of building around the territory. I know people."

"Any connection to the Gray Military?"

Kieran paused thoughtfully. "I'm almost afraid to answer that truthfully for fear it will lead to more distrust. However, the truth is that I tried to be friendly with everyone. You never know who will be on your ship when the winds turn. It's helpful to have friends in both ports."

"We have about two thousand warriors, with the faeries. Sigel believed they had roughly the same. Do you agree?"

Kieran shook his head. "They've at least five thousand Moherians in addition to however many Cedarmara men will fight on his side."

"Where are the Grays based?"

"Somewhere deep in the Dromdara Mountains, but I don't know where."

"Nothing useful has come from the Moherian prisoners," Brath ruminated. "I hoped we could use them against Shamwa, but they refuse to cooperate."

Briana knew if they didn't cooperate, they'd be killed. She realized she was getting over any queasiness about that possibility. She watched Brath consider all the information and formulate possible plans. Even Dara's whining to go out didn't interrupt his train of thought. Briana stepped to the door and shooed the dog out to do his business and returned to her husband's side. He seemed focused on the maps laid out in front of him. When he finally spoke, it was with certainty and determination.

"Sir Jameson, you'll be second-in-command while Sigel is incapacitated. We'll move to the castle in Firmara. I would prefer to win this conflict politically and with as little bloodshed as possible. Therefore, Kieran, I'd like you to be the official emissary to Cedarmara and the interim Cedarmara representative for the Evalon-Uisneach Council."

Kieran jerked forward in surprise. Briana looked to Sir Thomas, but his face was expressionless.

"Your Majesty, I..." Kieran started, but stopped when Brath held a hand up.

"I also want you to get word to Shamwa that you've only accepted the position to spy for him. And then I want you to tell him we'll be sending out multiple troops across Uisneach to replant faerie trees. Maybe we can divert some of his troops while we work on repatriating Cedarmara."

Briana maintained a calm demeanor, but inside she was conflicted about the decision. She was the one who thought he could spy, but being a double agent increased Kieran's personal risk. That was not her plan. A glance told her Epona was not happy with the idea, either.

"You want me to be a spy for both sides."

"Yes."

Silent communication between Kieran and Epona ended with her giving a nod and looking away while he gave his full attention to the king.

"I'll take the position, Sire, and hope that I can bring you something valuable in the war against the tyrant."

Brath reached out his hand and Kieran shook it.

"All right, then. We leave for Firmara tomorrow at first light."

The men and Epona filed out, leaving Sir Thomas, Brath and Briana.

"Are you settled with the plan for Kieran?" Brath asked Sir Thomas.

"I'm not absolutely certain I trust him. He could turn on us. Isabella would hang me for saying so, but he still needs to earn trust from me."

"And this is a way for him to do that."

Briana looked at Brath, her heart filling with pride and gratitude. Kieran could be a useful player in the Taranian army, but Brath was also creating an opportunity to heal old wounds.

"He'll prove to you he's changed, Sir Thomas." Epona said from the doorway. They turned. Her eyes expressed both sorrow and hope. "I came back to tell you that I trust him, and I believe you can as well. I also want to request that you let me go with him."

"Bloody hell, no!" Sir Thomas exploded. "He needs to prove himself to you too!"

"He doesn't need to prove anything to me," she argued. "We'll be married and…"

Brath moved to her side and took her hands. "Epona, I understand your feelings, but Kieran has agreed to do something dangerous and it would be better if you waited a little longer for things to be more secure. In any case, you're needed here to help manage the Winge troops."

"I won't let him go again," she insisted.

"No, I don't imagine you will, but let him do the job he's agreed to do. Let him prove to himself, to you and his father that he is worth the trust we're all putting in him. He might even come home a hero. Right now, he needs to focus on his assignment. You'd be a big help to him by supporting him from here."

"With all due respect, Your Majesty, that seems a bit hypocritical since you have your wife with you."

Briana felt herself flush. Epona had a point. She couldn't think of a good argument.

"You're right, Epona, it is a bit disingenuous. My apologies. Yet, I stand behind my advice to practice restraint and patience right now."

How did he do that? Turn something that should come across as totally wrong into something totally noble?

When the Winges and Epona left the room, Briana sat in the nearest chair. Brath came over and stood beside her. "Well, the good news is that we just got through an entire meeting and a bit of drama and you didn't do anything to make it worse."

She laughed and threw her hair back. "I marvel at my own self-restraint."

He squeezed her shoulder. "Didn't you and Cailleach want to go into the village?"

"I suppose, though I'm feeling more like a nap. Maker, I'm tired."

"Maybe you shouldn't stay up half the night."

She put a hand over his mouth. "Shh, someone will hear you."

He gently nipped the inside of her palm.

"You're incorrigible," she said quietly, removing her hand.

"You're both incorrigible," Cailleach said, amused. "The least you could do is shut the door. Briana, *are* we still going to Derryfeeny?"

"Cailleach, must you always slink around like that? Yes, we can go. I believe we're done here. Right, Brath?"

"Not by a long shot, my lady. But if you're going, let me pull together a detail to accompany you. Give me a few minutes."

⤳

As they rode to Derryfenny, Cailleach worried lines from the prophecy. "Two worlds collide. It really could mean anything."

"The obvious meaning is my world in Maine and this world," Briana said.

"Or it could refer to the battle between Brath and Shamwa."

"Hmm…" Briana stopped to snip a fern frond to use as a fan against the bugs, which seemed to be out en masse on the humid, summer day. "Or, it could be about the faerie world and the human world."

"The lines before and after don't help. One refers to ancient hills and symbols and the other speaks of treasure. Both references could mean Uisneach or your world. And who or what the cat is mystifies me."

Silas' face entered Briana's mind. Her great cat. She said nothing.

"Ah, we're here." Cailleach dropped the topic of the prophecy as they entered Derryfeeny.

Briana turned to Jonathan, not an arm's length from her. "Mr. Stark, I trust you remember the last time you were here." He didn't flinch. "Yes, I was interviewing for a job, I believe."

His cocky grin made her laugh. "Oh, ho. Is that what you call it now?"

The peaceful village was a hive of activity when the queen and the witch entered the main street. Briana insisted the guards stay at a discreet distance, having convinced Brath that being tightly guarded sent the wrong message to the people, suggesting they saw themselves as separate or above the villagers, or didn't trust them. Even so, children stared at her faerie companion, barking dogs went silent and shop owners came to the doors to gawk. A few remembered her and greeted her warmly. "Mrs. Jenks! I'm so happy to see you," said Briana as she hopped off Banrion. "How's my sweet Dauphne?" she cooed to the baby tucked tightly in the woman's arms.

"She's better than she was when you last saw here, milady—I mean, Your Majesty."

Briana automatically held her arms for the baby that several months before Cailleach had brought to her for assessment and treatment of the croup. Martha Jenks handed the now very healthy child to her. She was pink and alert and smelled like a baby. Tendrils of longing curled around Briana's heart. Oh, to have a child of her own. But then fear smothered the tendrils and Briana handed little Dauphne back to her mum.

They chatted a few minutes, but Cailleach was eager to get to the apothecary, so they bid each other a good day. Sage, lavender and sandalwood permeated the air as they entered the wild and natural world of Hapgood Broomesly-Wells' Apothecary Shop; Briana inhaled deeply of the sweet and savory scents. The shop seemed empty, though Briana could hear rustling behind the counter.

"Hello," Cailleach called out.

A red cap on top of wild gray curls popped up from behind the counter, followed by the short stout body of a gnome. "Cailleach! Queen Briana! Oh, how delightful to see you again! Welcome, welcome!"

He came around the corner of the counter to hug Cailleach's waist and bow to Briana, taking her hand and placing a courtly kiss upon it. "How is married life treating you, Your Majesty?"

Briana smiled. "Just fine, thank you, Mr. Wells."

His head wagged back and forth briskly. "Tut, tut. No Mr. Wells. It's Hapgood to you."

The apothecary nodded to Jonathan and Aya'emrys, who stood silently at the door. "Greetings, gentleman." He turned back to Briana. "I see you're well protected. Did the king not come with you, then?"

"He did not. He's seeing to arrangements for us to leave again tomorrow."

The gnome gave a disappointed nod. "Another time, perhaps. Have you come for something special?"

Cailleach rattled off several herbs. "And do you happen to have any topaz or jasper?"

Why did Cailleach want healing stones used for grounding and protection? The gnome scuffled to a high bureau and pulled out a long drawer.

Reaching inside, he lifted a tray arrayed with colorful stones. He handed a small, bronze obelisk to Cailleach. "Is this what you're after?"

Light glinted off the coppery patina as Cailleach turned it around and around as though gauging its potential effectiveness. Finally, she nodded. "It'll do just fine. Topaz?"

Hapgood produced a few chunks of raw, uncut topaz. Briana leaned forward next to Cailleach's shoulder, examining the deep golden depths.

"It's beautiful," she murmured.

"And will give a wee bit more energy to our friend," Cailleach whispered. They'd agreed to keep Sigel's incapacitation private for now to prevent anyone from using that information against them.

Cailleach and Briana perused the shop for other things they might need. Hapgood went to a tray and began chopping a handful of flowers. Briana wandered near to observe and discovered the lacy white top and hairy stem of Queen Anne's lace, or as it was otherwise known, wild carrot.

"Empty Cradle," Hapgood said, continuing to chop without looking at her. "You must not touch it, my queen, or your own cradle will remain empty."

"It's a contraceptive?"

He nodded gravely.

"Is it effective?"

He looked at her curiously. "Very. You must be careful around it. I'm sure you and the king are eager to start a family."

Briana looked toward a bin of dried mushrooms, pretending not to hear him.

He continued to work the herb until Cailleach said she was ready. He took the payment, wished the ladies well and walked them to the door. Cailleach stepped outside but before Briana made it through the door, she felt the gnome's hand grasp hers and place a small packet into her hand.

"It might give you some comfort to know you have a choice."

Briana glanced at the packet and knew right away what it was. Tucking it deep into her pocket, she gave him a confused look. "I don't know that I need it, but thank you."

"I hope you don't. I hope the next time we meet, you are as round as a barrel with a smile as wide as the sky. Many blessings to you, Queen Briana."

~

The rest of the time at Winge Mansion was spent preparing for the trip to Firmara. Epona was kept busy with the cavalry, the knights were either practicing or pulling gear together and she and Cailleach worked on making sure they had enough medicinal and trauma supplies, should they end up in a battle along the way. She or Cailleach checked in on Sigel every few hours, but in the middle of the night, when she couldn't sleep for worry over him, Briana went to his room.

She was admitted without question by a crow guard. The room was lit only by a few candles on the table near his bed. Sigel lay draped in eerie shadows, his breathing shallow, seeming more dead than alive. Someone had taken the time to trim his beard. Good.

She pulled a chair to the side of the bed. Cailleach had placed the crystals around him; their green and gold lights did seem to pulse with healing energy. Surely between her magic and the earth's natural magic, they could bring him out of this.

She took deep breaths. "I call on the wisdom and power of the tuathla," she said out loud and placed her hand on Sigel's lower leg. A hint of sandalwood, a weak pulse and a single flash of the stones on her ring. She looked from his leg to his face for any sign of rejuvenation. He remained unresponsive. She tried again. No change.

"Oh, Sigel, I don't know what to do." She picked up the spell book she'd left in his room earlier and rifled through the pages. Spells for every malady were inside; either she or Cailleach had tried them all. Nothing seemed to break Sigel's prison. Turning a page, her eyes lit onto a spell they hadn't tried: *Oak Door Spell*, to release someone from an imprisonment curse. Sigel's injury wasn't a result of witchcraft, though. Still, anything to do with oak doors resonated. Briana felt compelled to give it a try.

"Trapped behind the oaken door," she read aloud, imagining the tree that brought her from Maine to Uisneach. "Bewitched by witch or faerie lore. Say ye once, release and leave. Say ye twice this spell I weave."

She imagined Sigel opening his eyes and getting up out of bed. She called up images of him fighting the Gray Military in the fields around Cath Ardghal. She saw herself sparring with him in the training ring of Winge

Mansion. She remembered him walking her down the aisle to marry Brath. Nothing she said or envisioned made a jot of difference in Sigel's condition.

She glanced out the window as the first light of morning crawled into the room. "Please, Maker, heal him. Bring him back to us." She stared helplessly at her friend, mentor and protector. "Sigel, you have to come out of this. I can't bear the thought of losing you." Putting the thought into words released the tears held just under the surface. Resting her head on his hand, she let them fall. "Uisneach needs you, Sigel. Brath needs you." She made a muffled, chuckling sound through her tears. "Okay, I need you, too. You've become a father to me, and I cannot lose another person that I love."

"What's all the blubbering about," he said, his deep voice weak, despite its closeness to her ear.

She jerked her head up. "Sigel! You're awake! It worked."

"What worked?"

The crystals, the spells, her magic, her prayers? "I'm not sure, but who cares? You're awake! Oh, Sigel, we've been so worried."

"So it seems. Maker, I feel like I've been clubbed at least a half a dozen times. What happened?"

"You were hurt in battle and have been unconscious for days. Thank Maker, you've come out of it!"

"Let me get up."

"Not yet. I need to check something." She lifted the quilt from his feet. "Move your toes for me."

She waited a moment, but nothing happened.

"How's that?" Sigel asked, leaning up on his elbows to get a look.

"Try it again." This time she ran her finger up the sole of his foot.

"Well, everything working to your satisfaction?"

She leaned back in the chair and looked at him. Honesty was all he would accept. "No, Sigel, it's not working. The arrow apparently struck a vital center in your back and at the moment, you're paralyzed from your waist down."

He stared at her as though seeing her for the first time. "At the moment? So it's not permanent?"

"I hope not."

"You *hope* not! It bloody well had better not be permanent!"

"Sigel, sometimes nerve damage from this type of injury takes time to heal. The nerves have to regenerate and build new neural pathways…"

"What the hell are you talking about, girl?"

Even in his weakened state, when Sigel was angry, it was frightening, or would be to anyone else.

"Don't yell at me, Sigel! I'm trying to explain!"

He leaned back against the pillow, spent from the short outburst.

She tried again to explain the process of neural regeneration in simple terms. By the time she finished, he was staring hard at the ceiling. She waited for his response. When it came, she cringed.

"I would rather be dead than a cripple."

"You're not going to be either," Brath said firmly from the doorway, holding a plate of food.

Briana wondered how he knew that, because she certainly did not, and she had far more medical knowledge than he did. However, his hand on her shoulder provided some comfort, and that was what she and Sigel both needed in the moment. He handed her the tray. "Eat, love, the men are waiting. We need to go. Have you kept my wife here all night?" Brath asked his friend with a joking smile, trying to lighten the mood.

"How the hell should I know. I just woke up from my beauty sleep," Sigel replied, a little calmer, but clearly disturbed.

A valet entered and Briana sent him after broth for Sigel. While she wolfed down breakfast, Brath outlined his plans for Sigel.

"Who's replacing me?"

"No one. Don't you know, you're irreplaceable?"

Sigel just harrumphed. "Do you trust Kieran?" he finally asked.

"Time will tell. I'm willing to give him a chance. When you return, if you think it's not worth the risk, I'll reconsider."

"I *will* be back," Sigel said fiercely.

"You will," Brath agreed, patting his shoulder. "We need to go. Sir Thomas will be reporting to you every day. I think the both of you can keep things safe around here. Ready, Briana?"

She nodded, setting the tray aside and rising. She took one last look at Sigel's supine form. "Bye, Sigel." She didn't know what to say. "See you soon," was all that came to mind. She patted his hand and turned to follow her husband.

"Briana," Sigel said, his voice now tender.

"Yes?"

"You won't lose me."

He'd heard her. She choked back a sob and returned to his side. Leaning down, she kissed his cheek. "Get better fast." Unable to stand the moisture she saw in his eyes, she stood and turned away.

❧

The oak-lined avenue was quickly behind the armies as they marched north, following a small tributary of Long River. To the casual observer, it would seem Brath had only a small army. The thousand faerie soldiers were invisible to anyone other than those used to seeing the twinkles that surrounded the Taranian army. Even Captain Aya'emrys was a mere sparkle at Briana's side. Crows flew overhead, but their patterns seemed more random than militaristic. In an instant, what seemed a small group could become thousands strong. Briana felt completely safe amid such a magical entourage. The trail crossed the stream twice and Briana, on Banrion, made the crossing easily. As did Dara.

In Moiria, the took the ferry to cross the much larger Long River. Brath struck up a conversation with the ferryman and learned that a few Gray Military had been around in the past few weeks, but they seemed intent on finding something specific, and not finding it, moved on quickly.

"Likely searching for us," Brath said to Briana. "We can't stay in Moiria long. We'll rest the horses, eat and move away from the village."

They stopped at the Howling Wolf Tavern. Dara made good use of the outdoors water trough. Briana hoped she wouldn't have an awkward run in with Grania, Silas' old girlfriend. No such luck. Grania's coppery hair was the first thing Briana saw when her eyes adjusted to the darkness in the tavern. The woman saw her and glared before searching the rest of the group for... *Oh, let me guess, Silas?* The catty thought pounced through her mind before she could snare it, but she let it go and turned on her most queenly charm when the girl came to see them.

"Hello, Grania. Nice to see you again," she said.

The girl raised one eyebrow disbelievingly. The royal entourage was seated and ale poured all around. Mrs. McPhee came to the dining room.

Seeing her son, Sir Faolan, she raced to his open arms. Briana smiled at the warm reunion. Food appeared out of nowhere and the men dug in as though it were their last meal.

Grania came to fill their tankards and nearly spilled Briana's in her lap. "Sorry."

Right.

"Where is he?" the woman asked briskly.

"Who?" Briana pretended not to understand.

"You know who. Why is he not with you?"

"He's away. Personal business."

Grania frowned and moved away.

Brath said, "That seemed tense. You have history with her?"

"Brath, she's a tavern wench. Why would I have history with her?"

He tipped his head, eyeing her shrewdly. "I don't know, but that response is so unlike you that clearly you must."

She didn't respond, and he studied her intently, looked toward Grania and back at Briana. "Ahh," he breathed, realizing the source of their terse interaction. "Silas."

Before the conversation could become more uncomfortable, Brath noticed someone enter and turned away from her to his knights. Without any verbal communication, four of them rose and calmly ushered the bulky, dark-haired man out.

A Moherian. "Gray Military?" Briana asked Brath quietly. He nodded and turned back to the beef pie on his plate. Dara sidled up to Briana and she slipped him half her serving of pie. The knights returned shortly and whispered something in Brath's ear, then sat to finish their meals. The king and his men thanked their host and hostess and bid them farewell. On the way out, Briana caught one more glimpse of Grania and noticed a necklace flash in the candlelight, something that looked like a silver arrow.

"Briana, are you coming?" Brath said, sounding as irritated as she felt.

Sir Cruahan was on his mount, next to Briana.

"What happened to the Gray?" she asked.

"He wouldn't tell us anything and didn't want to join Brath's army."

She waited but he offered nothing else, leaving the disposition of the

Moherian to her imagination. She was certain they hadn't just let him go on about his merry way to tell Shamwa where they were.

For the next few hours they rode quietly through the forest beside the Fodor River. Brath was cool to her, probably irritated by the interaction between her and Grania, and since Briana had no soothing response to offer, she had to settle for letting him get over it.

They were on the short side of the afternoon when she recognized an orchard looming in front of them on a hill. To the casual observer, the apple trees, richly laden with red fruit, would seem inviting. Briana, however, recognized a certain energy emanating from the old fruit trees.

"Brath, hold up. We don't want to go through that orchard."

"No? Why not?"

When he heard her explanation, he nodded and rerouted the men north around the orchard. "We'll start looking for a place to make camp for the night."

She recognized the rough, hilly terrain as the route she and Sigel travelled on their way to Cailleach's cabin on her first journey across Uisneach. She managed the rock scrambles without difficulty and practically leaped across the small streams that crisscrossed the land. The darkness of the forest suddenly became a bit lighter when they entered a glen.

In the center of the space was a rounded hump of moss-covered, gray rocks. Druid's Grove! Where she met Silas. She could almost see him coming through the mist that day, his kilt swinging, carrying the bow that had just released the arrow that freed her from a Moherian's grasp. Her heart fell.

"Briana? Something wrong?"

"I'm fine. I just recognized this place. Sigel and I camped here once on our way to Ard Darach. I was just thinking how long ago that seemed."

They rode on, following the stream up the same ridge that she and Sigel climbed in search of the Gray Military. Looking down over the open field below, she was sickened by the results of Shamwa's destructive frenzy; hacked and burned stumps of faerie trees scarred the land. They hadn't even bothered to clean up their mess. Her throat constricted.

"Puts a whole new meaning to 'when the wheel of the seasons forgets to turn and the trees are nearly gone,'" she said, quoting the first lines of the prophecy.

"And there is not much we can do until the runes are returned," Aya'emrys said from beside her.

"We may as well camp here tonight, along the ridge," Brath said. "I'd like to leave again before sunrise."

Briana dismounted Banrion. Jonathan immediately took the reins and headed off to care for the mare. Brath led Briana to a nearby stream while men hustled around, preparing camp. This would be a short break and, wanting to keep as low a profile as they could, no tents would be set up, their fires kept small. Briana washed up as best she could in the water.

"You holding up okay?" Brath asked, sounding genuinely concerned.

"I'm fine," she answered, smiling, relieved he'd gotten over the tavern incident. "This is my element."

The evening passed quietly and being well guarded by crows and faeries, Briana fell asleep easily between Brath and Dara. She woke in the dark to a sound which turned out to be Aya'emrys whispering her name.

"What's wrong?" she asked, worried.

Brath remained asleep beside her, breathing regularly.

"Nothing is wrong, Tuathla. I want to show you something. Will you come with me?"

"Of course. Should Brath come too?"

"That is up to you. It is nothing dangerous."

She looked at her husband. He needed rest more than he needed whatever the faerie wanted to show his tuathla. She eased away from their bedroll and took the hand Aya'emrys offered to guide her through the camp. Several twinkling faerie lights accompanied them to the edge of the ridge. Briana looked out over what she expected to be a bleak and silent graveyard of faerie trees. Instead, tiny, shimmering lights blinked through a veil of mist over the field. Peering through the mist, Briana saw movement in the grass. Chanting reached her ear and the lights brightened a bit more. To the casual eye, it looked and sounded like insects, lightning bugs and something buzzing, but Briana knew the faeries were working magic. And she understood what kind of magic.

"We need your help, High Lady." Aya'emrys asked before joining his rich, timeless voice with the others.

Briana listened for a moment, feeling the cadence and the deep calling in the ancient words, even while she didn't understand them. Joining in the chant, she fell into the trancelike power of the magic. Waving her hand gently over the scene before her, she formed the words in her mind, *I call on the wisdom and power of the tuathla.*

In the faint light she witnessed a single tree trunk raise itself upright, its hacked branches rising and reattaching to the main trunk as withered brown leaves turned the color of eggplant, unfurled, and floated up to the branches. Finally, the flowers joined the living branches, their pearly mauve bells teasing the air with the sound of wind chimes.

"Oh, my Maker," Briana whispered, stunned by the resurrection of the faerie tree. She turned excitedly to her companion. "Aya'emrys, let's heal the rest!"

He shook his head. "It would be too much for any of us. When the runes come home, it will be easy to heal the trees, but it just took the combined efforts of every faerie here and you, High Lady, to repair the one. I simply wanted you to see what is possible."

They sat in silence, watching over the newly healed faerie tree as night slowly turned to day. She felt rather than heard Brath sit beside her. He kissed her cheek. Aya'emrys left the couple alone.

"Good morning. How long have you been awake?"

"A while. Look." She pointed to the tree.

"Did you do that?"

"I helped, I guess. Mostly it was the faeries."

Brath intertwined his fingers with hers. "It's beautiful. Someday, this whole field will be restored."

"I hope so," she whispered.

"It will."

&

"I can't help but wonder how that magic of yours can be used to defeat Shamwa," Brath said as they rode through uninhabited forests and fallow fields, seven days after leaving Winge Mansion.

Most of the Winge army and Evalon army travelled in magical form, so the ground troops appeared meager. Briana smiled at the subterfuge. In an instant thousands of warriors could materialize if Shamwa was foolish enough to attack. Brath had sent Kieran ahead with a small group of crows to open the castle and recruit staff to tend to the king and queen. By this evening, they should be settled in and ready to begin the political games to bring Cedarmara back into alliance with the Taranians. Conversation between Brath and the knights consisted mostly of how exactly to do that.

Just as Briana wondered if they would need to camp another night, the terrain started to slope downward and the trees thinned out. The trail curved around a rock post carved with the name Firmara and soon, before Briana's eyes lay the city so named. It reminded her of many towns along the coast of Maine, or Ireland, for that matter. Houses terraced down to the sea. What she was not prepared for was the fairytale castle that rose up from a small island in the middle of the harbor. Her jaw dropped.

"Firmara Castle has been the Taranian summer home for generations," Brath said," chuckling.

The multi-storied and sprawling angles of the structure made it seem bigger than it was, but size wasn't what kept her gawking. The setting sun cast a glow that made the castle's pinkish stone appear a brilliant rose-gold. Round towers stood as sentinels from every corner and turrets spired up gracefully from seemingly random positions across the stronghold.

"It's magical," she whispered.

"And completely defensible. Those sheer cliffs aren't the only means of protection. If intruders even thought of climbing the cliffs, they'd have to get through that." He pointed at the crenelated curtain wall that surrounded the castle. "They'd never make it through. Our archers would have them dead before they could get across the bridge." She nodded, appreciating the visible arrow slits lining the turrets. Windows dotted every side. While they were admiring the view, the Taranian flag unfurled boldly atop the highest of the towers.

"I suppose Kieran knows we're here then," said Brath. "Beautiful, isn't it? I'm glad we arrived late enough to see Firmara Castle it in this light."

She nodded wordlessly.

"King Brath, how do you want us to proceed?" asked Sir Stark. "Should the faeries and crows shapeshift and go in all at once, or do you want to keep it quiet?"

He tipped his head toward the flag. "Kieran's already alerted the towns-folk. Let's just stay calm and see what happens."

At a sharp command from Sir Stark, a sound like wind rose. Mini-tornados began to blow around Briana, whipping her hair around her head and face. Through the curtain of her hair, she saw the sight that never failed to both awe and repulse her: black wings flapped and twisted furiously as the crows started to shift, elongating and transmogrifying into a black-suited army of over a thousand.

Thankfully, the faerie transition was much gentler. Twinkling lights instantly became colossal golden warriors, a thousand-man army. Brath Taranian entered Firmara fully prepared to meet any threat.

They wended their way through hilly, cobbled streets. Prosperity had once allowed the people of this city to build multilevel homes and shops, some with gardens and courtyards. However, with the damage Shamwa had done with his economic sanctions, severe taxes and military operations, many shops were dark and empty, and most homes in disrepair.

Rather than the provocative beat of a war drum, Rippa's pleasing voice led the march down into the village, where people poured out into the streets with hesitant stares and hushed whispers.

"Fair Firmara, by the sea.
Greetings from your faithful king.
Banners wave in peace and promise.
Defend the realm, remove the threat,
To unity and prosperity.
Remember Uisneach, remember well,
When men and magic flourished.
Though fields lay fallow, hearts beat slow,
Your king brings hope, united story.
Of brighter days and magical ways, bards will tell."

Brath, riding in front of her, smiled and waved; some of the citizens waved back. Others seemed guarded, frowning uncertainly, their arms crossed over their chests. Briana felt a different sort of butterflies' flutter in her belly.

"I'm glad I've got you beside me," she said to Captain Aya'emrys.

"This does not feel dangerous to me," he replied, even while his eyes continuously scanned the crowd for any threat.

"I think we're fine," Jonathan Stark agreed, on the other side of her. "Kieran's just ahead and he doesn't look concerned."

Briana leaned sideways to see past Brath. Kieran was standing next to a tall, spare man in front of a tavern. When they were close enough, the Firmara man greeted them.

"King Brath, welcome to Firmara. I'm Governor Llewellyn. It would be my pleasure to have you join me at our tavern for supper before going on to the palace. I expect it will take your staff time to prepare. This will be easier."

Briana gave Kieran a questioning glance. He returned a slight nod. *Good, we have staff, Briana thought.*

"We would be honored to join you," Brath said, dismounting Ruark. He walked around to assist Briana. "Allow me to introduce my wife, Queen Briana."

The governor bowed low. "Greetings, Your Majesty."

"Thank you for the kind invitation, Governor Llewellyn," Briana said, straightening as she stood, trying to discreetly loosen the tightness in her back from riding. "I'm relieved not to have to put a household together this late in the day."

"Your Majesty," Kieran said to Brath, "If you are so inclined, the troops can set camp around the castle. There is food to feed them. Perhaps just the knights could stay with you."

The message was clear—you're safe enough, not totally invulnerable.

"Sir Jameson, see to those arrangements and then join us, please. You too, Kieran."

Briana walked beside Brath into the tavern, which was larger than it appeared from the outside. Servers ran to and fro, pulling together a meal to serve this large and esteemed group.

"Governor, I believe our emissary, Kieran, has told you of our reason for coming here."

"He has and while I am grateful for your attention to Cedarmara, I fear you will not find your reception easy in all places."

"So I understand. I hope you can tell me more about what's happened while I was under Shamwa's curse."

Briana smiled. That last statement was a purposeful attempt to remind the governor and anyone else listening that he was also a victim of Shamwa.

Refreshments were served and as they ate, the story formed. For the decade of Brath's imprisonment, things went from bad to worse in Cedarmara. For all the reasons that they'd already heard from Kieran, people were brought to a point of near starvation.

"Corruption and violence escalated in every part of Uisneach, but it seemed worse here on the west coast, maybe because there are more people here, I don't know. We'd never had to deal with such things before and no one knew what to do, or who to trust."

"Those circumstances were unheard of because the Taranians looked after the kingdom and managed with fairness and concern for all its citizens," Brath pointed out when the governor stopped to take a drink.

"Maybe so, Your Majesty, but with no Taranians available and the only government Shamwa's, we had no choice but to do what he wanted."

"Fair enough."

"So, when things got as bad as they could get and Shamwa suddenly gifts the cities with food, a halt on taxes and a promise to make trade routes safe again, the people welcomed him with open arms."

"But he was the reason the trade routes were unsafe in the first place and the taxes were so ridiculous," Briana argued.

The governor raised his hands. "I know, I know. And many would agree with you in Firmara. But Colmer Harbor, that's another story. They believe that regardless of who started what, Lord Shamwa made it right and deserves their loyalty. There are some that have sadly forgotten the leadership of your father, and they haven't had enough experience with how you might rule to trust you."

The sun was near to setting by the time Brath, Briana and their small entourage left the tavern. It seemed that the governor was hopeful about their chances to win over most of Cedarmara and certainly Firmara, so it came as a surprise to find a group of people crowded outside the tavern. They hurled insults and threats at Brath and Briana. Dara growled and in a rare show, bared his teeth. The knights immediately circled the monarchs while the governor attempted to calm their protest. Assuring himself of Briana's safety, Brath left the security of the knights to speak to the mob. His efforts were drowned out by their emotional outbursts and it soon became clear that escaping this throng was the only smart solution tonight.

"Your Majesty, we need to get you to the castle," said Kieran, laying his hand on the king's shoulder. "We'll start again tomorrow."

No attempt was made by Shamwa's supporters to follow them. They switchbacked down the steep, rocky shoreline to where a stone viaduct led across the harbor. Halfway across the bridge, Brath turned Briana back in the direction they'd come.

"Look over there," he said. A river of fire streaked down the side of the mountain to the south of the village. It took Briana a minute to realize it wasn't lava. A blood-red ribbon of water cascaded several hundred feet from the top of the limestone cliffs.

"It's called Fire Falls, for obvious reasons," he said. "It turns that red when the sun sets. Do you know of any modern science to explain it?"

"I'm no expert, but I imagine minerals from the limestone dissolve in the water and catch the light and turn it red. Whatever causes it, it is beautiful."

Once inside the castle walls, they dismounted and handed the horses to a young man for care and stabling. They passed through a magnificent stone archway into a narrow garden that seemed more eerie than welcoming in the torchlight. Several wide, stone steps led to double doors, twice the size of the tallest man in Uisneach, were opened and Dara walked through between two valets as though he owned the place.

"Sorry, sir," Briana said to one man, old and stooped over, dressed formally in a suit that had seen better days. "My dog seems to have forgotten his manners. Dara. Come here."

The servants didn't seem at all distressed by the arrival of the king, queen and nearly two dozen of their entourage. Brath greeted the two men respectfully and went with Briana inside. The knights, Kieran, Jonathan and Rippa followed. Dara slipped for a moment on the marble floor, then stopped and stared. Briana could see why. Counting the balconies, she realized the ceiling was six floors up, yet that might not be the most impressive thing in the room. A glorious replica of a faerie tree stood in the center of the vestibule, surrounded by a pool. Water rained down from the bell-shaped flowers in the tree's spreading canopy into the pool. A grand staircase to Briana's left curved up the entire height of the castle. Stained glass windows were spaced evenly all the way to the sixth floor.

I can't wait to see this in the daylight, Briana thought, marveling at the opulence and craftsmanship of Firmara Castle.

"Your Majesties," said an elderly man with a nasally voice, breaking into Briana's awed silence. "Allow me to introduce myself. I am Percival Pogue, your butler."

The sound of hurrying footsteps and heavy breathing drew their attention.

"Sorry, I'm late, ma'am," a young woman blatted, coming to an abrupt halt in front of Briana. She was likely no more than sixteen, all legs, arms and a frenzy of blonde curls that resisted her apparent attempt to contain them with a ribbon. She scratched the side of her nose with a long finger, and in the act, her lips parted, showing a row of terribly crooked but intact teeth, as she assessed them with her bright blue eyes. She curtsied a little too fast and would've toppled over, had Briana not caught her arm. "Thank you, ma'am, sorry."

"This," the butler said ruefully, "is Amelia Blackthorn." He sighed. "Your lady's maid." He looked apologetic, but Briana gave him and the young girl a winning smile, certain she'd love anyone who was such a hot mess.

"All right then," said Briana, are rooms ready for us and our men?"

"Yes, Your Majesty. The entire second floor has been prepared for your arrival."

"Wonderful. Then everything else can wait till tomorrow. Mr. Pogue, I understand we have enough staff to get the basics done, so I trust breakfast will be no problem in the morning."

"No problem at all. Amelia will assist you, and sir," he said, turning to the king, "I'll see to your needs tonight."

"Just show us to our room, please. We'll manage from there, thank you," Briana said in a kind but firm voice.

The old man looked up the staircase with some relief. "In that case, I shall have Amelia bring you up and I'll finish things down here."

The young girl tripped up the stairs, Dara hot on her heels.

"My goodness, Briana, you sounded like a real queen just then," Brath whispered to her.

She elbowed him. "I am a real queen."

"Oh, yes, I suppose you are."

Their men wasted no time securing rooms. Jonathan and Rippa elected to share a room near the king and queen.

Brath and Briana were ushered into a room twice the size of their chambers at home. "It won't be in the least cramped when you hold your staff meetings."

"Oh, there's a room readied for the king's business," Amelia said brightly.

Briana glanced around. "Now, I know where they came up with the phrase, a king-sized bed. This is humongous. I hope I can find you in there, somehow."

"No worries, my lady, I promise if you can't find me, I will most definitely find you."

Giggles issued from the other side of the room. When Brath and Briana both looked in Amelia's direction, she blushed. "I'm sorry, sir and ma'am. It's just that it was so cute, what you said. You must be very much in love."

Briana's throat went bone dry.

Brath stared at her but said nothing.

Amelia looked between them, a curious expression on her face. "Shall I help you with your gown, Queen Briana?"

"Uh, no. I'm fine, Amelia. We don't need anything tonight. I'll see you tomorrow and we'll have a chat."

"As you wish. Good night then." The woman breezed out the door, leaving Brath and Briana with the echoes of the awkward statement she'd made between them.

CHAPTER SIXTEEN

TAKING BACK UISNEACH

"Kieran," Brath said from his seat at the table in their chambers, "I'd have you go into the village and invite the governor and the town's leaders here for a meeting this afternoon for tea." Brath glanced hopefully at Briana, who shrugged, not sure if they had tea and food to offer. One way or another, the Taranians would be hospitable.

"Shall I offer an agenda?"

"The proposal of creating a unified Uisneach with representation from all the realms in the kingdom," Brath said. "We want them to elect or assign members to what we will call the Parliament of Peers."

Briana half-listened to these arrangements, her attention focused on Amelia Blackthorn, who was turning out to be more than just a lady's maid. She had delivered breakfast, made the bed and set out clothing for the monarchs and was now cleaning up the dishes. She flittered around like a drunken hummingbird. There was something else, though, that made Briana smile. As the sun filled the windows and candles were no longer needed, Amelia walked by and with a glance, extinguished the tapers. She paused before the fireplace and the flames picked up their pace, a good thing on a chilly morning. Earlier, when she noticed wrinkles in the gown she'd laid out for Briana, she'd swished her head from side to side and they vanished, leaving only smooth fabric.

She's got magic! Strong magic, by the looks of it. She would find out more about this unusual girl at the first opportunity.

A knock at the door and Jonathan Stark poked his head into the room. "Sire, a group of people are advancing up the bridge to the castle."

"How many?" Brath asked.

"About a dozen. They don't look angry."

"They're not," Amelia commented distractedly.

How does she know that? Their chambers were at the back of the palace. From the balcony, there was a beautiful view of the rocky shoreline of the island and the ocean, in its white-capped gray gown today, thanks to the rain. It wasn't possible for her to see who was coming from the front.

"Bring them inside," she said. "Get them dry by the fire." There was much to be done, but first things first. She grabbed Nua and secured her in the hip belt she wore attached her to the wrinkle-free, burgundy gown. "Amelia, come with us, please. Just in case."

"In case of what?" she asked, cocking her head.

Briana didn't know why. "Just come, please."

The girl nodded and followed Briana, tripping once on the way to the great hall. Heading down the stairway, Briana was enchanted by the many stained glass windows; though their effect was dimmed by the silvery light of the rainy day, they still managed to bathe the staircase and the entryway below with hues of rose, salmon, seafoam, and goldenrod. The colors would be different on a sunny day. Magical.

Great was hardly adequate to describe the hall. This room was three times the size of Ard Darach's great hall, bigger even than the ballroom at Winge Mansion. Taranian banners hung from the rafters. A fireplace, large enough to house a small cottage, lit one end of the room while braziers crafted to look like shields illuminated the other walls. The braziers were made from the same rose-gold stone as the castle walls. The room was warm enough that Briana wouldn't need the shawl she'd brought. A stone dais, centered on the wall opposite the double doors, held the thrones, both carved from rose-gold stone, bearing the same Taranian symbols along the backs of them as the oak thrones at Ard Darach.

Maker, I hope I don't have to sit too long in that. My butt's going to hurt like hell.

The thought had barely formed when Amelia zipped around her with pillows and placed them on the seats.

"Sorry," she muttered to Briana when she zipped back by.

Brath took her hand and together they stepped onto the dais and sat in the thrones. Briana had barely settled onto the cushion, that thankfully was thick enough to soften the feel of the rock-hard throne, when Pogue opened the doors to announce the visitors.

Holding her breath against the expected warriors or irate Shamwa supporters, Briana was much relieved when a raggle-taggle group of smiling citizens entered the room, looking around them in awe.

I know, that's what I thought too, Briana wanted to say to them, but instead only smiled warmly, hoping it would make them feel comfortable.

One man, a hearty-looking soul, stepped forward. "Your Majesties. We understand you need more servants."

Briana cringed. Partly because the idea of having servants still galled her and partly because she had no idea what they needed. At her ear, making her jump, Amelia whispered, "You only have me, Pogue, and Mrs. Pogue, the cook."

Briana quickly assessed the group of eight. "Your name, sir?" Briana asked the man.

"Dougal Donal, ma'am. I have been chamberlain of other households in Cedarmara and currently manage the taxing procedures in Firmara."

"Do you understand that we intend to make changes to that system?" Brath asked.

"Aye, Sire, I do. I sincerely hope you will. It's been long overdue."

Good then—a supporter, Briana thought. *Hired.*

Within an hour the palace was fully staffed, and Kieran returned with a response from the governor. He and the other top-ranking officials in Firmara would arrive late in the afternoon. Brath and Briana had a lot to do.

"Mrs. Pogue," Briana asked the cook, "can we be ready to serve a light supper to about thirty people this afternoon?"

"Of course, Your Majesty. We've enough help now to prepare a ball, if that's what you want."

Briana grinned. "No ball, just yet."

She left the cook and her kitchen staff to their preparations and went to check on the new housekeeping staff. Agatha, an older, no-nonsense sort of women had unofficially become head of housekeeping, with two youngsters,

James and Thurid, underneath her. Briana was stunned by the efficient spiffing-up they'd already accomplished and thanked Agatha for her attention to detail.

"Thank ye, ma'am, it's a pleasure. We've not enough fresh flowers to set about the great hall, but Finnegan, the groundskeeper, is hard at work cleaning up the gardens so the next time you receive company, it'll be better. Ah, it's lovely to have the castle opened up again. It's lovely to have you and the king here as well."

Briana's internal barometer spiked at the mention of working in the gardens, but her participation in that activity would have to wait for another time.

Nearly six hours passed before Briana saw Brath again as they were hastily changing into appropriate clothing.

"Nervous?" she asked him as she watched him lace up his boots.

He made an undecipherable noise which made her think he'd only half-heard her. She stepped over Dara and kneeled beside her husband. Putting a hand on his knee forced his attention. His eyes were dark with worry.

"It's going to be fine," she said gently. "I'm feeling the love from these people."

"Maybe you're feeling it from the staff. After all, they did come to us for work. However, that doesn't mean everyone will embrace our ideas or us. I worry that something will happen and I can't keep you safe."

"Should I bring Nua?" she asked, having decided earlier to leave the sword behind to avoid looking fearful or threatening.

He shook his head. "No, leave it. Aya'emrys is aware that should things turn sour, he is to remove you to safety at once. And I don't think we'll see violence today. Disagreement, perhaps, but nothing life-threatening." He lifted her hand and kissed the fingers before standing up. "How do I look?"

One side of her mouth curved in a sly smile. "Strong, self-assured and handsome as hell. I can't wait until this is all over and we can, uh, retire for the night."

He pulled her into his arms and rewarded her with a passionate kiss. "A promise of things to come," he whispered against her earlobe.

⤚

"Uisneach has been under the leadership of the Taranian family for generations. I have no intention of allowing Lord Shamwa to change that.

Before the prime minister put a curse on the castle and my person, we were a thriving, peaceful kingdom. You will recall our efforts to improve the roads, increase trade and implement new farming techniques that resulted in prosperity for everyone. It was Shamwa who increased taxes, shut down trade and travel and allowed his minions to terrorize your community. I promise you, we are going to change that."

Brath sat in the middle of a long table with Briana to his left and Sir Jameson to his right. Captain Aya'emrys sat beside Briana. The other knights Kieran and Jonathan filled in down the sides. The Firmara leaders faced the king from the opposite side of the table.

"I understand Shamwa has recently begun to relax his tyrannical policies and has even supplied food and supplies to Cedarmara. But you cannot have forgotten it was he who took them from you in the first place. His vision of Uisneach has not changed. What he's doing now is a tactic to ensure your loyalty as he seeks to rule the kingdom. His generosity and concern are an illusion. We must return to the pre-curse policies and projects of the Taranian government. The legitimate government!"

A wave of comments spread through the crowd, some in agreement, some in disagreement.

"I ask you this," Brath continued, "who in Cedarmara has been asked by Shamwa to help manage the kingdom? Who has been asked for advice or been given a position that would give them any authority to contribute to the long-term plans for Uisneach? Who has been included at any level in discussions about what is best for Uisneach?"

Silence was the only answer.

"I have already formed the Evalon-Uisneach Council, made up of representatives from all kingdoms of Uisneach. This council will meet regularly to discuss policy, create programs to benefit the kingdom and advise me on what is needed across the land. Mine is a vision for a unified and equal Uisneach, including Evalon, the realm of the faeries!"

Murmurs of surprise met this statement. Briana also heard a few dissenting voices spouting Shamwa's rhetoric about magic making the kingdom weaker. Brath must have heard it also.

"Magic once blessed this land, but the relationship with the faeries has waned over the centuries, and with the recent focus of Lord Shamwa on the destruction of the faerie trees, it is on the verge of extinction. Your queen," he turned and put a hand on Briana's shoulder, "is part faerie, and I have not only met with the faerie leadership but have seen firsthand how beautiful and beneficial magic could be to Uisneach. I have come to know the faeries as a truly wonderful and kind people. They want to help us and are in fact, part of our army, as you may have noticed."

All eyes turned to Aya'emrys, who remained attentive and silent. Briana saw the wonder in the eyes of those around the table. The faerie warrior was a sight to behold. *Wait until they see the whole army*, Briana thought, chuckling to herself.

"I know Shamwa tells you that faeries weaken Uisneach and they would take control of us. That's as much a fallacy as the idea that trading with other countries makes us weak. We have a strong army and we can be even stronger if we are united."

"So, King Brath. What do you want from us, and what is your plan?" Governor Llewellyn asked.

"I want to know that you stand with your king, that you are ready and willing to help us take back Uisneach, and that you will commit your hearts and your resources to winning this war against Lord Shamwa. Together, we can make Uisneach stronger and more powerful than ever before! Our plan is to create a people so unified in purpose that Shamwa will admit defeat and retreat on his own. I do not desire bloodshed. However, should he persist in his efforts to control you, I would meet his threat with all the power that the Taranian, Evalonian and Uisneach armies can raise, militarily and magically."

The governor looked to either side of him. Heads curled, they conversed in hushed tones. Brath looked at Briana with a giant question mark in his eyes. She smiled to assure him of his successful bid for support.

"Maybe you should speak to them, Briana," he said quietly. "Or is there something magical you can do to impress them?"

She thought for a minute and then cleared her throat. The Firmarians halted their considerations and turned their attention to her.

"Gentlemen," Briana said, with a confidence she didn't feel in the slightest. "You all know that I am the Mouse of the Prophecy and that I'm not from around here." There was an underwhelming response to her words, but their expressions indicated an awareness and a touch of awe. She took a breath and continued. "You don't know me, yet, and I realize I'm asking a lot from you to trust what I'm about to tell you. But I will ask it of you.

"I come from a place very different from Uisneach, a place that is too often led and run by men like Shamwa. His policies are not new to us, and have brought ruin upon the land, creating terrible hardships and suffering for many people. Suffering you cannot imagine and that I would hate to see come to pass in Uisneach. When I was kidnapped by Shamwa…"

A ripple of alarm waved across the table.

"I tried to tell him this, but he laughed at me and said his power came from ruling Uisneach through fear and victimization. He tried to coerce me to his way of thinking, but even though I didn't know King Brath, I had heard that his vision for Uisneach was much different. Now, I can say from experience that his plan is the right one. It is the one that will bring prosperity and peace to Uisneach." Recalling the effectiveness of singing "Crossroads" to the people across Uisneach, she adopted the same warrior stance and same tone of voice. "Will you support your king? Will you fight for Uisneach?"

It worked. The energy changed instantly and the mini-conclave between the leaders of Firmara fueled up. Briana sat down, received a warm pat on her thigh from Brath and waited. She didn't wait long.

Governor Llewellyn cleared his throat and stood. "King Brath, we're grateful for your visit to Firmara. We have supported the Taranians for as long as they have ruled, and we have no intention of abandoning you now. You have whatever we can give in terms of support. Just let us know how we can help."

Brath smiled. "First, I want your advice." As expected, his request surprised and delighted them. They discussed the situation in Colmer Harbor in greater detail. The mitten-shaped outcropping of land was about twenty miles from Firmara Castle, perhaps a day's journey for a heavily-laden group.

When the governor asked how soon the army could be ready, Brath responded, "they need a day to rest and resupply. I don't want to rely on the folks at Colmer Harbor to care for our army until we know they're with us."

The Firmara leaders worried about the delay. King Brath said he'd have a message sent to Shamwa suggesting the Taranian army was staying at the palace, awaiting more troops. While that raised a few brows among the city leaders, Kieran didn't even blink. Perhaps he did have the makings of a good spy.

Following a bit more planning, Brath decided to send a contingent of negotiators under Kieran to Colmer Harbor to try to bring them around to the Taranian side. Kieran would convey the king's offer to have his army rebuild their ruined roads—as long as they agreed to not aid Lord Shamwa in any way. Beyond that, small details about supplying the castle with food and other necessaries, paid for from Taranian funds, were addressed. The meeting concluded with Governor Llewellyn sending out couriers to spread the word of the pact, and Rippa singing what had now become Uisneach's anthem.

Rippa invoked the call to arms that "Crossroads" raised, his youthful voice asking were they ready to save the crown, free the nation and release Uisneach from the evil charms of Lord Shamwa?

"Yes, we will!"

"Will you rise?" he asked.

"We will rise."

"Will you fight?"

"We will fight."

"Will you come?"

"We will come."

"For Uisneach we will come!"

Platters of meat, vegetables and fresh bread were brought to the table.

Mrs. Pogue might well be a genius, Briana thought. Ale and tea were all they had to serve for beverages, but no one seemed to mind that.

Golden and amethyst twilight slipped through the window and braziers were lit. Noise from outside caught everyone's attention. Brath, Briana and the governor went to the window.

"Oh, Maker!" Briana exclaimed when she saw a huge group of people on the shore waving Taranian banners and heard them chanting the king's name. Chanting her name! Kieran led his men across the viaduct and was met on the other side with cheers as a small group of hastily formed militia followed him down the road to Colmer Harbor. The group wasn't large enough to look threatening, so Brath didn't recall them, knowing he'd be glad to have the extra hands if his plan worked, turning his military into a construction crew.

Brath's arm stole around Briana's shoulders and she wrapped her arms around his waist. When she looked at him, she found his hazel eyes as misty as an Irish field on a summer morning.

"You did it," she said, smiling.

"We did it," he said, looking between her and Governor Llewellyn. "I can't thank you enough."

"We hold the same goals for Uisneach, Your Majesty. It is my duty and responsibility to help you remove the scourge from the land."

The only downside to the plan was that Brath insisted Briana stay at the castle and get staff settled in while he and the army went to Colmer Harbor. They'd leave tomorrow and camp outside the town until an agreement was reached.

"Building relationships from within is just as important as confronting the opposition abroad," he said later, in the privacy of their chambers.

"You're just saying that to keep me from arguing," she said, but knew he was right. *I guess I'll count my blessings that I'm not still back at Ard Darach.*

He pulled her into his arms. "Admit it, you know I'm right."

Arguing at the teasing light in his eyes was impossible and foolish. Instead she pouted. "I'll miss you," she said.

He pulled her closer and kissed the crown of her head. "Not half as much as I'll miss you. I'm leaving a hefty group to look after you and Firmara. You should be safe enough. I hope."

She ignored the last comment. She wasn't worried. "You'll take Mr. Stark with you, right?"

He shook his head. "Now is not the time for reunions, Bri." When we have things settled, he can go visit the Connuckles. By the way, your lady's maid has a connection in Colmer Harbor."

"She does?"

"She is originally from Colmer Harbor and has family still there. She gave me a letter for them, in support of us."

"Wonderful. I hope it helps."

Dara's groan caught their attention. The hound was making tired circles on his bed. Finally finding the sweet spot, he plopped down and immediately closed his eyes.

The wolfhound's actions reminded Briana of something her husband had said to her earlier that day. She smiled wickedly at him. "Enough planning for one day. I'm ready to collect on your promise."

Chapter Seventeen

First Fight

Bergamot and pine. Bog water? The scent was confusing but could only mean one thing, which was confirmed when Dara's ears perked up and he barked. Briana dropped the magical spells book she'd been reading all afternoon and raced down the hall toward the stairs. Brath was on his way up, and they would've collided around the corner had he not caught her deftly by the waist.

"What are you doing home so soon?" she asked, hugging him tightly. He'd expected to be gone a week at least, and it had only been three days.

"It was a disaster."

He looked exhausted. She led him back up to their room. Meeting Amelia along the way, she asked for a supper tray to be brought up, as she and Jonathan had already eaten.

"Get those clothes off," she ordered her husband while pouring warm water from a kettle beside the fire into a bowl.

"Really, Briana, as much as I'd love to, I just don't have the energy right now," he said.

She turned around, stunned. "Not that, fool. You stink. Please wash."

"Oh." He pulled off his shirt and sat down on the footstool to remove his boots. She had a bowl of warm water and soap ready by the time he'd stripped out of his trousers. She wet a cloth and started to wash his face, when he took it from her hands.

"I may be tired, but I'm not a baby. I can wash myself."

Stepping away, she found clean clothes for him and took the dirty ones to a basket in the corner of the room. James or Thurid would get them tomorrow. On second thought, they would stink all night if she left them there. She opened the door to take them down to what she referred to as the mudroom and was met by Amelia with a tray of food, which she exchanged for the dirty laundry.

"I'm sorry, Bri. I shouldn't have snapped at you."

"Don't worry about it. You're tired. I get it."

He finished washing and donned the clean clothes. She sat with him while he ate, not asking any questions, relating the mundane and occasionally entertaining events of her days. When he pushed his plate away, she ended her tale by saying that she'd have to consider bringing Amelia back to Ard Darach with her.

"I'm growing quite fond of her," she said.

"Gael might not be too happy about that."

"It's a moot point, anyway. I think she's fairly happy living here and might be sweet on a local merchant."

"Thank you, Bri."

"For what?"

"Working your magic on me. I was pretty tense when I got here, but I feel much, much better. I suppose you'd like to know what happened in Colmer Harbor."

She nodded.

He sighed. "The good news is that Shamwa wasn't there. Nor were any Gray Military, though we did hear they were headed that way."

"The bad news?"

"Colmer Harbor fisherman are unmovable where Shamwa's concerned. We didn't even get to speak with their leaders. They met us in the village, armed to the teeth and prepared for a fight. Kieran met us outside the village to warn us, but I wanted to at least try to talk sense into them. Long story short, there was some fighting in which we ended up in a bog and I was presented with two options. Fight and spill Uisneach blood, or retreat."

Briana grimaced, knowing how he hated even the word.

"Not much choice, really. Killing the people I want to govern is not an option."

"Good, that's good," she assured him. "You made the right choice."

"Small comfort. I must find a way to get to them, and soon. My pulling back may have fueled their fire. I'm worried they'll come here, in which case, you aren't safe."

"I *can* defend myself and I *will* defend this kingdom!" she declared.

He smiled and ran a hand through a strand of her hair that had fallen forward. "My fierce warrior queen," he murmured.

His outstretched arm revealed a gash on his inner arm.

"Brath, you're injured!"

He turned his arm over to expose a laceration about four inches long, raised and red. She didn't see any drainage, but the redness was a worry. She rose and went for her kit of emergency treatments.

"Briana, I want to send you somewhere safe."

"No."

"Yes."

"There is nowhere safer than at your side with thousands of warriors."

"Baigsith is safer. They haven't attempted to move that far south. Besides, you could check on the gnomes' progress with the invisibility cloaks."

A knock at their door interrupted their discussion.

"Come in," Brath said.

Kieran entered, looking not disheveled or exhausted but as though he were ready for a photo shoot. *Maker, the Winges are ridiculously perfect*, Briana thought as she put the cover back on the ointment she was going to use. Tending to Brath's cut would have to wait a little longer. Their new spy was joined by Sir Jameson Stark.

"Sire, crows have discovered Shamwa setting up a defense along the Dromdara Mountains," Kieran informed him.

"Believing we are out and about planting faerie trees."

"Quite so, Sire. That seems to be the reason they're not in Cedarmara. However, that only buys us a little time. By now, couriers have surely been sent to alert him to what we're doing here."

"Right. Thank you, Kieran. You've done well to get that information to him. Sir Stark, are the men settled?"

"They are. Is there anything I can do tonight?"

"No. Both of you, get some food and rest and we'll meet in the morning to talk about next steps."

Briana was glad Kieran had come through. Maybe he'd prove his father wrong after all. Once Kieran and Sir Stark left the room, Briana went for the ointment and bandages again.

"This is a nasty cut, Brath," Briana said, pushing the sleeve of his shirt above the wound.

"It was the least of all the injuries our army sustained."

"Oh, no! I hope no one was killed. Who tended the wounded?"

He allowed her to spread some of the salve on the cut. "No one killed and a few local healers helped out. But, gaining support from Colmer Harbor is going to be far more difficult than I imagined. It's like he's poisoned them with his venom. This cause may be beyond hope."

"There's always hope," she replied, wondering at her own rare optimism. When did she develop that trait? "We just have to show them why they're better off with you." She ran her finger along the covered wound, silently forming words of healing in the power of the tuathla, before tying off the bandage and planting a kiss on top. "For good measure," she said, giving him a cheerful smile."

Another knock at the door. Amelia stumbled in with a pot of tea. *It's Grand Central Station in here tonight*, Briana complained to herself.

Brath rolled his sleeve back down, leaned back in his chair and sipped at the tea that the maid poured, nearly spilling it in his lap. "I wish there were a little…"

Before he finished the sentence, she handed him a decanter of whiskey.

He stared at her with narrowed eyes but took the decanter and poured a generous dram in the teacup.

"Oh, I meant to tell you we now have full casks of whiskey and wine in the cellar."

"You've been busy," Brath said.

"It's more like, ask and ye shall receive. Speaking of that—Amelia?"

The maid was busying herself with turning down the bed, but looked back at Briana.

"Amelia," Briana began again. "I've been meaning to ask, do you, by any chance, have magic?"

One corner of the girl's mouth lifted as she took the decanter from the king and set it back on the sideboard.

"Let me rephrase that," Briana said. "Why do you have magic, and why does it appear stronger than anyone else's? Are you faerie?"

"Witch," she blurted, and then covered her mouth.

"It's okay, Amelia," Briana assured her. "Some of the best people are witches and I'm thrilled that we have magic around us. Maybe you can give me a few pointers with mine. I'd love to possess the effortlessness that you have. Every time I use magic, it's a struggle."

The maid's shoulders relaxed. "Really, ma'am, you don't mind?"

"Of course not! You heard the king supporting the magic of the faeries, didn't you?"

"Aye, but most people don't like actually seeing magic done. It makes them nervous. I try to hide it, but it just sort of pops out of me."

"Well, I wish it would just pop out of me."

A soft snore drew their attention to Brath. His head had fallen against the back of the chair, his eyes were closed and lips parted slightly. Briana reached over and eased the teacup out of his hands before he dropped it. She and Amelia exchanged a glance.

"Good night, ma'am," the girl said quietly, and left the room.

"Brath," Briana leaned in and whispered. "Come on now, time for bed."

She stood in front of a very large pendulum clock. In the center of the clock's face was the same image painted on her shield, a tree and mouse and Nua, wrapped in ivy and feathers, superimposed over the trunk of an oak tree. There were no numbers on the clock. In the three o'clock position Brath's image stared out, and in the nine o'clock position, Silas' did the same. Back and forth the pendulum swung, making her dizzy and confused. She heard the ticking of time passing and wondered how much longer she would have to wait. What time was it, anyway? From the ethers she heard laughing, then crying. A baby crawled by, looked up at her and said, "There's no time to waste. Get on with it." She stared at the talking infant, not in the least surprised by its ability to speak, wondering what it meant. Sigel, his legs missing, suddenly appeared at her side, angry. He jammed a crown on her head and forced her sword and

shield in her hands. *"Dammit Briana, just make a choice, for Maker's sake. There's no time to waste."* She looked up at the two men on the clock. Their faces loomed over her expectantly. I can't choose. I won't choose. *"You must choose,"* said Sigel, who had now turned into a mouse with trembling whiskers. *"Face your fears and choose."*

She woke suddenly, consumed by dread, the words to a song she used to know floating in her mind. Silas was an immortal presence that would never leave her. She felt sick to her stomach. Sweat coated her body. Removing the covers slowly to avoid waking Brath, she slid out of bed and went to the balcony, inching the door open and slipping silently into the cold night. Her soul felt as dark as the night. *I thought I had chosen. I thought I...* Tears welled in her eyes, spilling over and splashing on the stone under her feet, the drops leaving big black holes like the one in her heart. *I can't do this anymore, Silas. I thought I was over you, but I will never be over you. Never.*

No, a mhuirnin. Please—don't give up. I'll find the runes and then I'll be home.

His voice was as real as if he were standing in front of her; and then he *was* standing there. He looked so different, dressed in jeans and a cable-knit sweater, a tweed driving cap resting on his beautiful blonde hair. He looked sad. "Silas," she whispered, into the darkness. Removing one hand from the rail, she reached out to him. He reached back, but they could not make the physical connection. A sob broke from her throat as she tried to touch him and she lifted one leg to climb over the rail. Strong arms reached around her, pulling her back and preventing her from completing the act.

"Oh Maker, Briana, what are you doing?" Brath's shaking voice broke the spell.

She looked at him blankly and then back at the ground below. Silas was gone. *No,* she wailed silently, *no.*

"You're so cold. Briana, what were you trying to do?"

"I don't know. It was a dream. Just a dream." Her words sounded hollow. She let him lead her back to bed, where he took her in his arms and covered them both with the blanket. She lay there, as cold and still as the standing stone at Shannon Abbey, wishing to Maker she had just been able to touch Silas.

Brath still held her when the sun came up. "Sorry about last night," she said. "That was a terrible dream. Thank Maker, you woke me."

"Briana, we both know that wasn't a dream. You meant to take your life last night."

Silence.

"You called his name."

"I was dreaming, Brath, that there was a clock and your face was on it and Silas' and…" She couldn't tell him that she was supposed to make a choice, or he would think she had chosen Silas. "I don't remember the rest."

He moved away from her to sit on the edge of the bed. "I thought we were doing well, Briana. I even thought maybe you were—I've been a fool to think you might love me." He hung his head in his hands. "If you are so unhappy, Bri, I will let you go."

She scrambled to sit up next to him. "I'm not unhappy, Brath. Honestly. I… I'm happy being your wife." *Why can't I just say the words he wants to hear?* "I really was dreaming. I'm not pining for Silas and I wasn't trying to kill myself." In the light of day, she wasn't exactly sure if any of that was the truth, but she hoped it was. She *was* happy with Brath. She was thinking less and less about Silas. So, what happened last night? Wasn't it just a dream?

Dara whined and went to the door just as someone knocked from the other side.

"A moment," Brath said, handing Briana a robe. He put on his trousers. "Come in."

Sir Jameson entered. "We've word from the governor that he would like to meet with you and the queen. He suggests breakfast in an hour."

"Fine," Brath said, his voice heavy.

Sir Jameson frowned. "Sire, are you all right?"

"I'm fine. Tell Llewellyn we'll be there on the hour."

The knight left, taking Dara with him, and Brath finished dressing.

Briana made the bed and looking for something to break the oppressive silence between them, asked him to hand over her bag.

He tossed her knapsack on the bed and started to turn until he saw the cloth pouch that fell out. He frowned when Briana hastily tried to shove it back in the bag.

"What is that?" he asked.

"Nothing."

"Briana you look like a deer who's seen the arrow loosed. You are quite possibly the worst liar in all of Uisneach, so I can't help but think that's something you're hiding from me." He looked shocked more than angry.

"It's my backup plan," she said, trying to sound nonchalant.

"For what?"

"It's wild carrot. Empty Cradle is what you call it. I got some in case I wanted to avoid getting pregnant."

"You don't want to have our baby?" He looked at her with a mixture of disbelief and disappointment.

"I haven't taken any. I haven't decided."

He gaped at her, but the pain in his eyes was what bothered her. She didn't want her uncertainty about pregnancy to hurt him. And yet it apparently had.

"It's just that it's so dangerous to have a baby here and I need to be sure I'm ready to take the risk."

"Then why haven't you taken it?"

"I don't know. I wasn't sure."

"Briana, if we don't have children, everything we're working for is for naught. There will be no Taranian dynasty to continue."

"Is that all I am to you, a vessel to carry on your legacy?" It was such a grossly unfair statement that even she was shocked at the words. He took several steps back. She was blundering so badly that she doubted she could make things any worse. "What if I die having a baby? What if the baby dies? What if I can't even have children? Would you just divorce me for another brood mare?" *Oh, I guess I can make it worse.*

She whirled toward the balcony and felt him come after her. "I'm not going to do anything to myself, Brath. I just need to breathe."

"Yeah, me too."

They stood beside each other on the balcony, letting the breeze cool their heated skin. Briana saw that she'd hurt him deeply but was afraid that anything she said would make it worse. Catching the glint of her ring in the sun, she considered using magic to fix this mess between them. *No,* she thought, *whatever happens here must be honest and true. Our marriage cannot be fabricated on magical manipulation.*

"Briana, we can't be held captive by our fears. There is too much at stake here. I can stay married to a woman who doesn't love me, but I cannot be married to a woman who refuses to bear my child."

"You'd risk my death for an heir?" She suddenly felt sad that they couldn't have met in another place and time without all the complications that had come with the prophecy, Silas and their responsibilities.

"Bearing a child is a risk, you're right. In this world and, I imagine, in yours. It's a risk women have been taking since the beginning of time."

"Well, also in my time, women have the right to choose if and when they have a baby."

He stared out at the sheep and the ocean beyond. "Are you certain that having a baby is what you object to?"

"I just said so."

"Maybe if it was someone else's baby, you would feel differently."

"That is not it, Brath. I keep trying to tell you…" She shook her head, frustrated by both her feelings and his reaction to all of this. "Bottom line. It's my body and my choice."

She saw him bite his lip and turn to go back in the room. "Where are you going?"

"We have to be at the tavern in half an hour. Please be ready."

She was, and they rode in silence across the bridge into town, surrounded by the knights and several hundred invisible faerie warriors.

The news at the tavern started out good. The governor had received a message from a colleague in Colmer Harbor that there might be a small contingent of Taranian supporters who were now ready to align themselves with King Brath. Llewellyn was prepared to hand over five hundred trained militiamen to help the military cause as well.

"Thank you, Governor. Every man helps."

They were eating breakfast and feeling fairly hopeful when Kieran swept into the tavern with a crow report.

"The Gray Military was spotted along the Fodor River just north of Druid's Grove. They must be marching to Cedarmara. I guess they found out we're all here."

"How many in the company?" Brath asked.

"All of them."

"Well, that changes everything. Governor, thank you for breakfast and I'll appreciate you getting your men ready by the end of the day." Brath looked to Briana, offering his hand, not saying anything.

He didn't speak to her all the way back to the palace. When they arrived, he left her in the great hall. "I have things to do. I'll see you later."

Her heart felt like an anchor.

She stood alone in the room until the squeaking of a small animal caught her ear. Following the sound to the fireplace, she saw a small mouse-hole near the wood box. Whiskers twitched in the opening. "Mouse?" she queried tentatively.

The body of the mouse followed his whiskers out the door. "You've really done it now, haven't you?"

"I guess."

"What will you do to make it right?"

"I don't know. Apologize?"

"I doubt that will do it."

"Hmm…"

"You could stop being stubborn about this. You could be honest about it instead."

"Honest? What do you mean?"

"You know bloody well that this fear is not about having a baby. It's about losing people you love."

"Oh, and how do you know this, oh, wise one?"

"That's not cute, Your Majesty."

It wasn't and she knew it. "I'm sorry."

"You're dancing around this whole thing and making it much bigger than it needs to be. You have lost much in your life, but you're not the only one. You must accept that life and death are irrevocably intertwined and that every breath you take involves a certain amount of risk. Everyone in your life will die at some point, including you. It doesn't mean you avoid the risks of loving someone or having a baby because you might lose them. You better face this soon, before you lose everything."

"I'll take this all under advisement."

"You're lucky I continue to look after you," the mouse said. "You don't make it easy."

"By the way, how did you get here?"

The sound of someone entering the room made the mouse squeak and run into the hole he had come from.

It was only Thurid with a load of wood for the fireplace. He dropped it, nodded to the queen and left as quickly as he came. Briana sighed and made the rounds of the castle. If they were leaving tomorrow, things would have to be done and supplies readied. At least she knew her job.

When she felt sure she had all the details taken care of, she went to change her clothes for lunch. To her surprise, Brath was in their chambers, writing something on paper.

"I didn't expect you here," she said. "But I'm glad you are. I need to talk to you."

"I need to talk to you first," he said, his tone clipped and emotionless. She cringed. *Now what?*

"After looking at the new information about Shamwa's whereabouts, I've decided it would be best to send you to the gnomes. You'll take Aya'emrys and the faeries with you, and we'll make do with what we have. I…"

"Wait! What? You're sending me away?"

"I can't guarantee your safety here, or that of the people of Firmara, for that matter. Shamwa will likely pounce on this city if he thinks he can defeat us. Crows can carry messages back and forth, so we'll be in touch. I'd like you to get the gnomes busy with the cloaks."

"Brath," she said, before he could continue, "this is ridiculous. You don't need to send me away. We'll work this out."

"This is not about what we discussed earlier. It's about…"

"The hell it isn't. You're pissed at me and this is punishment."

"It isn't Briana, though I think the distance will give us both a chance to think. I want you safe and I want those cloaks. If, while you're there, you decide you want to return to Maine, then I won't stop you."

Maine? What he meant was Silas.

She took a deep breath. A thousand thoughts and a hundred responses came to mind but what stuck was that she was a queen. His queen. She would not cower and simper. Straightening her spine, she looked him in the eye.

"I'm not going to Maine, Brath. I'm not going to Silas. I will go to

Baigsith and get the cloaks made. I'll take Rippa, so that we can stop and see his parents, and Jonathan, Aya'emrys and a handful of warriors to get us there safely. We'll leave tomorrow morning. When you're ready or it's safe, send for me and I'll happily return to your side and work on whatever issues we have. If you'll excuse me, I have some packing to do."

His speechlessness gave her no satisfaction.

CHAPTER EIGHTEEN

AISLIN

Silas, Hill of Uisneach, Loughnavalley, Ireland

Silas sat at the top of the hill near the royal palace, looking east. A fiery line of orange and gold split the purple and blue sky as the sun came up. Gray fuzziness turned into a field of wildflowers in the early morning light. He'd not been able to sleep. Dreams of Briana filled his night, which would've been nice if they'd been pleasant dreams. They were not. Always the dreams were wrapped in turmoil and confusion.

I miss her, he thought, wishing more than anything that he could go home and assure himself she was safe.

He was about to get up and explore St. Patrick's Well when the sound of heavy breathing caught his attention. Turning around, he saw Orla huffing up the hill, two take-away cups in her hands.

"Are you all right?" he called, starting down the hill.

She nodded, holding her hand up to stop him. In a few seconds she was there, handing him the cups. She was flushed and her breathing was labored, but she smiled and pulled a tube out of her pocket which she put in her mouth. She pressed the end and took a deep breath.

A few moments later she was fine. "A bit of asthma," she said. "Just needed a puff on my inhaler. I thought you'd be here when I didn't see the car at the O'Brien's. Brought you some tea. Last night was some great craic at the pub, wasn't it? I'm surprised you're up and about so early. But then, so am I."

Her laugh made him smile.

"Oh, and I found you a witch."

"Did you? Where is she?"

"In Tullamore. Name's Aislin. Believe it or not, she's open on Sunday. Fancy a visit?"

"Why, believe it or not?"

"Well, she ought to be in church. And by the way, I'll go with you, but for God's sake, don't tell me brother. He'll feel the need to do an exorcism on me."

"Since I don't know your brother, by whom I assume you mean the priest, I could hardly tell him."

"I was going to ask if you'd come to church with me next week. You could meet *Father Sean*," she said with a roll of her eyes.

"Do you actually call your brother "Father"?"

"I'd be a muppet to do that, now wouldn't I? Though Mum calls him Father." She rolled her eyes a second time. "Honestly, you'd think the sun rose and set on *Father Sean*. Will you come to church with me, Silas?"

"Sure, why not?" He wondered about modern religions and had planned to research a few while he was here. Christianity was as good a place to start as any.

They finished their tea. Orla wrapped the empty cups in a bag that she put in the small backpack she carried.

"It's too early to go into town to visit the witch," Silas said, "so as long as you're here, we might as well do some diggin'. We can skip the Catstone. I think we've exhausted that as a possible site."

᠅

"Here she is," Orla pointed to a shiny green and gold shingle hanging outside a row house on Kilbride Street that read, "Aislin-Practitioner of Magical Arts. Readings by appointment. Walk-ins welcome." Large pots overflowing with an assortment of flowers and vines sat on either side of a green door. "You do it," she said, pushing him ahead to knock on the door.

Silas rapped on the door and waited. No answer. He knocked again and the door opened before his hand was away from the wood. A woman of experienced years stood in the doorway, tucking a lock of curly gray hair behind her ear. Her body nearly filled the doorway and the tee shirt she wore with a pair of jeans had the same logo as the shingle in front of her house. The sound of a baby crying in the background made Silas wonder if they'd come at a really bad time.

"I'm lookin' for Aislin," Silas began tentatively.

She looked him up and down and then did the same with Orla. Her eyebrows jacked up and down as she considered them. "Ye've found her. Lookin' for a readin'?"

"Aye," he said. "It's of vital importance."

She nodded solemnly. "It usually is. Come in, then."

Silas followed her into the house, the room clearly meant to create a feeling of mystery and whimsy. A small, circular table with two chairs sat in the center. Wall hangings of the tree of life and a pentacle of braided vines hung on opposite sides of the room. Planters of sage and lavender, candles, crystals, porcelain angels and a large webbed hoop with stones and feathers tied onto the strings were set about the room in no particular order. The door to the main part of the home stood open, the smell of sausages and gravy wafting out.

"One moment, please," the woman said, and walked through the door.

Silas watched her turn off the burner of the stove. A stack of dishes waited beside the sink and a gray cat licked milk from a dish near a window. "Donnie, watch yer baby sister, please. I've customers."

"Yes, Granny," a young boy responded.

"I've me grandchildren with me," Aislin explained as she came back into the front, shutting the door behind her. "He knows when I say I have customers, it means to be quiet. Sit, please," she said to Silas, holding her hand toward the table.

Orla found a spot on an old church pew on the side of the room.

Aislin glanced at her, then at Silas. "Do ye wish her with ye durin' the readin'?"

"It's fine," he said, nodding.

"What's yer name?" she asked, pulling a deck of cards into the center of the table.

"Silas O'Mara."

"Is yours really Aislin? It means dream or vision, if I remember correctly," Orla said.

"Betty Murphy, actually. But who wants to consult a witch with an ordinary name?" She turned back to Silas, leaned forward and searched his eyes for an excruciating length of time. "An old soul." She paused before her next observation. "Women have drowned in those eyes."

"I guess," Orla murmured from the bench.

The witch glanced at her then back to Silas, intensifying her scrutiny. "But for you, there is only one woman."

Silas looked away, shivering at her insight.

"Mr. O'Mara, may I take your hands?"

He hesitated, now not at all sure he wanted her to see more deeply. Yet, his hands lifted. When their fingers touched, the witch closed her eyes and inhaled deeply. He felt a thrill shudder between them.

"Ahhh…" She released his hands and swept the traditional tarot cards in front of her clear off the table before rifling through a drawer and pulling out a different deck. "For you, these cards."

He saw the deck cover. *Druid Oracle Cards*.

Aislin glanced briefly at Orla before slanting a single eyebrow at Silas.

"We've not known each other long," he said.

Her lips curved in understanding. She shuffled the cards and then laid them out, upside-down, in a cruciform pattern with a corresponding straight pattern beside it, on the table.

She began to turn the cards over, one at a time.

"Blackbird is what is representin' the present time." She stared at the cards. "Gateway? Portal?" She glanced up at Silas. "Ye're not from around here, are ye?"

He shook his head.

She overturned the next card on top of the first. It was a Crane. "Ye've come here for a specific purpose, but it's wrapped in mystery and ye're missing vital information that will lead to success. Like the crane, ye must stand very still and be patient. What ye need won't come easy and ye'll find yerself frustrated in the process."

The next card was the Hare and she correctly commented that whatever he was searching for would reset the balance in some way. When she turned the fourth card over, a white swan floating on a lake, she looked again at Silas with a grin.

"No surprise here, lad. Yer future is wrapped in love."

Orla purred and Aislin turned to scrutinize the young woman. "Beauty is all around ye," she said, turning back to Silas. "It's a part of yer past, present and future. However, this card represents the kind of soul love meant for only one woman." Her glance at Orla was assessing. "Beauty and soulmates are not always one and the same.

"With this Salmon card showin' up in the place of goals and aspirations, I feel as though yer meant to connect with water in some way to access the wisdom ye seek. Rivers? Lakes? The ocean. I don't know, but look to water."

"Wells?" he asked.

She shrugged. "Perhaps. Wells are known to be magical. All of the energy around ye and these cards speaks of magic."

When the Seal card was turned, it started out upright, but slipped from Aislin's hand and landed in a reverse position. She sat back abruptly in her chair and focused on the card. Silas worried when she shook her head back and forth slowly.

"I'm sorry for yer loss, Mr. O'Mara. But it is not lost forever. Continue this quest for her sake. I do not believe ye will fail her or yer task in any way. But ye think ye might. Trust in what lies in the heart, not in what clutters the head."

Silas felt a tightening in his chest. He hadn't expected much from this visit, but she was damn good. He hadn't voiced his fears, of failure, of the loss of Briana forever, but they were there, always under the surface, coating his longing with an oily darkness. This witch had uncovered his deepest fears.

She moved to the cards that made up the staff. The first three cards, Wren, Raven and Fox, spoke of his need to be humble, smart and patient. This was apparently not to be an easy task, finding the runes. However, Aislin assured him that he was protected by the fiercest of warriors, the Morrigan. His success was almost guaranteed.

"If ye don't get distracted and lose yer faith," she said while turning over the last card. "Oh, goodness!" She jerked back, nearly toppling over in the chair.

"What is it?" Silas asked, panicked by her reaction.

"I've never, ever drawn a white raven. Powerful magic. Prophecy!"

Prophecy! This more than hit the mark.

She righted herself and took Silas' hands, now gripping the edge of the table. "Mr. O'Mara, I don't know who ye are or where ye come from, but ye're here for a reason. Ye must see this through and not be distracted by what is temporary." Her eyes slid sideways to the bench.

"Ye were right to come to me. In more than one way, ye'll need to rely on someone else's power to accomplish the task before ye. Don't be too proud to accept help in whatever way ye need it, and don't forget that this thing ye seek is much larger than yerself. Ye must finish and return to wherever ye came from. If there is anythin' else I can do to help, just stop by."

She turned her attention to Orla. "Would you like a reading, Miss?"

"No thank you," Orla said, more primly than was her style. "My brother would kill me."

Just then, a loud crash jarred them all into the present.

"Oh, dear. Usually, Donnie is so good about keepin' things quiet. Mr. O'Mara, it's been a pleasure meetin' ye," she said, hurriedly accepting the cash he slid her way, before rising to attend to her children.

He and Orla let themselves out. They were quiet as they headed toward O'Molloy Street to cross the bridge to the other side of the Grand Canal. They paused to watch the water drift under the bridge.

"Do you think she was for real?" Orla finally asked.

"Aye, I do," he said quietly. "Don't you?"

"I think she focused more on you personally than she did on your real question. I suspect she's a chancer, to be honest with you."

"You're the one who suggested her."

"True, but you never know about these things."

Silas suspected she was more put off by the woman's repeated reference to his being a one-woman man. He hoped she wasn't growing too fond of him. In any case, there was no point in arguing with her about it.

"Maybe you're right, Orla. She's probably a chancer."

CHAPTER NINETEEN

SPIRITUAL PLACES

"We could try the Shannon Pot, the source of the Shannon River. It's said there are faeries there. Or, the Hill of Tara, another magical place," Orla said, sitting in his living room on Thursday morning, perusing a book on faerie legends and sipping tea. "Oh, I've an idea. What about Rathcroghan? They say there's an entrance to the Underworld there."

"Really, Orla? Are you sayin' Catriona would've hidden the runes in the Underworld?" He whipped his head up with a disgruntled shake, before returning to the notebook he was writing in. "I don't think so. You shouldn't talk of the Underworld so casually. It's an evil place. Anyway, those places are too far away from the Hill of Uisneach."

"Silas, faeries live all over Ireland."

"Well, then if that's the case, Ireland is a big place and we have a poor chance of findin' them." *Shite*, he thought, looking up. He was thinking runes, not faeries. He'd almost given away that this hunt was for more than faeries.

She rolled her eyes and maneuvered around to sitting cross-legged on the sofa. "Why does it always feel like you're hidin' somethin'?"

He ran his hand over the map next to his notebook, pretending not to hear, touching place after place that they'd either searched or that seemed a waste of time. Nothing stuck out to him as a likely place to search. He ran his hand through hair loose and mussed from previous frustrated excursions by his fingers. "I'm a bloody druid, for Maker's sake! Why am I gettin' nothin'?"

Orla laughed out loud, reminding him that she was in the room. He was going to muck this up royally if he didn't pay attention.

"You're a gas, Silas O'Mara. But that reminds me, we might want to check out one of the druid ceremonies on the hill while you're here. I'll check the schedule when I go back to work. Oh, and I need to run to Dublin today. Fall registration opens for Trinners and I want to get my classes sorted. Want to go?"

He shook his head, still looking at the notebook. "I promised Finnegan to help him around here." His cell phone rang. Reading the name on the display, he saw it was Debbie. "I need to take this call."

"Privately?"

He shook his head as he answered, "Hi Debbie. How are you?" He listened to Debbie tell him about her recent research and smiled to himself as Orla wandered over to the couch, curled up and began checking her own phone for email. "Aye, Orla and I have spent a lot of time on the hill lookin'." A pause. "Orla?" She looked up and he shook his head. "She's a friend I've met here who is very knowledgeable about Irish history and myth. We've turned up nothin' as yet." After a short pause, Silas chuckled. "No worries, Debbie. I like your idea though. I'll run it by her. Thanks. Hey, how are you feelin'?" A longer pause. "That's great. I'll talk to her later today. Take care, Debbie."

He hung up the phone. "Debbie, Bri—uh, a friend of Katrina's, in the states. She wanted to check if we'd done the obvious and looked on the hill at night, when faeries are out and about."

Orla frowned. "Oh, aye, let's break in to a historic site that happens to be my workplace at night. Grand idea. I've never been arrested." She tapped her finger against her lips. Softly, she said, "I might say I lost my cell phone and we've been backtrackin' for hours lookin' for it. That might work." She nodded. "I'll be back from Dublin by dinner. Do you want to go tonight?"

"I'd like to."

"I'll pick you up at dusk."

"Thanks, Orla. That would be grand."

෨

Only one interpreter remained on site when Silas and Orla arrived, just before the last slivers of sun were about to set.

Jimmy said, "Orla, you'll not find your mobile in this light."

"Unlikely, I know, but I need to try. I can't be without it. I'll lock up when we're done."

"Fine with me, but you ought to shut the gates anyway, so no one drivin' by t'inks we're open."

"I'll pull it shut behind you."

Silas marveled at how easily she told the fib, the huge smile on her face completely natural as she locked up after Jimmy.

"Ready?"

They found a spot at the top of the hill and waited as the sun finished its descent below the broken line of small clouds, its orange-gold fire turning to softer shades of rose-pink, amethyst and indigo and finally black, pierced by the glittering lights of the celestial dome. In a rare moment, Orla was quiet. Silas welcomed the peace, but soon he was scanning the hill for small lights. His ears tried to pick up any trace of music that might issue from the wee folk's instruments.

"I guess we should go searchin'," he said, standing. He reached for Orla's hand to help her up.

"The Catstone?" she suggested.

"Good a place as any."

They walked slow and quiet, just in case, until they came to the monolith. Nothing obvious appeared or was heard. "You know, if the Gardaí find us here, we'll go to jail."

"I thought you had an explanation."

"Aye, well, the searchin' for the cell phone will only go so far."

He was about to ask if she thought they should leave when a hair-raising shriek tore through the darkness. Orla grabbed Silas around his midsection, pushing in as tight to his side as she could get. There was a split second when his body registered how good she felt against him. Then his stomach dropped to his toes.

"A banshee!" he whispered.

When a minute passed with no further screeching, Orla stepped away from Silas. "Had to be a fox," she reasoned.

"Would've happened more than the once. It was a banshee."

"Silas, seriously? Banshees are folk tales."

"Not where I come from; they're a bad omen."

She raised one eyebrow. "Where you come from? Where might that be, pray tell."

He realized his mistake too late, but the screech came again and with it, a gust of wind. Orla wrapped herself around him again.

"Jaysus and all the saints protect us," Orla said, removing one hand from his waist to cross herself. "Come on, Silas, whatever it is, it doesn't appear to be a faerie, so we might as well get the hell out of here."

He agreed. They hurried down to the gate. Orla had the key out of her pocket before they'd even come to the lodge. Once in the car, she turned to him. "You know, I just remembered an old family legend about banshees. You'll recall Brian Boru, aye?"

His body still felt the warmth of hers tucked beside him. He forced his mind to recall the details of an ancient king as a distant relative, or at least clan related.

"Brian's father was Cennétig mac Lorcain, which is modernized as Kennedy. Thus, I'm related to the high king himself."

"Yes, I remember you said so when we first met." The reminder was the cold water he needed.

"In Boru's time there was a holy well that belonged to Ayvinn, the banshee of the Dalcassians, his tribe. It was said that when the banshee was heard, a king would die."

Silas went white and felt his knees tremble. The first king that came to mind was on the other side of a magical tree. Could the banshee be connected to Uisneach? This was an emergency, wasn't it? He should try to reach her. He tuned out Orla and tried to focus on letting down the barrier to their telepathy. *Briana, are you okay? Is Brath all right?* Nothing, not even a ripple of familiarity. He tried again with the same poor result.

"Silas, what's wrong? You really do look as though you'd seen a ghost."

"I'm fine. Just a wee bit rattled by that banshee."

"Don't worry, I'll protect you," she said patting his thigh.

He jerked at her touch and she pulled her hand away quickly. She grew quiet as she drove. Silas' mind tumbled over her description of Ayvinn's well, which led him to Aislin's comments about water.

"Orla, could we find that well?"

"I don't know, Silas. It's more legend than tourist stop."

"We could try. At the least you could visit an old family village."

"No harm, I suppose," she said. "Oh, if we have no luck we could go to the cliffs. Have you seen them yet?"

"What cliffs?"

"Moher. Ah, they're magnificent and some say magical. Let's go tomorrow. It would be some great craic."

"Long as I can be home by the time I'm due at the pub."

"We've plenty of time. Well, here we are," she said pulling up into the drive that ran beside the O'Brien's home to his cottage.

He suddenly felt uncomfortable. Under normal circumstances, he'd invite her in; it was early, after all. Feeling himself quiver, he knew it wasn't a good idea at all.

Orla apparently had no such misgiving. "Silas, I know your wife passed on, but do you have a girlfriend somewhere you haven't mentioned?"

"No." He really didn't want to go down this path.

"Then it would be okay if we kissed good night. I don't mean to act the skank, but we've known each other long enough and I think you like me well enough. I'd really like to kiss you. Christ, I hope I'm not doin' this all arseways."

He didn't want to hurt her, but he was between a rock and a hard place, as Briana would say. *I might as well just be honest. As honest as I can be, anyway.*

"Orla, you are lovely, and I do like you. Very much. Under any other circumstances I'd have kissed you long ago. But it wouldn't be fair to start somethin' with you that I can't commit to. Once my research is done, there's nothin' to keep me here and I'll go home."

"But you said you have no one waitin' for you. Perhaps if we kissed, you might find a reason to stay."

He took her hand and kissed it. "That, Orla, is precisely what I'm afraid of, and I can't. I just can't. I think it best we keep this on the level of friendship."

He liked that she had the courage to look him directly in the eye when she said, "You probably really think me the skank now, don't you?"

✄

Silas spent a sleepless night staring at Briana's photograph, begging her forgiveness for the attraction he felt toward Orla. And then questioning his own foolishness for not moving on with his life. After all, Briana was married and out of reach to him, at least in this lifetime. Was he supposed to be a monk forever? He could barely open his eyes when his cell phone rang in the morning. He groaned when he saw the call was from Orla, wishing she'd chosen to cancel their date.

"Silas, you are the worst driver in Ireland, but it's your turn to drive. I'm ready to go whenever you are."

So here they were in Craglea, looking for a well that didn't exist, according to the curator of the local historical society. Orla dove right into a conversation with the scholar about the Dalcassians, the Tuatha De' Danann and a complete rundown of any faerie sightings in the last four decades.

He felt a little ashamed that she was working so hard to research information for a book that would never be written.

"Well, I guess that was a waste of time," she said, when they got back into the Toyota.

"No, not really. We can still go to the cliffs."

Her smile lit up the interior of the car. "Yes, we can! You're going to love this, Silas. It truly is one of the most inspirin' places in Ireland."

They stood on the cliffs in less than half an hour.

"Land, sea and sky," he murmured, looking out past O'Brien's Tower to the Aran Islands.

"Seven hundred and two feet above the ocean."

An army of tourists smothered the tower itself, so they walked up the cliff's Coastal Trail until they were on the dirt part of the path, away from most of the tourists. They found a spot where it was a simple step over the barricade to sit on the edge of the cliff. Waves crashed below; as they receded, they revealed one of the sea caves. They talked for what could have been minutes or hours until Orla made a funny noise in her throat. It had been sunny when they arrived but as they'd chatted, the weather had begun to turn.

"Look at the mist out to sea. The islands are nearly invisible now. Hope it doesn't rain. We didn't bring slickers."

"Do you want to leave?"

She stared at him. "No," she said. "I want to stay here forever."

He knew that look and turned away. He remained quiet, listening to Orla describe the classes she would take in the fall, letting her voice recede into the background as his gaze travelled down to the sea cave, where mist and fog were rolling in like the coating of a dream. He wasn't shocked when the dreamy miasma parted to allow the form of a woman, clad in leather trousers and vest with a large sword at her hip, glide across the water toward him. Her eyes seemed sad. Her arms floated out toward him.

"Briana."

"Briana?" Orla repeated the name. "Was she your wife?"

Her voice broke the spell.

Briana would never be his wife, but she was still a part of his soul. What was she trying to tell him? Was something wrong? Was that the message of the banshee? Or was she telling him to move on? He turned to the woman who'd made it very clear that she was interested in him and knew that if things were different, he could care for her too. He had no idea if he would find the runes. No idea if he would go back to Uisneach or stay in Ireland. Maybe he wasn't ready for a relationship, but he could at least be honest with Orla and let things unfold as they were meant. He looked into her bluebell eyes.

"Orla, I have to tell you somethin' that you are going to find very hard to believe, but I would never lie to you. I need you to understand why I can't become romantically involved with you."

To her credit, she listened without interruption. When he was finished telling her of Uisneach, the prophecy, the journey with Briana, the wedding and his offer to come and find the runes, fog had not only settled in the sea cave, but Orla's eyes were a little misty as well. She remained silent far longer than he thought her capable of, only tapping her lip in a rhythmic fashion. Finally, she spoke.

"So, you love this woman, but she is married to someone else. Could you be lovers?"

"No!" He sat back quickly, looking shocked. "That would get us both killed."

"Does she love you?"

"It's complicated."

"The circumstances of your relationship may be complicated but whether or not you love each other is not."

"Yes, then, we love each other." *At least we did*, he thought, wondering if she did still love him, or had fallen completely in love with Brath.

She studied something on her fingernails and said nothing for several minutes. He let her process his story.

"Am I to understand then, that because you *might* hurt me by gettin' involved and then leavin', that you don't want to have a relationship with me?"

He nodded. "It would be most unfair and very ungallant."

"Could you *choose* to stay here? Could you get the runes back some other way?"

"You believe me? I thought you'd have a more difficult time with this."

"I'm a historian, Silas, and although most of what you're tellin' me falls under the category of myth and faerie tale, I know you aren't a liar, so I suppose it must be the truth. So, my question remains. Could you choose to stay here?"

He shrugged. "I could if I didn't care what happened in Uisneach. But I do. As to gettin' the runes back another way, I have no idea if the runes, or meself, for that matter, can get home."

She stared at him as though trying to come to a decision about something. Then she put a hand on his cheek. "I'd like to take my chances on gettin' hurt. And shouldn't I have that choice?"

She was so close. Before he could decide whether to kiss her or not, her lips were on his. He sank into their softness. She tasted of gumdrops and minty toothpaste. She smelled like lavender and spice. Her hand slid under his shirt finding a resting place on his chest, over the tattoo that Briana so loved.

Briana. *Let me be,* a mhuirnin, *just for a minute, so I can enjoy this moment, the feel of a woman in me arms, soft and warm.*

"If she loves you, she'd want you to be happy, Silas."

He gave in to her gentleness, her desire, but kept his own held in with a tight rein. He cradled her dark curls with one hand, and held himself up with the other hand beside her hip. Heart beating fast, he tasted her, let her taste him and felt himself loosen the reins, just a little.

"How sweet," said an older woman in hushed tones as she walked by.

The words were like a bucket of ice on Silas. He jerked away from Orla. He stared at her for a moment, as though he were seeing her for the first time.

She looked dazed, her lips swollen from what had become a far more passionate kiss than he'd meant to share. Her eyes were a darker blue, more like the ocean just before the fog rolled in. He watched her lungs rise and fall with effort. Maker, he hoped he hadn't started an asthma attack.

"Are you okay?" he choked out.

"Oh, yeah. I'm really, really okay."

"I need to take you home. We've not eaten all day and I have to work tonight."

He stood, and she followed suit. He was about to turn in the direction of the parking lot when her hand on his arm stopped him.

"Silas, I have a feelin' that you'll tell me by tomorrow that you regret this, so, I'll be takin' full advantage of this moment."

Before he could grasp her meaning, she had her arms wound around his neck. Her mouth covered his and she stepped in closer, chest to chest and hip to hip, their lips connected. If there had been a dozen people standing around, he wouldn't have cared, though when he finally opened his eyes, they were alone.

"Maker, Orla, tell me how you really feel."

She laughed then. The tension broke and she stepped away. "Another time, perhaps. I'm hungry."

"I see that," he muttered, following her to the car, his heart fourteen shades of confused.

When they arrived at her house after what had been a quiet but not uncomfortable ride home, she looked at him. "I won't push my luck, Silas.

271

But I hope with all my heart, that wasn't the one and only time I get to kiss you."

"Are you comin' to the pub tonight?"

She pressed her lips together and shook her head. "Promised my mum I'd help pull things together for the baptism of my niece on Sunday. You're still comin' with me, aren't you?"

"Aye, I'll come. Well, good night, then."

She stepped out of the car. He shifted into reverse.

"Silas?"

He shifted back into park.

"Your songs. Are they for Briana?"

Honesty was what was needed. "Yes, Orla, they are."

She shook her head. "I can't believe she married someone else. It must have killed her. Good night, then."

∾

Orla had not come to the pub on Friday or Saturday, but here she was, at his door, at nine o'clock sharp on Sunday morning, dressed for church in a knee-length white dress that provided a crisp contrast to her dark hair. He realized now that he'd missed Orla's chatty presence. Not that it removed his resolve to refrain from a repeat of the kissing. It wasn't fair to her, or to him, for that matter, to become so involved that parting would be painful.

"You regret it, don't you?" she said, reading his expression correctly.

"Not regret, no. But I can't let it happen again."

She dropped the subject, put a smile on her face and they drove to the church to attend what she told him was a Catholic Mass.

He was introduced to her father and mother before the Mass began. Pleasant people, though her mother seemed a bit shy and her father gave him a thorough going-over. He wondered what she'd told them about him. The echoing of the church organ filled the cavernous sanctuary, ending their conversation.

He watched as people processed down the aisle with a very large cross, chanting, singing and carrying a large book. Father Sean, her brother, stepped behind the altar, leaned over and kissed it.

Silas noted the look of adoration on Mrs. Kennedy's face. Orla was not exaggerating her mother's regard for her son's avocation.

"The altar represents Christ," Orla whispered.

Father Sean greeted the people and made the sign of the cross. "In the name of the Father and of the Son and of the Holy Spirit, we come together to celebrate the sacrifice of Jesus Christ."

The words, prayers and songs celebrated a man they believed was the son of Maker, whose blood Maker needed to justify the sinful lives of all humanity. He didn't quite get that, but he was impressed with the love that seemed to glow from many people and their commitment to this weekly ritual. They asked for Maker's, God's, forgiveness and blessing. They sang prayers they claimed came to them from angels.

Silas felt a peace settle over him as he listened to the liturgy. The priest read from the big book, the Bible, and began to talk about the meaning of the words. Silas' mind began to drift. Darkness of sin. Light of the world. Darkness and light. Words that reminded him of the prophecy. Words that reminded him of his quest to find the runes.

"God sees every treasure on earth," Father Sean said. "Job tells us that he 'putteth forth his hand upon the rock; he overturneth the mountains by the roots.'"

Images of the runes under the Catstone flickered in Silas' mind.

"He cutteth out rivers among the rocks; and his eye seeth every precious thing. He bindeth the floods from overflowing; and the thing that is hid bringeth he forth to light."

Sweet Maker, is that a sign? Floods? Water? Is water hidin' somethin'? Aislin referred to water, too. Water in a hidden place. The priest's voice was a mere humming to him now as images of darkness, water and hidden places coalesced into a single image of a well. Somewhere in the recesses of his mind a memory sparked. Catriona had wrapped the runes in moss and hid them between the stones of a holy well on a hill. Was this a true memory or a message from some other place? If a sign, specifics would be handy. Which hill? Which well?

He followed Orla's example, on autopilot, as the people passed the peace, greeting one another in the Lord's name. More prayers, then the Catholics went up in a line to eat a small wafer dipped in wine, which was supposed to be the body and blood of their Christ. More prayers. *Maker, they pray a lot.* Finally, the mass ended and everyone left, except the Kennedy family and their friends, who stayed for the baptism of wee Margaret.

It was a lovely ceremony, but Silas was focused on the baptismal font, with water running through it. He had his own chant running through his head. *Well. Water. Well. Water. Well. Water.* How many wells were there in Ireland? Briana's ghostly visage from the cliffs wafted through his thoughts. And how much time did he have to find them?

CHAPTER TWENTY

RELUCTANT LOVER

hiz... Why... Whiz... can't... whiz... I... whiz... stop... whiz... thinkin'... whiz... about... whiz... her?

Arrows hit the bull's eye almost on top of each other in rapid-fire succession. Sweat glistened over Silas' bare torso. Breathing heavily, he pulled the projectiles from the target and turned around to start over.

Seeing Orla standing casually next to a tree, he paused.. "How long have you been standin' there?"

"Long enough to be impressed."

He set the arrows across the bow on the tree stump that served as a table and went toward the very source of his frustration.

"You seemed pretty intent on shreddin' that target." The glint of awe in her eyes couldn't douse the underlying fire.

I was pretty intent on tryin' to stop seein' your face in my head, he thought, while drinking in how beautiful her eyes were. "How are things at Trinners?"

Her blue eyes shone even more summery, if that were possible. "Great," she said. "Classes are full, the professors are savage, and I've got a ton of homework to do."

"You say that as though it's a good thing."

She pushed away from the tree and walked over to the stump, examining his longbow and arrow. He was glad he'd brought them to Ireland. Months away from practice would've killed him. "It is a good thing. I love my studies. However, it hasn't stopped me from workin' on your *research*.

If you're nearly done here, maybe you'd offer me a cup of tea and I'll tell you what I've learnt."

He shrugged into his tee shirt and gathered his bow and arrow. They went inside, where Orla began to prepare tea. He scowled. She was getting quite comfortable here.

"Had breakfast?" he asked.

She shook her head. He grabbed a loaf of bread Caitlin had brought him and cut off a few slices for the toaster.

They were quiet as they worked. Silas hadn't seen her since the baptism, over a month ago. She'd called a few times with ideas of places to search while she was away, always acting as though the kiss had never happened. He, on the other hand, couldn't stop thinking about it. She and Briana held equal space in his thoughts. Was it his lot in life to remain celibate because he loved a woman he couldn't have? Briana had encouraged him to move on and find love somewhere else. But how could she really have meant that, and how could he actually consider it? She was his soul, the only woman he would ever love. Aislin confirmed that when she read the cards. Yet, bluebell eyes and dark curls pestered him day and night, and now that she was here in front of him, what was he supposed to do about these unwelcome but persistent feelings in his heart and, well, other places?

"In Irish Gaelic, rún means mystery or secret. Same in Old English, although some sources interpret it as a miracle," Orla said, in between bites of toast.

"It will be a miracle if we find them," Silas grumbled.

"Some researchers believe that runes, in the earliest of times, were merely magical charms, but others say they're similar to the Ogham, and were likely used as a way of communicatin' through writin'. They were not, as most people think, originally used as divination tools as they are now."

She will be a great professor one day, Silas thought. *She tells everythin' like it's a lecture or a documentary.*

"Well, in our case, they hold the key to restorin' magical energy to our kingdom."

"Do you really believe that, Silas."

"Of course I do. I live there. It's the truth, Orla. I have to find them."

She looked amused.

"Do you think I'd honestly spend this much time searchin' and," he looked down at his feet, "putting meself in so much emotional turmoil, if I didn't."

"Emotional turmoil, is it?"

They stopped talking. When he looked up again, he saw a flicker of hope in her eyes. He turned back to his toast, saying nothing more.

"Did you go to any of the places I told you about?" she asked, before picking up her cup for a sip of tea.

"Aye, I did. Oh, I found a magical road in Louth. I put the car in neutral, turned it off and when I took me foot off the break and gas, I rolled backward, uphill!"

"I hate to burst your bubble, Silas, but there's a reasonable, scientific explanation for the *magical* hill. It's an optical illusion."

"Now who's alterin' reality?" Silas said with a slightly mocking tone.

She narrowed her eyes, before carrying on with the theory. "It's a place where an obstructed view of the horizon alters how the objects that aren't quite perpendicular to the ground appear. Thus, a road that appears to be slopin' uphill is actually slopin' downward. Your car wasn't actually rollin' uphill. It was rollin' downhill."

He shook his head vehemently. "I was there, Orla. I saw it."

"Optical illusion," she insisted in a sugary voice, before taking another bite of toast.

"Why can things never be as they appear to be?"

She tilted her head and quirked her head back. "What's that supposed to mean?"

"Nothin'," he said, taking his empty plate to the sink. "Where are we goin' today?"

She raised her eyebrows. "Did I say I was goin' anywhere with you, then?"

"Come on, Orla. You wouldn't be here if you didn't plan on helpin' me."

"That's where you're wrong, boyo, but aye, I'll help you. Let's visit the Shannon Pot. If it's magic you're wantin', you might find it there."

"Let's go, then. I'll just fetch me keys."

She was rinsing the dishes when he returned from his bedroom. "That's odd," he said. "I always put the keys in a wee dish by the bed and they're missin'. The dish is empty." He took his coat from the closet and checked the pockets but came up empty-handed.

Orla moved a book on the coffee table. "*Modern Military Tactics?*" she grimaced. "You off to war?"

"Not in this kingdom," he muttered, as he checked the sofa cushions for his keys.

When silence was the only response, he straightened up and looked at Orla, who was staring at him, her eyes cloudy with sadness. He met her gaze but said nothing.

"Should I double-check your room? Sometimes a second pair of eyes, you know."

She would see Briana's picture by his bed, but maybe it was best she did, as a reminder. "Sure," he said as he rummaged through some papers on the bookshelf.

She came out seconds later, jangling his keys in her fingers.

"Where on earth…"

"In the wee dish beside your bed. Beside her picture."

He took the keys. "Thanks. You know, this is the third time somethin' like this has happened in the past two weeks."

"Well, you seem a bit distracted, Silas. Maybe you're just misplacin' things."

"Maybe. You ready?"

⤙

In a little over two hours, they were in Derrylahan, opening the white wrought iron gate. They headed down the path through green fields to the pond that was nearly as round as a well, the source of the Shannon River. It wasn't terribly impressive, a small, deep, dark and—frigid, Silas learned when he stuck his hand in—pool of water. Willow and hawthorn trees encircled the pond, a light breeze through their leaves adding a bit of natural music to the scene.

"Hard to believe this little bit of water is the beginnin' of the Shannon," Orla said. Finding a patch of grass that pleased her, she sat down. "There are underwater caves not far from here that feed into this pool."

Silas explored every inch of the bank. For what, he didn't know.

Anything that would stand out as a clue. Nothing did. Finally, he plunked down beside Orla.

"I suppose you know the legend behind the river."

"Of course," she replied, and without hesitation sprang into the story of Sionnan. "She was the granddaughter of Manannán mac Lir, the god of the sea. She came here to eat the forbidden fruit of the Tree of Knowledge. As she was dinin' on her delicious fruit, the Salmon of Wisdom became angry and caused the waters of the pool to rise over her. The bad news is that she died. The good news is that the Shannon River was born."

"Poor lass. All because she wanted to be wiser."

"That's your take, then? Me, I think she just wanted what she couldn't have."

"Could be. Women can be like that."

She tipped her head sideways and widened her eyes. "Is that so? Men can be like that too, Silas."

He flushed; her point was well-taken.

"Do you need time to intuit?"

He chuckled. "I do."

They sat quietly until Silas took Orla's increased fidgeting as an indicator that she was tired of *intuiting*.

"There does seem to be a nice energy here, even if she did drown."

At that moment, a fish jumped clean out of the water. Seemingly suspended in mid-air, he stared at the pair on the bank before diving down with a loud splash!

"A salmon! That was deadly!" she exclaimed, her eyes the size of saucers.

"Not a salmon, a trout, but a wee bit of magic for our effort."

"We've time to hike to Garvah Lough, if you like."

They followed a stream a short while, then wandered down roads and through meadows painted with summer flowers. The sky suddenly turned from brilliant blue to black and without warning, rain fell mercilessly from the sky. Before they could take cover in a nearby abandoned and half roofless cottage, they were both soaked.

"Not expectin' that," Silas said, shaking water off his hair.

"Neither was I," Orla said, pulling off her shirt, under which she had a tank top with thin straps and a dangerously low neckline.

He saw, for the first time, the full tattoo on her bosom, a coin-sized rendering of a Celtic cross. Amidst the fine, Celtic weavings nestled a tiny heart. The work was tasteful and skilled. *I shouldn't be starin' at her chest*, he thought, but it, the tattoo, was gorgeous. He started to reach a finger to touch the ink but jerked away at the last minute. Orla was watching him and, he could tell, holding her breath. When his hand fell to his side, she let out her breath.

"It's a beautiful tattoo. What does it mean to you?"

"I wanted Christ near me heart as a reminder of me faith."

"That's really lovely, Orla," he said, finally tearing his eyes away from her bosom. He walked to the window and peered outside, trying to settle the tension in his body. He was nearly calm when he felt her body press against his back and her arms wrap around his waist.

"Silas."

Not statement. Not question. Just a breathing of his name. Maker, she felt good against him. Good, but not right. Much as he might have wished it so.

"Orla," he started to say, as he turned to her. He stopped, confused by the look in her eyes. Part passion, part fear and part sorrow, he thought. *Oh, this is not good at all.* She had not released her hold on him and he felt her fingers tighten on his back.

"I'm fallin' in love with you," she blurted out.

"Orla, I…"

"Please. Hear me out. I know you love her. God, I can't even say her name. That's so juvenile." She shook her head and started again, with what sounded like a rehearsed speech. "I know you love Briana, but she isn't here, and you don't know for sure you'll get back. I'm willin' to take me chances on gettin' hurt. If it turns out that you find the runes and decide to go home, I promise not to hold it against you. I won't be a tool about it and make a big scene." She took a breath but had more to say. "I read people pretty well and I think you're interested in me. In fact, I think you care for me. Why shouldn't we enjoy each other as long as we can and see what happens?"

"Because I do care for you, and as I said the other day, I don't want to treat you disrespectfully, and secondly, I don't want to fall in love with you and then leave. I'm far too close to that now for comfort and I *am* going home, Orla. Whether Briana and I are ever together isn't the point. In fact, I don't see how we ever could be. But I have to get those runes home. I will only hurt you and maybe me, too, if we get involved. I don't want to do that."

"We're already involved," she said. "Can you deny that?"

The sound of his cell phone jolted them both apart. Silas reached in his pocket, pulled out the device and looked at the caller identification. Katrina.

"I have to take this, Orla."

She gave an aggravated grunt and walked away.

"Katrina," he answered the phone curtly. "No, I'm fine. Are you okay?" he shuffled his feet as he listened. "I see. Katrina, listen, can I call you later? Orla and I are out explorin' the Shannon Pot. Yeah, I will. Talk to you soon. Bye."

He slid the phone back in his pocket. Orla was standing by the door.

"The rain has stopped. We should probably go back."

"Orla, I'm sorry."

She turned around and he was grateful to see she wasn't crying. He couldn't have stood that. "Guess it's a good thing that Briana's family and friends check in with you so often. That alone will keep you out of trouble." She turned toward the door.

He was surprised at her cattiness, but he understood. She was hurt. He could only imagine how difficult it would be if they did become lovers. He let the comment slide.

"You were right about one thing," he said, taking hold of her arm and turning her around to face him. She wouldn't meet his eyes. Gently, he took her chin in his hand, forcing her to look at him. "I do care for you. I do. You're not alone in feelin' torn up about us."

She searched his eyes. "I won't do this again, Silas. You have my word. But should you ever change your mind, all you need to do is bring your toothbrush to me house."

He nodded. "Thank you, Orla. That's fair enough."

She turned around and took a few steps toward the door. "Unless, of course, I've been swooped up by some other handsome man."

"I have no doubt that you will be, and it will be my loss, milady."

᪥

Silas lay on the sofa in his cottage, giving Katrina an update on their lack of progress today. She told him of her recent card readings, studded with bow cards, which are generally good, but she was worried about the Guardian turning up, an indication of a prevalent fear. He rubbed his temples as he listened to Katrina tell him that for Uisneach's sake, and Briana's, she hoped he found the runes soon. Silas agreed, but did not share his current worry that that if he stayed here much longer, he would not be able to withstand his growing affection for Orla. *I'm only a man, am I not*, he consoled himself. *How much can a mere mortal take?*

He hung up the phone and sighed. The ride home with Orla had been tense and she left without any indication of whether she was coming to the pub tonight. In any case, he needed to shower, change and get himself there.

The pub was full when he got there, with Seamus pouring rounds and grinning from ear to ear.

"Damn, it was a fine thing, hirin' you, Silas. Business has tripled since the handsome bard arrived."

Silas waved him off. "Seen Orla?"

"No. Here you go, lad," he said handing a pint across the bar to a "lad" of about ninety winters. "I expect she'll be in soon," he said to Silas. "You want dinner? Bangers are grand tonight."

"Sounds good, thanks." He wasn't at all sure that Orla would come tonight and almost hoped she didn't. Maybe they needed a break from the tension between them. He tuned his guitar and ate the sausage and mashed potatoes, which did in fact taste grand. He finished the first set. Still no sign of Orla. The always together foursome, Grady, Tommy-boy, Jinx and Eileen pulled him to their table during his break, but they hadn't seen nor heard from Orla. He was getting ready to step back up on stage when Eileen asked if he would play one of his originals.

Orla's absence gave him an opportunity to sing one he'd written recently. He'd been hesitant to perform it, as she would certainly know it was for Briana.

He strummed a few lines and checked the room once more. No Orla.

"In my mind, I feel you, my hands ache to touch you.
I hear your voice call across the void.
Unexpected strength, unseen forces keep you
Closer than a heartbeat, further than the sun.
Souls bound by time, held fast by gravity.
Torn by a world that won't understand.
From heather to ocean, mountains to stream.
Unconditional love bindin' our hands.
Closer than a heartbeat, further than the sun
Time means nothin' to souls that are one.
Some day, some way
Our hearts will beat as one."

He strummed a break and then continued with the next verses.

"Speak to me softly, call out my name.
Winds blowin' over the mists of my dream.
If wishes were horses, and there was no shame
I'd lay down beside you, gilded by beams."

He was lost in the song, thinking of the woman he loved, the queen of his homeland, when he sang the last lines of the chorus, "Some day, some way, our hearts will beat as one."

Looking up he was utterly dismayed to see Orla standing in the doorway near the bar, tears sliding down her face. *Oh, Maker, Orla, I am so, so sorry.* He set the guitar down and stepped from the stage, intending to go to her, but by the time he caromed through the tables and chairs, she was gone. He made it outside in time to see her halfway down the street.

"Orla," he called, but she only ran faster.

It was time to call it a night anyway, so he went back in long enough to let Seamus know he was leaving. Then he went after Orla on foot. Near the bridge, voices caught his attention. Deep, threatening voices and one higher pitched, pleading.

Around the corner, he saw three good-sized young men pinning Orla against the railing. Rumbling chuckles came from two of the lads as one stroked Orla's hair. She jerked her head back, which only made the boys laugh. Silas gritted his teeth. He didn't see any weapons. Still hidden in the darkness, he eased his hand down for the knife he always kept in his boot. The big guy, the one touching Orla, would have to go first, and then he'd take the other two out, but he'd need to surprise them. He took a breath and sharpened his focus. Stepping out of shadows he walked slowly to the group, his hand tightening on the knife hidden between his hand and his leg.

"Ah, now, lads, that's no way to treat a lady."

Four heads turned to the sound of his voice. Relief sparked in Orla's eyes.

"And who might ye be?" The shorter of the boys took a step toward Silas.

Silas mentally adjusted his plan in case this one had to go first. The bigger one moved in closer to Orla. Silas' eyes narrowed at the sound of Orla's fear. He edged closer.

"You do know that you've chosen a poor spot to assault someone. The bloody light is shinin' right on you. Should the guards drive by, you're made."

One of the boys looked up and grimaced. He took a step back.

"Why don't you stop harrassin' a defenseless woman and take on a man your own size?"

The big guy, his hand still on Orla's shoulder, made a rude sound. "She's got more to offer me than you do, boyo."

"Oh, I can offer you plenty, if you're man enough to take it."

Bushy eyebrows raised in surprise.

Silas fingered the handle of his knife.

"Maybe we should just walk, Liam," the smaller fellow said, sounding nervous as his eyes travelled from the lamppost to the area around them.

Liam threw him an aggravated look. "Go on then, coward. I'll take on this wanker, and then I'll have the lass to meself."

This was all the smaller boy needed to make a hasty exit. Down to two. Better chances. Silas took a step closer, one eye on Liam and the other on Orla. Her eyes were two round blue saucers.

Silas felt something shiver up his spine that he hadn't felt since leaving Uisneach. If not for that fact that Orla's safety hung in the balance, he'd really enjoy the thrill of danger, the opportunity to do battle. He was ready to take Liam on and hand him his arse. The grin that spread across his face served as the gloved slap to Liam, who growled and let go of Orla.

Liam advanced toward Silas, his smaller sidekick also taking a step in his direction. Silas waited until they were within grabbing distance.

"Go on home, lass," he said calmly to Orla. "I've got this."

She moved back a few steps, though not far enough for his comfort.

Liam threw a punch, which Silas deftly caught and twisted violently, turning the boy on his heel. Holding the lad against his body with one hand, he brought the blade around to his throat.

"Whoa!" The smaller boy exclaimed, backing up three steps.

"Bobby, get the guards," Liam shouted, his voice trembling.

"No need," Silas said quietly, "if the two of you just walk away and swear never to bother a lass again. If you can't do that, then I shall absolutely, and without any guilt, slit your throat." He dug the point of the blade in just enough to draw blood.

Liam squealed. "I promise."

"On the name of the savior and on your mother's life?" Silas tried to hide a chuckle as he adjusted his stance in case the boy should decide to fight once he was loose.

"Yes, yes. Let me go!"

"All right, then. Run along now. You might also consider goin' to church on Sunday and repentin' of your sins."

He relaxed his grip, ready for anything, but as soon as he let go, Liam and the other boy ran as if the devil himself were after them.

He turned his attention to Orla. "You okay?"

She was silent.

He stepped toward her. "Orla, are you all right?"

"What the hell, Silas? You break my heart in one minute and save my life in the next." She shook her head. "What am I supposed to do with that?"

Silas thought she was angry until he saw tears slipping down her cheeks and realized she was trembling from head to toe. He put an arm around her shoulder and pulled her close, without saying anything. When her shaking subsided and she was breathing normally, he stepped away, holding on to her hand. "Come, on, Orla. I'll see you home safe."

CHAPTER TWENTY-ONE

A WICKED, WEE MAN

Golden, early morning sunlight, misted through the tree branches, settling on her naked body, which rested on a mossy bed in the center of the glade. She smiled up at him with soft eyes. His finger traced a line from her cheek down her neck and along the length of her shoulder and torso to her hip and thigh. Velvety skin covered toned muscles. Flowing, ashen hair nestled around her gentle breasts. As he let his fingers explore the magic and mystery of her body, she lifted graceful fingers and traced the arrows inked over his heart. He closed his eyes, savoring the feel of her hands on his chest. Bliss. I love you, a mhuirnin. I love you, my great cat. Overhead, songbirds serenaded, and a hint of breeze whispered through the leaves. A new sound emerged from outside the thicket. Drumming. Cymbals. Strumming. He looked down at his love, regretting even this sweet music, for it meant they were not alone. His gaze travelled to the edge of the trees and was horrified to see another woman under a willow tree, with bluebell eyes and raven hair. While she beat the bodhran, small faeries danced around her feet, playing their miniature instruments. Her eyes, moist with tears, tore at his heart. He looked down at his love and knew she judged him not. The music grew louder and the woman, part of his soul wafted away, until his arms were empty. Don't go, a mhuirnin. I love you. But she was gone. He turned to the woman at the willow, but she too had disappeared. Only the music remained.

Silas clenched his eyes shut, not wanting to wake, hoping his love would return. The weight of consciousness was a burden, taking away all but the music. He lay very still in the bed. If he moved a muscle the music would stop, and he wanted to figure out where it was coming from. It had woken him for the last few nights. Or mornings, rather, as a slow glance at the clock told him it was four a.m. Laughing? That was new, and it was not a pleasant laugh, more like a deep cackle. *What the hell?* Ever so slowly, he eased the covers away and sat on the edge of the bed. The music came from the center of the room, but there was nothing there. When he stood up, it stopped.

He lay back down and rolled on his side, curling one arm underneath his head. He stared at Briana's picture. *I miss you, a mhuirnín. I never thought I'd be this long away, never imagined it would take this long to find the runes. The thing is, I don't even know where to look. They have to be on the hill, but without excavatin' the entire place, how am I ever going to find them?*

He should make another trip to the hill this morning. Showering and dressing in a plaid, button-down shirt that would keep him warm against the chill October air, he poured a bowl of cereal and sat at the table, eating breakfast and reading *The Art of War*. He wondered, as Orla had, why he was drawn to reading military books. That would've been Sigel's thing. He should be reading books of poetry and magic. But the military books were interesting, and he had learned a few things that might be useful to Brath and Sigel. Recalling Brath's name automatically led him to Briana and he sighed, seeing her so sweet and natural in his dream.

He put the book down, set the empty bowl in the sink and went to get his guitar and music journal. Seamus had asked him to play a song he didn't know and he wanted to work on the chord progressions. The guitar, Briana's guitar, stood in its usual place beside his bed, but when he reached for the journal on the nightstand, it wasn't there. He kneeled beside the bed and looked around the stand and under the bed. It wasn't there. He growled in frustration. Yet another thing had come up missing. Where the hell were these things going? Everything that had come up missing in the past few weeks, eventually turned up, so what was going on? Was he losing his mind?

His search was interrupted by a knock at the cottage door. Walking into the living room, he saw Caitlin at the door, a cheerful smile on her face, waving with something in her hand. He motioned her in.

"Good morning, Silas. Guess what I've found?"

"A lottery ticket?"

"No, of course not. I don't buy those."

"The runes?"

"Oh, don't I wish. But close."

He was intrigued.

She handed him an old, worn, leather book, tied with fraying ribbon. "It's my mother's journal! At least one of them. I just found it in a box of things in the shed. How it got in there, I can't imagine."

This was good news. Maybe.

"I've read it, but not much makes sense to me. It's mostly drawings, symbols and some language I don't know. I'm hopin' it's Uisneachan language, or at least you recognize some of the drawings."

"Will you sit and have a cup of tea while I read through?"

"No, love. Finnegan and I are goin' to church, but I'll check in with you when I get home. Oh, Katrina called this mornin'. She has had a few queries about the house. Nothin' serious, but a bit of movement, anyway."

Silas frowned. He still felt terrible about her putting the house on the market. It seemed sad to think that her home, the only one Briana had ever known, would belong to someone else, and that Briana could never come home again, even if that were possible.

"She says to tell you she'll call you later in the week." She leaned over to kiss his cheek. "See you for supper?"

"Thanks, Cait. I'd like that. Maybe I'll have some good news from this," he said, holding the book up.

After fixing another cup of tea, he settled on the couch and opened the book. The first image was a tree and some squiggles on the trunk that could be interpreted as a door. *Well, she came through the same way the rest of us did*, he thought. Some of the words Caitlin noted were in the old language of Uisneach and he could only translate a few words. A hastily drawn hill caught his eye, but the symbols surrounding it were unfamiliar.

His cell buzzed on the table. Glancing over, he saw it was a text from Orla. His lips thinned as he recalled her teary eyes in the dream. *It was just a dream, man, let it go.* He forced himself to focus on the journal in his hands. Perhaps she would have seen some of these symbols in her research. Once she had calmed down from the incident in the pub, she was still willing to help him, though she had been a little distant. School helped. She was truly devoted to her studies and it gave her a reason to back off. A series of texts later and an agreement was reached that she would stop by after church with some books she'd found in Dublin. She also mentioned she would be home for a few days working on her thesis.

It was a little after noon when he answered her knock at the door.

"Hey," she greeted him.

"Hello, come on in."

She set the bag of books on the table and lifted them out one at a time. One was a very thick, worn volume on Irish mythology. The other two were more like booklets than books.

"These look a bit more digestible," she said, pointing to the smaller books. "This one is way more than you need, but there are a few sections on faeries that may be particularly useful. By the way, I told you I'm writin' my research question, but what I didn't tell you is that I'm rewritin' it. The old thesis was going to be about the impact of Brian Boru's leadership in Ireland. It will now be about the truth or myth of faeries in Irish history."

"I've made a convert of you." Silas grinned.

"Let's just say that I'm intrigued enough to make it the focus of my work. And it allows me to do my research more locally. I'll be home more." She gave him an exaggerated wink.

"That'll be nice," he replied with polite vagueness. He didn't want to encourage any romantic notions she might still be entertain'.

"And there is a precedent for the research. In 1911 Dr. W. Y. Evans Wentz, an American scholar who studied at Oxford and worked with the likes of Yeats, published research on faeries. His book, *The Fairy Faith in Celtic Countries*, describes the four theories of the day and set out to establish scientific proof that faeries exist."

His ears perked when she mentioned that one theory claimed that faerie belief rose from the folk-memory of druids and more specifically, druidesses.

"However, this pretty much lost credibility since there is no evidence that there were druidesses, and if there were, they would've played a subservient role to the druids."

Silas frowned. "It's false in any case, since faeries existed before druids."

She set down the book in her hand. "Is that what they taught you in druid school?"

"I didn't actually go to a druid school, but every Uisneachan knows their lineage. The faeries definitely came first to the island through the Uisneach Tree."

She tapped her finger against her lower lip, a sure sign she was considering whether or not to believe him. Finally, she shook her head. "Well, anyway, I have research to build upon and I have an eyewitness." She screwed up her mouth. "Or do I? I wonder if the origins of faeries in Uisneach equate to the faerie kingdom here?"

"Dunno, but since the runes came from there to here, there has to be some connection."

They spent a couple of hours skimming through the books, mostly looking at pictures, catching up on the last few weeks.

"I think I have somethin' in the house messin' with me," Silas told her.

She twisted around to face him on the couch. "What do you mean?"

He told her about the missing objects, the music in the middle of the night, and the occasional feeling of someone's presence. He'd initially attributed the feeling to Briana trying to connect with him, but when he opened himself to her, nothing happened. Now, he was considering other explanations.

She put a finger up and then grabbed the big book and started flipping pages. "Hang on, I did see somethin' here that might explain." She paused, grimacing at him. "I can't believe I'm about to suggest this."

He moved closer to her to see what was in the book and drew in a breath at the feel of their shoulders sliding together.

Jamming her finger on a picture, she looked sideways at him. "What you may have here is a leprechaun. The Gaelic name, which I shudder to pronounce, is translated as either shoemaker or small-bodied. They're pure genius at findin' treasure and such."

Silas looked at the wee creature, who appeared part human and part gnome, lacking even gnome stature. The figure was only about six inches high, with a wrinkled face and a bulbous nose. He was dressed in brown with an apron and a red cap that looked like the ones worn by the gnomes back home, and had silver-buckled shoes.

"What I don't understand is why they would prank you. That sounds more like their evil cousin, the clurichaun. Now *he* might be more inclined to create a bit of havoc. Nasty-tempered beings, accordin' to the book. And drunks, to boot. It does say if you want to attract them, it's best to offer a bit of food and drink, preferably strong spirits."

Silas sighed. While it all sounded strange, he had no other explanation. He leaned over the book when he suddenly realized he was almost in her lap and could feel her breath on the back of his neck. He straightened and slid away, noting the pinkness in her cheeks and the glint in her eyes. She ran the tip of her tongue over her lip. Neither spoke.

The beeping of his cell phone broke the tension with a text from Debbie. He thumbed the message open and read out loud.

"What are the runes made of? If not stone, they could have disintegrated. Know Catriona brought them through in the forties, but were they much older?"

He spoke his response as he typed. "More questions than answers. Don't know. Understood them to be stone."

He was quiet, waiting for a response. Orla had taken their cups to the sink and was rinsing them.

The message he received was not much help but he read it out loud too. "Might need to rely on their energy to guide you."

"I would think that fairly obvious," Orla sniffed.

Debbie and Katrina were doing all they could from Maine to help. Silas knew she was irritated by the frequent calls and texts. He thought it best to ignore her.

After silently responding, he put the phone down. "Do you have the rest of the day free?"

"Aye, I do. I won't start workin' on the thesis until tomorrow."

"Want to go for a walk and supper?"

She nodded, her smile returning, along with the sparkle in her eyes.

After leaving Caitlin a note that he would not join them for dinner, they were on their way.

᷈

Silas and Orla found a seat at the end of the bar and ordered pints.

"It's jammers in here. I can barely hear myself speak," Orla said. "What's the story, Seamus?"

The bartender shook his head. "Can't say for sure, but since Silas started, it's been like this. Or perhaps they're just fond of me cookin'."

"That'd be reason enough for me, Seamus," Silas said, bringing another forkful of gravy-drenched pot roast to his mouth.

"Pardon, me, sir, but might ye be Silas O'Mara?"

Silas turned to see a spare old man leaning on a can behind him.

"Aye, I'm Silas." Can I help you, sir?"

"I believe 'tis I to be helpin' ye, lad. I've heard ye be lookin' for anyone with faerie stories."

Silas turned all the way around on his stool. "You heard right."

"What I've got to share with ye is a long and some would claim wild tale, but it's the pure trut', it is. The noise in here is deafenin', so I wonder if ye'd be so kind as to come to my home out past t'e water treatment plant and t'e ruins. I might even be able to convince me wife t'at visitors deserve a drink of t'e good stuff." He winked at Silas.

"We'd love to come," Orla agreed, before Silas could get the words out. She stuck her hand out to shake. "I'm Orla Kennedy, Will and Janet's daughter. Aren't you Mick Sullivan?"

"Ah, wee Orla. I've not seen ye since you was a wee chisler. I saw your da last week."

Silas waited until the proper reacquainting was finished before putting his own hand out to Mick. "We'd be happy to come to hear your story. How far is it? Do we need to get the car?" He looked to Orla, as they had walked to the pub.

"I've me car with me," the gentleman said. "I can take ye and I'll bring you back to yer home."

"It's not that far to walk from yer house to where Silas and I live," Orla answered.

"Oh, so ye live together? Are you married, then?"

Before Silas could prevent his heart from hitting the floor of his stomach, a voice muttered gleefully behind him, "Not yet."

Silas threw Seamus a stern glance. Orla didn't miss a beat.

"No, we don't live together. We live near each other, though."

"My apologies, lass," Mick said.

"No need. Maybe you've the sight and have seen into the future."

Silas closed his eyes and sighed. Was he the only one who thought this a totally inappropriate conversation?

Mick brought his beer to the bar and waited while Silas and Orla finished eating. The three of them drove the couple of miles down a very narrow lane not meant for car travel, past the dark outline of castle ruins to a small cottage lit from the inside.

"Me wife, Becca," Mick said, as the small woman took their coats and hung them on pegs behind the door. "Hardly even need these coats, it's such a fine evening." She put a kettle on to boil and uncovered a bottle of Jameson's, poured three cups and handed them around.

"Ah, come on, Becca. We don't have company often. Pour yerself one, too, love."

Becca giggled and poured herself a dram.

Silas and Orla settled onto an overstuffed couch draped with a floral slipcover. Silas adjusted a pillow behind his back and stretched out his legs. Orla sat daintily beside him. The lamp cast a drowsy light on her eager face making her look even younger than she was. *She must have been a darlin' wee chisler*, he thought to himself before his attention was turned to Mick, who cleared his throat, ready to tell his story.

"Most folk don't admit to believin' in the Good Folk, but I got good reason to. Ye see, one night, shortly after Becca and I were married, I'd gone to the hill—of Uisneach," he smiled at Orla.

Silas noticed he pronounced it 'Ushna.' Many things were pronounced differently around here by different people.

"It was a raw night in April with a stiff wind, but a friend of mine who lived on t'e edge of the hill had a ewe about to lamb and she'd come up missin'. I was out helpin' find her. I'd gone as far as t'e top of the hill, near the old rath, when I heard the sound of music. I called out to Jimmy, but t'ere was no answer.

"Now, I swear to ye I wasn't off me face. I'd not a drop to drink t'at evening. And it wasn't t'e wind. T'ere's a big difference in the sound of a storm and such lovely music. I followed the sound to a hawthorn tree, but I didn't see a bloody t'ing.

"I decided to sit still a bit and see what happened. Well, and don't you know, I was rewarded for me patience. After a bit, t'e wind died down before it stopped altoget'er. Unnaturally quiet it was. A tuft of grass at the base of t'e tree began to move and to me amazement, a wee man stepped out. How I kept from jumpin' straight in t'e air, I'll never know, but I kept still and t'e wee man was followed by a woman, as tiny as hisself. They wasn't what you'd call pretty, no. But t'ey didn't look like goblins, neither. Just a couple of homely wee folk, who appeared to be headin' out for a stroll atop t'e hill. He carried a fiddle and she some kind of stringed instrument, strange to me. T'hat must have been where the music came from.

"Suddenly, the auld man sees me and jumps straight in t'e air. He pushed the auld woman behind him and wit' his tiny, wee fist pumpin', he glares at me and says, 'And what might you be doin' up here on such a wild night?' 'I've lost a ewe,' I say to him, and he puts his arm down, does a complete circle and points to the Catstone. 'Down there,' he says. 'You'll find her and her wee'un down there. Now, get on wit' you and leave us be. We've work to do.' 'What kind of work?' I asked, trying to be pleasant and interested. 'It's none of your affair, but I'll tell you. We're gat'ering berries for a pie.' I didn't believe him. 'There's no berries in April,' I say to him and he steps toward me as t'ough he'd do me harm. 'T'ere is, if you know where to look. Now, get on wit' ye. Tend to yer own business.' Well, I did t'ink it best I do so, and left the auld ones to t'eir business. I went back a few times over t'e years but never did see 'em again. Never heard t'e music neither, but as I live and breathe, t'at night, I met faeries, or leprechauns, or whatever t'ey were." Mick took a long swig of his whiskey. Becca went to pour tea.

"Was he right about the sheep?" Orla asked.

Silas chuckled. Only Orla would want every loose end tied up.

"Oh, aye, of course. I led the sheep and her babby to me friend. But I never forgot t'e meetin' with the auld folk." He looked to Silas. "What do ye t'ink? What were t'ey?"

"Don't sound much like faerie, but perhaps the leprechaun. And since Orla and I just did a bit of studyin' on them a few hours ago, I'm intrigued by the fact that you appear to us now with such a rare experience. It seems like a clue to me. Do you think so, Orla?"

She nodded gravely. "We were meant to hear about this now, for certain."

She and Silas accepted a cup of tea and for the next hour heard stories of odd events in and around Tullamore. Srah Castle, the ruins Silas had seen on their drive in, and Kilbride Church were the source of many stories of ghosties, banshees and the like, but Mick had never seen a thing around either and claimed to have studied every inch of the ruins.

"I always wanted to run into Cromwell's ghost at Srah and put t'e bugger into his eternal hell. Never did see him."

Finally, unable to sit a minute longer, Silas mentioned that he and Orla should go.

"I'll take ye back." Mick stood slowly and reached for his cane.

"No, no, we can walk," Orla said quickly. It's a fine night. Besides," she said, looping her arm through Silas', "I've this fine braw man to protect me from any banshees." She winked at Silas as they both knew it might be she calming him down from any banshee howls.

They thanked their hosts, bid them a good evening, and headed down the path in the dark.

"Are you thinkin' what I'm thinkin'?" Silas asked her as soon as they were away from the door.

"Grab the car and head to Uisneach?"

He slung his arm around her shoulder and hugged her. "Perfect!"

At the hill, they left the car down the road and walked the short distance to the site to avoid any curious speculation. Orla unlocked the gate. They slipped inside the park.

"We'll leave the flashlights off until we get up the hill a bit. Don't want to attract any unwanted attention. Besides, I could walk this hill in me sleep."

"Orla, we don't need flashlights at all," he said, pointing up toward the bright silver disc of moon that flooded the path with light. "In fact, we'll be lucky not to be seen."

Orla stumbled and Silas chuckled. "In your sleep, huh?"

"Feck off, Silas," she swore at him, but moved closer when he tucked her arm in his.

Focus, Silas. Disregard the fact that her breast against your arm is about to drive you mad. You're here to search for faeries and keep her from breakin' her leg. He chanted this mantra several times until she pulled away herself.

"I can walk myself. Your walkin' like a bloody tin soldier is more likely to trip me up than the dark."

He let go but slowed his pace, so they could pay better attention. Up the hill and around the bend they walked until they made out the hawthorn trees next to the site where the ancient ringfort would be. The clumpy tufts of grass tripped them up more than once while the looked around the earthworks.

"So, what now?" Orla asked, running a hand along the side of a wicker lodge before bending down to peer inside. "Nothin' here."

Silas sat on the ground in the center of the fort site. *This will attract a faerie, piss a faerie off, or nothin' will happen,* he thought. Teaguen popped into his mind. Briana had said that simply by intention, she could call Teaguen to her.

"Teaguen?"

"Huh? Who's Teaguen?"

"Shhh… I'm intuitin'."

"Right."

He repeated the name several times before, to his shock, there was movement in a grassy hillock near the hawthorn. "Teaguen?"

"And just who might this Teaguen be?" said a wee man from the base of the tree, his voice a harsh growl.

Orla shrieked. Silas jumped straight up from his seated position on the ground.

"What's this all about, and what are the two of ye gawkin' at?"

Standing with all the haughtiness that his six inches would allow, the man stepped in front of Silas and looked up, jamming his hands on his hips. Silas recovered quickly. The elder gentleman was finely dressed in a white frilly shirt under a red, long-tailed jacket with silver buttons, red breeches, and black stockings that disappeared into leather slippers. Moonlight glinted off the large silver buckle on his belt, from which hung a wooden cup. A tall black hat plopped on top of snow-white hair. The man lifted a hand and ran it down the sides of his long, white beard, returning Silas' hard stare.

"Who's Teaguen, then?"

"Who are you?"

"I'm not sayin'."

"Neither am I."

Silas wondered why he felt the need to be so adversarial. Something told him not to give an inch.

Silence created an opportunity for Silas to check Orla's reaction. Her jaw was hanging slack as she clung to the wicker house. Silas walked over and took her hand. "Come on, I don't think he'll hurt you," he whispered.

She shook her head vehemently and pulled back, unable to produce a single word. Orla, speechless, was more disconcerting to Silas than the leprechaun—at least, what he presumed was a leprechaun.

The little man stomped over to within a foot of them and peered closely at Orla. A mean smirk crossed his face and he jumped at her with a growl, landing on her foot!

"Sweet Jaysus and all the saints and apostles!" she cried out, crossing herself before skittering behind Silas.

"Knock it off!" Silas demanded of the man. "And tell us who you are, or I'll…"

"You'll what, Your Lordship?" The fellow whirled on Silas, lost his balance and nearly toppled over.

Silas paused, wondering what would make the leprechaun behave. "I'll leave," he said archly.

The wee fellow stepped back and considered that with a frown.

"And you won't get what you want," Silas added for good measure.

The leprechaun's frown deepened. Then, as though none of the previous nastiness had occurred, he swept off his hat and bowed low before Silas. "Me name's Áed. And you, kind shir, who might you be?"

"Silas," he replied politely, noting the slurred speech and thinking he needed to keep control of this situation. "This is me friend, Orla."

"Might ye have a drop of any kind of libation on you?"

He had taken on a tone and attitude that would satisfy any sweet tooth, but Silas was wary. "Where did you come from?"

Áed cocked his head sideways. "You saw me with yer own two eyes, did ye not?"

So much for a change in temperament. "I've no idea where you came from and I'll give you nothin' till *you* give *me* a little information."

Áed stomped a foot down in anger, wagged a finger at Silas and screeched, "Give me somethin' to drink and I'll tell ye." When Silas didn't respond, he brought his leg back and gave a mighty whack to Silas' shin, no worse an insult than a mosquito bite. Silas reached down and picked the man up by his shirt collar, holding him up and out in front of his face.

Orla's giddy laugh startled the men, causing Silas to lose his grip on the squirming leprechaun and drop him. Áed landed in a heap in the grass.

"He's drunk!" Orla stated. "He's not a leprechaun, Silas. He's a clurichaun!"

"She's brilliant, that one," Áed grumbled, scrambling to his feet and holding out his cup. "Are ye goin' to give me a drink, or what?"

"I don't have anythin' with me," Silas said. They were getting nowhere.

"Well, what in Patrick's name are ye doin' up here in the middle of the night, then?"

Orla, having found her courage, stepped forward, glaring at Áed. "Look, you wee arsewipe, what we're doin' is none of your affair. You're nothin' but a cranky, off-your-face, wannabe leprechaun, and if you're not goin' to be civil and talk to us, you can just go back where you came from."

In an instant, the little man shocked Silas and Orla by disappearing. He reappeared in a branch of the hawthorn tree, inches from Orla's face. She didn't even flinch. "I'm not afraid of you," she said.

Maker, Silas thought, seeing another side of the woman, *when she gets angry, she's a force to be reckoned with*. He wanted to laugh at the sight of the two, face to face, neither willing to back down.

"No, not afraid, are ye? How about now?" Before anyone could react, he'd lifted his hands and flicked his fingers at Orla. Fire shot out of them, not much bigger than a match flame, but it startled her. She raised a fist to the wee man.

"Hold on," said Silas, lowering Orla's arm. "Áed, you want somethin'. We want somethin'. Perhaps there's a deal to be struck here."

"I'm listenin'."

"You want whiskey…"

"Wine or beer would do, as well."

"Well, I don't have any on me, but I know where to get some if you can help us find a certain treasure that we seek."

"Treasure, is it? I *might* know a thing or two about that." The clurichaun leaned up against the trunk of the hawthorn. "You'll need to tell me a bit more about it."

"Don't tell him a thing, Silas. He can't be trusted."

Áed raised his fists again, but Silas pushed them down with one finger. "No more of that, Áed, or any deal is off. Orla, be nice, please. We may need his help." He sighed, feeling more like a referee than a treasure hunter. "I'm goin' to trust you, Áed, and tell you my story. If you can help, then I'll bring you back some whiskey *and* beer. Fair?"

The wee one nodded and sat down, his legs dangling over the edge of the branch.

When Silas was done, Áed ran his fingers through his beard and scratched his head. "Well, Mr. Silas, I've not heard of these runes, to be honest. However, I might be able to find some information for you, through my connections. You say ye'll be leavin' when you find them. Ye'll be goin' back to Uisneach?"

"Aye, I hope so." Stealing a glance sideways, he saw Orla's jaw tighten at this.

"I want to go with ye," Áed said.

"What? Why would you want to do that?" Silas asked.

"I'm lookin' for a wife, and there's none to be had around here."

Orla huffed and received a glare from the clurichaun.

"I can't promise to take you to Uisneach. I'm not even sure I'll be able to get back, but I will promise to see what I can do to help you find a lady."

The little man paused, considering, then stuck out a gnarly hand. Silas took it between his thumb and forefinger, giving it a gentle shake to seal the deal.

"How do I find you again?" Silas asked.

"The same way ye did tonight, ye gowl."

Silas shook his head. Nothing about working with this fellow would be easy. He was about to call the deal off when a bright light blasted into the circle of three, followed by a deep, authoritative voice.

"And what might you two be doing up here?"

Silas turned to see two gardaí, holding flashlights on them.

"Good evening, officers," Orla said smoothly. "I'm Orla Kennedy, an interpreter for the hill and I'm assistin' my friend, Silas O'Mara, with research for a book he's writin'."

"In the middle of the night?"

"Well, this part of our research ponders the question about whether or not it's possible to find faeries at night. We're testin' this hypothesis, you see. I have permission from the board to do this."

Silas was impressed. She sounded so professional and confident that he had no doubt they would be left alone.

"Well, then, why did you leave your car down the road? Huh?"

"Oh, well, to avoid any nosey eyes, don't you see? I failed to consider our very trustworthy and faithful gardaí would easily see through that ruse. You gentlemen are the best. Truly. I will be sure to let my supervisor know how well the hill is protected."

That did the trick.

"Well, then, you two be careful. The moon may be bright, but you never know what lurks inside a ringfort at night."

Indeed, Silas thought. *Try a nasty little clurichaun.*

"We'll be careful, sir. And thank you again," Orla said, pouring on the sweetness.

The guards left, muttering to each other and chuckling. Silas and Orla turned back to the hawthorn tree, but there was no trace of Áed. "Where'd the wee muppet go?" Orla asked grumpily.

"Honestly, Orla, you do have a terrible mouth on you, sometimes," Silas commented with a grin.

She shrugged. "That nasty little man could bring the worst out in anyone. What now, Silas?"

"I don't think there's much else to do here tonight. We might as well go home."

Orla chided him most of the way home about being too trusting and contributing to the delinquency of a magical creature.

"Would you like to come in for a drink?" she asked, while they were yet a couple of miles from her home.

Just then, his phone buzzed with a new text. It was Debbie. He let it go until he pulled into Orla's drive and parked. He read the text aloud, assuming it would have to do with their search. The text asked if he had checked St. Patrick's Well on the hill.

"That would seem a logical place," Orla said neutrally, though Silas didn't miss the rolling of her eyes.

But then, Debbie mentioned having found a notebook of songs that Briana wrote, that he might be interested in, and wondered if he wanted her to send it to him. Once he started reading it out, he couldn't very well stop, and the mention of Briana's name had the expected effect on Orla.

"I think I'd like to take a raincheck on the drink, Silas, if you don't mind. I've a bit of headache coming on."

"Orla, I wish you wouldn't be like that. You can't be gettin' upset every time I talk with Debbie or Katrina, or when Briana's name comes up. That's hardly fair."

"I'm not upset. I'm just tired, that's all. I'll see you tomorrow, maybe."

He sighed. "Okay, Orla. Talk to you tomorrow."

She let herself out of the car and sprinted to her door.

What a shame to end such an interesting night on such a sour note.

Minutes later, he was in his own apartment, removing his boots, when a flash of red caught his eye near the backpack he had tossed on a chair.

"Áed?" he asked incredulously. The little clurichaun sauntered around the pack and jumped to the floor. "What are you doin' here? How'd you get here?"

"None of your affair in the how, but I'm here, and any decent host would offer a man a drink."

"Aye, I'd like one too," Silas said. He poured himself a few fingers of whiskey before filling the wee cup Áed was holding out.

"*Slàinte*," Silas toasted him.

"*Slàinte mhath.*"

Silas sipped his drink, but Áed gulped his and thrust out the cup for a refill.

"Fine, but this is it for you, little man."

He poured a bit more. "Are there really no clurichaun women in Ireland?"

"I never said none were here, I just can't get meself one. They'll have naught to do with me."

Silas wondered if he treated them the way he had been treating Orla and him.

"Well, I don't know about gettin' you to Uisneach, but I might be able to help you be more, um, attractive to the female persuasion here."

Áed shimmied up the leg of the couch and settled on the cushion next to Silas.

"I'm listenin'."

"Well, I assume you know that women like to be treated as though they are special."

Áed screwed up his face. "They're women, not fiddles."

"Fiddles?"

"Fiddles are special, women are, well, women, meant to be servin' a man."

Silas rubbed his temples. He had a lot of work to do with Áed and he was too tired tonight to begin.

"Áed, do you think the runes could be in St. Patrick's Well?"

"Now, why on earth, would she have hidden faerie runes in a Christian well?" Áed said, snuffing as though he'd smelled something foul. "Ghormin' wankers, faeries are."

Silas took that as a swear word and derogatory toward the faerie race. "It's no wonder you can't get a wife, Áed. You have a nasty mouth. I advise you to try and curb that a bit, if you want *anyone* to like you."

The clurichaun shook his fist at Silas. "And what about your girlfriend? She swears a red streak. Have ye taught her to be nice? Not much to look at either, now that I think of it."

"You out of your mind? She's a beautiful woman. And Orla's almost always nice and doesn't usually swear that much. You bring out the worst in people, you know? And she is not me girlfriend. We're friends."

Áed bellowed. "Do I look blind, lad? She muckled on to you like she owned ye, sure enough. And yer defense of her is a bit more than friendly, me thinks. More whiskey."

"No, you've had enough."

Áed whirled around and around, stomping his feet, jumping from couch to table, pushing papers and banging his cup on whatever he could find, throwing a spectacular temper tantrum.

"This is exactly why you can't find a woman, Áed," Silas said, trying to catch him. The clurichaun was fast and could disappear and reappear anywhere he liked. Silas pretended to be done trying until Áed laid himself lengthwise on top of the book in front of Silas. Like an arrow loosed, Silas snatched the little guy. "Now, if you don't behave, I am goin' to stuff you in me knapsack and throw you in the river. Understood?"

With a clever grin, Áed disappeared, leaving Silas holding air.

"You're a wicked wee man, Áed!"

Sighing, he picked up his phone and texted Orla. No response. He sighed again and traded the phone for his journal, and headed for bed, intent on making a few notes about where and how he might find the runes on his own.

Later, as he was about to succumb to sleep, a horrid clattering brought him back awake.

"Stuff it, Áed. Go to sleep."

The noise stopped abruptly.

"Ye wee gomeral," Silas muttered, sliding back down into dream.

CHAPTER TWENTY-TWO

PROUD REUNION

Briana, Tollemy Farm, Appleduir, Uisneach

"The farm looks exactly the same, Rippa," Briana said.

"Aye, well, yer Majesty, it's only been a few months since you were here last."

"Oh, my goodness, it has, hasn't it? I can't believe how much has happened in two months!"

Rodnner Tollemy, silhouetted by the afternoon sun, strode up the hill.

At the sight of his father, Rippa glanced at Briana.

"Go! Go!" she encouraged him, with a wave of her hand.

"Pa!" Rippa shouted and raced into his father's outstretched arms.

Dara barked enthusiastically and followed Rippa down the hill.

"It appears they have missed each other," Aya'emrys said, beside her.

Briana smiled and led her small army of faerie warriors and Jonathan down to Mr. Tollemy and his wife, Gertrude, who, babe in arms, joined him with tears sliding down her face.

"Your Majesty," Rodnner said, once Briana dismounted.

Briana gave him a long-suffering look and opened her arms for hugs from him and his wife. "We've brought your son home for a visit."

"A visit, is it?" Rodnner said, his mouth curving down.

"Well, at least to get formal permission for him to stay on as bard at Ard Darach."

"What's happened to the old one?" Gertrude asked.

"It's a long story."

"Then we can discuss it over supper." Rodnner stretched his eyes over the clan of warriors.

Briana quickly introduced Aya'emrys and Jonathan.

"My men and I will circle the farm. We will provide for our own needs," Aya'emrys said to both the farmers and his queen.

Briana nodded in agreement. "Can you manage to put up with just us three stragglers?" Briana asked, and saw Gertrude relax at once.

"And how is my wee Penelope?" Briana crooned, relieving Rippa's mother of the squirming bundle. The infant burrowed into her neck, melting her heart with the innocence of her trust.

"Come inside, then," said Gertrude.

While Gertrude added a few more vegetables to a pot of stew and sliced more bread and cheese, Briana sat at the table, bouncing Penelope on her lap as she talked with Rodnner about their plan for Rippa, pending their consent.

"Where is your husband, then?" Gertrude asked from the hearth, where she stood, stirring the pot.

Briana froze. She hadn't prepared herself to answer questions about why she and Brath weren't together. What to say?

"He's defending Firmara and wanted the queen at a safe distance," Jonathan Stark said, not looking at his queen.

The young man seemed to sense something was amiss and, as usual, stepped up to protect her. Perhaps he'd noticed the tension between the king and queen when they parted yesterday with a peck on the cheek instead of a hug and warm kiss goodbye. Briana had been determined to present a strong façade on this journey despite a long, sleepless night at camp last night, surrounded by faerie warriors and two young boys.

"Yes, that's right. The citizens of Colmer Harbor are putting up some resistance to Brath's resuming his role as king of Uisneach. He and the army are trying to restore relationships there while defending Firmara against Shamwa's supporters. He felt I would be safer in Baigsith."

Briana could see the skepticism in Gertrude's eyes, but she returned to stirring the stew.

"So, what do you both think of Rippa staying in the king's army?"

"It's yer army, too," Rippa said, making his allegiance clear.

Rodnner settled his head on folded hands as Gertrude stepped behind him and laid a hand on his shoulder. They stared at their son, who held his breath, his eyes pleading.

"It's what ye want, Rippa?" Rodnner asked.

"Aye, Pa. I want to serve Briana, uh, Queen Briana."

"And King Brath," Briana remarked pointedly.

"Yes, him too."

Seeing a shadow cross Gertrude's face, Briana suddenly felt terrible, taking their only son from them. She started to say something, but Rodnner spoke first.

"I was not happy with Rippa for running off to Ard Darach. But I told ye, Queen Briana, that we would do whatever we could to help the king restore Uisneach. If it means our son can help by using his Maker-given gifts, then so be it."

Rippa whooped with joy and after a hug to his parents, turned to Jonathan. "I told youz they'd let me stay!"

"You did, Rippa. You were right," Jonathan agreed, his face split in a wide grin.

Briana was glad the boys had developed such a close friendship. Gertrude went back to the pot and frowned. Briana wondered if she was worried about having enough to feed the extra bodies. Taking a breath, she thought the words of magic, made a few motions with her ringed finger and hoped something good would come of it.

"Rippa, while we're waiting for supper, why don't you tell your father about what's happened during your time with us."

The lad kicked off his shoes and went immediately into bard mode, weaving a colorful tale of being at the skirmishes at Art Aron and Dun Lura and the injuries sustained by Sigel. In the middle of describing Winge Mansion, Gertrude uttered a shocked exclamation from the fireside.

"Maker above, would ye look at that! The pot is full of twice as much meat as I had and half the garden of vegetables! How did that happen?"

"Oh, probably Briana," Rippa said nonchalantly, using the interruption as an opportunity to take a sip of the cider his father had poured him.

"Ye have magic?" Rodnner asked.

"A bit. Sometimes. I'm still learning how to use it."

"I thank ye for practicin' here, then," Gertrude said, wide-eyed, as she looked inside the bountiful pot.

When the meal was ready, they gathered at the table and Rodnner steepled his hands in a position Briana recognized as preparation for grace. She bowed her head.

"Maker, we give ye thanks for the bounty before us and for the safe return of our son. A…"

Gertrude cleared her throat.

"Uh, and Maker thank ye for our faithful king and queen. Please bless them with all they need to secure Uisneach and give power back to the Taranian king. A…"

A louder throat clearing. Briana shifted her eyes subtly, to find Gertrude staring at her husband. He took a breath.

"And, Maker, we do thank ye for the new life that grows within me wife's womb. We thank ye for the blessing of children. A-men," he said forcefully.

"What!" Rippa and Briana exclaimed at the same time.

"Youz are havin' another baby, Ma?"

"'Tis true. Due in the Hawk Moon," she replied. "Or, perhaps the Harp Moon, but more likely the Hawk Moon."

Winter, about January, Briana translated in her head. "Congratulations, both of you."

The meal was seasoned with conversation about Rodnner's wish that he could join the army, which was immediately nixed by both Gertrude and Briana. The queen suggested they grow more food to supply the army.

"I'll need to plow more fields, but that's easily done," Rodnner said, looking pleased that he could make some contribution.

"Well, now, that's settled," Gertrude said, with audible relief.

"Rippa didn't say what happened to the old bard," Rodnner asked.

It was the second time Silas was referred to as the old bard and Briana wanted to laugh. Twenty-five years was old? But then, he'd been the bard since his youth, so perhaps longevity made him an old bard.

"Rippa wasn't there when all that happened," Briana said, before launching into the tale of the Uisneach-Evalon meeting and the discovery that the runes had to be found and brought back to Uisneach before magic could be restored.

"But ye have magic," Gertrude pointed out.

"Well, yes, some. I was granted special powers by a magical pool in Evalon."

Dara was fed bits of stew and bread from every person at the table, until Briana reminded them that his belly could only hold so much. The hound responded to her statement with a look of extreme disappointment.

"Sometimes I think he understands every word I say," she commented, as he turned away with a huff, which prompted laughter around the table. Head hung, he headed for the door and whined until Rippa let him out.

After supper, Gertrude insisted that the queen and her entourage stay the night and head for Baigsith in the morning. Briana spoke with Jonathan, giving him instructions to relay to the faerie captain. While he was gone, Briana took Penelope from her mother and rocked her in the chair as Gertrude poured ale for everyone except herself.

"Ale, or goat's milk, Briana?" she asked, one eyebrow raised.

"Ale is fine, thank you."

"Ye'll make a wonderful mother," she commented, noticing Penelope snoring softly in Briana's arms. "Is the king anxious to start a family?"

Briana swallowed hard but answered the question. "He is. I guess it will happen when it's meant to."

"True enough."

The men, not inclined to talk about babies, continued a discussion about the weaponry being used against Lord Shamwa and how skilled an archer Jonathan had become. Briana desperately wanted to join that conversation, but Gertrude had other plans.

Taking Penelope from her, she handed the sleeping infant to Rodnner. "I want to show Her Majesty the lambs."

Briana and Dara dutifully followed Gertrude to the barn, where a ewe was lying in with a set of twins. Dara promptly laid down in front of the stall, staring at the sheep.

"Oh, my, they are so sweet!" she said, watching the lambs vie for their mother's attention.

"It was a difficult birth, but the ewe did a grand job and with Rodnner's help they were born safe. Both are faring well."

The mention of difficult birthing revived images of the cottage in Inis Fáil.

"What is it, Briana? I can see something troubles ye. Maybe I can help."

The story poured from Briana, from the difficult delivery to her thoughts of taking the herbs to prevent pregnancy, leaving out only the disagreement between her and Brath and his decision to send her away.

Gertrude clucked and nodded sympathetically throughout. When Briana finished, she stood quietly, allowing the air to settle around them as the lambs nursed lustily from their mother. Finally, she spoke.

"That was a terrible thing, Briana, and the truth is, it happens sometimes. Surely ye know that. Didn't ye tell me your mum is a midwife?"

Briana nodded.

"So ye know nothing is predictable in the world. But that shouldn't stop us from living, having families and such. Death is a part of life that doesn't just happen on the battlefield. Ye must risk it to live fully."

Briana stared at her feet, tears pricking at her eyes.

"Yer a natural mother, Briana. I've watched ye with Penelope and Rippa. If it's not meant for ye to conceive, well, then there's nothing to be done about that, but to avoid it out of fear is not something I can imagine ye doing. Yer much stronger than that, and you would rob yourself and the king of a great blessing if you purposely chose not to have children out of fear."

Briana leaned over the boards of the stall, watching the two lambs nestled into their mother and felt something stir in her own womb. Perhaps Gertrude was right. Maybe fear *was* robbing her of something precious.

"Thank you, Gertrude. I do think talking with you has helped."

"Good, then."

The evening finished off with fiddle playing, song and story, and for Briana, another mug of ale. Sleep wasted no time in coming, even though she was in the bed from which she'd been abducted by Shamwa's henchmen only a day into her journey to Dromdara and King Brath.

Maker, Dara snores a lot, was her next to the last thought. *Good night, Brath*, was her last thought.

CHAPTER TWENTY-THREE

DECISIONS

Rippa hardly said a word as they left the Tollemy farm and frequently swallowed hard. Jonathan rode at his side, honoring his need for silence, offering comfort when he could.

This was exactly what she'd been worried about when she offered him the job. He was so young. He belonged with this family.

"Do you want to go back, Rippa?" The boy shook his head. "I belong with youz," he said. "I just feel bad, knowin' I won't be there when me little sister is born. I'll git over it."

"Maybe we can stop on the way back to Firmara," Jonathan offered, stealing a look at his queen. "Of course, we'll stop," Briana agreed. "And Rippa, if you decide to stay with them and help on the farm, it's okay. We need good men all over Uisneach, doing all kinds of things to support the cause."

Just then a whoosh of black wings glided over her head and the crow landed between two birch trees fifty yards away. He twisted and turned into a Winge army warrior. Aya'emrys, riding in front of Briana, held up the entourage.

"I come from King Brath," the crow warrior said. "He wishes to know how the queen fares?"

Irritation pricked at her heart. *Oh, he does, does he? How good of him to enquire.* "Please, tell His Majesty that we are fine and that there is nothing to be concerned about. There's been no sign of Shamwa or the Gray Military.

I'll send word when we reach Baigsith." She turned away from the frown appearing on Jonathan's face.

The messenger bowed, then began the machinations of shifting. He flew off.

"Come on, then," she said, before anyone could comment. "I want to get to Baigsith by lunchtime. They make the best oat bread."

Baigsith was only a few hours away from the Tollemy's. However, there was the little issue of crossing Long River. As far as Briana knew, the only crossing was over a magical bridge. Could she get across again? Could the rest of her group?

She spent the next hour noodling ideas to get them across and was deep in thought when she realized they were less than a mile from the river.

"Captain Aya'emrys, would you send a messenger to the village to ask Jack Wells if there's a way across the Long River other than the rainbow bridge."

One of the faerie guards made the luminescent transformation and drifted away to Baigsith. The rest of them carried on. Briana suddenly felt goosebumps on her arms. Looking to Aya'emrys, she saw that he too sensed something out of order.

"Captain?" she whispered.

He put a finger to his lips before lifting it above him, making some sort of designs that she was unfamiliar with. The faerie army moved around her. Jonathan Stark eased his sword from the scabbard. Briana followed suit with Nua. Something was amiss, though there wasn't a sound to be heard beyond the hoot of an owl. An owl? In broad daylight? *Damn! That's no owl.*

The queen and her faerie army moved as one down the path, hoping to get to the bridge before the attack. Hopefully, Jack would be there with a way to cross. But then the gnomes would be at risk. Baigsith could be the next Inis Fáil!

"Wait," she ordered Aya'emrys.

"There's no time, High Lady."

"We need to meet them here. I don't want Baigsith involved."

The decision was taken out of their hands when the trees began to crawl with bodies that had been hidden by the forest, gray vermin, singular in their battle cry.

Knowing she was momentarily well protected, Briana took the opportunity to call up her power. Pointing around her in a circle, she allowed the ring to create a wall of protection around her troop.

"Shields up! Archers ready!" Briana ordered. Several Grays bumped against the invisible barrier. How long would it last? "Knock...draw...loose! "Arrows arced into the air, angled just enough to drop into the swarm of fighters on the other side of the invisible shield. Fatalities on the enemy's side mounted as the hive of faerie warriors moved Briana forward down the path. Just in case, she kept her shield up and Nua handy.

Within minutes, the Gray Military lay heaped along the path. Her army had not suffered one loss.

"Great job, men!" she pronounced heartily, feeling quite pleased with the outcome of this skirmish.

She and the faeries remained on alert as they continued toward the river. As she suspected, a colorful, transparent bridge lay between her and the large group of gnomes on the other side.

"Jack, I thought for sure you'd have made something a bit more solid by now."

"Ho, there, Queen Briana! It's a joy to see you again. You and your men, come on over."

"Really, Jack? The faeries can get over and I might be able to, but how do I get the boys across?"

Danger was suddenly written on the faces of the gnomes. She turned to find a second wave of Gray Military, larger than the first, running at them from behind.

"Bloody hell!" She needed to think quickly. Lives depended upon it. "Captain," she turned to Aya'emrys, "between us, can we make a bridge?"

What had been tiny sparks in the air turned instantly into seven-foot-tall golden warriors who built a line between Briana, Jonathan and Rippa and the Grays.

That buys us time, she thought, jumping off Banrion and pulling Nua out of the scabbard. Jonathan raised his bow and aimed through a small aperture in the faerie ring. He loosed several arrows, but it was like spitting in the wind. There were too many Grays. They needed a bridge, and fast!

"Throw Nuada across the gorge," Aya'emrys instructed.

Briana's eyes went wide. "Are you crazy! I can't throw Nua away!"

"Say the words and throw the sword!" he ordered. She turned to the chasm and focused all her energy on the colorful band across it, ignoring the din of battle behind her. When she raised Nua, she felt its heat travel up the steel to her hand, making her ring glow. The power continued up her arm, spreading throughout her body to her core. She felt like a living thunderbolt. From her peripheral vision, she saw Aya'emrys, beside her, pointing his sword in the same direction. Drawing on the energy inside, she entreated all the powers who were listening, and raised Nua high in the sky. "I call on the wisdom and power of all tuathlas before me to turn this bridge to solid wood. Now!"

At a cue from Aya'emrys, they flung their swords. She watched in fascination as the swords arced through the air, elongating as they turned end over end. They shifted from metal to two long planks of wood that reached from one side of the gorge to the other, attaching to posts that seemed to appear out of nowhere. A solid bridge. The energy required to manifest the magic had her sweating profusely. While power coiled in her belly, her legs began to weaken.

"Mr. Stark. Rippa. Take the horses across. Go! Hurry!"

The boys obeyed without question and were across the bridge in seconds. The clatter of swords behind Briana caught her attention.

"Go, Tuathla. Do not worry about what is behind you."

She nodded and stepped onto the bridge when an idea came to her. "Aya'emrys, call back your troops and let the Grays come."

His eyes widened but he sent out a whistle that caused the faerie warriors to shift to light energy and float across the gorge.

Shamwa's troops were startled into inactivity long enough for Briana to make it nearly to the other side. The Grays poured onto the wooden bridge. She had one foot on solid ground and one on the bridge when she turned back and forced her remaining energy to reverse the magic. Wood immediately turned back to steel just as Briana brought her other foot off the bridge. The horde of soldiers were dumped, screaming and flailing, into the Long River, hundreds of feet below. Nuada flew up into her hand, but not before one of the Grays grabbed her ankle. Jonathan immediately grabbed her arm. Realizing what was about to happen and not wanting Jonathan to be hurt, she jerked her arm away. "Let go, Jonathan!"

She heard screams from above and looked to see that her squire had not released her and was descending alongside her. Falling through air was painless and gave her a sense of exhilaration that freed her to think with extreme clarity. Her only thought was to save a twelve-year-old boy who had an entire life yet to live. "Nua, help!" she called out once more, hoping the sword would do something. A glance down told her that the floor of the canyon was looming close with every millisecond. *Oh, Maker, I don't think we're going to make it... Oh, I'm so sorry. Silas. Brath. I...* She closed her eyes in a prayer that was more images than words.

Suddenly, she felt the freefall turn into a float and opened her eyes to find herself in the arms of Captain Aya'emrys. "Jonathan!" she cried out.

"Is fine," said her captain, pointing with his chin to where Jonathan was scrambling out of the arms of another faerie warrior.

"I'm not a baby," he grumbled, pulling away from the faerie.

"Mr. Stark!" Briana scolded him.

"Sorry," the boy muttered.

Broken bodies littered the banks and floated by in water reddened by their blood. She must have caused the death of at least a hundred of Shamwa's soldiers. She shivered and looked up. Gnome faces and one black-haired, freckled face were peering over the edge of the cliff.

"Jack, can we get that bridge built now?"

Cheers from above filtered down below.

In seconds, Aya'emrys and his subordinate had her and Jonathan united with the others at the top of the cliff.

Briana knelt on one knee to receive the warm hugs and kisses from Jack and Genevieve Wells. "I'm so happy to see you," she said.

"Aye, 'tis a blessing that you're here and safe now," Genevieve replied.

"Your Majesty," Jack said, with a bit of jig. "I taught you how to climb those cliffs for a reason. You could've climbed out yourself."

She rose and placed a hand on her hip. "I've graduated from that, Jack. I have faeries who do the heavy lifting for me."

He harrumphed, but one corner of his mouth lifted. "In any case, it's good to have you back, milady. I mean, Your Majesty. Come along, we must let Governor Wells know you have returned. He won't want to be kept waiting."

Briana turned back to the cliff, looking down once more. Any sense of joy at her reunion with the gnomes, any jocularity about the rainbow bridge, dissipated at the massive loss of live that she herself caused. She bit her lip.

"In times of war, lives are lost," Aya'emrys said beside her. "You are not to blame."

"I know. I just wish it didn't have to be this way, or at least, I wish it was Shamwa down there and this could all end."

"Shall I send a message to the king advising him of your arrival and what has happened here?"

"Let him know that I am here safely. Say nothing of what's gone on."

Aya'emrys frowned. "A lie by omission is still a lie, High Lady."

"I respectfully disagree. He is to be told that we are here and we are safe. That is the truth. He needs to focus on what he's doing, not be anxious about what's already been handled."

"Very well," he said and left to give the order for a messenger to go back to Firmara.

⁂

The gnomes had the heart and will to aid their kingdom. They just needed a proper leader, which they found in Captain Aya'emrys, who, with the help of Jonathan Stark and Jack Wells, started training them in battle skills soon after the queen's entourage arrived in Baigsith. The shire became a hub of activity, with some gnomes training while others continued producing the invisibility cloaks for the army. Briana was pleased to find stacks of cloaks when she arrived, but more were needed, so she happily rolled up her sleeves and joined the production line.

Two days later, a crow arrived during the military drills. Briana was called out of the shed where they were working on the cloaks. Practically the entire village gathered in a circle around the queen and the crow, anxious for word from the king.

Briana waited for him to finish shapeshifting, her jaw tight, butterflies fluttering uncomfortably in her belly.

"Your Majesty. The king wishes you to know that he is grateful for your safe arrival and that all is well in Firmara. They ride to Colmer Harbor in two days."

Briana nodded and waited, but no further message was delivered. She dowsed the disappointment that threatened to incite tears. *If that's how he wants it, that's how it will be.*

"Any return message, Your Highness?"

"Wish him a safe journey and a successful campaign," she croaked out past the lump in her throat.

"Will that be all?" The crow seemed uncertain about the short message.

"Tell him that the cloaks are in production. And, tell him not to worry about us," she added, realizing when she said it how bitter it sounded. "Refresh yourself, please, before you go." She turned and walked back to the table of cloaks they were working on, feeling the weight of every eye on her back.

Things remained quiet in the sewing circle that afternoon. It wasn't until after supper and discussion turned to the prophecy that Genevieve brought up the king again.

"I wonder what happened to the missing pages," she said, when Briana told her of that discovery.

"Hopefully, Silas will find something on the other side that sheds some light on that."

"It must drive you and the king fair batty to know there are pieces of the puzzle missing."

"It is frustrating. It could be that with the missing information, Silas would be able to find the runes quickly and we could have all the magic we need to take care of Shamwa and fully restore Uisneach. We just have to work with the information we do have."

"And that requires you and the king to be apart?"

Briana thought it a grand time for a bite of oat bread.

"You must miss each other terribly," the gnome pressed.

Yes, she missed him. Terribly. Did he miss her? Probably not. He was so angry with her when they parted. Would he ever want her back? Maybe she *should* go back to Maine.

"Who could have imagined that at the end of your journey, you would find a wonderful man to love?"

Briana looked at Genevieve, who regarded her speculatively.

"Yes, who knew that would happen," Briana agreed vaguely. She refused to engage in this discussion, but her mood had headed south since the crow's visit and didn't promise to improve.

❧

In a week's time, the gnomes managed to produce one hundred invisibility cloaks, using a combination of local materials found nowhere else on Uisneach and a bit of highly specialized gnome magic. Briana marveled at the gossamer capes. Once on, they became totally invisible from the magic imbued in them.

"The king will be pleased, to be sure," Genevieve commented, surveying the table heaped with the cloaks.

Briana nodded with the pasted-on smile she had perfected since leaving Firmara. Every couple of days, a crow arrived with another brief message about the status of the Taranian and Winge armies and Briana gave the same short message back: invisibility cloaks in production and everyone safe. That was all.

Briana plodded on, directing the production of cloaks, practicing her own magic, helping where she could around the village. However, after almost ten days of village life, ten days away from Brath with no hope of things improving between them, ten days with factual, emotionless messages cycling between her and Brath at sunrise and moonset, she was sinking down into a dark hole that her practiced smile could not hide.

Fuzzy edges of a dream that she thought included Silas faded as Briana ascended out of sleep into darkness broken only by the light of the half moon through the window. Worries about Brath shooed off any lingering vestiges of the dream. In an hour, the village would wake, and she'd be smothered again in attention and speculation. What she craved, with a hunger that would not be denied, was solitude. She glanced toward the stairway. Aya'emrys would be stationed at the bottom for protection. There was no hope of evading him to go for a walk all by herself. Or was there? She spied the invisibility cloak folded on the bedside chair, meant to protect her in the event of an attack. Well, this was an emergency of another kind.

If I don't get some alone time, I'm going to lose my freaking mind! It worked for Harry Potter, I should hope it will work for me.

Easing out of bed, she dressed, cloaked herself and grabbed her boots. "Dara, you have to stay here. Please don't make any noise," she whispered. Dara looked at his mistress doubtfully. "I'll be careful, I promise. Please don't give me away." He groaned, sighed and curled up on his bed, though his eyes stayed open. She slid Nua into her scabbard. She was taking a risk but would not be foolish. She needed some protection. A quick glance in the mirror confirmed that she was imperceptible. Tiptoeing down the stairs, she held her breath and slid sideways past Aya'emrys, who stood wide awake at the foot of the stairs. He didn't seem to notice anything unusual. It wasn't until she got to the door that she released her breath, but then realized he would see her open the door. What other route of egress? An open window provided the answer. It wouldn't be the first time she escaped confinement through a window. Slowly, carefully, she lifted a leg over the sill. The rest of her body followed without a hitch and she paused outside the window long enough to breathe in the smell of freedom.

Pink washed the eastern sky as she wandered away from the cottage to the path leading out of the village and up to the ridge. Every so often she looked behind to see if she was being followed. Not a sign of anyone. She breathed a sigh of relief when she squeezed through the twin boulders to the ridge trail. Not so long ago she'd entered Baigsith along this same trail. Out of sight of the village, she removed the cloak and wrapped it around her waist. As she hiked, she felt the weight of responsibility lift from her. She didn't have to smile and pretend everything was fine. She didn't have to give orders or deal with any of the never-ending issues. She didn't have to face the crow messenger with another factoid message from her estranged husband. However, she now had to face her own inner grief and the fact that she missed Brath like crazy and feared they would never return to the promise of a happy marriage. She ignored the intermittent tingle she felt on her arms and the back of her neck. *Just feeling guilty about sneaking away.*

Her feet wandered with her thoughts until she heard the sound of Faerie Falls. She paused long enough for a drink of water from the pool. *Wish I'd thought to bring food*, she thought as her belly rumbled, nearly matching the noise from the falls.

Time ceased to exist as she as she followed the path through a forest that thinned out to meadow on one side of a familiar river. On the other, side a forest of yews, hawthorn, pine, birch and rowan stirred a memory. She recognized the stone wall and the bench where Genevieve had once sat so demurely. The only difference was that the lonely, nearly dead faerie tree now flourished. Her heart hammered in her chest. She knew exactly what she would see when she turned around. Swallowing, she slowly turned her body to the oak tree. Tears pricked her eyes as she stared at the green door with a silver handle. *No*, she thought, *this can't be. Why did I end up here?* She heard Brath's words clearly in her head: *If you want to return to Maine, then I won't stop you.*

She could walk through that door and be home in as much time as it took to walk down one set of stairs and up another. Her mother lived on the other side of that tree. Silas was there. The sound of her agonized breaths filled her ears. Dizziness washed over her in waves. She reached out her hand, nearly touching the handle. She paused a millimeter from contact. She heard her heart ripping in two. Legs too weak to hold her folded and she sat before the door, tears now rolling down her cheeks.

"I love you both, so much. But I love Brath too, and I belong here." She whispered the words, almost begging them to forgive her.

Sorrow and regret overwhelmed her, and she curled up beside the tree and cried out the pain of her choice until she felt a hand stroking her hair. Jerking upright, she pushed tear-dampened hair away from her face to find Aya'emrys sitting beside her, watching her with concern.

"It was you I felt! You've been with me all along!"

He nodded.

"Why didn't you make yourself known?" she demanded, embarrassed and angry that he'd witnessed her meltdown.

"I needed to protect you, but you needed to believe yourself alone."

"You should have told me."

"That would have defeated the purpose you set yourself to."

She wouldn't have left the cottage. She wouldn't have come here. She wouldn't have had to make a choice. But she had. Finally, and irrevocably, it turned out. When she glanced at the tree, she found the door gone.

"Let's go home."

He reached out his hand to help her up.

"Thank you," she said, meeting his eyes.

They made it as far as Faerie Falls before they met up with the search party, headed by Jonathan. Dara barked out a greeting and sailed over the brook to his mistress. After a cursory sniff assuring her security, he stood silent beside her.

"Mr. Stark is angry with you," Aya'emrys said softly in her ear.

It didn't take magical powers to see that. His eyes were blazing. She hopped across a few stones in the stream to where he stood, feet apart, shoulders squared and glaring at her.

"What is the meaning of you running off like that?"

"I went for a walk."

"A walk! You're miles away from the village and you told no one where you were going."

"Mr. Stark!" she interrupted his lecture. "I believe I am still the queen here. I do not have to ask permission to go for a walk."

"I believe I am still the queen's protector," he countered. "And I cannot bloody well do my job if you don't follow the rules."

"What rules? I make the rules," she countered, growing angry herself.

Aya'emrys touched her elbow and stepped forward.

"My apologies, Squire Stark, for not informing you of our decision to go out, but as you can see, I was with her and she is well and safe."

Three seconds of silence ensued, time enough for Jonathan and Briana to take a breath and calm down.

Briana looked around at the rest of the search party: Jack Wells, John Wells, the master builder, and Ebenezer Wells, the governor, along with half a dozen other Wellses, and Rippa, looking insulted, worried and relieved. "I'm sorry I worried you all," she said, putting a hand on Rippa's shoulder.

Aya'emrys stepped forward. "Shall we all go back to the village and have breakfast? I believe the queen is near to starving." He moved to lead the group, saying something in Jonathan's ear as he walked by.

The young man looked at Briana, nodded curtly and held back until Briana was next to him. Walking side by side, neither spoke for some minutes. Briana finally broke the silence.

"You know, you kind of reminded me of Sigel back there."

He tried to hide his chuckle behind a cough before he looked at her. "Seriously, Briana, you might prefer the captain's protection, but I take my job seriously. If something happens to you, I won't need to worry if King Brath is going to execute me. I'd kill myself."

She didn't know whether to admonish him for the familiar use of her name, laugh at the ridiculous notion that Brath would execute him, or hug him for his loyalty to her. They had a special bond and he was one reason she knew she'd chosen correctly. As much as it hurt to decide against going home to Maine, she really did belong here, and she was happy. Well, not counting the rift between her and Brath, but maybe that would work out. Peace replaced any twinges of remaining doubt in her heart.

"Mr. Stark. I do not *prefer* Captain Aya'emrys. I did not even invite him. I had the invisibility cloak specifically to avoid *anyone* following me. He just happens to have more magic than you do. And," she glanced down at Dara, "I suspect this traitorous fellow ratted me out. I appreciate your allegiance, Mr. Stark, and in future I will promise to tell you when I am going out, but you must honor my need to be alone sometimes. I simply cannot live in an aquarium."

"A what?"

Explaining an aquarium allowed the conversation to turn away from her escape. By the time they reached Baigsith, they were chatting up a storm about the merits of archery over sword fighting.

A group of children were huddled near the chestnut tree in the middle of Baigsith, laughing and cooing at something in their midst.

"I wonder what they're up to," Briana said.

"One of the dogs has had pups," Rippa informed her. "I saw 'em this morning, before we came lookin' for youz."

Briana wandered over and the gnome children parted, giving her the opportunity to see the huddle of squirming brown and black puppies, four of them. The mother, a hound by the looks of it, gave Dara the evil eye, as she would any male dog, and moved into the midst of the puppies. No sooner had she laid down than the pups tumbled into a line at her teats, each one latching onto a nipple and sucking for all it was worth. Briana felt a tingling in her own breasts as she watched the mother nurse her young.

"These are all she had?" Briana asked one of the children.

"Yes, ma'am."

"None died?"

The child gave her a queer look. "No, ma'am, of course not."

Briana sighed. A successful birth. She continued to watch mother and puppies, feeling something shift in her.

"Captain Aya'emrys," she called to the faerie guard, who stood nearby talking to John Wells. "I need you for one more thing."

She felt Jonathan stiffen beside her. "This is just something I don't want you involved with, Mr. Stark. It is not a reflection on your capability as my first protector."

"Fine," he said. "I'm going to find breakfast."

"Save me some. I'm starving."

"Aya'emrys, I need to go get something and I want you to accompany me to the river."

She didn't wait for an answer, but ran to her room, past the enticing smells of food being set out and grabbed the pouch of herbs from her knapsack.

Racing back out, she took the path to where the gorge emptied into a wide, fast-running part of the river, impossible to cross, perfect for dissolving unnecessary herbs.

CHAPTER TWENTY-FOUR

RIVER OF LIFE

The river flowed by, serenely accepting the course of its life. No struggle. No resistance. *I wish I could do the same*, Briana thought. The bench along the river had become her daily haunt. A place to think deep thoughts, solve problems and miss Brath. She sacrificed her sorrows to the river, which accepted them as gracefully as it had the small packet of herbs she tossed in almost a month ago. *It's been more than a month since I saw him*, she thought, remembering the hurt in his eyes when he'd kissed her hand and said, "Good bye, my lady. Makerspeed."

Sunlight sparked across the water like diamond drops on glass, temporarily blinding her and preventing her from noticing that her guards, Aya'emrys and Jonathan, had moved away. The sudden smell of pine and bergamot raised the longing in her to a painful pitch. A familiar shadow set her heart hammering. She held her breath.

"May I sit with you, my lady?"

She'd forgotten how his voice sounded like fine whiskey and peat fire.

She forced herself to turn and speak calmly. "The crow didn't tell me you were coming."

"I wanted to surprise you. Actually, I didn't want to give you time to deny my need to come and grovel at your feet."

Not what I expected, she thought.

"I'm sorry, Briana. Sending you away was the stupidest thing I've ever done in my life. Will you forgive me?"

Tension drained from her shoulders, along with the breath she'd been holding.

"Only if you forgive me. I hurt you, Brath. I've been hurting you since we met and I am so, so sorry."

"We'll forgive each other, then," he said, taking her comment as permission to sit beside her. "I've done a lot of thinking since we've been apart."

"Me, too."

"I can't say I don't care if we have a child. I do, but I was wrong to dismiss your fears and uncertainty so quickly."

"I was wrong to let my fears rule me."

"Keep your herbs, Briana. Take them if you must, until you are ready to have children."

"They're gone, Brath. I threw them in there," she said, pointing to the river.

They watched the water in silence for a while, letting the current clear away the mistakes and hurt feelings of the past.

Briana was the first to speak. "Brath, I need to tell you something."

"I'm listening," he said, turning enough on the bench to take her hand.

His eyes almost undid her. So deep and green. She wanted to fall into the future she saw there. She ran her tongue across her lower lip. She had to say this right, so that he knew without a doubt that she was sincere.

"What is it, Briana? Are you okay?"

She nodded and grasped both his hands, holding them like a lifeline.

"I'm almost glad that we separated for a while. It's made me realize how much you mean to me. I've been an idiot about everything. I…" She watched hope rise in his eyes. "I love you, Brath."

His eyes became mossy pools. "You have no idea how I've longed to hear those words from you."

She forged on. "As to having a baby, I've been so stupid about this. Women have children every day. Here, like in my time, some live and some die. Call it acts of Maker, fate, or accidents of time, it doesn't matter. Life is unpredictable but that doesn't mean we shouldn't live as fully as we can with whatever circumstances we're dealt."

"I've thought a lot about your fears of getting pregnant. Your life, since arriving in Uisneach—no, since you lost your father, has been one trauma after another. Delivering that baby dead was perhaps just one more reminder of how uncertain life is."

"Maybe."

"I've also given thought to how I'd feel if, for whatever reason, we couldn't have children. I don't know how we'd carry on the Taranian legacy, but I know I wouldn't trade you in for another *brood mare*."

The last was infused with humor and they smiled at the phrase she'd used in anger.

"Briana, I've missed you so much."

She stood and stepped between his legs, settling herself in his lap. "I missed you, too," she whispered against his lips. His arms encircled her, holding her tight to his chest.

Only the loud throat-clearing of Captain Aya'emrys reminded them that they were not completely alone. Her guards remained out of hearing, not out of sight.

Hands entwined, they walked back to the cottage while he told her what had happened in Cedarmara.

"The battle at Colmer Harbor was pretty hot but ended in successful negotiations with the local government, no small thanks to your lady's maid."

"Amelia?"

"She has many connections in Colmer Harbor and convinced many of our honest intentions. Most, if not all, of the folks have agreed to support us against Shamwa. And the idea of a Parliament of Peers is really striking a chord. Firmara has already assigned a representative."

"How do you know they aren't just blowing smoke and will tell Shamwa the same thing?"

"Kieran is staying there as the emissary to the EU Council. He's worked his arse off to stay informed of everything that's happening in Cedarmara. I have full trust in him now, Briana. You were right to give him another chance."

"I'm glad to hear that. Hopefully, Sir Thomas will see it as well."

"He made a visit and I told him how trustworthy the man has been. I think he's coming around. Oh, and speaking of coming around, apparently, Sigel is making some progress. He is able to feel his legs again and is walking with help."

"That's awesome! Oh, thank Maker for small favors."

"I guess he's been a beast and Cailleach is ready to pull her hair out, but a beastly Sigel is better than a bedridden one."

Briana grimaced, imagining how difficult a man like Sigel would be through rehabilitation. "Poor Cailleach. Poor everyone at Winge Mansion."

"How are the cloaks coming?" Brath asked.

"Wait until you see. In fact, I can show you," she led him toward the production shed, built specifically for the new work of the gnomes. Brath had to duck underneath the lintel. Sunlight from many little windows fell across a long table of neatly folded invisibility cloaks.

"My goodness, there must be hundreds here!" Brath exclaimed, his eyes wide. A huge grin spreading across his face.

"Three hundred and forty-two, to be exact. As of this noontime's count."

"This will be a huge benefit to the army. We can easily sneak up on Shamwa at the place of our choosing." He put an around Briana and pulled her close to his side. "Thank you, darling. I'm sorry that it came because of difficulty between us, but you certainly came through on this."

"Not me. It was all gnome magic and elbow grease. I'm just the supervisor around here. They hardly let me do anything, but they also never let me out of their sight." *Well, except for the one time they didn't see me leave, but now is not the time to get into that.*

"Glad to hear it."

When they reached her cottage, a party was in full swing. It wasn't every day that the king of Uisneach made a visit to Baigsith. Brath and Briana were escorted to their seats at the head of the table. Kegs of ale were rolled out, steaming tureens of stew and platters of meat, vegetables and loaves of oat bread were set about the long table.

"I'm so hungry, I hardly know where to start with this feast," Briana said, even as she reached for a slice of bread.

Brath gave her an odd look, which she correctly interpreted.

"No, I'm not."

"Just wondered."

A line of knights, led by Sir Jameson Stark, filed past Briana, patting her shoulder or offering a courtly bow with a verbal expression of affection.

Lively notes floated from the corner, the young bard's effort to contribute to the party.

"Rippa, come to the table and eat. There's plenty of time for story and song after supper." Briana twirled her finger, pointing to the empty chair, which he wasted no time sliding into, hastily tucking his bare feet underneath the rungs.

She was not about to waste time scolding him for a habit he might never break, so she just shook her head and turned her attention to the roomful of people, her family. She was happy to see everyone enjoying the meal, happy to be sitting beside her husband, happy for the first time in weeks.

Brath had many questions for Captain Aya'emrys, and the faerie warrior was able to answer all of them without giving away anything of the real events of the last few weeks. Most of the king's questions to him had to do with preparing the gnomes for defense.

"Your Majesty, are we to leave in the morning?" Sir Glendon Cavanaugh asked, brushing back his perfectly coiffed strawberry-blonde hair.

"We are. You'll have to get up early, Sir Cavanaugh. No sleeping in for any of us."

Briana narrowed her eyes. "Are you telling me you just arrived and you're leaving again?"

He grasped her hand under the table. "*We're* leaving tomorrow. I'm not going anywhere without you ever again, Briana."

She was giddy with relief and gave him a grateful kiss on his cheek.

No one hurried through the meal. Candles had been lit by the time gnomes cleared away the dishes. Rippa returned to his seat near the window and picked up his fiddle again. He played a few tunes as everyone settled themselves.

"Rippa, I assume you have a story to tell about the journey from Firmara to here?"

Rippa stared helplessly at the queen who had commanded them all not to tell Brath of the battles or the bridge crossing or her wandering off to the tree.

Briana sighed. She couldn't let him lie to the king's face. She waved a hand at him nonchalantly. "Tell your story, Rippa, all but my trip to the forest. I'll tell His Majesty that story later."

Brath looked at her questioningly.

"Later," she repeated. "Go on, Rippa, it's okay."

"Still can't get shoes on him?" Brath whispered in her ear.

"I've given up."

Rippa's tale of the two battles, falling into the gorge, being saved by Aya'emrys and the death of a herd of Gray Military soldiers, brought looks of respect and loud clapping from the knights. Brath wasn't as enthusiastic. He'd gone pale halfway through the telling, his jaw set and eyes dark. He said nothing, which seemed worse than if he'd scolded her outright.

Briana wondered what he'd say behind closed doors. She didn't have to wait long as knights, gnomes and faeries pleaded fatigue.

Aya'emrys confirmed that he would have the faerie warriors ready at daylight and put a hand on Jonathan's shoulder. "Come along, Squire Stark. I believe the king can protect your queen tonight."

Briana nodded. "Get a good night's sleep, Mr. Stark."

Genevieve, the last to leave, bobbled over. "Is there anything else you need? No? Good. I've smoored the fire. Go on up when ye wish, you'll not be bothered tonight. Good night."

"Oh, one minute, Genevieve. I have something for you." She reached into her pocket. When she held her palm out to the gnome, it held a single seed. "When you feel the magic return, and it will, plant this faerie tree here in Baigsith."

"Aye, lass, I'll do it," Genevieve said, tucking the precious seed into a little bag on the waist of her dress before leaving her and Brath alone.

Briana drank the last sip of ale in her cup and looked at her husband. "Are you tired?"

He pushed a lock of hair behind her ear. "Not too tired to hear the story of the forest adventure, but let's go up and you can tell me in bed."

Oh, this is so not a bedtime story, she thought, fearing how he might take it. "Maybe we should save it for tomorrow?"

He stood and taking her hand, pulled her up with him. "I'll hear it tonight and I won't bother scolding you. It can't possibly be any worse than what I've heard already." They were heading up the stairs when Dara bounded past them. "Besides, I have a confession of my own to make."

"Oh?"

"I wasn't entirely forthcoming with you. There's the little matter of being abducted by Shamwa supporters and held captive on a boat for twenty-four hours."

"What! You didn't think that was important to tell me?"

He paused on the step and leaned against the wall, giving her a wry smile. "Really, Briana, after what you've withheld, you're going to reprimand me? What say we call it even?"

She flushed. "Okay, then. Even."

They undressed quietly. Briana turned the bed down, nearly tripping over Dara, who was snoring soundly despite their chatter while Brath placed their swords against a chair within easy reach. She slid under the quilt, scooching next to the wall while he worked his tall frame into the not very long bed.

"Tight fit," he remarked.

"I don't mind," she said as she squirmed into the arm he was sliding around her.

"Nor do I. Now, tell me about the tree."

"The short telling is that I used an invisibility cloak to sneak off by myself. I was feeling smothered and I needed to be alone to just deal with things."

He squeezed her shoulder.

"I ended up at the tree."

"What tree?"

"*The* tree. The one I came through. And the door was there."

His arm convulsed, but he remained quiet.

"I knew if I just opened the door, I'd be in Maine with my mother."

Though she hadn't spoken his name, Silas loomed between them.

"I *wanted* to stay here. I wanted to work this out between us. I wanted to tell you I love you and that I wanted us to have a baby."

She felt his shudder as he rolled on his side to face her. He kissed her. Long and deep until she had to pull away for breath.

"Thank you, Briana. I thank you with all my heart."

They held each other, quiet, coming to terms with the past, readying themselves for the future.

"Why don't you tell me about your abduction," she said, content for the moment to lie in his arms and listen to his voice. He told her how a dozen men snuck into camp and were able to lead his guards in one direction while four others crawled under the tent and overpowered him, dragging him off to a boat, which they then sailed out of the harbor. "Their entire goal was to hold me ransom; they needed the money to pay taxes to Shamwa. I don't get it. They'd rather fight the man who can release them from the burden of the taxes instead of joining him to eliminate the man forcing the taxes."

"Who saved you?"

"I did. I talked them out of it. You know, using my great diplomatic gift and natural charm."

"Charm? I didn't think you were too charming when you sent me packing."

"I was an ass, Briana. I am so sorry. I should have kept you with me, though all things considered, you've been relatively safe. How can I make it up to you?"

She slid her foot up his leg and let her fingers curl in the hair on his abdomen. "I have a few ideas."

❧

Briana took Nua from Brath and slid her into the scabbard, though the baldric wasn't yet secured to her person. "Come on, Dara, breakfast first. I'm starving." The wolfhound raced down the stairs as his mistress and her husband followed. Her reflection in the mirror caused Briana to stumble. She would've fallen had Brath not caught her by the waist.

"Look, Brath. This is the Mirror of Truth."

Both their reflections were there, but instead of the lean, warrior queen that was ready for breakfast, a full-cheeked and full-bellied queen looked back.

She saw tears in his eyes. His arms encircled her, which in the mirror, encompassed their unborn child. "I am a blessed man."

"I guess we can stop worrying about whether or not I'll get pregnant. The mirror doesn't lie."

CHAPTER TWENTY-FIVE

MOONLIGHT MADNESS

riana listened to the morning briefing with half an ear while she marveled at how well things had come together in the past three months with this raggle-taggle group of what Brath finally referred to as staff, instead of servants. It had been a huge effort to change his habit, but he finally got the hang of honoring her wish to dignify their work.

Hearty fires blazed in the hearths and braziers, creating a cozy barrier against the drizzling rain outside. Through the window of their chambers, Briana watched Fire Falls stream down through filmy fog, a mere blue-gray ribbon without the sun to turn it into liquid fire. Mr. Pogue kept mugs filled with tea and cleared away the remnants of Mrs. Pogue's bannock and bacon breakfast. She forced her attention back to the discussion at hand.

Brath turned to Kieran. "This plan puts Cedarmara at risk, but I see no other way to clear the way to Aurum Castle."

"This is the best way," Kieran agreed. "We have close to five thousand soldiers now, Your Highness. We have supplies, the cloaks and plenty of equipment to defend Cedarmara and launch the offensive in Dromdara.

"Once there, we hide in the forest and begin tunneling toward the castle. Even with the man power, it will take some time, but within a few weeks, I believe we can surprise the prime minister in his own lair.

"I'll get word to Shamwa today that all your troops are here in Firmara. Although he won't likely leave the castle himself, he'll send his Grays here. Tonight's gala is the perfect ruse to make him believe you're hunkered down.

While the party is underway, we can spirit you and the queen out of here and on your way to Dromdara. I estimate that we'll have three days from the time I get word to Shamwa until Cedarmara is crawling with his troops."

Something about the tunneling plan bothered Briana, even though it had been her idea. Her knowledge of modern warfare had come in handy on more than one occasion. However, a prick of uncertainty wouldn't leave her alone.

"I don't understand why we don't just leave now. Why do we need to be at the gala at all?" she asked.

Brath answered, "Because if there are any spies in our midst, we want them to see us here. We'll leave the celebration wearing invisibility cloaks, so that no one knows we've left or where we're headed. I'm not convinced, though, that having you at Aurum Castle is safe or useful. I'm leaning toward sheltering you in Tynan Ibor."

Briana jaw clenched with the effort to hold her tongue. He had told her he wouldn't leave her behind again and already he was waffling on that promise. They would talk about this later.

"And we're absolutely certain that the majority, if not all, of Cedarmara is going to back us?" Brath asked.

Kieran nodded toward Briana. "According to your lady's maid, Cedarmara now understands which side of the bread is buttered and will support King Brath."

With no other suggestions or arguments forthcoming, Brath made a final decision. "Okay, Kieran, get the message to Shamwa. Briana, carry on with tonight's plans as though nothing is out of the ordinary, but pack a bag. Sir Stark, you'll meet discreetly with your men to determine who stays in Firmara and who rides to Dromdara. Captain Aya'emrys, I would have you with your tuathla." He glanced at Briana. "Wherever she may be."

Well, that's good. Doesn't sound like my being left off somewhere is set in stone, Briana thought with some relief.

"Pardon, Your Majesty, but there is a courier from the Governor's mansion to see you and the queen," the butler said, from the doorway.

"Thank you, Pogue. Have him meet us in the great hall."

"Anything else, gentleman?" he asked. All heads wagged in the negative. He turned to Briana. "My lady? Any further concerns?"

Not to be discussed here, she thought, but shook her head.

"Good. Then let's you and I see what the governor wants with us."

The messenger, a young, sharply dressed lad, sat at on one of the benches, staring around the great hall in awe. He jumped when the king addressed him.

"What message has Governor Llewellyn for us?"

"Aye, sir, yes, sir. He asks for the aid of the queen."

His eyes flittered around the room and his ability to deliver his message seemed to be waning with each moment in the castle. Briana had to prompt him.

"How can I help?"

"It's his son, ma'am. He's very ill, near to death. Governor Llewellyn has heard you're a healer and wonders if you would come and see him. The local healer has already been tried, but the boy is worsening by the minute. The governor is desperate, he is. Will you come with me?"

"Of course," Briana said. "Give me a few moments to gather some things and alert my staff. Wait here. Amelia," she said to the young woman who seemed to appear out of nowhere, "could you please bring my cloak."

"I'll go with you," Brath said.

"Great. Maybe you can distract Llewellyn while I tend to the boy."

The king, queen and a few knights arrived at the mansion, no worse for the weather, and were led immediately to a room where the governor sat beside a boy Briana gauged to be about six years old. Drawn curtains made the room dark. Briana asked Brath to pull them so she could see the boy more clearly.

He lay in listless pallor in a bed that practically swallowed him. A sheen of sweat dotted his forehead and his eyes were closed. Wheezing alternated between a tight cough and an occasional moan.

"What is his name?" she asked the governor quietly.

"Cedric. Please, your Highness, can you heal him?"

"Cedric?" She eased down on the edge of the bed and attempted to rouse him rather than answer the question. The boy's eyelashes fluttered open. "Do you hurt anywhere?"

"All over," he replied weakly, shivering a little with the effort.

She felt his forehead. He was feverish. She felt his pulse. It was barreling along. "I want to have a listen to your chest." She pushed aside the front of his nightshirt and lay her head against his ribby frame for a few seconds. "Does your chest hurt?"

"Aye, sometimes. It's a sharp pain when I breathe."

In her time, pneumonia was relatively easy to manage with antibiotics. In Uisneach, she imagined it could be deadly. However, the treatment would be the same.

"Make sure he drinks water or broth. Preferably both. Peppermint tea would be good to ease his lungs and raise the mucous." She reached in the little travel bag of remedies she had taken to carrying on visits. She handed a packet to the woman standing quietly nearby, who she assumed was the boy's nanny. "A little willow bark tea might help him feel more comfortable. Besides that, just let him rest. No need to keep it dark in here. Sunshine and fresh air will work their own magic. He'll recover in a week or two."

The young woman nodded. "Yes, ma'am. Thank you, ma'am."

"Are you sure?" Governor Llewellyn asked, wringing his hands.

"He's got a respiratory infection. Pneumonia. A lung illness. He'll get better if he stays hydrated. I mean, as long as he drinks plenty of fluids. And he does need to rest and let this work out of his system." She addressed the nanny. "He'll feel better if you give him a wash; get some of the sweat off him and change the sheets every day if he's feverish."

Briana closed her bag. "Cedric?"

He opened one eye at her voice.

"You're a strong lad and you're going to get better very soon. You have to drink, though, even if you don't feel thirsty. Promise to do that?"

He gave a feeble nod and closed his eye again.

Outside the room, the governor took her free hand inside his big hands. "I can't thank you enough, Your Majesty. His mother died giving birth to him and he is all I have. I don't know what I'd do without my Cedric."

Briana squashed a tremor of anxiety at the mention of a maternal death. She leaned into the hand that Brath placed on her lower back in a gesture of understanding and comfort.

"You're most welcome, Governor. I hope you're still coming to the party tonight."

"Oh, I'm not sure that I could leave Cedric for an evening."

"Well, of course you must decide what's best for your family, but I promise the boy will recover from this." *At least I hope he will.*

"There's a bit more to this than just a party, Governor," Brath said. "Is there somewhere we can talk privately?"

They were ushered into the governor's office and when they left an hour later, Governor Llewellyn, now thoroughly apprised of the plan, committed to coming to the gala. Brath had promised a detail of warriors to guard the mansion if the Gray Military showed up. The Governor's worry was for his son, who would be too ill to travel to safety. It was a concession that wasn't really a concession at all, since Brath had already planned on protecting the castle and the mansion at Firmara.

⤸

A hurried knock and the door to Brath and Briana's room opened. Amelia burst in and rushed to Briana's side, tripping on the carpet edge and nearly knocking Briana over as she fell into her.

"Sorry. Sorry, I'm late."

"Amelia, if you sorry me once more, I'll, I'll, I'll send you to the kitchen." The lady's maid screwed up her face. "Why the kitchen?"

"I don't know," Briana said, with a fair amount of exasperation. "So, Mrs. Pogue can deal with you, I guess."

"That makes no sense."

"Amelia, can you just tend to this corset, please? We've guests arriving in less than an hour and *I* certainly don't want to be late. Do you know where Brath went?"

"He's downstairs, meeting with Sir Stark."

"I'm right here," the man himself said, coming through the door. "Did you need me, Briana?"

"I always need you, but at the moment, I *think* I have help." She turned halfway around to give Amelia a vexed look. "Ouch! Are you trying to kill me?"

Amelia stamped her foot. "Aye, I am, so the castle will be minus a queen… again." She stepped away from Briana and headed to the door. "I'll just go on to the kitchen, where I'm appreciated."

"Wait, Amelia. I'm not hooked up here!"

Using two fingers, the maid drew a little spiral in the air above her head. Briana felt the hooks attach snugly behind her.

Briana growled as the door shut behind Amelia. "I swear, I don't know what I did to deserve such a contrary maid. And it's not fair that she has more magic than I do."

Brath watched his wife with an amused smile. "She is different."

"Different? She's a wretch." Briana started laughing. "But she's my wretch and I couldn't do without her. And how is it that with magic waning across the kingdom, she seems to have more magic than either Cailleach or me? It's effortless for her."

"Are you nervous about tonight?" Brath asked, grinning.

"A bit. We've been back three months, and this is the first time we've opened the castle for the public. Will they think we're slackers?"

"Not sure what a slacker is, but I believe they'll understand that we've had a lot to do, getting the castle in entertaining order and securing the loyalty of the region. And by the way, might I remind you that Amelia's contribution to that effort at Colmer Harbor was not insignificant. She may be eccentric, but her letter to her family did help quite a bit."

He was right. Amelia's three uncles made it clear that if she felt inclined to back King Brath and Queen Briana, they would do likewise. Their support seeped through the rest of northern Cedarmara and, as if by magic, all of Cedarmara was on their side.

Briana slipped the rose and gold gown over her undergarments and smoothed out the satiny fabric. "How do I look?"

Brath looked her over with a critical eye.

"Hey, it shouldn't be that difficult to answer."

He erased the space between them in two steps and pulled her into his embrace. After a tender kiss he held her away a few inches. "You look beautiful and I am so proud to be your husband."

She gave a half-hearted smile and stepped away.

"What's wrong?"

"Nothing," she said, not looking at him. She turned to reach for the tiny flask of scented oil on her dressing table, but a sharp pain turned interrupted the task. She pressed a hand to her belly with a grimace.

"Your cycle started?"

She looked at him sideways. "Yes. I'm sorry. I don't know why I'm not getting pregnant."

"It's okay, love. When it's meant to be, it will happen. I—"

A knock at the door ended the conversation.

"Come in," Brath invited. "Can we talk about this later?" he said to Briana.

She shook her head. "No need."

A crow warrior, impeccably dressed in black formal wear, stepped in. "King Brath, I bring a message from Winge Mansion."

Anticipation flooded through Briana. *Oh, please let it be good news.*

"Sire, I am to advise you that Lord Marshall Sigel is fully recovered and is on his way here."

"That's wonderful news!" Briana exclaimed.

Brath groaned.

"What?" Briana was surprised by his lack of enthusiasm.

"It's great that he's well, but he should not come *here*, Briana."

"Oh, right." They would not be here.

"Please, take word back to the lord marshall that he should meet us in Moiria in three day's time."

Music and dancing were already underway when the king and queen entered the great hall. Everything and everyone stopped as the couple was introduced, and Briana felt no small amount of relief at the resounding applause that met their entrance. It could have gone the other way. Their efforts to secure the alliance had been worth the effort. As Brath had said some time ago, trust had to be built from the inside, from the ground up. She glanced at him and felt herself filled with pride. He was handsome, smart and most importantly, kind. No wonder the people found him easy to follow. Once they understood his commitment and concern for them, it was impossible not to respond in kind.

They were seated upon the Firmara thrones and the music began again. Dara, who had faithfully followed them in, found a spot he approved of, curled twice and lay down.

Briana looked around the room. She'd seen the staff making the hall ready for the event, so wasn't surprised by the tapestries that had been dug up from trunks in the cellar, dusted off and hung around the hall, each one telling a story of Cedarmara's history. Arrangements of evergreens and holly bushes were her idea and she liked the effect of bringing the outside in. What made her breath catch was the sight of so many men and women dressed in their finest suits and gowns, dancing and chatting under glowing candle chandeliers. Adding to the magic was the smell of balsam in the braziers, tables of food and spirits and the sound of musicians, including Rippa, playing on a small stage set up for the occasion. Her eyes cast downward at Rippa's feet. Shoes on. *Good lad!*

"I'm pleased to see so many people turn out for this," Brath said beside her. His expression did not radiate the same emotion. He seemed disturbed or distracted.

"You'll have to work a bit on your smile to convince anyone of that. What's bothering you, Brath?"

He shook his head. "If the Gray Military attacks, these good people would be at risk. I hope we haven't made an error in judgment by holding the ball."

She saw his point, but everyone on the team believed this was a risk worth taking to throw Shamwa off-track. Part of her wished Shamwa himself would show up. She'd give anything to have the chance to connect with the Dar Morch.

Their worries were curtailed by the suggestion that the king and queen lead a dance. Rippa, a harpist and a young lad with a lute-like instrument struck a chord and began to sing a love song. Brath took her in his arms and whirled her around the dance floor. It was the first time they'd danced since their wedding and she was once again reminded of what a smooth dancer he was, and tickled by the fact that it had been Sigel who taught him to dance.

"You're thinking of Sigel."

"You're reading my mind now?"

"You get this funny grin on your face whenever you're thinking of him. That, and I know you are probably remembering him as my dancing tutor."

She laughed. "I would love to have seen those lessons."

"I wonder where Dara is going?" Brath asked as the hound brushed past them and out the door of the great hall.

"Who knows? Probably he has to pee."

They held each other and finished the music in simple enjoyment of the dance. When the music ended, he loosened his grip. A second song started immediately.

"Sire, may I have the privilege of dancing with your lovely wife?" It was the governor. From his arms she was passed to Kieran Winge, Sir Stark and many other guests. Brath danced with a few of the wives present, but mostly engaged in short conversations with the governor, the knights and other members of the court. After nearly an hour, Briana wanted a break.

"Brath, I need some air." She was already heading toward the open door to the balcony.

He was right behind her. "Wait a minute, Briana. I want to go out with…"

"Your Majesty, I need to talk with you," Kieran Winge interrupted.

"Briana, please wait."

"I'm just stepping out for air," she said, laughing off his overly concerned tone.

The autumn air dried the sweat on her neck and face in seconds. She drank in the pine scent, grateful for the rare moment of solitude. Sounds of celebration drifted out from the hall. She smiled, even though she knew the joyful noise was a façade meant to trick Shamwa. *We're faking it until we make it to being a truly carefree Uisneach*, she thought. Shamwa would be in for a surprise when they dug a tunnel right under his nose and into his home.

Suddenly, she felt as though ants were crawling all over her. The breeze stopped abruptly, and the moonlight darkened a shade. She looked up to see the light half of the moon covered by half of Shamwa's face. She could just make out his features darkened in the other half. The eye in the light burned red. His lips curled back in a mock smile. She shuddered. The thud of something heavy drew her attention to the balcony's balustrade. She leaned over to investigate. Whatever it was, it didn't bode well for her and she turned away. "Brath!" Her words were smothered by a hand over her mouth and a band-like arm around her torso that pinned her arms and secured her to a large, broad and soaking-wet chest.

CHAPTER TWENTY-SIX

HUNTER OR HUNTED?

Fury that the security of Firmara had been breached and that this goon was getting her gown all wet launched Briana into action. "Ay... cmm... n... wsomn... prr... fff... trula," she mumbled the magical words through the rancid-smelling hand smothering her, followed by a hefty stomp on his foot. The soldier yowled but did not loosen his grip. She bit down on his hand. That worked the first time she'd been kidnapped, but this dude was apparently much tougher. The sound of celebration in the great hall covered the muffled sounds of the struggle between Briana and her assailants. Her stomach jolted in sudden anxiety as a third body pressed against her. How had they scaled the wall to the balcony? Ropes? Ladder? Sandalwood scented the night air and Briana felt a surge of power course through her.

Thank you, Maker, she thought as she tensed her arms next to her body and then forced them apart with enough faerie strength to break the soldier's hold on her. She jumped forward and whirled around with a powerful kick to the man's gonads, dropping him. Not sparing a second, she flung her finger forward toward the other two men. Flames erupted in a straight line at them, sparking their coats on fire. They howled in fear and danced away from her, furiously beating out the flames. But Briana had only begun.

"I am so sick of this!" She advanced on them like an angel of death, one arm cocking to release a superhuman jab at the jaw of one, snapping his head back with an audible crunch. Simultaneously, she whirled and kicked a slippered foot into the middle of the chest of the other. Both men fell dead at her feet. Turning back to the man she kicked in the groin, she grabbed his head in-between her hands and closing her eyes, gave a mighty jerk, ending his breath. In the glimmer of Fire Falls, she saw yet another man making his way over the balcony wall. She sighed regretfully. "Hate to do this, bud, but…" She flexed her wrist and with the flat of her hand butted the man's forehead with force enough to send him flying down from whence he came with a heavy thud. She leaned over to check for more attackers, but the string of soldiers seemed to have ended at four. The herbal smell, and her powers, receded, and a feeling of emptiness filled her. She turned, meaning to find Brath and tell him what happened, only to see him standing at the balcony door, his mouth hanging open, his eyes wide as saucers. Beside him, Aya'emrys grinned, making him appear more human than faerie warrior.

"Thanks for the help," she said, breathless.

"Sweetheart, I think I would have only been in your way," Brath said quietly with a look of anxious admiration in his eyes.

"I'm okay."

"Yes, I see that." He sucked in his breath and took the few steps that separated them. Wrapping her in his arms, he whispered against her ear. "Amelia has nothing on you in full tuathla power."

"It does seem as though I'm getting stronger, but Brath, I think I need to sit down." She took one final look at the mayhem on the balcony. "I really hate having to kill people," she thought out loud.

"I know, love." Brath led her to a seat inside the hall where others, now aware that something had happened, were gathering. "Only a few minutes, Bri. We need to leave."

She nodded. "Just give me a second." While she was collecting herself, he started giving orders.

"Mr. Stark, stay with the queen. Captain Aya'emrys, send your warriors to scout the perimeter of the castle and take care of any other Grays out there. Kieran, have an escort get Governor Llewellyn home safely. Send half your troops to the village and find any of Shamwa's men that might be creating a problem there."

"The other half?" Kieran asked.

"Our escort to Druid's Grove."

The young Winge commander responded with a clipped nod and left to carry out his orders.

"I'll have the horses readied," Sir Stark said, already anticipating the role of the knights in getting the king and queen to safety.

"I'll be right back, Briana. I want to have a word with Governor Llewellyn before they take him. Don't move." He kissed the top of her head before striding away to take care of these last-minute details.

She began taking deep breaths until she felt herself grounded again. "Mr. Stark, I need to change my clothes. I'm going upstairs."

She didn't wait for a response but headed out of the hall to the staircase and raced up its curve to her suite, Jonathan Stark and Dara trailing after her. She entered the room and her eyebrows shot up when Amelia came toward her with an armful of invisibility cloaks. *How did she know?*

"I thought you might want these," she said, tripping on the edge of the carpet, sending the cloaks fluttering into space before landing in a heap at Briana's feet.

"Well, yes, we do need them," Briana said, choking back a laugh. She helped retrieve the jumbled cloaks.

"Sorry, Your Majesty. I'm not terribly graceful, you know."

Briana instantly felt bad that she'd even been tempted to laugh, but when she caught Amelia's eye, the lady's maid was grinning at her own clumsiness.

At least she can laugh at herself, Briana thought, as she helped Amelia and Jonathan refold the garments. "Grace may not be your strong suit, but your intuition and magic are off the charts," Briana said aiming to bolster the girl's confidence.

"Thank you, ma'am."

"Please excuse us, Jonathan."

He looked uncertain. "King Brath said I should stay with you."

"Oh, okay, but I'm changing my clothes."

He went scarlet and looked between her and the door. "I'll be right outside. Please yell if something happens."

"You have my word, Mr. Stark."

When the door was shut behind the young man, Briana engaged Amelia in the task of outfitting her for a swift journey on horseback into the night forests of Cedarmara.

Amelia was just securing the buckle on the baldric that crossed Briana from shoulder to hip and protected Nua, when Brath walked in.

He paused, his eyes sweeping over her tunic, vest and trouser-clad body.

"What's the word you use for a man you think is attractive?"

"Hot?"

"That's the one. You, my lady, are totally hot. But didn't I tell you not to move?"

He wasn't mad and his joking relaxed her into a giggle. "Too bad we need to be on our way."

"Too bad, indeed. However, we do. Ready?"

"Yup! Lead the way, Your Majesty." She turned to a goofily grinning Amelia. "Hold the fort, would you Amelia? You are the one person I trust with the ability to do so."

The lady's maid's grin disappeared as her eyes flared in surprise and pride. "Yes, Queen Briana. I will do whatever it takes to protect Firmara."

Briana took one long last look at the room where, in some ways, she had truly become Queen of Uisneach. Maps that she'd poured over with Brath and the knights remained spread across the table, a ríocht board that Brath had crafted out of local sandstone from Fire Falls still sat in mid-play. The massive bed where she and Brath had made up for their time apart sparked a heat in her belly. She loved the palace at Firmara and had grown fond of the staff and the villagers. *Maker, please keep everyone safe here*, she prayed before tilting her head at Dara and Jonathan and followed her husband out to the waiting horses.

⋘

Briana yawned for the fifth time. "I must be getting old."

Brath looked at his wife in the rose-tinted light of dawn. "Why do you say that?"

"I used to be able to stay up for days on end when I first came to Uisneach. I hardly ever had a full night's sleep on the road. I've gotten too soft at Ard Darach and Firmara."

Brath looked at her oddly. "Briana you've only aged by six months. That's hardly put you into the elderly category."

"Six months?" She counted back on her fingers and looked at Brath, her mouth dropping open. "I've lived an entire lifetime in half a year? I've gone from having no boyfriend to wondering why I'm not pregnant. That's crazy!"

"I'd like to say that things will calm down, but I doubt that will be true any time soon." He turned Ruark closer to Banrion, who huffed indignantly at the stallion's intrusion into her personal space. He scrutinized his wife's face, particularly her eyes. "You have been through a lot, darling. I worry about you sometimes. You're so young to have to endure this much change in so short a time."

One side of Briana's mouth lifted mockingly. "And you, my ancient husband, haven't?"

He touched her hand and smiled. "I'm used to changes. And I'm a man."

Her mocking grin changed to open-mouthed indignation. She narrowed her eyes. "Do you know what a male chauvinist is?"

He laughed. "I can guess."

"Sire," Sir Stark called back from the front of the line. "We've reached Druid's Grove."

The sun was just coming up, casting magical colors over the open glade. The moss-caped gray humps that once startled her stood in the same position they had when she mistook them for people. She breathed a sigh of relief which lasted approximately two seconds before her eyes filled with the image she had dreaded. As though it were only yesterday, the sunlit glade filled with mist and a blonde-haired archer emerged with catlike grace into the center, his rose, brown and gray kilt swinging casually against his leg, his booted feet barely making a dent in the earth. His quiver, minus the one arrow that had impaled her attacker and freed her, hung carelessly from his shoulder. She had dreamed of him for so long and here he was, with a face more beautiful than any she could have imagined.

"Briana?"

Brath's voice broke the trance. She sucked in her breath and turned to her husband.

"Are you all right?"

She gulped and nodded. A second wave of relief washed over her when she glanced back to find only the misty glen. She was the last to dismount, needing a moment to let the tumultuous feelings from the vision resolve. Brath took her hand and they walked together to the druid stones. As she got closer to them, nausea rose in her stomach and her knees wobbled. Breathing deeply failed to dispel her anxiety. She looked around at the forest surrounding the glen but saw nothing out of the ordinary. As much as she hated to be a Nervous Nelly, her companions needed to know something was amiss.

"Brath, I feel something here, something that doesn't feel good."

Every hand, including hers, went to their swords.

"What is it, Briana?"

"I don't know, but it's spooky as hell."

A tremble travelled up through the ground and through her legs. Looking around the group, she asked, "Do you feel that shaking?"

As they all shook their heads, she felt herself grow weaker and more unsteady. She moved closer to the stones and put a hand upon one to rest. Nausea turned to a full-forced need to vomit. Her knees gave out and she saw Brath reach for her just as she felt herself slipping away. "Brath, help me!"

⁓

She woke to total darkness and dank, musty cold. *Like a cellar*, she thought. *Where am I?* The foul taste in her mouth clued her that she *had* vomited about the same time as her fingers slipped in something wet and vile.

"Gross," she muttered, wiping her hand on her pant leg and her mouth on the sleeve of her tunic. "Deep breath," she coached herself, trying to ignore the scurrying, scratching sounds in the dark.

Her ring was still on. She said the words that would raise her power. Seconds later the smell of sandalwood covered that of her stomach contents and she focused on mentally calling up light. Her fingers became the glowing candles by which she could see her surroundings. Gray, furry critters scrambled for cover as the room lit in an emerald-hued circle.

"I knew it!" she exclaimed as she took in the obscene cache of wine casks, dried food, furniture, metal crafts and chests. Standing in full strength, she lifted the lid on one of the chests to find it chock-a-block full of coins. She growled as chest after chest revealed the wealth of Uisneach's people stockpiled in Shamwa's—whatever this was. She bit her lip. *I think I'm in the cellar of Aurum Castle! The druid stones must have acted as a portal to bring me here. But, why? And why now, and not the first time I encountered the stones?* The answer that made the most sense was that she wasn't infused with magic before. Whatever the mechanics, she was here and would take advantage of the opportunity to gain information about Shamwa's status and strategy. Time to explore. Her anger grew as she found farm equipment, horse tack, spinning wheels, pots and pans, anything her people could give him to meet the tax burden. *He's robbing them blind!* Directing her finger around the room, she found stairs. *Ready for Round Two, Shamwa? I'm coming for ya and when I'm done, this stuff is all going back where it belongs!*

Ignoring Brath's warning voice in her head, she headed up the stairs. Halfway up, she paused and chuckled. *This is where I tell the protagonist to take off her shoes and stop making so much noise. Luckily, my boots don't make noise.* She chided herself for the flippancy. If she wasn't careful, she could end up another victim of Shamwa's cruel vengeance. The thought tripped her heart rate up a notch. A heavy black latch secured the door at the top of the stairs. *Lights out,* she instructed her fingers, hiding herself in darkness once again.

Slowly, she lifted the handle up and eased the door open a crack. Pressing her ear against the opening, she listened for sounds outside the door. Hearing nothing, she took a breath and pushed the door open enough to slide through. Heart pounding, she slid through the open space and carefully closed the door behind her. A sharp *click* made her cringe. She reached for Nua but came up empty-handed. *Great, I have no weapon,* she thought. Finding one became her top priority.

"You'd best not muck that bread up," a woman's voice warned. "His Lordship will have your head."

"I never made a loaf that wasn't to 'is likin'," a huskier voice replied cockily. "Just you tend to the eggs and we'll both keep our heads."

Briana tiptoed around the corner to find herself in a vast kitchen. In the cavernous fireplace, a large turkey spun on a chain and a pot bubbled with something savory. Two women stood with their backs to her over a table preparing their respective dishes, unaware of her presence. Scanning the room, she saw an open door leading out of the kitchen. She slid against the wall soundlessly until she reached the door.

"Mayhap we should add a bit of a surprise to his eggies," the one said quietly.

The other made a shushing noise. "You best mind your tongue, Miniver. What if His Lordship heard you?"

Talking ceased abruptly and Briana choked on her breath, thinking they'd seen her. But they went on with their chatter and she slipped out of the room into a hallway.

Looking both ways and finding nothing, she acted on pure instinct. *Damn, what I wouldn't give for an invisibility cloak. Where's Dumbledore when you need him?* She kept close to the wall and when footsteps sounded behind her, she raced on her toes to the nearest door and opened it, praying to Maker that no one would be on the other side. She was just in time as she heard steady, firm steps walk past. For all she knew, it could be Shamwa. A huge bed draped in red and gold velvet and brocade took up half the room, its canopy soaring nearly to the vaulted ceilings. Gilded braziers burned on each wall, which could explain the sweat popping out on her forehead. A table was set with a gold decanter and goblet. Everywhere she looked, gold! Even the crystal ball sat on a gold filigreed base of gaudy flowers. Crystal ball? Why would Shamwa, who didn't believe in magic, have a crystal ball? A carved oak chair, more like a throne, graced a corner with ermine mantles slung over the backs. The opulence sickened her.

"You can pretend to be king all you want, Shamwa," she whispered, "but it ain't ever gonna happen. You are nothing but a crude, egotistical thug!" Being in his bedroom made her queasy, so she hurried out.

Back in the long hallway, she considered her options. There was no clear indication which door led to the salon, where she knew there were items she could use as weapons. She saw two elegantly dressed servants come toward her.

Damn! She was caught! The back of her mind took curious notice that they did not react and in fact, never changed pace or expression as they got closer. They seemed almost like zombies. The front of her mind panicked and she opened the first door she reached.

She slipped in, intending to barricade herself inside, but before she could even locate something movable, she heard them pass by. *Like they didn't even see me.* How was that possible? When her pulse and breathing slowed and she could assess her surroundings, she smiled. She knew where she was. It was the room Artanin had brought her to when they'd kidnapped her. Which meant two things. The first was a sickening awareness that she and Shamwa had been sleeping right next door to each other. Goosebumps raised on her skin. *He could have come in and raped me any time he wanted.* The other thing that dawned on her was that she knew how to get to the salon. Wasting no time, she cracked the door open and listened for activity. None. She made it nearly to the end of the hall before a dog barked and someone commanded it to shut up!

What the heck? She never saw a dog or any other pet here. So many mysteries to solve, but finding a good hiding place trumped them all. Briana tried to open the door to her left. It wouldn't budge. She had to heft herself against it before it even opened a crack. The sharp voice grew louder. Briana stumbled into the room and closed the door quickly behind her. Directly in front of her stood a long, wooden table with metal handcuffs and stained leather straps. *Is that blood?* She edged closer for a look and a sniff. Yes, it was blood. Human or otherwise, she had no idea. Along the wall were chains, thumbscrews and a metal mask with screws hanging from the eye sockets. Dried bits of something she didn't want to consider plastered the wall behind the torture instruments. The place smelled rancorous. It was enough to make her veins freeze. Her eyes narrowed with another thought.

For Maker's sake, if they can make this, they can make armor! She searched the room until she found a weapon, a knife. She grabbed it but groaned when she felt the edge and knew it wouldn't cut butter. As many tools of torture as this room held, it was ridiculous that she couldn't find a sharp knife. Maybe she could rely on magic. *But I'd feel a whole lot better having something heavy or sharp in my hand.*

She was in a bad position. Her anger thermometer rose steeply. Boldly, she flung open the door and walked into the hall, heading for the salon. On the way, she realized she had two choices. She could try to reach the garden and hopefully a route of escape, or she could find a weapon, find Shamwa, and end him. She was inclined toward the latter—until she heard footsteps behind her. Intuition and the hair raising on her arms told her it was him. Fear doused her bravado. She needed to find a way to protect herself. She wasn't far from the salon. She could make it. Taking off at a sprint, she rounded a corner and made it to the door. With a little luck, he hadn't seen or heard her. Shutting the door, irritated that there was no lock on the inside, she went for the window. Using both hands, she heaved against the sash. It wouldn't budge. She grounded herself and whispered, "I call on the wisdom and power of the tuathla." She tried again, but the window would not even crack.

Unexpected chortling whipped her around. The same shawl-wrapped creature who helped her escape last time was now mocking her with the eyes of the witch she'd thought was dead. "Ealga!"

The gnomish figure shrugged and cackled in response. Cailleach had been right to worry that Ealga somehow lived on. "Not for long, you hypocritical bitch," Briana swore.

Bootsteps sounded closer. Briana swept the room for a weapon. Like manna from heaven, she saw a bejeweled box sitting on the desk, an ornate gold key beside it. Next to the box lay an emerald-handled dagger. Her eyes narrowed suspiciously. It could be a trick. However, nothing ventured, nothing gained. "Tuathla powers protect me," she whispered, as she grabbed the box and key in one hand and the knife in the other.

For a moment she saw fear flick across the gnome's eyes. Steeling herself with the reminder that the gnome was only kept alive by an evil spirit that needed to be fully dead, she thrust the dagger into the space between the creature's eyes. Her shoulder protested as metal struck bone, but she pulled out the weapon and drove it in again, into the gnome's chest. A spindly whine escaped her. Briana doubted Shamwa could have heard it. What was left of the host shrank into a lifeless pile as a vapor, probably Ealga's spirit, rose. With the athletic prowess of a Red Sox outfielder, she leaped into the air and caught the vapor in the box. Slamming it shut, she locked the box and thrust it and the key into her baldric. She searched for a hiding place, but there was nowhere he wouldn't find her. She held the dagger before her and called upon all the power she possessed as the door was flung open and Lord Shamwa filled the doorway. Even in this state of urgency, she still responded to the sight of his Herculean body, blue eyes and honey-blonde hair. *Damn! Someone so evil just shouldn't be so sexy.* She banished the thought, just as she had the first time they'd met. He might be gorgeous on the outside, but his soul was the sort of ugly that went straight down to the bone.

"Well, Briana, oh, pardon me, *Your Majesty.*" He taunted her with a courtly bow. When he rose his eyes were a freakish red. She took a step back.

"Ah, you noticed. How does the Dar Morch look on me?"

"I liked you better before."

"Really? Did you? I wish I'd known. Maybe I'd have tried harder to woo you."

"Don't get excited, Shamwa. You and I would never have worked out."

He moved toward her. She read his intention and backed up, stumbling over the pile of bedding that held the gnome's remains. She didn't fall, but it jarred the knife out of her hand, sending it clattering across the floor, far out of reach. Shamwa smirked before noticing the flat pile of shawls. "What have you done with her?" he snapped.

"Who?" Playing dumb might buy her a bit of time while she found another weapon. Keeping her attention on Shamwa while looking for a useful object was difficult, but the snap of a pine log in the fireplace drew her attention to two golden andirons. That looked promising. She slowly paced backward.

"You know who I'm talking about."

The honeyed tone of voice was gone, replaced by pure venom. "No matter. I don't really need her. I do marvel, though, that you had the guts to destroy her. So, Briana, I won't waste time on diplomacy. Let's get to business, shall we? I called you here for a reason."

There was no way to hide her shock. *Called me here?*

"How do you think you got through the portal? Hmmm… It seems you have a connection to the Dar Morch, and well, that's a problem for me. He is much too distracted by you and I can't risk losing him. Much as I hate to do it, especially since I do think there might have been a chance for us, you must be, shall we say, done away with."

Visions of being strapped to the wooden table in the torture room with the eyeball-puncturing face mask made her stomach clench.

Summoning all her courage, she adopted an air of haughtiness. "Look, let's sit down and talk about this. We're intelligent adults who can surely find common ground and a way to move forward for the benefit of Uisneach. We don't have to be enemies."

He laughed. "Right. I don't think you understand. I don't need to join you. I need to destroy you." Without warning, he lunged for her.

She jumped sideways and yelped as her hip banged painfully against the desk. Using it as a shield, she edged toward the andiron and called up her power.

"I call on the power and wisdom of…" she met Shamwa's eyes and had an idea. "The Dar Morch!"

Shamwa jerked backward. He looked panicky as he stumbled to his knees. He shook violently and made a sound, part cry, part growl.

The air around him shimmered red. What should she do if the Dar Morch wanted to enter her? She might gain more power, but didn't have a clue what to do with it. But the fact remained, Shamwa would be powerless. Her lips curved as she realized she might be about to put an end to the evil prime minister.

Shamwa rose up with a hiss. His eyes were fully red now, and his power seemed even stronger.

Briana was inches away from the andiron. She grabbed for it. Wielding the heavy instrument over her head, she planted her feet and let him come at her. She realized her mistake when he towered over her. She wasn't tall enough to use the andiron effectively against him. She needed more of the tuathla's magic. Frantically whispering the words, she breathed a short sigh of relief when the smell of sandalwood permeated the room and her ring began to hum.

But Shamwa was in full Dar Morch power and before she could defend herself, he wrapped her hair in one large hand and grabbed the andiron with the other. He held her fast and pulled back his arm to take a swing with the andiron that she knew would kill her. She lurched away, feeling hair being pulled out by the roots but not caring a bit, and kicked as hard as she could at his crotch.

Not expecting her to counterattack, he was knocked sideways and grabbed between his legs.

She stumbled back and Ealga's soul box fell out of her baldric and skittered near the fireplace.

"What's that?" Shamwa snarled.

Before she could retrieve it, Shamwa advanced on her. He was a powerful man without the Dar Morch, absolutely petrifying when fully possessed by it. Even without the faerie's power, Shamwa could easily kill her.

"Come out of this man and come to your tuathla!" she commanded.

Again, Shamwa wavered, but maintained his control over the Dar Morch.

Briana scooted back. With a stretch she was able to get her hand on the jeweled box. However, she was now blocked in by the fireplace, with Shamwa a few feet away from her. Only her tuathla power could save her. She turned to the fire and imagined it coming to life. Flames roared and danced wildly. Briana directed them toward Shamwa. They came in her direction instead! Heat surrounded her and drew her toward the flames.

Shamwa laughed hysterically as Briana clawed and kicked to resist the draw into the fireplace. Her stomach folded over on itself.

Not a good time to feel like puking, dammit. She swallowed the rising ball at the back of her throat. If she didn't figure out what she'd done wrong, she would die—in about three seconds, by her calculation. She fought with every ounce of faerie-infused strength she had. It bought her a few more seconds, but her choice was soon clear. Give in to the fire or die a torturous death at the hands of the psychopath above her.

Relax, High Lady, Tuathla of Evalon. The faerie's voice was as serene as a lake on a summer morning.

Briana clutched the spirit box tight against her, closed her eyes and gave in to the faerie who seemed to have everything under control.

CHAPTER TWENTY-SEVEN

POET'S GAP

Cold, hard ground. Briana's heart hammered a hole in her chest, paced for a three-minute mile. A crackle and snap turned her attention to the orange and red glow of a campfire. Fire! Frantically running her hands over her body, she found no sign of injury. Patting her baldric confirmed that the spirit trap was safe and sound.

"'Tis break of day and lonely yet, the sun comes… no… wait… the golden orb… no, that's not it," said a man with a creaky voice who sat by the fire. "One… two… and three… four… five… six… seven… ah, eight measures."

Humming ensued. Briana strained to see the shadowy shape. "'Tis break of day and lonely yet." The man paused. "The sun a brightly shinin' orb. Oh dear…"

She saw nothing but gray stone around her and what might have been the dark opening of a cave. Could be nighttime. Briana pushed herself up from the prone position she'd landed in. Squinting, she peered toward the flashes of firelight to get a better look at the person whose cave she'd crashed.

"Greetings, Queen Briana, Tuathla of Evalon. Are you all right?"

Briana bit her lip. *Friend or foe?* He sounded old, so perhaps no physical threat. He knew who she was, so might be magical. She remained still and silent, thinking through her options.

"I wouldn't hurt a mouse, Yer Majesty." His rheumy laugh supported his claim.

"Who are you?" she asked. "And how do you know who I am?"

He rose from his place beside the fire. Bent at a ninety-degree angle, the gentleman shuffled slowly toward her. Mostly bald with a whimsical crown of white hair that stuck out at various angles, he seemed to have forgotten the purpose of a comb or brush. He had deep-set eyes as old and wise as the cave he inhabited, under downward-slanting lids. He had the nose of a gladiator and the mouth of a professor, both draped by folds of skin softened from eons of living. His pants, a colorful hopscotch of wool squares, came to the top of ankle-high boots made from animal skin. A grubby, linen tunic hung from his wizened frame.

"Well," he said, rather impatiently, "What rhymes with orb?"

"Absorb?"

He stared at her. "That's it? That's all ye can come up with?"

Shrugging, she nodded.

"Perhaps we could introduce ourselves," she broke in, wanting to get on with the situation at hand. "I'm…"

"Queen Briana, yes I know who ye are. Have you at a disadvantage, do I?" He chuckled when she grunted a response. "They call me the Poet."

"The Poet?"

"You mean to say ye've not heard of me?" He shuffled closer until the crown of his head was almost touching her chin and stared up. "Hmmm… Ahhh…" he crooned, giving no clues as to the implication of his intonations.

Briana held her breath, not daring to give any sign of her discomfort. She let him study her as long as he needed to.

He snorted dubiously and stepped back. "Not exactly what I expected, but ye'll do."

He scuffled back to the fire, pointing to the kettle and two bowls beside the fire. "Come on now, Yer Majesty. Have a bowl of stew with me, hmmm?"

"Expecting company?"

He chuckled under his breath as he ladled soup into the bowls. "You don't really need the baldric on in here," he said, as he filled her bowl. "You and… any of your belongings will be perfectly safe here."

The sharpness in his expression made Briana wonder if he somehow knew exactly what was in her baldric. However, that didn't mean she needed to confirm it. With a blank expression on her face, Briana plopped down cross-legged beside the old man. He handed her a steaming bowl of chunky potatoes, carrots and stewed meat.

"Uh... Mr. Poet," she addressed him, wondering if there was a less awkward name, "I'm pleased to meet you and appreciate your hospitality, but I have something I need to do, so I best be going."

The ancient blue eyes bore through her. "To reach a destination, you first need to know where you are. Come on, sit with me a while. Yer friends will work out where ye are and come for ye. In the meantime, perhaps ye'd help me with this blasted rhymin'."

"My friends don't know where I've been, or where I am. I really need to get home, Mr. Poet."

He smiled patiently.

She could ignore the savory stew no longer and took a spoonful. It was wonderful. Several more bites followed. The warmth of the soup and the warmth of the fire relaxed her. "Are you some kind of druid or magician?"

He seemed to consider the question seriously. "No."

Going back to his word-crafting, he seemed to forget about the queen's presence. "'Tis break of day and lonely yet, the sun a brightly shinin' orb. On hilltop high, he gives his heart of pain his to absorb." Pushing up an errant, patch of flat hair, he grumbled, "Drat. Bloody terrible."

While she ate, he repeated the same phrases over and over until she thought she'd lose her mind. Briana blurted out, "'Tis break of day and lonely still, the sun awakens all. Atop a hill there sits a man, alone, afraid to fall. Oops, sorry. It's your poem, not mine."

"No. No. That's good. Let me see. Alone, afraid to fall. Hmmm." Briana took another bite of bread. He continued. "'Tis break of day and lonely still, the sun awakens all. Atop a hill there sits a man, alone, afraid to fall. His grieving heart laments the past... Do ye have any idea how many different kinds of poems there are?"

She shook her head, only half-listening. She needed to get out of here and get back to Brath.

"I don't either, but there's a lot. This one here is soundin' like an elegy and I hate elegies. We've got to turn it 'round."

"Mr. Poet, I don't mean to be rude, but I am the queen and need to get back to King Brath. Would you mind awfully taking a rest from the poetry-writing so I can have a little quiet in which to think?"

"Poetry is much like life, really. It can be one thing in one moment and somethin' entirely different the next. Take yers for example."

"My what," she replied, pushing one hand through her hair in frustration.

"Yer life. 'Tis like a poem. It started out in epic fashion, comin' through a tree, goin' on a journey to save a king..."

"No," she interrupted hotly, now completely irritated with the old man. "I'm pretty sure mine is a haiku you know, a poem without rhyme or reason. Or better yet, a limerick. 'There once was a girl in a tree, who fell for a bard, though not free. She got her heart broke when he left without hope, never more to be seen in the shire.' Well, that last line clearly needs some work. Didn't quite turn out that way."

"That's my point, exactly! Things rarely turn out the way we think they will."

For an instant, Briana saw behind the absentminded persona to the wise old sage sitting imperturbably in front of her. "I'm sorry, that was rude," she apologized, irritated with herself for losing control and sad because she obviously did see her life as a parody of sorts.

"Yer Majesty," he began again when it was clear she was through. "As I say, life is like poetry. Some are epic adventures, some are sonnets and yes, some are pure satire. The ex-prime minister comes to mind on that one." He grimaced. "But it's a poem that never gets finished. Keeps on writin' itself every day ye live."

She yawned deeply, thoroughly exhausted.

"So, where am I?"

"Deep in the Dromdara Mountains, south of Aurum Castle."

She shook her head dejectedly. "I'm clear across Tynan Ibor. We were on our way to Moiria. Brath won't know where I am!"

"Did ye not use a portal to get here? Might there not be another to take ye back?"

"I didn't create the portal. It appeared on its own and took me. I can't just make them appear."

"No?" The old man peered at her over his bowl. He raised one scraggly eyebrow.

"Can I?"

"Yer Majesty, ye are the most powerful woman this side of Evalon. Or that side, for that matter. Ye just need to trust yerself. But mostly, ye need rest. Ye look done in." He pointed to a pile of straw and blankets she hadn't seen before.

It had been a long, stressful night. A power nap wouldn't hurt. Crawling over to the bedding, she curled up and closed her eyes.

The poet continued to weave his words, changing words and meter as he deemed necessary, yet never happy with the results. The cadence relaxed her. During a momentary pause, she asked, eyes still closed, "How long have you lived here?"

"Longer than these mountains have been here."

"Are you being funny?"

"No."

"Why has no one spoken of you?"

"Why, indeed? Perhaps they don't consider me all that important."

Strange, she thought, that an old man would live alone up here, and no one would think to check in on him from time to time.

He took up his crafting again and she gave up any attempt to stay awake.

⤨

"'Tis break of day and lonely still, the sun awakens all."

"You aren't seriously working on that same poem," Briana said, yawning as she sat up on her pallet. Light shone through the fog that covered the mouth of the cave. She must have slept through the night.

"Perfection takes time to complete. Speaking of completion, don't ye think ye ought to be figurin' out the prophecy?"

"The prophecy has been fulfilled," she said arching an eyebrow at her new friend. "I'm the queen now, remember?"

"Only part of the prophecy is completed. Remember the lines,

> 'Two worlds collide in time,
> Treasure lost the cat must find.
> Dark and light now must meet,

River battle ends one part, brown king protects to death'?"

Briana said, "The second line refers to our bard going to Maine to find the lost runes. The first and third Cailleach is working on, and the last, well, I don't *even* want to think about the meaning of that."

He shook an arthritic finger at her. "Ye *need* to think about that line if ye don't want to be taken by surprise."

He was right, of course, but her gut told her it had evil portents and she wasn't ready to go there just yet. She stared at the fire, letting the snap and crackle of logs fill the silence.

"Have I ever told you the story of the Dar Morch and how he must be conquered by ridin' his horse into Scáil Meanoiche?"

"We've just met. I don't believe you have."

"Well, a long time ago, there existed among the faerie warriors a great leader named Dar Morch. He fought fiercely against the Moherians but in the last of the great wars he was seduced by a goddess of the Moherians who turned his fealty to them. As a result, a curse was placed on him by Urelian, the first faerie queen. He was exiled to Scáil Meanoiche, the Underworld, where he would remain a prisoner for eternity.

"If he has somehow escaped his imprisonment, 'tis only the faerie queen or the tuathla who can banish him back to Scáil Meanoiche."

"How?"

"The quickest way is to ride him back down."

"Sure, like Brath would ever agree to that."

"Well, dear heart, the Dar Morch is *your* servant after all. You will have to figure it out. The Dar Morch is feedin' power into Lord Shamwa and if ye don't end that, he could destroy us all."

Briana dropped her chin into her palm, her mind whirling with thoughts of getting back to the Druid's Grove, or wherever Brath was, and of how to send the Dar Morch to Hell.

"Death comes to all in its own time.
The grave seems ever silent.

But veils are thin and in night sublime.
Could prove yon death not violent.
No, not violent, that's terrible. Is faerie death reliant?
Yes, that works."

"A little dark, but yes, poetic," Briana said, distracted. She remembered a comment about portals. Her eyes traveled around the cave, searching for such a tool to get her back where she belonged. Circles surrounded her. The campfire-oh, no way was she going back through fire. The round pot containing the stew. *Maybe I could dump what's left out and use my magic to make the opening bigger.* She looked up to see the Poet staring intently at her. Just behind him was the mouth of the cave. A nearly perfect circle. Swirling gray mist slowly dissipated, revealing something that made her mouth drop open in its own perfect oval. The Poet was staring at her with a slight smile, his eyes alight.

Bright sunlight lit a grassy glade draped in ferns, decorated with leafy trees and low-hanging hawthorn branches. Feathery grasses clumped around an ivy-mantled stone door. Just a door. No house, castle, room or any other dwelling behind it. Just a door.

"I believe ye could walk through it and get where ye wish to go. If ye've a mind too."

She weighed her options. Open the door and go wherever it took her, or stay here and listen to more poetry, leaving her people to wonder where she was. The choice was clear. She stood, patted herself down to see if anything useful had magically appeared, and with a shrug, headed for the door.

"Thanks for the food and rest, Mr. Poet. If they come looking for me, it means I didn't get where I meant to go. Please tell them I'm... somewhere, looking for them. I'll come back and visit you one day."

"That would be lovely," he said and then, remembering something, attempted to snap his fingers. The action produced a dull slide rather than a sharp snap. "I did finish the poem. Would ye mind havin' a listen?"

She pressed her lips together. Courage wouldn't stay with her long but after all he'd done, she ought to return the favor. "Of course," she said, forcing her lips into a smile.

"'Tis break of day, the golden sun.
Hearkens forth their love.
A man, his wife and baby born.
A blessin' from above.

Happy three in yonder days.
No longer seems a dream
A music man and majesty
A lad beside the stream.

In every life a poem dwells
Each stanza tells a tale.
Seem it may, a sad lament,
Until she lifts the veil.

'Tis break of day, the golden sun.
Smiles on all their hearts.
A haiku—no, nor elegy,
A ballad, wrote in parts."

Briana stared at him, tears starting to form. "It's beautiful," she said sincerely. "Terribly, wonderfully beautiful."

"Do you understand it?"

"No," she replied honestly. "But I feel it."

"Fair enough. Go now, and be well, Yer Majesty."

With a brisk nod, she walked forward toward the cave opening and the stone door. Just as she reached the door, she stopped and turned around with a wide grin. "Here's one for you. Caution to the wind, she throws. Through the portal door she goes. Where she lands, nobody knows."

To the sound of his laughter, she put her hand on the cold rock and...

CHAPTER TWENTY-EIGHT

MODERN-DAY DIVINE PRACTITIONERS

Silas, O'Brien cottage, Tullamore, Ireland

"Short of bulldozin' the entire hill, I don't see how I can find the runes. It's been months and I'm still empty-handed."

"You need to find some real magic." The clurichaun sat against a stack of books on the table, his short legs splayed out carelessly, chewing on a portion of the sandwich Silas had given him. He reached for the shot glass of lemonade, smelled it, screwed up his face and set it back down.

"Yeah, I do. I *thought* you were the one with magic. You haven't been all that helpful, Áed."

The little man shrugged and took another bite of bread. "What's this stuff anyway?" he asked with his mouth full.

"It's peanut butter and jam."

Áed made a sound that might've been appreciation or disgust, Silas wasn't sure. He moved the clurichaun aside to retrieve Catriona's journal. Áed resettled himself and continued working on the sandwich while Silas leaned across the pages of the journal and the pages of a book on ogham, the ancient Irish alphabet. Orla had suggested he try to find any similarities between Uisneachan and ogham. So far, he had not. He hoped the symbols might reveal something from the mere studying of them. However, nothing was happening, so he traded the journal and history book for the daily newspaper. He grimaced when Áed made a rude noise followed by a smell that was much more powerful than should have come from such a wee personage.

"Really, Áed, is that necessary?"

"Me mam always said, 'Better out than in.'"

The clurichaun stretched out beside the stack of books.

"What are you doin'?" Silas asked.

"What's it look like I'm doin'?" he retorted grumpily. "I'm gonna have a nap."

"Well, at least you'll be quiet for a bit," Silas muttered under his breath. He focused on the paper. Between the sports, weather and obituaries he found an interesting post.

"It says here," Silas said, startling the wee man out of a post-sugar reverie, "that there is to be a gatherin' of druids at the Hill of Tara tonight to honor Samhain. I wonder if I might find a skilled practitioner of the magical arts there?"

"Maybe so. Takin' the lass with you?"

"She's at school."

"I'll go."

Silas raised an eyebrow in response.

"The Sun God falls to his slumber. The earth rests in darkness. The veil between the worlds is thin. This is the time of year we honor the ancestors and seek to hear their voices on the wind as they travel to the Summerlands. It is Samhain."

The sing-song voice led Silas up the grassy hill to the place where the ancient kings of Ireland had been crowned in ages past. Orla would be proud. He'd done his research. Half a dozen people in long robes of white, gold, silver, black and orange stood around a blazing bonfire. This small group was ringed by a larger group of observers, non-druids, he assumed, who watched and listened in rapt fascination. Silas found a place among the spectators.

A drum beat out a rhythm and the druids began chanting words that made supplication to those who had died before. A tall, lithe woman with a tambourine joined the chant and entered the circle in a twirling dance meant to symbolize the constellations of stars in the darkening sky above. A wreath of dried leaves sat atop her head. Her necklace of chestnuts and crystals swung against her chest in rhythm with the skirt of her dress that swayed with her twirls, hops and slides around the fire.

Silas looked around to see pumpkins carved into grim faces lit by candles, baskets of apples and gourds piled up in the four directions. The smell of dried oak and apple wood, as well as sage and nutmeg, floated in the air.

"We call upon the Crone and the Consort to join us and bless us with their presence. Hear us, wise ones, as we offer our gratitude in the form of offerings."

A short, round, dark-haired man in a white robe shared a story of the origins of Samhain, presumably for the benefit of visitors. Producing a candle from the folds of his robe, he lit it from the bonfire and lit a larger pumpkin "to represent the lighting of our doorsteps to guide the way for the dead and any unseen guests."

More songs, prayers and dancing and then a woman in a gold dress adorned in sparkling bits of stone and glitter stepped forward. Her bright red hair captured shards of light from the fire, making it seem that her head was on fire. She moved so close to the pyre that Silas worried she would light up like a torch.

"I want to warn all the wee lads and lassies here, to be on guard for the wee folk. Samhain is the time they want to play pranks on us humans. They've been known to cause all manner of trouble and ill, so watch well, children, and keep your doors closed tightly this night."

A harrumphing sound issued from Silas' coat pocket.

"Shhh, be quiet, Áed, or you'll just prove them right."

Silas hadn't wanted to bring Áed, but the wee man pitched such a fit that Silas gave in, demanding the clurichaun keep his comments and tantrums to himself.

Silas watched the celebration in respectful silence. It was a lovely ritual and he appreciated the intention to bring alive the ways of ancient worship. But this extravaganza wasn't *really* how things were done, at least in Uisneach. It seemed to him a lot of drama without much substance. Certainly, no magic.

When the last prayer and blessing were offered, hot cider was passed around and the celebrants visited with the people who had come to watch. The woman with red hair found him sipping his cider.

"I brought you a pumpkin cookie," she said, handing him a fragrant orange cookie.

"Thank you," he said. His eyebrows rose a notch when her fingers lingered purposefully on his.

He took a generous bite. "Um, good. Did you make them?"

"No, Serena did," she said, nodding to a young mother near the bonfire nursing an infant and talking to one of the male dancers.

"Hello friend," said the man who led the ritual.

He moved in beside the red-haired dancer, pushing her close enough to Silas that he could feel her hip against his. Pumpkin spice competed with the patchouli she wore. Silas took a step back.

The druid leader stuck out his hand. "Coran."

Silas grasped his outstretched hand in a firm shake. "Silas O'Mara."

"What brings you here, friend?"

"I was curious how this kind of ritual is done here."

"Ah, you're not a druid, then?"

"Aye, I am. Where I come from. But we do things a bit differently."

"Oh? And where are you from?"

He was caught in his own trap! Faint sniggering came from his pocket. He tapped it gently but pointedly with his finger to hush the wee traveler inside. "Well, I suppose I'm more bard than druid."

"Do you belong to the OBOD?"

"The what?"

"The Order of Bards, Ovates and Druids?"

"No, I don't think so. I don't really belong to any group."

"Oh, so you're a hedge-druid?"

Silas hadn't heard of that so didn't dare agree to it. "No, I'm just a bard, I guess."

"Do you play an instrument?"

"Aye, a few."

"Would you be inclined to sing a wee song for the group here? It would be nice to continue the celebration a little longer. A tale or a song would go a long way."

Silas hadn't planned on performing, but he supposed it wouldn't hurt. "It would be an honor. May I borrow a guitar?"

The woman hurried over to where a young boy was plucking strings and making a minor cacophony. After exchanging a few words, she procured the instrument and brought it to Silas. He found a log stump near the fire and sat down, strumming a few chords before beginning a story that had roots in Uisneach.

> "Upon the dark of night and full of moon,
> Memories of ancient lords and ladies fill the air.
> Our hearts recall the days when men sang songs,
> Of faerie magic, home and love true fair.
>
> But times have changed and so have we,
> And battles rage across the land.
> The faeries have all left the earth,
> Replaced by swords held in fiery hands.
>
> Will times return when trees of faeries bloom?
> When home and hearth are happy yet?
> 'Tis Maker's hope and man's to do,
> Peace returns, crossing out the threat.
>
> Upon this dark of night and full of moon,
> Call us upon the lords and ladies fair.
> Restore the days when men sing songs,
> Of faerie magic, home and love true fair."

A sigh rippled around the bonfire's circle as souls responded to the images Silas called up with the ballad. A tear wet his own eye as he thought of Brath and Briana working toward that very end, to bring the magic of the faeries back to Uisneach.

He stood and handed the guitar back to the lad, who stared at Silas as though he'd been placed under a glamour. Turning to Coran, he returned the man's wide smile.

"You're a bard all right. Would you consider joining our community?"

Silas knew that wasn't possible but was curious about what it entailed.

"You spend at least a year, maybe more, depending on your level of knowledge and skill, which seems significant if that performance was any indication, learning the history and craft of bardic druidry. There's an initial membership fee and then annual dues to support the organization. You would have a partner, or tutor, if you will, to help you along the journey."

"Does your community believe in faeries?"

Coran and the redhead chuckled.

"Well, some do, some don't," Coran replied. "Mostly we imagine they might exist, but don't really believe in them."

"Witches? Do you believe in them?"

"Of course. But witches have their own covens and practices and we don't usually worship together. At least not in this order."

"Coran!"

Coran turned to the person calling to him from across the bonfire. "I guess I'm needed for something. Nice to meet you, Silas. Do consider joining us. You'd be a welcome addition."

The redhead stepped away with Coran and said something in hushed tones. The druid leader glanced at Silas and nodded. A few more words and he strode away but the woman came back.

"By the way, I didn't introduce myself. I go by the name, Fedelma, in memory of the druidess who served Queen Madb of Connacht."

"Pleased to meet you, Fedelma. I enjoyed your dancin' and storytellin'."

"I'm glad I pleased you," she replied, her tone taking on a huskier hue. She moved a step closer.

Silas thought it odd that none of these people sounded Irish. *Maybe Americans?*

"I asked Coran and he said it would be okay to invite you to our private gathering tonight, after everyone leaves."

"Oh? What's involved at that celebration."

"We continue our worship, but in the old way."

Silas wondered if this would be more to his liking, more like how he honored Maker in Uisneach. "The old way?"

"We worship sky-clad." At his look of confusion, she smiled and added, "Naked."

"You would want me to take me clothes off in front of people—ladies, to tell stories?" He took another step away from her, unable to hide his shock.

"It's not sexual, Silas. Worshipping nude helps us feel a greater connection to nature and promotes uninhabited access to our energy."

Though her words seemed genuine, the light in her eyes as they traveled up and down his fully clothed body offered another message. She clearly hoped he would say yes.

"Miss Fedelma, I have been worshippin' Maker me whole life and have never felt the need to remove me clothes to do it. I thank you for the invitation, but it wouldn't be for me."

"I didn't mean to offend. I'm sorry if I did."

"No offense taken."

She gave him one more disappointed perusal. "I best get back to the group."

And I best get home, before someone else tries to get me naked.

❧

The next day, coffee in hand, Silas strolled by the gray façade of Father Sean's church. *It's a bloody fortress*, he thought, staring at the red door, peaceful glass windows and sacred statues, all behind a metal fence and gated parking lot. It seemed holiness here came at the price of security. He wondered if he could get in. Finding a nearby waste receptacle, he swallowed the last of the coffee, threw the cup away and headed for the red door. To his surprise, it swung open. The sanctuary was bathed in rays of colored light from the slanted window on one side of the room and the round stained-glass window overseeing the altar. The heavy scent of old incense hung in the air. He wandered down the aisle between the pews, his boots echoing under the vaulted ceiling, to a place near the front where the priest would perform his sacramental duties. The seat was hard, but he tried to relax, closing his eyes, hoping to feel a guiding presence or a comfort for his lonely spirit. The room was silent. No angels made themselves visible, no murmuring of

371

what Orla called the Holy Spirit. Just the vast emptiness of a cold, stone building. *How did God make himself known to people here, anyway? Could you just ask the man to appear and he would? Did you have to do the finger crossing on your head and chest? Wasn't he everywhere, all at once? Didn't he know what a man needed without his asking?*

"Hello, Mr. O'Mara."

Silas jumped and looked up to see Orla's brother, Father Sean, standing next to him in the aisle.

"Sorry. I didn't mean to startle you. Were you at prayer?"

"I suppose I was."

"I'm very sorry, then. I'll leave you to your…"

"No, no. It's okay. I'd about said what was on me mind, anyway."

"What brings you here, Mr. O'Mara? Besides a need for prayer."

"I don't honestly know. Orla finds peace here. I suppose I was lookin' for a little of that."

"And did you find it?"

"No offense, but honestly, no."

The priest was quiet for a time. Silas began to wonder if he himself were waiting on a word from God. The silence was burdensome, even to a man who was quite at home alone in the forests and glens of the mostly uninhabited landscape of Uisneach.

"Sometimes God speaks to us in surprisin' ways. Perhaps using a wordless language, perhaps usin' messengers that we aren't expecting. I think sometimes we offer our prayers to God and he takes some time to consider how best to respond."

Silas thought that an all-powerful Creator would hardly need to think about how to respond to mortals, but not wanting to insult the priest, he kept the thought to himself.

"I'll be on the lookout for any ministerin' angels that seem to want to bring a message," he said with a smile.

The priest sighed.

Being the human mouthpiece to God must be a difficult and thankless job. Silas wondered if he sometimes felt disappointed in the meager counsel he could provide.

"I was surprised when Orla brought you to the service and baptism," Father Sean said. "She's never brought a lad to church."

Silas took his turn at a sigh.

"You know she cares a great deal for you."

"Aye. I care for her too."

"I would hate to see her hurt."

"She's a lovely woman and my friend. I have no intention of hurtin' her."

"That's good. I'm glad to hear it."

There seemed nothing more to say. Silas thanked the priest for his time and the two men shook hands before Silas walked back down the aisle to the door. Turning back, he glanced at the stained-glass image once more, where Jesus stood with arms outstretched in blessing.

All you gave me was more to worry about, but I thank you for your time.

Squinting at the change from darkness to full sunlight, Silas paused outside the church to get his bearings. He automatically headed for Convent Road but realized he didn't want to go home to Áed, and Caitlin and Finnegan had gone to visit friends in Kilkenny. Turning about-face, he headed for Kilbride Street.

He was still trying to figure out where he meant to go when he found himself in front of Aislin's shiny green and gold shingle. He was staring at the flower pots, wondering what to say when the door swung open and the gray hair and generous body of Betty Murphy, a.k.a. Aislin, materialized, looking not the least bit surprised to see him.

"Hello, Mr. O'Mara."

"Are you a real witch?" He knew how desperate that sounded and realized he felt that desperate.

"I can be no other than I am."

"I need your help, but I can't tell you what kind of help, or why. A real witch would know, wouldn't she?"

"Have you ever worked with a witch?"

"The best one that ever cast a spell."

"I see. I'm to compete with the best, then?"

"Can you help me?"

"Come in, Silas."

He followed her into the room and breathed in the same scent of sage and lavender. Why did the tree of life and dreamcatcher seem so much more comforting than either the robed druids or the stained-glass windows? Why did he feel like he might actually leave here feeling better?

Aislin closed the door to her kitchen.

"The grandkids?"

"Not here today. I was doing a little housework, but you are a welcome interruption. Let's not waste time, Silas." She sat in one of the chairs at the circular table and indicated that he should sit in the other.

"You despair of completin' your quest and feel terribly alone in the trying."

His body jerked convulsively. She certainly didn't waste any time. And she hadn't brought out the cards.

"What you seek will be found, but as with all things on the Wheel of Life, it takes time and patience."

"Sometimes I feel like givin' up."

"Druids don't give up."

"I never said I was a druid."

"No? I thought you had."

When he didn't reply, she smiled serenely and leaned over to turn on a CD with some restful harp music. She adjusted the volume so the music was very low. "I can't help you find what you're lookin' for, but I can ease your spirits a bit. Have you ever done guided imagery?"

He stiffened. Of course, he had, with Briana, when she was so badly injured in the fight at Ardghal. Memories of her rising above him to bury her sword in the soldier who was trying to kill him, her terrible injury and the vision he'd conjured to get her mind off the pain, flooded through him, adding to his angst.

"I see you have, and maybe the experience wasn't completely pleasant."

"It was under gruesome circumstances."

Aislin nodded understandingly. "Well, let's see if we can't go on a journey that will take away some of your sorrow. I'll give you a moment to center yourself."

He sat back in the chair and took the breaths to settle himself. Closing his eyes, he nodded his readiness.

She spoke to him in tones just above the serene harps in the background, guiding him to let his true self, his inner being, escape the confines of his body. "And now, I want your spirit to walk along the path you see before you. As you walk, look around at the landscape. What do you see? What do you hear? What do you smell?"

The path took him into a forest of old yew, oak and ash trees. Birds twittered and sang to each other. A hawk screamed somewhere overhead. Earthy smells of decay and of life, rotting tree stumps and mushrooms breaking through the dirt. The scent of pine needles mixed pleasantly with mossy stones in a nearby stream.

"Relax, Silas. Let yourself rest in the beauty and contentment you find here."

Peace infused the joints and muscles of his body. She let him stay in that place of total well-being for what seemed like a long time.

"Look around to where you will find somethin' to serve as an altar or table."

His inner eye lit upon a tree stump surrounded by green and yellow ferns. A mouse sat at the base, chewing on a seed, watching spirit-Silas with no apparent concern.

"Silas, allow your spirit to rise above the scene. Keep it in your sight but view it from a place of objectivity and detachment." She paused. "Now, turn your attention to the quest that you have undertaken. What is the most likely path forward? See the answer to this from this place of detachment."

His inability to see any way forward was not changed by the peaceful surroundings and a view from above. Maintaining his sense of well-being grew more difficult with this task. Anxiety began to replace peace.

"Breathe, Silas. Allow your spirit to access the place of all wisdom and understandin'. Every quest has challenges and concerns. See yours. As you list them in your mind, set them on the altar."

His first concern was not finding the runes. Looking around the scene, he found three small stones that he picked up and placed on the altar. His second concern was more difficult to put into a concrete thought. He was worried he'd never see Briana again, that she wasn't happy, and that she'd forgotten about him. He ended up wrapping his concerns about Briana in the single thought that he was lonely for her. His third challenge was what to do about Orla. He didn't want to lose her friendship, but he didn't want to hurt her by keeping it.

"Silas, you have laid the challenges and your worries at the altar. You must now let them go. Trust that the One who is above all and in all will take care of them, and that things will unfold exactly as they are meant to unfold in their proper time."

She gave him a minute to adjust to the idea of letting go of his fears.

"And now, you are to receive a gift that will help support you on your journey. Look again to the altar and see that the worries are gone and in their place is somethin' meant to help you and bring you peace. What is the gift?"

He stared at the stump and at first saw nothing. *I guess Maker has nothin' for me,* he thought. Just as he was about to bring himself out of the imagery, he saw the tree rings on the pillar shift and realign to create two separate hearts. He was surprised that the hearts were not connected. Was this gift telling him that he was released from his bond to Briana? Overwhelming sadness mingled with unexpected relief. Maybe he could move on. Maybe he was meant to move on.

"Silas, it's time to come back to the present. You will return with a renewed energy for your journey and a sense of well-being. The image of your gift will give you strength and courage to stay on the path until you complete your quest. Let your mind rest, focus on my voice and as I count back, ready yourself to become completely and fully in the present. Ten... nine... eight..."

By the time she had finished the count, his eyes were open, he was fully grounded and could honestly say he felt better.

"Thank you, Aislin," he said pulling bills out of his wallet and handing them to her. "Your magic might be just what I needed."

"Come anytime, Silas. I wish you Godspeed on your journey."

Outside, he took a deep breath, clearing away any vestiges of his trance. *Maybe Orla's right. Maybe we should simply enjoy whatever time we have together without any long-term expectation. We should have that conversation again.* The hearts appeared in his mind again, but this time took on the form of two hearts, entwined in bone. His fingers went to his neck. *But what about Briana?*

CHAPTER TWENTY-NINE

DEAD STOP

Belvedere House in November had few visitors. The famous gardens at the Rochfort estate in Mullingar, Westmeath, were cut back for the winter and the maple leaves were beginning to fall, prompted by the recent rain and winds. It was a good time for Orla to interview the grounds curator about the public's increasing interest in faeries and the faerie gardens at Belvedere, background for her thesis. Silas was happy to enjoy a peaceful walk by himself while she conducted her interview. Though the forecast had been for more rain, the sky was blue as blue could be. Orla joined him on the grounds when her meeting was over. They searched for a good spot to eat lunch.

"Silas, what time is it? I still need to get back to Dublin tonight for classes tomorrow."

Silas glanced up at the sun. "About two o'clock." When he looked back down, she was staring at him and shaking her head. "What?"

"You're an odd man, Silas O'Mara."

"How so?"

She reached out a hand to pat the place on his wrist where a watch should be, but wasn't.

"Most people just look at their watch, but not you. For some reason, you feel it necessary to use the sun to tell time. It's a gas, but strange."

The hairs on his wrist rose where she'd touched him. Other parts of him were considering doing likewise and he stepped away. *It's been far too long since I've loved a woman*, he thought, wishing the desire wasn't making an appearance now.

Another jag of coughing brought him around. Definitely not a good time to get romantic. "Orla, are you sure you don't want to go see the doctor? You've been coughin' and wheezin' all day. Do you think being out here is good for your asthma?"

"I haven't had an attack in over a year. It's just a cold. With the asthma, it sounds worse than it is. I'll be fine. Hey, look at that!"

He followed her pointing finger to a break in the trees, where a stone gazebo stood, minus its roof, in a small clearing. She should sit for a minute, so he led her in that direction.

"Silas, we could..." *ah choo...* "have our picnic there."

He agreed. She needed to rest and he was getting hungry.

After checking out the lion statue inside the structure, they sat on the edge of the gazebo's platform. Orla pulled a thermos of tea and sandwiches out of her backpack.

Silas took a bite of his. "Umm, ham and cheese." He took another bite and chewed, eyes closed, making undistinguishable noises of appreciation.

"Are you always such a noisy eater?"

"Only when it's very, very good. You're a good cook, Orla."

She swatted his arm. "It's only a sandwich, Silas. One of these days, I'll cook you a proper meal."

Silas glanced over at her, wondering what it would be like to have her cooking meals for him. And doing his laundry. And having his children. He scrunched his eyes to push away the thought. Since his visit to Aislin, he was thinking of her along those lines, more and more, and wasn't sure he liked it. Was she the gift he was being given, or was he simply lonely and drawn to this lovely woman? One part of his mind was trying to pay attention to what she was saying, something about not finding any possible hiding place for the runes here at Belvedere House. The other part was thinking of how he could create a scenario between them that would end in bed. Maybe they could take a drive down to Dingle and stay somewhere overnight.

"Silas, are you listenin' to me?"

"Aye, you were sayin' you thought... ah, I guess I missed the last part. Orla, would you want to go with me to Dingle next weekend?"

"Dingle? What's down there? Surely you don't think Catriona went to Dingle to leave the runes?"

"No, I don't. I just would like to see the place and thought maybe we could take a trip together." He was about to suggest an overnight trip when he saw her bite her lip and look away. "What's wrong?"

"Nothing. I can't go next weekend."

"No? Somethin' goin' on at church?"

She shook her head, still not looking at him.

He frowned at her obvious discomfort. "Orla, what is it?"

She took a breath and looked up, meeting his eyes. "I have a date next weekend, Silas. Ned Turner asked me to dinner and a play in Dublin."

His heart flopped like a fish on a hot beach. He didn't know what to say. He looked away. He knew Ned Turner from the pub, a decent fellow, an accountant, if Silas remembered correctly. "I see." A sickening thought struck him. "You said you have a date next weekend. Dinner and theater in Dublin would be a late night. Will you, uh, be gone all weekend?"

She gave him an evil eye. "No, you eejit, I'm not plannin' on stayin' the weekend with him. What kind of slag do you take me for?"

"I don't think that of you, Orla. I'm just taken by surprise, that's all."

"Are you now? Well, I have every right to go out on a date, Silas."

"Aye, you do," he said with a sigh. Was he supposed to ask her not to go? Was this his do-or-die moment? He sighed again. Any response was curtailed by a clap of thunder.

Looking up, he was stunned to see that the skies overhead had gone from a peaceful blue to a murderous black. Orla pulled her sweater around her as the wind suddenly whirled around them.

"Gonna rain in about ... now," he said as the first drops fell.

Orla was already shoving things back into the backpack, even as she coughed in unison with the next rumble of thunder. He grabbed the backpack and threw his jacket over her shoulder against her protest. The gazebo sat along the edge of Lough Ennell and parking was all the way to the other side of the grounds. Silas hurried Orla as much as he could to avoid the downpour, but the more she hurried, the more she coughed.

Rain and wind grew fiercer by the second. They were both soaked by the time Silas unlocked the car and Orla slid in. She was coughing hard, her face a pale pink.

"What can I do?" Silas asked with grave concern.

"No-thing," she wheezed out. "Just... drive."

They were only about half an hour from home, so Silas drove as fast as he could through the driving rain.

Orla's wheezing sounded worse and she had gone pale, sweat popping up across her forehead and cheeks.

"I'm takin' you to the hospital."

She nodded, reaching inside her handbag for something. Pulling out her inhaler, she was just taking the cap off when Silas turned a sharp corner, jarring the canister out of her hand. It fell under his legs. He reached down underneath his seat, feeling for the medication and just touched it when he heard her tight scream. His eyes had only been off the road for a fraction of a second, but when he looked up, the raindrops on the windshield had turned to diamond shards from the headlights of an oncoming vehicle. He swerved hard to avoid crashing into the car. Dark brown ribs of a massive tree trunk replaced the vehicle in his line of vision. Cursing his ineptness as a driver, the rain and his decision to leave Uisneach, he threw his arm across Orla in a futile attempt to shield her from the impact.

CHAPTER THIRTY

THE GROVE

Briana, Cailleach's cabin, Tynan Ibor, Uisneach

I'm not going to puke, was Briana's first thought as she stepped out of the portal that had formed at the mouth of the Poet's cave. That was a happy improvement. Her initial disorientation turned to recognition when she found herself beside a cascade-rich brook with mossy rocks and a bittersweet memory of Silas. The protected forest near Cailleach's cabin. Relief settled her quaking guts. She whipped around to catch a glimpse of the opening that brought her here.

"If portal-hopping is going to be the new thing, could you at least show me how to use it?" The shimmering doorway between two birches was fading fast. Pointing her tuathla ring at the portal, she said the words, felt her power rise, and looked for some response from the opening. There was none. Instead, with a final *blip*, it was gone.

Swearing at the now nonexistent door and the unseen powers controlling it, she flipped her hair back and turned to the brook, specifically to the stone where she and Silas had spent an afternoon alone, fishing, talking and falling in love. The afternoon they *almost* held hands. The afternoon they *almost* kissed. The afternoon he told her there could never be anything between them. She skipped across the stream and sat on the rock, letting her feet dangle in the water. Just for a moment she released the tight control she kept on her deepest feelings and allowed herself to think of him, to miss the one who shared her soul. Longing, a deep and unquenchable ache in every cell of her body, consumed her. It was a terrible, beautiful ache that brought him nearly close enough to touch, yet infinitesimally far away. Remorse hitched a ride to the longing. She was married. She loved Brath. Why could she not forget Silas? Why couldn't she be free of this longing? Suddenly, she wondered if her mother had ever loved anyone besides her father? Would she understand this impossible hole in her heart that only Silas could fill?

"Where are you, my great cat?" she whispered, and gasped when a trout pirouetted out of the water. For a split second, he seemed suspended in air. His bright scales flashed as a ray of sun splintered through the trees. She recalled Silas' fishing advice, that she must be patient. Then time ticked on and the fish splashed heavily in the water and dove to the depth of the pool. "Patience, my ass," she grumbled. "We need you here now, *with* the runes."

Forcing her thoughts back to the portal as a possible tool to use against Shamwa, she tried to recall every moment, before and after, of the times she'd traveled these gateways of time and space. Excluding her initial entry into the tree to Uisneach, which seemed singular, these trips were sudden, without any awareness of the in-between place, usually followed by nausea, vomiting, or both. She hadn't commanded a portal to appear. She didn't know she could. She hadn't any say in where she went. Who or what was causing this to happen? Could *she* control it? Questions piled up without any corresponding answers.

Knowing where she was didn't help much, either, since she didn't know where Brath was, or how much time had passed. She tried visualizing another entrance in a rowan bush to take her to wherever he was. Not so much as a shimmer. Staring at a spot in the water where three stones converged into a miniature dolman, she spoke words adapted from a protection spell. "From harm I seek to be removed. Between the misty halls of time. Surround me with protective grace, yet make a way to leave this place." Nada. Water continued to run around and over the stones, heedless of her desire.

She stared at the forest, searching for anything that might respond to magic. Her efforts to spell, image, pray or order an opening went ignored. "I suppose, then, it must be that some supernatural being is overseeing all this and decides when a portal is needed. You know, I really hate leaving my fate to chance, some discerning god or goddess, or randomness. A little control would be nice."

A deep bark startled her, and she jumped up in time to be blindsided by Dara.

"Sweet Maker, do you have to knock me down, Dara?"

"Briana!" Brath was running through the forest, effortlessly clearing boulders and blowdowns to get to her.

He was here! He found her! This man who loved her, who had given her time and space to come to terms with her choices and who'd forgiven the times she'd hurt him. This man who would move heaven and earth to protect her. This man who loved her unconditionally and had the patience to wait until she loved him back. The portal seemed to know what it was doing, after all. The hole in her heart covered itself in mourning and allowed the other parts to pulse with gratitude and love.

"Slow down, Brath," she cautioned, "before you fall and break your leg!"

She met him halfway in a bone-crunching embrace. "Brath, I missed you, too, but you're squeezing the breath out of me."

He held her at arm's length. "Are you okay? I've been worried sick! Where have you been?"

"Well, let's see. I took a tour of Aurum Castle, had a fight with Shamwa, went through the fireplace and ended up with the Poet in Dromdara Mountains. And now I've just come through a lovely little portal to here."

Brath was pale. "Are you okay, Briana?" He scanned her from head to toe. Dara continued to sniff her as well.

"I'm fine," she reassured them both.

When he embraced her a second time, she felt his trembling and thought maybe he was close to tears. She ran a hand down his back. "Brath, I'm really fine. Shall we go to the cabin, and I'll give you the good news and the bad news. By the way, how did you know to find me here?"

"Dara went berserk, and I thought he must sense you around, so I followed him."

"Good boy," Briana said, patting the wolfhound on his scraggy head. "Where are the rest of the troops?"

"A few are back at the cabin, but the perimeter of this forest is surrounded by faerie warriors and the Taranian and Winge armies."

"We're safe, then?"

"Between the troops and Cailleach's protection spell, we're as safe as we can be. Come on, let's get you fed."

Dara beat them back to Cailleach's, so an entire entourage of people met them on the porch and under the yew tree. Sir Jameson and young Stark stood side by side, their matching sea-green eyes staring at her with concern. Kieran Winge hunkered over a stump, sharpening his sword, but looked up and nodded in greeting. Beside him stood Captain Aya'emrys, who didn't seem at all surprised to see her, and Sir Niall Harkin, who maintained a sentinel-like pose that was belied by the sheer relief in his eyes. Rippa, shoeless, was on her with a hearty squeeze around the waist.

"Are ye okay, Bri—Yer Majesty?"

She patted his head. "I'm fine, Rippa. Really, everyone, stop worrying. I have a lot to tell you as soon as you all stop making a fuss over me."

"Well then, get your fanny in here and tell us your tale."

"Sigel!" Briana tore herself away from Brath and raced up the steps to where the lord marshall leaned against the post. He stumbled sideways when she threw her arms around him.

"Whoa! You mean to knock me on my arse?" he said, but held her embrace for a couple of seconds before extricating himself.

"I'm so happy to see you. You're back to your old self, thank Maker."

A shadow momentarily darkened his features. "Nearly, yes."

When he headed inside, Briana saw the limp.

She looked to Brath who responded with a grim nod. She wondered if it would affect his ability to perform his duties, but answers to that would have to wait as she was hustled inside, where Cailleach was preparing a meal. "Welcome back, Briana. I trust you are in one piece."

"I am. I have so much to tell you."

"I know you do, but not before we tend to you, lass. You men can go amuse yourselves for a bit while Briana gets cleaned up."

The men, except for Brath, filed out, with Sigel the last to go. Although his limp wasn't horrible, it was enough that Briana knew it must be a source of frustration for him. *Maybe it will get better in time*, she hoped.

She turned to find her husband filling a large basin with hot water from the fireplace. She lifted an eyebrow.

"I'm not going anywhere. I'll help you, Bri."

Cailleach went to fetch a clean dress for Briana from the loft.

Briana started to remove her baldric. "Where's Nua?" she asked Brath.

He nodded at the corner of the fireplace, where her sword stood, waiting for its owner to return.

Briana fished the jeweled box and key out of the baldric, and was showing it to Brath when Cailleach returned with the dress. The witch paused, her jaw clenching. Briana felt the tension in her.

"Let me have her," the witch said, her voice dark with regret. Cailleach took the box and turned it every which way, her mouth thinning in a tight line and her eyes moistening. "It must be destroyed. Tonight. I don't want to take any chances on her escaping again."

"How do we destroy it?"

"We take it to the sacred grove of the Uisneach Tree. Nionon will help us." She looked at Brath. "You can escort us to the grove, but you'll have to wait outside the circle. Only Divine Practitioners can enter the presence of Nionon."

"I don't like you being left without protection. Surely the dryad will allow us in for safety's sake."

"No, Brath, you will not be allowed."

"Sigel is a druid," Briana said. "He should be able to enter. And Aya'emrys. Faeries are permitted inside the circle."

Brath looked uncertain. "I'd feel better if..."

Briana didn't let him finish. "Brath, Sigel likely needs to feel he's needed and useful. You won't be far away."

"Fine, but I will be as close as the dryad will allow me to get."

"And I'll yell if something happens," Briana assured him, with a kiss on the cheek.

"In the meantime, I'll keep this close to me," Cailleach said quietly, putting the spirit trap in the pocket of her skirt. She returned to the task of putting a meal together.

Brath helped Briana wash and change while Cailleach sliced bread and set out platters of meat and vegetables. Briana wondered where all the food came from.

"The men have not been idly waiting for you," Cailleach said, reading her expression.

"How long have I been gone?"

"Just since yesterday," Brath answered.

Okay, so time hadn't changed while I was away, just location. She filed that piece of information away for future consideration.

The men were called back in. Cailleach wouldn't let Briana talk until she'd eaten, so the meal was dispatched swiftly.

Brath sat her beside the fireplace and pulled a footstool next to her. Inwardly, Briana chuckled. He hadn't been more than three inches away from her side since her return. It was nice now, but she hoped he would relax before too long.

She told her story from beginning to end with only a handful of questions asked during the telling. Silence followed her recounting. Brath seemed to be weighing possible responses.

"The tunnel needs to be a priority," he finally said. "I want to see every last cart and apple returned to the citizens of Uisneach."

"I've been thinking about the tunnel, Brath. I know it was my idea, but I realize now that with the invisibility cloaks, we could just go upriver and walk right into Aurum Castle." Brath started to argue, but she held up a hand. "I know what you're going to say. How do we hide the boats? All we need is about two boats full of men to get in the castle. Shamwa doesn't have a lot of staff there and I didn't even see soldiers around. He's relying on the protection spell, which does not cover water, and the Dar Morch. We can sew together enough cloaks to cover the boats, get inside the castle via the garden, kill Shamwa, break the protection spell and leave by the front door."

"How do you know we can break the protection spell?"

"If we kill Shamwa, the Dar Morch will be at my command and he can remove the spell."

"That might be so, Your Majesty," Aya'emrys commented. "But only if the Dar Morch knows the spell. Since Lord Shamwa was not in control of the Dar Morch at the time the spell was applied, he may have no power over it. The more likely way to break the spell is through the natural Uisneach magic in the Divine Practitioners, which will be fully restored once the runes are returned."

If, not once, Briana thought. Pessimism wouldn't help here, so she kept the thought to herself.

"We should at least send Kieran and a few crows to the river to see if they can get past the spell," Sigel said.

"Sigel, I got out," Briana reminded him.

"Didn't you say you got out through a portal?"

"I don't mean this time. Last time, when they kidnapped me."

"Briana, first of all, you got out, not in. Leaving the barrier is naturally going to be easier than getting in. Secondly, Artanin helped you escape, remember?"

He was right of course. On both counts. "We could at least try."

"Which is what I'm suggesting," he said, his eyebrows curling together at her.

"Right." She rubbed at her temples as fatigue she hadn't noticed suddenly hit her.

"So," Brath said, standing and bringing Briana upright with him. "We have a plan. Sigel, ready the men to leave in the morning. Kieran, you and your crows check out the river near Aurum Castle. If it's doable, send them to Baigsith for two cloaks big enough for boats."

"What are we going to do while they're doing that?" Briana asked.

Brath stretched his legs out in front of him and stared into the fire. Briana noticed new worry lines around his eyes.

"We visit the Uisneach tree."

⚬

An eerie glow bathed the sacred grove as moonlight mixed with the green, gray and brown of moss-cloaked boulders and yew trunks. The circle of stones that birthed Nuada stood silent in the sepulchral amphitheater, protecting the sacred Uisneach Tree and its arboreal guardian, Nionon.

Brath reluctantly waited outside the circle with Dara and a small army as Briana, Cailleach, Sigel and Aya'emrys approached the massive ash tree. Briana stepped across the tinkling brook that ran between the stones, feeling the increase of energy around her as she and Cailleach drew close to the tree. Sigel and Aya'emrys remained close enough for protection, but outside the immediate presence of the holy dryad. Musical chimes accompanied the materialization of Nionon's face. As the ash trembled and turned, rows of bark divided, allowing her to emerge in a slow process. Golden hair swayed around her nut-brown face as she detached from the tree's trunk. Slender, branching arms and willowy legs followed until the dryad stood before Briana in all her magnificence. In one graceful movement, she bowed before Briana.

"Greetings, Your Majesty. It is wonderful to see you again."

Her voice, like wind chimes, resonated through the forest, filling the space with the sound of beauty. Briana felt it wash over her.

"We come bearing bad news and seek your help."

"You come in support of another's sorrow," the dryad said, turning her attention to Cailleach. "Greetings, Crone. I share your sadness over the loss of your sister."

Cailleach inclined her head toward Nionon. "Thank you. Your sympathy gives me great comfort."

"Are you prepared to do what must be done?"

"I am," Cailleach replied, sounding more determined than sad.

"This will destroy her soul, forever," Nionon said.

"As it must be."

Briana looked at Cailleach and the realization of what they were doing hit her. *We're about to kill her sister. Her family.* Having grieved her own father's death, Briana couldn't imagine how they could carry out the killing of this woman, even if she was evil to the core.

"Cailleach?" she whispered.

Cailleach raised a hand to stop her. "It must be done, Briana. I will have no regrets." She pulled the beautiful box out of her skirt and placed it on a flat stone.

Briana felt Nuada heat up at her side and pulled the sword from its sheath. The blade glowed brightly.

"Cailleach, you will repeat the words I give you over the box," said Nionon. "Briana, when we have spoken the words of obliteration you will need to complete the physical act by stabbing it with your sword. Are you both ready?"

They nodded.

Nionon moved her wraithlike arms over the box. Cailleach followed her example and together they spoke magic that would end Ealga's wickedness forever.

"In the name of Maker and in service to the Five Blessed Realms, may this soul of darkness, be destroyed into infinitude. May the evil that it intended for this kingdom and those who serve it, be cleansed by fire and turned to ash. And may your healing grace grant peace to those who carry out the deed."

Nua burst into flame, taking Briana's breath for a moment.

"Now, Briana, finish the act!" Nionon instructed, with startling urgency.

Briana held the grip with both hands and plunged the fiery blade into the box, not once but three times. The wood caught and burned with the ferocity of the furious soul inside. Jewels sparked color into the pyre. Briana was taken by the terrible beauty of the scene until a tormented screech issued from the fire. She dropped Nua and covered her ears. Cailleach stood stalwartly as her sister's soul entered oblivion. Only when Briana saw her close her eyes and lower her head, did she know that Cailleach's pain went deeper than any words or action could reveal.

The screeching stopped, and silence filled the grove. What remained of the box and Ealga, ashes, were absorbed into the stone, leaving no physical trace of Ealga's soul.

"She is forever dead to this world or any other," Nionon pronounced flatly.

Cailleach nodded.

Briana and Nionon stayed still until Cailleach herself indicated a readiness to move on.

She straightened her back and looked at Nionon. "Are you aware that the Dar Morch has been released into the realms?"

The dryad tipped her head in acknowledgment. "Someone reversed the spell. I felt the tremble through my roots when it happened."

"Ealga?"

"That is possible, though I cannot say for certain. Will our troubles never cease?"

"Not as long as Shamwa breathes," Briana said fervently, and cringed. When, exactly, had it become so easy for her to consider the death of others? When had she decided that there was evil incapable of rehabilitation? Whatever had changed her, she now believed it was true. Also true that hard decisions came at a steep price, one Cailleach just paid.

"Queen Briana, it is your responsibility to remove the threat of the Dar Morch," Nionon said. "He is bound by his very nature to serve you, the tuathla of Evalon. He must be sent back to Scáil Meanoiche or we risk annihilation of all of our hopes for Uisneach's future."

"But I was face-to-face with the Dar Morch and he didn't respond to me at all." That wasn't quite true; she had felt something from the Dar Morch, but nothing had come of it.

"The Dar Morch is confused by the one who contains him and the one who truly holds the power. You must release him from Lord Shamwa and return him to the Underworld."

"Nionon, is that what is meant by the lines of the prophecy, '*Dark and light now must meet. River battle ends one part, brown king protects to death*'?" Cailleach asked.

The dryad's body undulated. "The prophecy lends itself to multiple interpretations, does it not?"

As an answer, Briana found it lacking. Cailleach seemed unperturbed by the ambiguity.

"I met the Poet," Briana said. "He told me I had to ride the dark horse into the Underworld to re-imprison the Dar Morch."

Nionon's lips parted in a fibrous smile. "The Poet is fond of theatrics. That is one way, of course, but there are other ways to accomplish the goal. Find the summoning and banishing spells of Urelian."

"The first queen of the faeries? Are you kidding me? With all due respect, it would be far easier to steal the horse and ride to the Underworld."

"Captain Aya'emrys?" Nionon called.

Briana had almost forgotten he and Sigel were so close by. The golden warrior stepped forward and kneeled before the dryad.

"Do you have any knowledge of Queen Urelian's grimoire?" Nionon asked.

"I have heard that it disappeared when Catriona left the kingdom."

"Well, there you go," Briana said, her hand flapping impotently at her side. "Catriona must have taken it with her for safekeeping."

"Then you must ask her where it is."

"How am I supposed to do that? She's been dead a long time."

Nionon smiled indulgently. "Death is only a barrier if you believe it so."

The dryad was already moving back into the Uisneach Tree, her brown skin blending with the bark of the tree, her hair becoming the nurturing veins of the trunk.

"Nionon, please, my lady, tell me how to reach Catriona."

Cailleach put a hand on Briana's arm. "Come, lass. We'll think of a way."

Briana stared back at the tree that no longer held any hint of the dryad within. "This is the problem with Uisneach. So many magical beings who give you impossible quests with only smidgeons of clues," she grumbled as she stepped away from the tree. Sigel walked ahead and Captain Aya'emrys behind the two women, until Sigel stumbled against a small boulder. Briana moved up beside him, ignoring the look of irritation he flashed at her.

"Brath should be right behind those pines," she said, pointing to a copse of scrubby baby pine trees. Voices confirmed her statement and in the next instant she was standing in front of him.

"Well? Were you successful?"

Her nod was enough to communicate that Ealga was dead, and he was wise enough to let it go at that. As much as she wanted to tell him about the Dar Morch, instinct advised her to hold off until they were alone.

Once inside the cabin, under the light of a few candles and the hearth fire, Briana saw the grief etched into Cailleach's face.

"Can I fix you a cup of tea, Cailleach?" Briana said softly.

The witch patted her shoulder. "No, thank you, lass. 'Tis sleep that's needed. There's no telling what tomorrow will bring."

"I can tell you what it will bring," Sigel said bursting through the door. "A crow was waiting to tell me that the Gray Military is just outside of Moiria. Lord Shamwa is with them."

Briana turned to Brath, who was biting his lip as he stared at her.

Unspoken communication passed between them. Sleep would have to wait. Discussion about Shamwa and Dar Morch would happen sooner rather than later. Even though it was probably playing into Shamwa's hand, there was no way they were going to let Moiria become the next.

"Saddle the horses, Sigel," Briana said, not taking her eyes off Brath. "We ride to Moiria."

CHAPTER THIRTY-ONE

HOWLING WOLF TAVERN

"There is *no* way I'm agreeing to you riding into Scáil Meanoiche or confronting Shamwa. Briana, seriously, are you out of your mind?"

Briana removed her cloak, tied it to the back of her saddle and rolled up her tunic sleeves. The October sun had risen toward noon, baking the land and her body in an unusual heat wave. Brath had already removed his cloak and the soldiers were all in shirtsleeves. They stood just outside Moiria, waiting for Sigel and his men to check the village for any sign of Shamwa.

Overhead, a harsh, wock-woc-a-wock of a magpie caught Briana's attention. She frowned. It sounded like a warning.

"Brath, I'm the only one who can command the presence out of him."

"I understand that, but you also said there was a spell for that. That sounds much safer than going face-to-face with a man who has tried to kill you. Twice! Whatever made you think I'd agree to that plan?"

"I didn't think you would," she grumbled under her breath, blowing a strand of hair away from her face.

Their argument was curtailed by the sound of harried hoof beats.

Orion, Sigel's stallion, skidded to a halt in front of them. "Moiria is crawling with Gray Military. Something is going on inside the Howling Wolf. That black stallion Shamwa's riding is tethered outside."

Briana touched Brath's elbow. "I should call the horse to me. Then Shamwa is stuck."

"And he would be alerted to our presence. I think the better option is to use the invisibility cloaks to walk in and grab him. Captain Aya'emrys, organize your warriors in a circle around the village. Mr. Stark, pass out cloaks to the knights. Briana, the knights, and I will enter the tavern and get him. Cailleach. I think you and Dara should stay hidden by this tree. I don't want to have to worry about Briana and you."

She narrowed her eyes. "I still do have a bit of magic, lad. I'll be fine. I'll put a stop to anyone trying to escape past me."

Dara lowered his head, hearing his name coupled with stay.

"I need you to protect Cailleach," Briana told him, trying to ease the pain.

"Sigel, you and the crows position yourself just inside the trees, ready to stop any of the Grays who try to leave."

Briana saw Sigel's jaw tighten, knowing he couldn't join them in the tavern, where the space would be tight and difficult for him to maneuver. With a few hand signals he had the crows fly to the trees surrounding Moiria, ready to shift at his command.

Briana took her cloak from Jonathan and slipped it over her head.

"Damn, that's eerie," Brath said. When Briana didn't reply right away, he reached toward her. "Briana, are you still there?"

She heard barely controlled panic in his voice. Clearly, her teleportations were making him skittish.

"I'm here, Brath," she said, reaching a hand out from under the cloak.

"And just as I think your invisibility is weird, I see only a hand. Maker, this is bizarre."

Briana saw his point when he swished his cloak overhead and blinked out of sight.

"Oh, yes, I see what you mean," she said, with a totally inappropriate giggle.

When no one could see anyone, Brath gave the order to move. A chorus of "ouch," "oh, excuse me" and "sorry" peppered the air as they bumped and caromed off one another.

"Hey guys, let's all whisper something every few seconds so we'll get a sense of where we are in relation to one another," Briana suggested.

"Brilliant idea," Brath said. "I knew I kept you around for a reason."

"I'd like to think there's more than my military genius."

"Uh, that would be the least of the reasons I want you around," he said before being kicked out of flirt mode by Kieran Winge.

"We're almost to the tavern," Kieran said, from Brath's left side.

"Time to get serious, love," Brath whispered to her. They passed by the three-goddess fountain that poured water, sparkling from the sun, into the pool below the goddesses' feet. Flowers bloomed fervently in bunches and cascades of color. If not for the absolute absence of human activity, Briana could believe it was a day like any other.

"There's the arsewipe, right in front of the bloody window." Sir Cruahan's deep voice came from just behind Briana.

"Sweet Maker, he's got Grania!" Briana was shocked to see one of her nemeses holding the arm of another.

"He knows we're here," Brath said, with that dangerous calm that sent a shiver up Briana's spine.

Cailleach spoke up. "I imagine the Dar Morch alerted him. He very likely feels Briana's presence."

"Shit!" Brath swore. "Kieran, you and Jonathan get her out of here!"

"Brath, no! I can help! You guys get Shamwa and I can get Grania to safety."

Brath growled in frustration. There was no time to argue the plan or change it.

"Let's go then, while we still have some semblance of surprise," he said. Shamwa was using a citizen of Uisneach as a human shield. They were not about to let him get away with that!

"Knights, on my count to three, we rush the door. Cruahan and I will grab Shamwa and Briana will move the woman out of the way. As soon as we've secured him, we'll remove cloaks and finish him."

Briana's heart was pounding. Would this work? Or, would they tumble in and around each other? And would they really, after all this time, capture Shamwa? Finish him, Brath had said. Would they kill him, ending his terrorism and getting Uisneach on the path to a better future? These thoughts raced through her mind as they moved, miraculously, as a unit, toward the door. Without fanfare, Brath pushed the door open and Briana heard boots moving toward the target. Briana felt a moment of triumph as Shamwa's expression turned from smug to confused. Then Brath's cloak caught on a chair leg and slid away, revealing him. He wasted no time in tackling Shamwa. Briana, still covered, grabbed Grania's arm. The young woman, eyes wide with fear, pulled away. Briana grabbed a second time and tried to pull her out of harm's way, but damn, if the woman wasn't a scrapper. During the struggle, Grania found an edge of Briana's cloak and it dropped to the floor.

"You!" Grania went feral and attacked Briana.

"Grania, there's no time for this. I'm trying to save you. You need to come with me."

"I'm not going anywhere with you. You're the reason Silas is gone!"

"Silas is gone because he's trying to save our kingdom," Briana growled back, pinning Grania's arm behind her. "And if you want to see him again, you better work with me here. Defeating Shamwa is our best hope of getting Silas back, so what say you help us instead of trying to beat the hell out of me?"

She could see Grania trying to figure out what to do. Briana stole a glance at the struggle between her husband and Shamwa. All cloaks were off now, and a handful of Grays were piling through the front door. It turned into a melee. Brath landed a fist in the middle of Shamwa's face. Blood spurted across the king' shirt. In response, Shamwa brought his foot up hard to Brath's crotch, causing him to stumble backward.

Briana went ballistic. "You bloody bastard. I'm going to kill you myself!"

"Oh, did I nearly wreck the chance for an heir?" Shamwa's maniacal grin and ghoulish red eyes made him possibly one of the handsomest jack-o-lanterns Briana had ever seen. He grabbed a kettle from the heart and swung at Brath.

With no time to think, Briana shoved her ring finger at Shamwa. "I call on the wisdom and power of the tuathla! Fire back!" The kettle reversed direction. As it arced back at Shamwa, it flashed into flames. With a flick of her finger, the flames leapt and caught Shamwa's shirt. She'd only meant to stop him, but he went up like a Roman candle. She turned for Grania but grabbed air as the woman swept past her, thwarted by a flaming Shamwa. The dry wood of the building and furniture made good kindling and within seconds, the tavern was completely engulfed in flames and smoke.

Briana tried to pull Grania away, but a heavy curtain of smoke swirled around Shamwa and the tavern maid, making it impossible to separate her from him.

Crash...

Briana turned in time to see the back wall of the tavern fall in. At the same time, she heard a keening sound from Shamwa's direction. Intuition told her it was the Dar Morch trying to escape the burning body it was trapped in.

"Come to Mama," Briana hissed to the entity. She felt nothing. She was about to try again, when a strong arm pulled her away. She knew it was Brath and that it would be futile and dangerous to resist.

She let him lead her out of the burning building and cried out when the wolf, moon and red letters of the tavern's sign fell inward, followed by the remaining walls. Flames reared up, momentarily blinding Briana, but she didn't have to see the fire to feel the whoosh of something living sweep past her. She thought she heard Shamwa's laugh, but that would be impossible. He was burning up right in front of her eyes. Wasn't he?

She turned away from what she was sure the end of Shamwa. And of Grania. Tears pricked her eyes. Whatever stupid rivalry they'd had didn't warrant this! She couldn't hold back and buried her face in Brath's chest to avoid seeing anymore. As her tears fell into his shirt, her rage rose. She was angry at Shamwa for being so bloody evil. Angry at herself for not being able to stop him on the two occasions she'd stood in the same room with him. Angry at Grania for resisting. And angry at Silas for not getting back here with the runes.

A thought jolted her out of remorse and she pulled away. "Brath, where's the Dar Morch's horse?"

Brath swiveled around to survey the area. Villagers were frantically trying to put out the fire before other dwellings caught. Soldiers wrangled captured Grays. But there was no black stallion other than Orion to be seen. His eyebrows rose and lips puckered as he shook his head. "That's a good question. Cailleach, did you see the horse?"

She shook her head. "He did not come this way."

Turning to the crowd he hollered out, "Did anyone see a black stallion with red eyes and smoke possibly issuing from his nostrils?"

Lots of head-shaking and twittering, all to the negative. Until Rippa stepped around the corner of a shop. "I seen the beast, headin' away from the village with that girl on 'is back. The one from the tavern with the black hair and the big…"

"Grania!" Briana said, tugging at Brath. "How could she possibly have gotten away? She was right in front of me with Shamwa. They were both on fire!"

Brath rubbed the stubble on his chin.

"Brath, if he left on the horse, we should be able to catch him," Sigel said.

"Yeah, unless the horse uses some magical powers to disappear or something," Briana said with a flick of her fingers in the air.

"Kieran?"

The young captain of the Winge army stepped in front of the king. "Yes, Sire?"

"Take your crows to Aurum Castle. See if you can find any trace of the horse, Shamwa or the girl on the way. If you find the girl, bring her back. If you find the horse, let it go and if you find Shamwa, destroy him! If you get to Aurum Castle, see if you can get in via the river. If so, keep the troops there and send word for us to follow. Sigel and I will take a small detail and get the queen to Winge Mansion and await word there. Sir Stark, I would ask you and the remaining Taranian army to stay here and help clean up this mess. Sir Faolan, you stay here and help your parents get settled somewhere until the tavern can be rebuilt."

"Yes, Sire. Thank you," the gentle knight said, focusing his one eye on his king while the other might have been looking at Briana. Or Rippa. Briana wasn't sure.

She offered him an encouraging smile in any case. "Please, tell your parents how sorry I am about all of this," she said, wondering what had happened to the McPhees. She'd have thought them nearby during the disaster. Brath was already on the move, so seeking them out was out of the question.

Within minutes they were on the road again.

∽

Briana sat in a high-backed chair at Winge Mansion, stroking Dara's head and staring into the fireplace. They'd arrived at the mansion in less than three hours. A small legion of servants had them bathed, dressed in clean clothes and fed in another two hours. The Winges, including Epona, now sat in the library in front of a fire that Briana couldn't imagine would bring comfort, and yet it did. Sir Thomas drilled questions at the king. Brath told him how impressed he was with Kieran and assured him that the man had been nothing but loyal and committed to the Taranian cause. Briana saw relief and pride soften the Winge clan chief's eyes. Epona smiled widely, her dark eyes also gleaming with satisfaction. She and Sir Thomas exchanged a glance that Briana read as "I told you so," and "Yes, you did."

Lady Isabella had seen to their every need and now sat beside her husband, listening carefully and asking insightful questions. When the information about the Dar Morch was shared, she summed up the dilemma.

"It seems you have a choice. Allow Briana to lure the Dar Morch to Scáil Meanoiche or find Catriona and Urelian. Briana, do you have any idea how to make that connection?"

"Not a clue."

"Cailleach?"

She shook her head.

"She is not going to take on Shamwa or ride the black beast to the Underworld. Not happening."

"I wonder if you can take someone to help you?" Epona asked, sounding eager for the chance to be that person.

"I think I'd have to do it alone," Briana replied, leaning back and closing her eyes.

Unexpected images surfaced from her subconscious. A magical map. *The Book of Leaves.* Silas walking out of a ghostly mist. A fire-breathing black stallion. Red eyes. The torture room at Aurum Castle. Keys. A golden-haired dryad. Ornately carved runes. The Queen's Pool. Herself, racing alone across a moonlit landscape on Banrion. Kailen's Castle. Fighting. A bloody knife.

"Bri, wake up, love! It's just a dream."

"Huh, oh, Maker. Oh, no." She opened her eyes to see Brath kneeling next to her and Sir Thomas and Lady Isabella staring at her with worry-filled eyes. Dara's head lay on her knee, equally as concerned.

"I am so sorry," she said. "I must have dozed off."

"You were dreaming," Brath said.

She drew in a deep breath. "Yeah, I guess I was. But I don't remember it."

"Come on, then. Let's go to bed."

She was dead on her feet, but she knew that look in his eyes. It did not mean "let's go to bed and sleep," and she was all in for what he had in mind. Sometimes the only thing that could soothe what they'd been through in the last seventy-two hours was sex.

She took his proffered hand and returned his smoky gaze. "Let's."

"Good night, Your Majesty," Sir Thomas said, giving her a hug. Epona and Lady Isabella did likewise before blowing out the last candles as they all left the library. Brath led her to their room, where a fire burned low in the hearth and candles shed a peaceful glow on the turned-down bed. Briana sighed with anticipation at the comfort she knew would come in that bed and in his arms; she looked at Brath, already removing his shirt. She looked at the sleeping gown on the bed, stole a look at her husband, who was stealing his own look, and moved the gown to a chair.

"Would you mind untying me?" She said, turning her back to him.

Clothing was swiftly dispensed with. Brath crawled in next to her and, wasting no time, rolled on his side, drew her body close to his and kissed her with passion held in tight control. Her lips and tongue demanded more. She wanted to be taken, not as a victim, but as a victor. She wanted to feel powerful even while uncertainty swirled around them. She wanted to meet him in sexual battle, stroke for stroke, and feel her lifeblood surge through her, freely giving, freely taking.

"Are you sure you're not too tired?" he whispered against her jaw.

"I'm exhausted, as are you, but there is nothing I want more than to love like the warriors we are."

His breath came out as a *whoosh* against her neck a split second before he released the fetters of restraint.

Their lovemaking was fast, hard and alchemical, turning all their fear, frustration and tension into reassurance, relief and reconnection.

Afterward, he blew out the candles and held her against his chest.

"I feel like a Rolo," she said.

"A what?"

"A Rolo. It's a candy that has a hard chocolate shell but inside it's filled with gooey caramel."

He laughed out loud. "I don't think 'gooey' is a very romantic term."

"How about gummy? Or gelatinous? Or chewy?"

"Gee, Briana, you have such a way with words. How about—soft?"

"Um, yeah," she cuddled in closer. "Soft. That works."

She was soft. Sated. And as near happy as one could be under such a tenuous state of living. Not far away was the thought that tomorrow would likely bring a new worry and that tonight she might take a deeper dive into the terrible dreams of a subconscious attempting to resolve a plethora of problems.

⤜

Dara's wet nose on her cheek woke her just before the loud knock at the door.

"Give us a minute," Brath hollered and turned to her. "I don't want to leave this bed, Briana. I want to make love to you again and again and forget about Shamwa, battles and the saving of Uisneach, but I'd bet my last coin that whoever knocks on that door doesn't bring happy news."

She put her hands on his face and kissed him lightly. "You're probably right and so we must get up and get to work. But tonight, my love, when the last problem has been dealt with, we'll return to this bed or some bed, and I'm going to love you like you've never been loved before."

He smiled into a final kiss. "I'll hold you to that," he said before throwing back the covers and reaching for his trousers.

In record time, they were dressed and opened the door to admit a grumpy Sigel and amused Kieran.

"Do you have time to meet with us, Your Majesty?" Sigel asked, eliciting a squeak from Briana, who was trying not to laugh out loud. He glared at her. Really glared. Her amusement disappeared.

"Come in," Brath said, leading them to the table and chairs in the long end of the room.

Briana's lady's maid, Claire, followed the men in with trays of food and an urn of tea.

"Cailleach and Sir Thomas will be along momentarily," Kieran said. Briana found it odd that he would refer to his father as Sir Thomas but supposed he was trying to keep their fragile relationship professional for the time being.

After making sure that everyone was served, Claire headed to make the bed. Briana touched her arm on the way by. "Thank you, Claire."

"My pleasure, Your Majesty," she murmured, and went about her duties with a smile.

"Good morning," Sir Thomas greeted everyone. "Feeling better this morning, Your Majesty?" he asked of Briana, dropping a light kiss on the crown of her head.

"Much, thank you."

Cailleach, coming in behind him, nodded at Briana and Brath and took a chair next to Kieran. Briana noted lines of strain and fatigue in her face and frowned. She understood Cailleach's grief, having lost her father and Silas. She would find a way to comfort and offer support to Cailleach, but for now, they had to focus on Kieran's report.

Claire finished with her duties and left, shutting the door quietly behind her. Briana was always amazed at how staff could be so attentive in such an unobtrusive way. Dara, sensing a meeting about to convene, curled up with a big sigh at Briana's feet.

"Well, I have one piece of good news on top of a mountain of bad news," Kieran started.

"Go on." Brath picked up his tea and took a sip.

"First of all, the cloaks worked. We were able to get very close to the castle without being seen by anyone."

"But?"

"You can't get to Aurum Castle by river."

"Why not?" Briana asked.

"I don't know, but after Shamwa took the girl inside the castle, we tried, and it blocked us."

"Grania is alive?" Briana sat back hard in the chair.

"She is. She dropped this on the ground near the castle. Anyone recognize it?" He threw a gold pendant shaped like an arrow on the table.

A grunt came from Sigel's side of the table. "It belongs to Silas," he said, giving Briana a narrow look.

"Oh," she said, with full understanding. A flash of irritation stabbed her, followed by a wave of guilt. *I have no right to be jealous of their history,* she reminded herself. She forced a look of indifference on her face.

"With the Dar Morch's power, it is quite possible that Shamwa created an illusion of his and Grania's death while using a stolen cloak to escape. The question is whether or not Grania is a victim or an accomplice."

"Oh, I don't believe she is a willing partner in this," Briana said, earning a pair of raised eyebrows from Sigel.

"Then we'll give her the benefit of the doubt and assume she needs saving," Brath said. "But how? We can't get in."

No one had an answer or idea.

"We have to go on the offensive, but when and where is critical." Kieran's statement was met with unanimous agreement.

Briana picked up the pendant from the table, turning it over in her hand. It was Silas', all right, she could feel his imprint on it. "I'll hang on to this and get it back to Grania, or Silas, whomever turns up first."

Brath seemed not to hear her. "Let's think this through. We need to avoid the strongest part of Shamwa's army and attack the weakest."

Plotting took until lunchtime. When Lady Isabella came to invite them downstairs for the noon meal, Sigel stood to summarize the plan thus far.

"We move forward with the tunnel project. The Winge army will patrol and protect the west while half of the faerie warriors begin tunneling from the southern foothills of the Dromdara Mountains. The rest will return with the king and queen to Ard Darach."

Some of the Taranian army would be housed as inconspicuously as possible near Ratskillen. Small groups wearing invisibility cloaks would travel back and forth to the digging site and work in shifts. Some Winge soldiers would join the diggers and watch for any sign that Shamwa was aware of their activity.

Sigel carried on with more specifics, but Briana's mind was stuck on the tunneling. It would take forever to dig a tunnel to Aurum Castle, even with faerie magic. They needed help from another source and Briana knew where that could be found. If she could just communicate better with digging animals, they'd have an entire army of diggers. She knew she had the magic for it, inherent in her faerie blood, but so far, she'd only been able to talk with a few birds, a deer and a mouse. The mouse! He was the key to this, she was sure of it. He had shown up at Ard Darach and Firmara. If he was somehow traveling around with her, then he should be here too. It would be way too busy during the daytime, but she promised herself to get up early tomorrow morning to see if he would show himself.

"There's one more thing we have to consider?" Brath said tightly. "If Shamwa has an invisibility cloak, he is an even bigger danger. He could walk among any of us at any time and run a knife through our back. Every single one of us must always be on high alert. None of us is safe if he's able to go invisible."

The room went dead quiet.

"It's imperative that we get the queen and Cailleach to Ard Darach while we know Shamwa remains at Aurum Castle. We'll leave tomorrow morning."

Tension followed the group to the dining room and Briana was surprised when Sigel limped past the door. "Sigel, aren't you going to join us?" she asked.

"Not hungry," he said, and kept walking out the front door.

Briana frowned. She made a mental note to find time to talk with him about what was causing this uncharacteristic surliness, though she was pretty sure she knew.

﹏

Maneuvering out of bed without waking Brath wasn't easy, but her promise of loving him unmercifully had been kept and he never moved a muscle as she slid out of the warm comforter, lit a candle and crooked her finger at Dara.

The candle threw ghostly shadows on the walls as she made her way to the library, where a fire had already been stoked, creating a cozy ambience. She settled herself in a chair, wrapped a throw over her shoulders and waited for any sign of the mouse. Her thoughts and Dara kept her company. She and Cailleach had to find the summoning and banishing spell to deal with the Dar Morch. Briana had no idea where to even start, but hoped inspiration would come from somewhere. She'd assigned herself a private task, learning how to control portals. If she could manipulate the portal, she could find Catriona and the spells. She could also get back into Aurum Castle.

Tiny scratching caught her ear and she returned her attention to the present and her furry gray friend. He found a warm place beside the fire and looked up at her with his beady eyes and shivering whiskers.

"Hello, Mouse."

"Your Majesty." He tipped his head in acknowledgment.

"How is that you manage to travel with me without my knowing?"

"Why is it you always look a gift horse, or mouse, in the mouth?"

"Touché. I need your help."

The mouse cocked his pointy head. "Really? How unusual."

"No need to be snarky."

"Snarky?" the mouse asked. "I don't believe I know the word."

"I believe you know what I mean."

"What, pray tell, can I do for you, Your Majesty? Need help with your love life? Need a friend to bolster your self-esteem? Need me to tell you how much magic you really own?"

"Did you get up on the wrong side of the nest? Or do you really see me as so insecure?"

"Well, you have needed a fair amount of hand-holding, Queen Briana. However, I admit, you seem to be maturing a bit."

"Oh, well, thank you. That means the world to me."

"Now, who's being snarky?"

"Can we get down to business, please?" she asked.

"Please do."

"I need you to rally the digging animals to help us tunnel through to Aurum Castle."

"Oh, just that. You ask for so little."

She ignored his continued sarcasm. "I know I can communicate with some animals but it's still pretty random and I don't know how to get the word out to enough of them. Surely, you can manage that for the kingdom?"

With his tiny hind foot, he scratched behind his ear and considered her request. "You want me to recruit badgers, foxes, otters and weasels, any of whom would be happy to eat me rather than help me?"

"And rabbits and moles," she added. "Anyone who can move dirt."

The rodent took so long answering that the sound of a door shutting somewhere in the castle made her jump.

"I'll tell you what I'll do. I'll tell the rabbits, who won't eat me, and the moles. I will encourage them to spread the word. I'm not going to promise you the entire animal kingdom will answer the call, but maybe you'll get some help."

"Thank you, Mr. Mouse." She thought about following up with his comments about her insecurity, but then she might just prove his point. "I appreciate your help. So, will you be going to Ard Darach with me?"

"Back to that, are we?" He made a squeaking noise. "Maybe."

"Briana who are you talking to?" Brath said coming up behind her.

She started to tell him no one, but changed her mind. "The mouse. He's going to help us recruit animals to help dig the tunnel. Aren't you, Mr. Mouse?"

The creature stared at her and the king, whiskers trembling and one foot scratching, but said nothing.

"Perhaps he won't speak when I'm around. I don't know how to speak mouse."

"Well, you're not faerie, Brath."

"No, I'm not, but you are." He sat in the chair next to her and held his hands out. "And since it's still very early and no one is up yet, why don't you come over here and make a little magic with me?"

Briana glanced toward the mouse who took his cue and scurried away. Briana accepted her husband's invitation and moved over to settle herself on his lap, wrapping an arm around his neck and leaning in for a good-morning kiss. When his hand settled across her waist, the warmth from the fire became a mere whisper compared to the heat that spread through her midsection.

"Since everyone is still sleeping, maybe we should go back to bed and practice our baby-making technique."

"I suppose we have an hour before we have to leave for home," he agreed without hesitation.

CHAPTER THIRTY-TWO

BREAKING POINT

Silas, Midland Regional Hospital, Tullamore, Ireland

Beeping sounds dotted the wasteland of his brain. Unfamiliar smells leaked into his subconscious. Pain shrouded his body. With supreme effort, he opened his eyes to blurry images of machines and tubes, and Orla sitting hunched over beside his bed. As the fuzziness cleared, he saw she was asleep, a book lying haphazardly on her lap.

A nurse came in. "Oh, we're awake, then?"

Orla's head snapped up and she leaned in closer. "Silas? How do you feel?"

"Like I've been run over by an army."

The nurse bent over him, examining him from head to toe. Her familiarity with his body was more than a bit uncomfortable. "Does that hurt?" She poked at his leg.

"Hell yes, it hurts. What's banjaxed me leg?"

"It's broken, Silas. Be still," Orla advised. "Let the nurse assess you. You've been out cold for a week with a severe concussion."

"What's a concussion?"

The nurse glanced up with an odd expression.

"It's when your brain slams against the skull, which it did when you hit the tree. It..."

He sat up, much too quickly. He moaned. "I'm going to be sick," he choked out in a panic. He grabbed the basin the nurse handed to him. What little sat in his stomach erupted into a greenish pool in the pan. He shuddered and handed the pan back to the nurse. Orla offered him a damp cloth to wipe his mouth.

"I'm sorry," he said to Orla.

"It's okay, Silas. It's normal to be nauseated when you move too fast after…"

"No, I mean I'm sorry for the accident. Are you okay?"

She waved him off. "I'm fine. Once the emergency crews got me breathin' under control, I was fine. You took the brunt of the collision with the tree."

He'd never have lived with himself if she'd been hurt as a result of his careless driving. He took a few moments to get his thoughts back in order. She sat quietly watching him.

"How was your date?"

"My what?"

"Your date with Ned Turner."

Her blank stared turned angry. "You come out of a coma and that's the first thing you think of? What kind of a wanker do you take me for? I'm supposed to leave you here, half dead, and go out with another guy? Jaysus, Silas. I seriously don't understand you."

Silas didn't quite understand it either but was saved from further reflection by Katrina saying, "Well, well, the bard wakes."

"Katrina! What are you doin' here?"

"I was supposed to wait in Maine to hear whether you lived or died? Where else would I be?"

"Was I really in danger of death?"

"It was a nasty head injury," said a man who quickly identified himself as Dr. Moran. "It was touch and go for a while. If you ladies will excuse us, I'd like to examine my patient."

Katrina and Orla made a hasty exit. The doctor lifted the sheets from Silas' legs. It was only then that Silas saw the bulky black thing secured around his lower leg. How in hell was he supposed to get around to search for the runes like this? "When can this come off?"

"You'll need to wear the walking boot and use crutches for four to six weeks. You were lucky the fibula fracture wasn't worse, so this, and physio-therapy when the boot comes off, are all that's required."

The doctor must've seen that Silas had no understanding of these terms and he tried again. "You broke the small, supportive bone in your lower leg. Since it wasn't a complete break and didn't break through the skin, you didn't need surgery. This boot will keep the bone stable and minimize pain, allowing it to heal. You're young and strong so I doubt you'll need more than four weeks on crutches. After that, the physical therapist will show you exercises to strengthen your leg to full recovery. For the next few weeks though, no driving or any exercise that would stress that leg. Understand?"

Silas nodded, disgusted with what looked like an obstacle to his search. The doctor finished his exam and stepped back with a pleased smile.

"Youth and health are on your side. I see no evidence of any neurologi-cal or cognitive changes from the concussion. You are a very lucky man, Mr. O'Mara."

Silas wasn't feeling lucky but at the risk of sounding ungrateful, he simply nodded.

"I'll have the nurse relieve you of all this extra equipment. You can get out of bed, but do it slowly. A week in bed makes you a bit unstable. Don't want you taking any falls, then, do we?"

The doctor left, replaced by a petite but militarily efficient nurse, who relieved him of what she called intravenous access and unhooked the elec-trodes from his chest and arms that were monitoring his vital signs.

Maker, you need to be a doctor to understand their language, he thought testily.

Finally, she left the room and Orla and Katrina came back in.

"They'll discharge you tomorrow, if all goes well," Katrina said.

"I'll have to find a way to pay them," Silas said.

"I'll take care of it, Silas," said Katrina. "You just focus on healing and getting back to the task at hand. I've some errands to run, but I'll be back later tonight. Mum and Da want to come and visit. I'll bring them along."

He nodded at her encouraging smile.

When she was gone, he turned to Orla, who was busying herself arrang-ing his water pitcher and pulling the bed linens down over his toes.

"You don't have to play nurse to me, Orla."

"I know, but I've never had the chance to be someone's nurse. I rather like it."

"I don't."

She paused in her ministrations, stood and put a hand firmly on her hip. "Tell me you're not going to be one of those cranky male patients nurses talk about."

This scene seemed so intimate, like they were a couple. Part of him was intrigued, part pleased, while yet another part was terrified.

"Orla, I am so sorry I caused that accident. I could've killed you."

"You didn't cause the accident, Silas, so don't batter yourself. I was the gobdaw who waited too long to use my inhaler. If anyone is at fault, it's me. Anyway, it was an accident, pure and simple. Luckily, we both live to tell the story."

"I wouldn't hurt you for the world, Orla."

They both went silent, understanding that he was speaking on two different levels.

"I know," she finally said.

෴

"Chestnuts roastin' on an open fire," crooned Silas. "Jack Frost nipping at your—"

"Enough with the Christmas carols," Orla groaned as he launched into the sixth song in a row.

"What else would I be singin' then, with you puttin' all them colored balls on the tree? Besides, I've got to have these down for work. They'll be expectin' Christmas songs, won't they?"

"Couldn't you learn somethin' a bit more contemporary? What about 'All I Want for Christmas'?"

"Mariah Carey, is it? Hmm… For you, dear Orla, I'll learn it." Her responding blush and raised eyebrow perplexed him. "What is it?"

"You might want to read the lyrics before you go singin' it for me."

He picked up his phone and typed in a few words. The song lyrics popped up and he read through them, consternation rising with each verse. He left his eyes on the screen long after he'd finished reading. What should he say now? Singing it for her might sound like a promise he wasn't ready

410

to make and yet, the image of them holding each other under the mistletoe was more than a little appealing.

"Relax, you wee gombeen, I'm only teasin' you. Flip that switch, would you?" She pointed to the electrical cord with the tree lights plugged into it. Silas reached over.

"There, would you look at that?" she said, standing back to admire her handiwork. "Now you've a proper Christmas tree."

Silas had to admit, the twinkling colored lights were pretty and cheered him in a way not much had lately.

"Thank you, Orla. It's a lovely tree." While she picked up the empty boxes and put them in the trash bag, he watched her. She'd been incredibly supportive during his rehabilitation. In between classes and homework, she spent all her time at his place or driving him to appointments, trying to cheer him up. He had, in fact, been one of those lousy patients she mentioned, and bad as he felt about it, couldn't seem to snap out of it. The boot had come off four days ago and the physical therapist was nearly ready to discharge him on a home maintenance program. Even that piece of good news couldn't chase away the dark cloud of depression that hung over him.

Orla, growing quite comfortable in his cottage now, responded to the knock at the door. "Come in."

Katrina, arms filled with packages, entered. Orla took a few of the boxes out of her arms and put them on the table.

"I'd help if I could, but..." Silas had meant it to be funny. He hadn't time enough to get up and help since Orla had responded so speedily. However, Katrina apparently didn't find the humor.

"And you could, if you wanted to."

He was stunned at her snippy response. "Everythin' okay, Katrina?" he asked, leaning forward on the sofa.

Orla, with uncharacteristic intuition, intervened. "I'm glad you're here, Katrina. I need to get home and finish an assignment, but how do you like Silas' tree?"

"It's lovely, Orla. I assume you did it. Very nice of you."

An uncomfortable silence hung over the room. Orla moved the boxes under the tree. "I was hopin' to cheer him up."

Silas didn't like how apologetic she sounded. "And you did, Orla. I thank you."

"I thank you for the Christmas carols," she said, sounding as though she were defending him.

What was really going on?

"Well, Silas, I guess I'll see you later," said Orla. "I'll be by Wednesday to take you to work." She patted his shoulder, then grabbed her purse and headed for the door. "Don't forget to check the water in the bowl every day and add more water if it needs it."

When she was gone, Silas turned to Katrina. "Can I get you some tea?" She shook her head.

"Katrina, what's botherin' you?"

"Okay, I'm going to be honest with you, Silas. Since the accident I feel you're less and less interested in finding the runes and more and more interested in pursuing a relationship with Orla."

"That's not fair, I…"

She put a hand up to stop him. "Let me finish, please. It's your business if you've fallen in love with Orla. She's a fine girl and I wouldn't wish you a life of loneliness because you and Briana can't be together. However, as long as Briana's life is in jeopardy, you do not get to give up on my daughter."

Anger flared in him. How dare she suggest that he'd give up on Briana. "I have done no such thing!"

"No? Have you gone through those trunks again? Have you made one trip to the hill since the accident? Did you even help Orla get this tree up?" She was staring at the tree and Silas was startled to see tears forming in her eyes. "You do not get to give up on my daughter, Silas O'Mara. You need to get your ass in gear and find the damn runes." With that she whirled, and left Silas with his mouth hanging wide open.

On the one hand, she was right. He hadn't looked through the trunks or gone to the hill. But for Maker's sake, he couldn't drive with this bloody boot on. He was dependent on Orla or Briana's family for everything. On the other hand, he honestly didn't have the heart for searching anymore. What use was it? He'd been over that hill with a fine-tooth comb and come up empty. It was most likely that the Runes of Evalon were nothing more than a legend. What was the point in expending energy he didn't possess on a wild goose chase? And if that were the case, why didn't he just say so and muckle on to Orla with both hands? Or go home, empty-handed and a failure?

He sat alone in the darkening room, the blinking lights of the Christmas tree offering a sense of holiday cheer he simply did not feel.

Only the blinking message on his phone, a text inviting him to come over to Caitlin's for supper, broke the stupor he found himself in. Any thought of ignoring it would only bring Katrina after him, so grabbing a light jacket and putting on boots, he headed across the drive to the main house.

Light chatter couldn't disguise the somberness of the O'Brien family. Katrina was quiet, though polite enough. Caitlin seemed sad and Finnegan continued to chatter on about local news as though nothing murky was swirling underneath the surface.

As Cait cleared the supper dishes, Katrina finally made eye contact with Silas. "I'm sorry about earlier today."

"It's fine, don't worry about it."

"No, it's not fine. Nothing's fine. I'm just so frustrated, Silas. I want to know that my daughter is okay. Can you understand that? What if Lord Shamwa kills her?"

"Brath won't let that happen," Silas snapped, his tone sharp with resentment he'd thought buried. He gave her an apologetic look. "Of course, I understand. I worry about her—them—too. And I feel like a bloody gobdaw that I can't do the one thing that would ensure their future and restore magic to the kingdom."

Cait returned with an aromatic cobbler and spooned it out into four bowls. "I wish I could remember somethin' helpful."

"Everyone just stand down," Finnegan ordered firmly. "This search has gone on much longer than anyone thought it would, with nothin' to show for it. But it's not Silas' fault. It's not anyone's fault. So, let's let the lad breathe. Silas, I do think yer a bit depressed and need to do somethin' besides work and sleep. Why don't ye and Orla go away somewhere?"

Grim silence met his statement. Silas looked around the room. While Finnegan was looking at him straight in the eye, the women stared down at their plates. Silas frowned.

"I'll just speak to the gorilla in the room," Finnegan continued, practically and patiently. "We would all love to see Silas find the runes and go home to save the kingdom and be reunited with Briana. But, even if he does find the runes, Briana is married and Silas will, presumably, remain a bachelor. I don't know about ye two," he pointed to the women, "but I'd like to see the lad happy, with a family of his own. Orla's a fine girl and she cares for ye, Silas. I think ye care for her too. Get on with life, man. Keep searchin' for the runes but don't let the opportunity to fall in love slip away. A good wife is a blessin'." He smiled affectionately at Caitlin.

The tender roast beef that Caitlin had served now sat like a brick in his gut. He looked to Katrina, who nodded through misty eyes.

"Every time I read the cards, I see you and Briana together, but it may not be together in the romantic sense. I may be reading my own desires into the spread. Orla is sweet, kind and totally over the moon about you. Go for it. Maybe that will make you feel better and renew your enthusiasm for the quest."

"I'm not all that comfortable with you all discussin' my love life like it's a family matter up for a vote, but I appreciate the thought behind it. I don't know meself where things are with Orla, but I can promise you I'll get me head back into the search. I'll go through the trunks tomorrow. And now, if you don't mind, I've got some songs I'm workin' on for the pub and need to put some energy there as well."

Back in his cottage, he turned on the Christmas tree lights. It really was pretty, so kind of Orla to put it up for him. She'd be a good girlfriend or wife and maybe a good mother too. He was crazy not to let her in.

His phone dinged and he saw a text from work.

Christmas Party Invitation. December 18th at 7 p.m. Food and drinks provided. Band hired. Not you, Silas. Bring a date. RSVP ASAP.

"Oh, a party. How grand," Áed said, looking over his shoulder.

"Where the devil have you been, man?"

"Around. Didn't think you needed me."

"I don't."

"Ungrateful, wanker."

"Ungrateful for what, Áed? All the help you haven't provided? All the support you've failed to offer?"

"Well, you had the lass to help. You didn't need me."

"True, but here you are. What is it you want now?"

"Nothin'. Well, a wee dram wouldn't go unwelcomed."

"You're going to wreck your liver, you know that?"

The clurichaun shrugged and held out a thimble-sized cup. Silas poured the little man a dram of Tullamore Dew. He started to recap the bottle, but sighed and poured himself one too.

"You got woman problems?"

"I wish everyone would stop worryin' about me love life."

"Well, maybe if you'd stop sighin' like it's the end of life and mopin' around like a heartsick eejit, we would. What's going on? The wee cracker mad at you?"

"No, Briana's grandfather thinks I should forget about Briana and accept Orla's affections."

"Affections? Such a gallant way of puttin' it."

Silas glared at him.

"No, I'm serious. You bards have a way of sayin' things that sounds so pretty. Anyway, the auld man's right. You're wastin' a perfectly good woman, I can't believe I just said that, on a dream that may never come true. You should invite the cracker to the party."

Silas sipped his whiskey. *I've failed me quest,* he thought morosely. *I can't go back to Uisneach and face them. I should just accept me lot here and move on.*

"Áed, if you're finished with your drink? I think I'd like to be alone."

In a huff and a blink, the clurichaun was gone.

Silas picked up the phone. Before he could change his mind, he tapped out a text.

Work is throwing a Christmas party on the 18th. Would you care to be my date?

In seconds he received a reply.

Yes, well, who else would you take, then?

He couldn't help but smile. For not being a bard, she did have a way with words herself.

He downed what was left in the glass and went to his bedroom. As soon as he turned on the lamp beside the bed, Briana's face smiled up at him. Another morose sigh escaped his lips.

"I will never stop lovin' you, Briana. You are a part of me soul that I couldn't deny, even if I wanted to. But I can't spend me life alone and that means I must make a really hard choice here. I hope you will understand." Kissing the picture once, he put it in the nightstand drawer. Reaching behind his neck, he unlaced the warrior bones and laid them on top of the photo in the drawer.

CHAPTER THIRTY-THREE

LETTING GO

"Sorry, Silas, but I'm not ready yet," said Orla. "Had an emergency at Mum's house. She's babysittin' wee Maggie, and the lassie is vomitin'. I went to help her. I'll be just a couple of minutes. Make yourself comfy." She pointed to the sofa.

He took a seat and picked up a magazine from the coffee table. "Take your time, Orla. If you were ready, we'd be early. *Faerie* magazine? If you're not careful, you'll end up a believer."

"I never said I didn't believe in them," she called from the other room. Her bedroom. She'd left the door open. He could hear drawers sliding open and hangers rattle together as she rifled through them. "And, well, Áed convinced me that the little people are in fact, a reality."

"A pain in the arse, is what they are," he muttered.

"What? I didn't hear you."

"I said," he said, turning his head to project better Orla walked past the door in a pair of black linen slacks and a pale pink, nearly transparent bra that plunged between the fertile valley of shadowy cleavage. Silas completely forgot what he was going to say. Her generous breasts swayed gently as she moved across the foot of the bed and reached for something behind the door.

Heat spread from his hardening groin to his face, and his mouth went bone dry.

"Silas?"

He couldn't answer. What the hell was he thinking, denying himself the gift of her heart—and that gorgeous body?

"Silas, are you all right?" She came out of the room, smoothing the edge of the rose-colored blouse over her hips.

"I'm fine," he lied. "Lost me train of thought."

"It's excitin' that you can drive tonight. How does it feel?"

"Great. Freedom at last." If she noticed his nervousness, she didn't say anything.

She slid into a pair of black half-boots, fluffed her hair once and grabbed her purse. "I'm ready."

Yeah, me too, he thought miserably.

"Hey," she said, taking a step back and studied him. "Where are your hearts?"

"I took them off."

"Why?" she asked in a breathless whisper.

"It's time to move on from Uisneach," he answered, looking her in the eye. Seven simple words that were about as complicated as the feelings that had guided him to say them.

Orla's look said she knew exactly how earth-shattering the statement was.

They said little on the drive to Seamus' pub. Just as they pulled into the parking lot, Orla spoke without looking at him. "Silas, you can't give up on the runes. We're going to find them and somehow get them to Uisneach. However, at the risk of soundin' totally selfish, I do think you're right to let go of a woman who can't ever be yours. That's all I'm goin' to say about it." She opened her door and stepped out.

They entered the pub to find the party already in full swing. Seamus met them at the bar, and slid drinks into their hands. "Orla, darlin', you look beautiful. Silas, well, at least you're upright and no extra legs to help you walk. What do you think of the band I've hired for tonight?"

The musicians seemed to have a knack for taking Irish classics and creating arrangements that hovered somewhere near folk and rap with a dance mix beat. An interesting combination.

"Good choice!" He glanced at Orla, taking a sip of her wine, and hoped like hell he could dance with her. At least to the slow ones.

He took a swig of Guinness. "Seamus, might you want to pour me a shot of the *uisce beatha*?"

"Of course, lad. In a partyin' mood, are ye then?"

Silas accepted the healthy pour of amber liquid and downed it, following it with another swallow of the black stuff.

Orla cocked her head in his direction. "I understand you might wish a little emotional fortitude but gettin' langers may not result in the outcome you desire."

He choked on the beer. The outcome he desired was to be in her bed, burying himself in her lush body. The outcome he desired was to do it without thinking of Briana Brennan-Taranian. He wasn't completely certain he was ready for either, but man, oh man, did he desire to be.

When the band switched from a gully mix to a restorative ballad, he held out a hand. "Care to dance with me, my lady?"

Her smile cracked his heart. The feel of her in his arms when they came together on the dance floor broke it wide open. He closed his eyes so he could feel her better, smell her more deeply. They moved well together on the dance floor, making him wonder how they would move in bed. Her breasts pressing against his chest fanned the flame that was growing in his belly.

She made a sound and the feel of it whispering against him almost undid him. He pulled only far enough away to tilt his head to look down at her. She looked up and it was understood. His mouth captured hers with conviction and urgency. His hands buried themselves in the only appropriate place they could, her thick, black hair. Eventually, they broke apart to suck in some oxygen.

"God, Orla," he whispered into her face.

Her eyes were bright and shining, her lips wet from his kisses. For once she was speechless, though the sound of her breath was articulate enough.

"I don't think I want to stay at this party," he said.

"Neither do I."

They stopped briefly at the bar and paid the tab and put up with Seamus' comment that it was about bloody time.

She said nothing but laid her hand on his thigh when they got in the car and never removed it. She was killing him, but it was a death worth dying for. Silas drove as fast as he dared to her house.

He put the car in park and turned to Orla. Taking her face in his hands he kissed her again, aching with the sweetness of it. "I wish I'd brought me toothbrush," he joked lightly.

"No worries. I bought a spare, just in case."

"Demon-child, that's what you are."

She shrugged. "I will be what I must for you, Silas."

Sweet Maker, she's serious. She was willing to do whatever she must to be with him. Was he ready for that responsibility? The silver package in his pocket that was currently burning a hole through his slacks said he was.

His heart was hammering as she led him inside and turned on a small lamp beside the couch that cast a soft glow in the room, making her look almost angelic, in a sexy sort of way. He pulled her into his arms and held her without kissing her. He needed to feel her and know that he was doing the right thing.

Her hands wrapped around him and one began to rub his back. It was an odd sensation, like a mother comforting her child. Conflicting emotions battled within as he realized he needed the comforting as much as he needed to make love with her. That she intuitively understood that humbled him.

Time passed and it came to him that he needed to do something to ease her mind about his intentions. He moved so that they were watching each other. Slowly and gently, he slid his hand up her ribcage to her breast and caressed her. Her eyes dilated with passion and her lips parted. He teased the nipple and she gritted her teeth.

"I want to make love to you, Orla."

"Thank Jesus and all the saints," she ground out between clenched teeth.

She stepped away, capturing his hand, and led him to her bedroom. Sitting on the bed, she eased her legs apart and moved him between. Untucking his shirt, she made swift work of the buttons and slid the material off his shoulders. Cool air on his bare skin made his nipples harden and she rubbed her fingers around them in a way that nearly dropped him to his knees. Her hands and lips explored every muscle and bone on his torso until he felt he needed to feel the same on her body.

She read his eyes and in one swift motion, lifted the hem of her blouse and removed it over her head, throwing it on a nearby chair.

The translucent bra only magnified the bounty beneath. Silas wrapped both of his large hands around her breasts. She arched her back and he deftly flicked the front clasp apart, releasing her to his full gaze and touch.

"You're beautiful, Orla." It was time to let go of Briana and give all of himself to this angel.

He eased her back on the bed.

She looked up at him with eyes so loving, so trusting. "Are you sure, Silas?"

CHAPTER THIRTY-FOUR

PORTENTS

Briana, Gardens at Ard Darach, Dromdara, Uisneach

"What the…" Briana jumped away from the widening circle of shimmering space in between two rose bushes. For a moment she stopped breathing as molecules formed a looking glass the likes of which she'd never seen. Its polished wooden frame slowly emerged, suspended an inch above the grass. In it, she saw not her own image and garden, but an entirely different landscape, darkness punctuated by spectral spirits floating in the air along a dark river of sludge.

"Cailleach." She turned to the witch who was bent over a large spell book. "It worked."

Cailleach glanced up, her eyes rounding and then turning to slits. "What have you called up, girl?"

"I don't know." "I was thinking about Scáil Meanoiche," she whispered in awe. "Is this the Underworld?" She took a step forward and reached toward the looking glass.

"Briana, stop! Don't touch it. We don't know how secure this portal is. It could suck you in and not let you out!"

Briana stepped back, suddenly anxious about what she'd conjured. She was right. Magic being as weak as it was, this portal might not be stable. Before she could decide what to do, it vanished.

She and Cailleach exchanged looks of excitement and trepidation. "It worked, Cailleach." The implications were enormous. She could potentially find Catriona and the spell or enter Aurum Castle at will. And, as the cavernous image had shown her, she could use it to get the Dar Morch back to Hell.

"Aye, but you need far more control over it than you possess now."

"Is it an issue of needing more skill or a stronger source of magic?"

Cailleach shook her head. "I honestly don't know, though I suspect 'tis the latter. You've gained good skills, Briana, but there isn't enough of the energy source to maintain this level of magic."

Briana had mastered some of the spells to move small objects and her fire-starting ability had made waking to a cool morning a thing of the past.

"I need to go tell Brath what happened." She started to head for the great hall but paused. "Maybe that's not a great idea. He probably won't like it."

Cailleach smiled. "He worries about you."

"Like a mother hen. But he should know what we've accomplished. If you don't see me by dinner, come and release me from wherever he's locked me up, for my own safety," she said, punctuating the air with quotation marks.

She hurried away to the witch's laughter and teasing comment. "Drama queen."

The great hall was empty. She hurried upstairs to their room where Brath was likely working. Just before she reached the door, Sigel's angry voice halted her.

"I'm not a damned invalid, nor am I an old horse to be put in the pasture!"

He hadn't been himself since Moiria. The limp remained significant. She'd also noticed the occasional grimace as he rubbed his leg, but he refused all of her remedies, so he was getting no relief.

Brath's calm and quiet voice was hard to hear so she took tentative steps forward.

"I'm not suggesting you should be put to pasture, Sigel. I'm simply offering another detail that might be a little less strenuous on your leg. I'm trying to help you."

"I don't need any fucking help. I've not let you or anyone else in the Taranian army down."

"No, of course not. But, I'm not blind, Sigel. Your leg hurts and I would not have you suffer like that when there's an alternative."

"Being on the queen's protection detail is not a solution. I might as well just lay down and die."

"Are you suggesting that Briana's protection is not important?"

Brath is handling this all wrong, she thought. "Of course, her protection is important. You insult me by insinuating I might think otherwise, but I am your right hand, Brath. I am the leader of your army, not a squire. If this is an order, then you will have my resignation and I will leave Ard Darach."

"Maker, Sigel, why are you being so stubborn? There isn't a soul in this kingdom who would think less of you for doing this."

"Really? Why don't you step down from being the king and become, oh, let's say, the head groomsmen? Would people think less of you?"

"That's ridiculous, Sigel. I'm the king."

"And I'm the lord marshall, not Jonathan Stark."

They took a breath and Briana thought maybe she should interrupt. Making her steps a little louder, she took the last few to the room and opened the door with a wide smile.

"Hey, you're both here. Great! Guess what I just did?"

Both men stared at her, their argument still reddening their faces.

"I just created my first portal!"

Brath scrunched his eyes together and rubbed the center of his forehead. "Do I even want to hear this?"

Sigel stared at her a moment then said, "That's great, Briana. Mind telling me about it later?" He left brusquely, nearly slamming the door.

Briana sat in the empty chair at the table and tilted her head to Brath. "You heard?"

"Yeah. And I cannot imagine what you were thinking, Brath."

"He's in pain all the time. He's trying to keep up as he always did and it's killing him. I was thinking I would make things a bit easier for him."

"And you thought Sigel would be happy to have things made easier?"

"What am I supposed to do, let him keep struggling?"

"Yes."

Brath shook his head. "That's foolish."

"It's what you do for a proud man, a warrior. You *know* that. He'll work it out."

Brath said down opposite her. "I hate that he's in pain."

"Me too. I've offered medicine, but he'll only take the mildest dose. I've offered massage, which would probably help a lot, but he refuses. It frustrates me to know I could ease his discomfort and he won't let me. He'll do it his way. But Brath, even with this disability, he's no liability to our troops. He can still lead."

"I know that. That isn't my issue. It truly is just the pain I see it causing him."

"Let him be, Brath. I'll try again with the massage and medicinals, but otherwise, he must know that you have every confidence in him. In other words, you need to go apologize and assure him he is still the only man you'd have at your side."

He nodded. "Very well. I'm not sure it's the right thing, but I see your point. The last thing I want is for him to go out anywhere feeling insecure."

"Are the troops heading out?"

"At some point. But not today. Today you need to tell me about the portal you've made, which I'm most assuredly *not* going to let you go through."

She told him about the portal and as predicted, he ranted about her staying away from it. He in turn updated her on a message delivered via crow about how the tunneling was going.

"You'll be happy to know that the animals are showing up in droves. It seems your recruitment efforts have paid off. The tunnel is almost finished."

"That's wonderful. I'll have to thank Mr. Mouse next time I see him. Will we go and visit the site?"

"No. Kieran thinks it best we stay away. He has also gained intelligence that Shamwa has spies keeping an eye on Ard Darach, to make sure we stay put. I want him to think that's what we're doing. I've got to meet with Donnelly and go over some financial stuff. Please promise me you won't sneak through any mirrors or any other variety of portal today."

"Promise. I'm going to look for Dara. He's gone off on another jaunt, apparently. I haven't seen him all day. I want to know what he's up to."

"Good luck, darling. I'll see you at lunch time." He kissed her, but she could tell his mind was already on the next task, so she left him to it.

Rippa, Jonathan and a few of the knights were in the great hall, Rippa practicing one of his stories, and if their rapt faces were any indication, it was a doozy. The story stopped when they became aware of her presence.

"Have any of you seen Dara?"

"Aye, milady," Rippa said. "'E's down to the stables with the babies."

"The babies? What babies?"

"His babies. He and the yella bitch 'ave some puppies."

"What! Why wasn't I told?"

"Sorry, milady," Rippa said. "I thought youz knew."

She raced out of the castle and down to the stables, where Riordan stood looking over the edge of a stall door.

"Hello, Your Majesty. You've come to see the pups."

"I've just heard about them." She leaned over the door to find a yellow hound with six hairy yellow puppies and one dark gray one, lined up at her teats. She seemed bent on ignoring the spectators. Dara, on the other hand, sidled in beside Briana and looked at her with canine pride in his eyes.

"So, mister, this is what you've been about for these past few months. You could have told me, you know."

Dara cocked his head sideways, which she interpreted as "*You've been a bit distracted by your own issues lately.*"

He was right. She'd hardly paid attention to the dog, or Banrion.

On cue, the mare whinnied, and Briana went to her. They shared a little love and Briana promised to take her out for a ride soon. She returned to the pups and watched them wiggle and squeak as they nursed and felt a wave of regret ripple through her. When would she produce an heir for the kingdom? On the heels of that ripple came an urge to go to the garden and specifically to the place where she'd made the bramble hearts. Denying everyone the possibility of knowing how things were with Silas because she didn't want to risk feeling things she shouldn't suddenly seemed foolish. They needed to know if he was bringing the runes home. Her feet seemed to travel through the gates to the garden of their own volition. She barely heard the birdsong warbling around her. She swept past the moon trees, sun dial and even the young faerie tree that waited for the return of magic that

427

would allow it to come into its own. Silver birches marked the spot where she had turned old gorse bushes into two connected hearts as a reminder that she and Silas would never be completely separated, even as their lives took separate paths. They shared a soul which allowed them the unique gift (or curse) of telepathy. She sat on the bench and focused her attention on the hearts. With a swirl of her ringed finger, she called up Silas' image. Her heart warmed as she saw his blonde hair, blue eyes and charming smile fill the space inside the hearts. *Oh, Silas, I've missed you. Have you found the runes? Will you come home soon?* The image remained, but without any answering voice in her mind. She began to wonder if anything would happen when she saw the image shift and another face joined Silas', a woman with dark, curly hair and bright blue eyes moved into the hearts. Curiosity held her and she watched as Silas leaned toward the girl, wrapping her in an embrace and kissing her warmly. *She's pretty.* Feeling like a voyeur but unable to look away, Briana asked again about the runes, but received no answer. If she were meant to take this literally, she would say that Silas had moved on and might not be coming back at all. Sick to her core, she finally turned away from the heart, overwhelmed with personal grief that he had let her go, but more importantly, she reminded herself, sorrow over the certain fate of Uisneach if the runes did not come back and magic wasn't restored. *I can't tell anyone about this. It would destroy all hope. for the kingdom.* It seemed hope was being dashed in all areas.

She and Brath had been married nine months, and still she wasn't pregnant. Watching the dog with her puppies only made Briana's longing for motherhood stronger. She'd assumed that once she was ready, it would happen. She frowned and tapped her fingers. *Wait a minute. My cycle should have started five days ago! Am I pregnant?* She asked the question to no one in particular, but the answer was swift and sure. *Yes!* She felt the nascent stirrings, like a flower breaking through the earth in early spring. That would account for the nausea she'd felt the last few mornings. "I'm going to have a baby," she whispered to the garden, and smiled. Maybe there was a reason for hope after all.

❧

She decided not to say anything to anyone just yet. After all, she was only a few days late. She didn't want to get Brath's hopes up prematurely. She checked in with her body constantly to detect any new feelings of pregnancy. She examined her breasts for any changes, though it was too early for anything to be noticeable. She did wake up vomiting two days in a row, which beyond the discomfort, filled her with excitement.

On the third morning she barely made it to the closet before heaving her guts up. *Okay, now it's getting old.* Brath was already gone, as he had been every morning, for a week. She was just finishing dressing when he came in, followed by Gael, with a breakfast tray.

Brath kissed her quickly and sat down.

"Aren't you going to eat?" he asked. "Not very hungry this morning," she replied, wondering if this was the right time to tell him.

"I have some news that might stimulate your appetite."

She doubted that sincerely.

"Kieran's here with news that they broke through to Aurum Castle."

"No kidding? That's wonderful. And did they execute Shamwa?"

"That's the bad news. He wasn't there. The troops cleaned out the cellar and are distributing the goods across Uisneach, even as we speak. The castle was torched and Shamwa will have nothing to come home to. I can only imagine his fury when he discovers that he's been ransacked and left homeless. End of protection spell, too. At least, I assume that with no castle, there will be no protection spell."

Briana mulled over the implications. Shamwa was homeless, but he was also on the move, and that might make him even more dangerous. She hoped burning down Aurum Castle was the right thing to do.

"Aren't you happy?"

"I am," she assured him. "He's vulnerable, but I'm just worried that his vulnerability could threaten our own security."

"It does. However, we are going to scour the kingdom and take him down. He is done, Briana."

She gave her most cheerful smile. "Then we must celebrate."

"Maybe we should wait until we have him in hand. And we still need either the runes or the spell to repair magic."

"Then, let's celebrate something else," she said, moving from her chair to slide onto his lap.

He put his half-eaten scone down and wrapped an arm around her waist. "Oh? What are we celebrating?"

She moved his hand over her belly. "Say hello to your son or daughter."

It took a second for him to grasp her meaning but then a grin spread across his face from one temple to the other. "You're pregnant?"

She nodded and kissed his forehead. "We're going to have a baby in a little over eight months."

"So, you're just barely pregnant. Are you sure, Briana?"

"Oh, I'm sure."

He tightened his hold on her, laying his head on her shoulder. "Thanks be to Maker," he whispered. "We will have a celebration. Tonight!"

They stayed wrapped in each other and the moment. When she felt Brath trembling, she pulled back enough to search his face. "What's wrong?"

Tears were slipping down his cheeks. "Nothing is wrong. Everything is wonderful. It's just that I've wanted this moment to happen for so long, and I was beginning to lose hope. We're going to have a baby, Briana. Nothing in the kingdom could make me any happier."

"I'll finally fulfill the prophecy and deliver the next king."

He shook his head vehemently. "I don't even care about that. I bet he'll be beautiful, like his mother."

"He? You sure about that? It could be a queen and not a king."

"Doesn't matter. Son, daughter. It will be the child that we created, and he or she will be just perfect."

They stayed cuddled in each other's arms until Gael came in to take away the breakfast dishes.

"Wait a second. I could eat now," Briana said, swiping a scone and a cup of tea before waving away the rest.

The maid took the platter with a knowing smile.

Covertly, Briana, Gael and the Flannigan sisters planned a celebration for that evening.

Brath found reason to see her throughout the day and she took great joy in the smile that her pregnancy had brought to his face. He wouldn't stop whispering to her how much he loved her, how excited he was to be a parent. Everyone in the castle should've guessed what was going on, but when the great hall was brimming with people, the focus was on the victory over Shamwa.

Briana was pleased to see Lady Seraphina and Sir Stark sitting side by side in a cozy chat. There had been little time for her and Seraphina to talk, but apparently, she and Jameson Stark had made time. She knew Seraphina had long hoped for something to develop between herself and the widower knight. Perhaps her hope was being fulfilled.

Rippa had already come up with a few verses about the victory. The knights made a great show of rattling their swords and swearing their allegiance to Uisneach. Briana caught sight of the mouse sitting unobserved by the hearth, in a somewhat expectant pose. Just before the meal was served, Brath stood to say a few words.

"This victory over Shamwa is worthy of celebration, though we must remain vigilant. While he still breathes, he is a threat."

"He'll not breathe long," Sir Cruahan shouted out and received a hearty "hear, hear," in return.

When the din died down, Brath continued. "Queen Briana and I have other news that we hope you will find worthy of celebration."

Silence fell across the room. Brath took Briana's hand and raised her to stand beside him.

"We are pleased to announce that we expect to greet a son or daughter in the fall. Queen Briana is with child!"

Cheers filled the room. Briana looked to Sigel, who was, for the first time in months, smiling. His eyes were moist as he came to her side and kissed her cheek.

"Congratulations, Your Majesty." Turning to the hall, he raised his glass and they followed suit. "To King Brath and Queen Briana. May the prophecy be fulfilled!"

From a spot near the fireplace, Briana saw Aya'emrys smile and bow to her. She wondered what this child would mean to Evalon.

As their friends and family cheered again, Briana looked to the mouse, who wiggled his whiskers in acknowledgment before scurrying behind the fireplace.

Rippa began to sing to the accompaniment of a harpist.

"With hopeful hearts and joyful voice,
We celebrate this day.
New life has found a home.
Taranian name continues on,
Rejoice, we all, rejoice.
A happy day, in every way. A happy day."

Rippa held the last note for several beats. A wailing wove into his voice and rose to an ear-splitting cry. Shouts of alarm rang out when a grayish wisp of energy floated through the window. A ghostly woman, her long hair trailing wildly behind her, flew around the room, keening. Briana wrapped her arms around herself to ward off the chill that invaded the room.

The spectral visitor finally departed through the main door. Briana saw Brath and Sigel staring at each other, bookend expressions of grim dread on their faces. She turned to Cailleach.

"What was that?"

"A banshee. An evil portent of the worst caliber. Someone is going to die."

"Banshee's aren't real. They're myth."

"No, Briana, they are very real, and this is the worst possible omen at the worst possible time."

Briana stepped close to Brath, looking to him for reassurance, but his jaw was set in a bleak line.

This can't be happening, Briana thought. Someone would die? Maybe it was a sign that Shamwa would be killed. Maybe it was metaphorical, relating to the clear separation between her and Silas. Surely it couldn't literally mean that someone she loved was going to die. Her hand rested protectively on her still very flat stomach.

CHAPTER THIRTY-FIVE

EU 2

"In Maine, it's called a baby bump," Briana told Gael, sliding a hand over the tiny hump on her abdomen. "The question is, can we find something to fit over it?"

"It's not that big, Your Majesty. You can wear anything in your wardrobe." She pulled out two gowns and held them up. "Which do you prefer?"

Briana bit her lip. King Kailen would be here, as would Teaguen and a host of faeries from Evalon. She wanted to look her best for the second meeting of the Evalon-Uisneach Council.

Gael sighed for the third time in this dressing process. "The violet would look stunning with your eyes, but the gold makes you look regal." She arched her eyebrows, waiting for the queen to make up her mind.

"Given that it's an official event, I guess I'll wear the gold," she said with a firm nod.

"Thank Maker," Gael muttered, putting the violet silk away.

She was tying up the back of the dress when Brath entered, already dressed in gold and green trousers, a green tunic and gold vest. His hands carried two crowns, the smaller of which he handed to her. "Here you go, Bri. You must not forget this."

A king, handing her a crown. A distant, dreamlike memory fluttered in her mind, taking her breath away and leaving her off-kilter. Déjà vu. Prophecy.

"Whoa there, sweetheart," Brath said grabbing her arm in support when she stumbled. "Feel sick?"

She shook her head, drinking in a large gulp of air. "I dreamt about you handing me a crown," she said, closing her eyes, attempting to recapture the image. It faded away.

"Hmm…" she murmured, accepting the gold and jeweled symbol of her office. "I'm ready."

Together, they walked down to the great hall. Brath assisted her to her oak throne, which she hadn't seen in some time. It was only brought to the great hall on royal occasions. Once again, she marveled at the exquisite craftmanship of the carvings of the Uisneach tree across the back, along with the white weasel and the gold-braided crown and holly. She settled into the red brocade cushion and let her eyes roam around the hall, at the fiery braziers, the banners of the Five Blessed Realms and the mouse who sat quietly by the hearth. She nodded, and he wiggled his tiny pink nose. Hopefully, no one else would see the creature and decide to take a broom to him. Captain Aya'emrys, the only faerie present, he took his post beside his tuathla.

Jonathan and Sigel were also beside the king and queen, both wearing stern expressions. Briana wanted to tell them to lighten up. It was only a meeting with the Evalon faeries. Only Rippa seemed at ease with the energy in the room, his smile adding a touch more light to the space. Briana smiled in return, glad to note that he had shoes on his feet. He was starting to mature a bit, doing a fine job of replacing Silas as Royal Bard. Well, in some ways, he was. The ghost of Silas was forever a fixture in this hall and in Briana's heart, though he was heavily guarded in the latter.

Hair stood up on her arms, alerting her to a change in energy in the room a moment before she heard drums and whistles outside. When Sir Niall Harkin and Sir Glendon Cavanaugh swung open the doors, a line of faeries, led by the spritely Teaguen, processed down the middle of the room to the thrones. Teaguen, always a joyful spirit, smiled and winked at Briana, then bowed formally before her tuathla, Queen of Uisneach. Gaily colored faeries trooped in behind her and spread out across the front of the dais. And then, King Kailen entered in all of his magnificence, taking Briana's breath away. It still wasn't easy to accept that her great-grandfather was the king of Faerie. He was as tall as Aya'emrys and as golden as the brightest sun. He came to stand before the thrones. Brath and Briana stepped down off the dais in front of him. After the expected bowing and curtsying, King Kailen embraced his granddaughter. "I hear congratulations are in order. I am so happy for you both."

"Thank you, Your Majesty. We couldn't be happier. Thank you also for coming today."

"We have much to discuss," he said, turning to Brath. "Shall we begin?"

The faeries were led to the long U-shaped tables to discuss how best to respond to Shamwa's latest tactics.

As mead and cider was poured, Brath offered a summary of where things stood.

"Thanks to the hard work of the Taranian and Evalon armies, along with an army of badgers, rabbits, mice and other willing animals, Aurum Castle was breached two moons ago. Our troops were able to return all that Lord Shamwa had stolen to the people of Uisneach. The castle was razed, leaving him essentially homeless. We believe that he and his army have a fortress somewhere in the Dromdara Mountains, perhaps underground, but we cannot find them.

"Gray Military have continued attacks on small villages and have destroyed yet more faerie trees in Tynan Ibor. The Winge and Taranian armies have met them in small battles all over Uisneach, with casualties on both sides, though I would say our troops have fared better. We have prisoners being held in Ratskillen, but they provide nothing useful and we have not been able to turn any to our advantage."

"And the Dar Morch? Does he still reside within Lord Shamwa?" King Kailen asked.

"We believe so," Brath answered. "Queen Briana and Cailleach have worked diligently to find the spell to extricate the spirit and send him back to Scáil Meanoiche. They believe Queen Catriona has hidden it somewhere. So much of what we need depends on restoring magic. There's been no word from Silas of Cedarmara regarding the runes."

"If Catriona knows where the spell is, you must find her, granddaughter."

Duh, Briana wanted to say. She turned to King Kailen. "I assume that if you could contact her, you would've done so by now." He nodded. "I haven't had any luck yet, either."

Discussion continued about the effectiveness of the faerie army across Uisneach and a request for continued support, which was readily given. They were discussing the terms of that support when the doors to the great hall opened, admitting Kieran Winge and Epona.

Maker, they are a magnificent couple, Briana thought as the black-leathered warriors entered side by side. Kieran was given the floor.

"Crow scouts have discovered Gray Military near the border of Evalon. They seem intent on cutting down and burning every tree, faerie or otherwise, in Evalon."

An uproar ensued. The knights stood as one, swords drawn, and thumped on the table, a statement of their readiness for war. Brath held up a hand to quiet them.

Kieran continued. "However, on our way here from Winge Mansion, we discovered Lord Shamwa heading this way with a second army."

"Thank you, Kieran and Epona, for the report. Can you send Winge troops to Evalon and get word to all Taranian troops to return to Ard Darach?"

"King Brath, if I may," King Kailen interrupted. "Lord Shamwa's threats against Evalon are empty. We can send faerie warriors to barricade the realm. He will not cross the border.

"He could, however, hit Ard Darach hard, and if he knows that the queen is with child, he will do his best to kill her to prevent the fulfillment of the prophecy. I suggest you send her to Kailen's Castle for safety, and then be ready to meet Shamwa here, on familiar ground. Since Captain Aya'emrys will be needed with the faerie warriors along the border, I would send Teaguen with the queen for additional support and security."

Brath considered this idea for only a moment before nodding.

"Brath," Briana began, but his look stopped her.

"We'll talk later, Briana."

She knew any argument to stay with him would go unheard. If Kailen thought she was safest in Evalon, then Brath would send her there. She stole a look at Teaguen, who had moved closer to her, her expression transformed to that of a trained warrior, intensely focused on her duty.

Brath continued to issue the orders that would get the faeries to the border and the Taranian and Winge armies organized at Ard Darach to meet Shamwa's force. The faeries would leave immediately, the crows would fly out and bring Taranian forces home, and Briana's group, cloaked in invisibility, would leave at dawn.

The new development changed the day's agenda and mood. Food was served and eaten quickly. King Kailen and his entourage left without the usual pomp and fanfare, escorted only by Brath and Briana to the garden portal. Night had fallen and the path was lit by groves of moonflowers that reflected the light from a nearly full moon.

"Speaking of portals," Briana said, as they walked between blooming night roses and silver-tipped evergreens. "I conjured one, but it seemed unstable and possibly dangerous."

King Kailen rested a hand on her shoulder. "Granddaughter, the time is not right for you to work that kind of magic. When we have conquered Shamwa and magic is restored, I will help you devise a portal to remove the threat of the Dar Morch from this land."

Briana stole a glance at Brath, whose jaw set told her that he didn't care if Maker offered to help her go to Scáil Meanoiche, he wasn't signing off on it.

"But we can't control Shamwa as long as he's being powered by the Dar Morch," she argued.

The faerie king patted her shoulder. "I believe that we can, my dear. Let us see what happens in this campaign."

The boulder guarding the portal entry slid away. After a hug and a bow, the king and his guards reentered Evalon, leaving Teaguen behind.

She and Brath hadn't been in their chambers more than a few minutes when there was a knock at the door.

"Come in," Brath said, giving Briana a look that said the last thing he wanted was company.

Sigel limped in and shut the door behind him. "You didn't exactly tell me where I'm to be in this campaign," he said, staring at Brath defensively.

Briana didn't give Brath the opportunity to err a second time. "I would think that obvious, Sigel. Brath is not going with me, so you, as his lord marshall, will remain here at Ard Darach at your king's side."

Both men gawped at her. She held Brath's stare, daring him to contradict her.

"Briana's right. You'll remain here with me."

Briana relaxed her shoulders and waited through the silence that followed.

"Very well. You'll be all right, Briana?"

"I'll have excellent protection, Lord Marshall. Please don't worry."

He nodded and stared down at the space in front of his feet. When he looked up, his eyes held a shimmer of gratitude and acceptance. "When you come back here, I'd like you to work on this leg for me."

"I'd be happy to," she replied, without hesitation.

"Thank you," he said, turning to leave. "Thank you both."

His exit was followed by Gael's entrance with a decanter of whiskey. She turned down the bed and asked about any further needs, then bid them good night and left.

Finally alone, Briana turned to Brath, who was pouring them each a drink. "Yeah, that's a good idea. I could use—oh, shoot."

"What?"

"I can't have whiskey. What was I thinking? I'll have Gael, bring some of the weak ale." She started for the door and stopped. "On second thought, I don't need anything but to be in that bed with your arms around me."

Something in her voice prompted him to look up from untying his boots.

"Hey, love. Don't cry." He kicked off the boot and went to her, wrapping his arms around her shaking shoulders.

"Oh, Brath, I don't want to be separated from you."

"I know, I don't, either, but we have to trick him, Briana. This could be our chance to end the bastard and I want you to be as far away and safe as possible."

That only made her cry harder. "Honey, what is it?"

"I'm scared, Brath."

"What are you afraid of?"

"Of everything. Of losing this war and Shamwa taking over Uisneach. Of losing you or the baby. Of Silas not getting back with the runes. Of magic being lost forever. What if this is the end for us?"

He led her to a chair and eased her down. Kneeling in front of her, he took her hands. "Briana, this is not the end of anything. It is the beginning of a new age for Uisneach and for us." He pulled a handkerchief and handed it to her, waiting for her to blow her nose. "Do you remember, before we married, that I told you I married you to fulfill the prophecy and save Uisneach?"

She nodded, hiccupping and wiping at tears, still sliding down her face.

"That was a lie. Well, partly a lie. The truth is that I have always known that there was one woman who would be brave enough, strong enough and committed enough to stand as my wife and lead Uisneach. From the moment I saw you, I knew, even though you looked as vulnerable as that wee mouse over there," he said, pointing to the bottom of the bedpost where Mr. Mouse sat watching them.

Briana frowned and shooed him off. "This is not your affair, sir," she reprimanded him. With a sniff of his whiskers and blink of his beady eyes, he did an about-face and pattered off.

"I knew," Brath continued, squeezing her hands for emphasis, "that you were that woman."

Tears streamed down her face. She buried herself into his shoulder.

"The fact that you were drop-dead gorgeous was just a boon I was all too happy to accept."

She laughed and he hugged her tight. "Come on wife, let me show you all the reasons we have to win this battle and why we need to do it as fast as possible to get you back here."

She stood and began to undress.

He did the same but paused, barechested, and called her name. "Briana."

"Yes," she said with a lingering sniffle.

"I promise you, I am not going to let Shamwa destroy our happiness or threaten our family." He stepped close to her and settled his hand on her bare belly. "He will not win. Uisneach will be free. Magic will be restored."

Looking into his eyes, she believed his promise.

They climbed into their bed and pulled the curtains, shutting themselves away from everyone and everything but their hearts and bodies, thrumming with need for each other.

Lengthwise, they faced each other. Brath ran his hand down her ribcage, brushing her breast with butterfly softness to the bone of her hip, before sliding the same hand to the firm flesh behind her, pulling her closer, letting her feel his strength and desire.

She arched into him, sliding her leg over his hip to fit him to her with no space for even a sliver of light. Her hands traced the taut muscles of his back and neck, losing themselves in his hair. She was drowning in the smell of bergamot and his male muskiness. His breath against her collarbone hardened her nipples, sensitive from pregnancy. Desire turned to excruciating need. She pressed his head to her breast and moaned when he took her in his mouth, swirling his tongue around the nub.

He jerked against her and turned with her until he was over her. Emerald-green eyes met steel-gray ones, holding the stare while the two became one.

Her breath was coming in sobs as he rocked her, gently at first, and then with more and more urgency. Her arms and legs gripped him like she was riding the wind. He loved her like it was the first time, and the last, they'd ever be together. She met him, thrust for thrust, asking for more and giving everything she had in return. Promises of love floated between them, while promises of tomorrow remained unspoken.

She reached the edge of the precipice and began to fall over. He came right behind her, holding on to her, vowing never to let her go. And then they were free-falling through air. Down. Down. Down. Their landing was soft and peaceful.

The lay quietly side by side, allowing their hearts to slow. When she believed him sleeping, she turned her head to study the strong features of his face. As her husband, he excited her and brought a contentment to her life she would never have believed possible. As her king, he inspired her with his grasp of the complexities of war and his ability to take information from a multitude of sources, evaluate it and craft a solid plan. His steady, calm leadership was a model she could only hope to emulate. Maybe in time, when Shamwa was no longer a threat, they would enjoy more carefree moments. For now, he had the weight of three worlds on his shoulders, and the best she could do to help him was dig deep for her own inner strength and be the partner he needed in these dark times. She sighed.

Brath took her hand, entwining their fingers until they were one hand. "Are you still afraid?" he asked, without opening his eyes.

"I fear nothing," she said, and curled into his side, embracing what sleep and security she could get in the remaining hours.

CHAPTER THIRTY-SIX

Teaguen and Jonathan sat together near the door of Kailen's Castle, sharpening arrows, saying absolutely nothing. Cailleach was just as focused on her task, the *Book of Leaves* open before her on the kitchen table, though she muttered aloud every now and then as she read.

"Checkmate," said Epona, leaning back in her chair near the fireplace.

"Whatever."

"Come on, Briana. You're never this easy to beat. What do I need to do to get you out of your head?"

"That's easy. Find Shamwa. Kill him and get me home to Brath."

Epona reset the ríocht board without responding. They were all worried about what was going on at Ard Darach. Despite the fact that their journey to Evalon was accomplished without difficulty, even knowing that Kailen's Castle was about the safest place she could be, worry remained Briana's primary occupation, and nothing really distracted her. They restricted their communication to urgent messages to reduce the possibility that Shamwa would discover her location. So far, no crows had been sent to, or from, Ard Darach.

"I suppose no news is good news," Briana said, walking to the window. Dara, who refused to leave her side for a second, followed. The sky was as blue as blue could be. Too blue. The kind of blue she'd learned as a child to associate with terrorists flying planes into skyscrapers, burning down cities and turning her world into a scary place. She shivered and wandered to the fireplace. It wasn't cold outside, but the chill that invaded her body the moment she left Brath had remained stubbornly fixed. She looked around the room. Epona was still making a show of resetting the ríocht board but her dark eyes were focused on something unseen. Briana still couldn't get used to seeing Teaguen in warrior garb, silver breeches, a blue tunic and knee-high boots of white leather, with a jewel-studded baldric hung empty across her chest. A sword carved with runes sat beside her, glowing like quicksilver. Her hair still spiked about her like tiny silver daggers, but the cornflower eyes, which sparkled gaily in that other realm, were now focused shards of glass, alert for any noise or change that would threaten her tuathla.

"From hill to hill an ancient symbol taken." Cailleach's muttering caught Briana's attention. "Two worlds collide in time. Which two worlds?"

"Cailleach, I thought we already figured that out?"

"Interpreting this prophecy is like looking at a gemstone. Every time you turn it, a different aspect presents itself. I wish we knew for certain what it meant. I'm still stuck on the river battle line, too. The only river battle was the one you were involved in at Appleduir. But it's followed up by the brown king, which must mean Brath, unless it's a twisted reference to Shamwa, protecting someone or something to death. The runes? Protecting the runes?" In an uncharacteristic display of vexation, the witch pushed the book aside. "It would've been easier to find the runes in the Pool of Queens."

The Pool of Queens. The idea sparked something in Briana. She joined Cailleach at the small table and knelt before her. "Cailleach, I think you just hit on something. Perhaps I should make a visit to the pool and see if I can get anything from its magic."

"That is an excellent idea, High Lady," Teaguen said, surprising Briana, since she hadn't allowed her to leave the room since their arrival.

"She, we, need to wear the invisibility cloaks," Jonathan added, already standing to fetch them.

"Good idea," Epona said.

Sensing something afoot, Dara went to the door. Briana bit her lip.

"We're going to have to put your party gown on, Dara," she said. They'd crafted a form-fitting cloak for the hound, but he'd whined and fidgeted all the way from Ard Darach, clearly hating the confinement. He whined now at the mention of it.

"It's that or you stay here."

With a huge sigh, he hung his head and allowed Teaguen to secure the cloak.

"Keep one hand outside the cloak so that we can see each other. The noise of the falls will prevent us from talking to each other," Briana said.

Laughter rippled around the group as five hands appeared in thin air.

"Best just a few fingers, I guess. Floating hands might be noticed."

Adequately camouflaged, they headed through the forest toward the falls. Briana led the way because she was the only one who had been there, but Jonathan and Epona flanked her so tightly that they bumped into one another more than once. "Watch your footing," she warned, as they approached the ledge. "It's slippery up here. A little more room between us or we'll be pushing one another over the edge."

Finding the cave entrance, Briana stepped inside and removed her cloak. The others followed her example. For the first time since leaving Ard Darach, she smiled at the looks of wonder on their faces. She'd almost forgotten how stunning the grotto was with its soaring ceiling and stone floor. The pool, filled by the cascade and heated by a subterranean spring, danced with ripples of water and steamy wisps of steam.

"Watch this." She knelt by the pool and put her ringed finger in, taking a deep breath when the water turned luminescent green. This was magic that could impress even faeries, witches and shapeshifters, it seemed. Their collective awe floated through the cavern.

"Do you want to be alone, Briana?" Cailleach asked.

"Well, I need to get in the pool." She turned a meaningful eye on Jonathan.

"Come on, lad," said Epona. "Let's you and I guard the cave from the outside." Dara glanced between the two groups before following the guards.

"Briana?" Cailleach prompted again. "What do you need from us?"

"I think you can stay. I don't want to do this alone."

"If you do manage to connect with Queen Catriona, please ask her who the brown king is? And ask if the outcome of the prophecy, as we know it, is certain?"

Briana thought that an odd question but agreed to ask. Wasting no time lest she chicken out, she laid Nua on a nearby boulder, tugged off her tunic and stepped out of her breeches. Naked, she took a step toward the water, her heart racing. Sucking in a bolstering breath, she touched one toe in. She heard Teaguen and Cailleach gasp as the tiny lights sparked into life around the cavern, melding with the green water, transforming the grotto into a living emerald.

Tremors zipped through her body and her finger began to thrum. Looking down, she saw the shimmer emanate from her body. The smell of sandalwood filled the air. As the warm water embraced her, she felt power build and surge. Everyone and everything else blurred into non-existence. Water gently swirled around her, the runes on her finger throbbing to the pool's rhythm.

Words came, a summoning from her soul.

"Come to me, Queen Catriona, once guardian of this kingdom. Bring to me your story and your wisdom. Help your granddaughter in her time of greatest need." She felt an almost painful twisting of the runic lines on her finger as they burned with power. Closing her eyes, she allowed the feeling to flow over her. She felt simultaneously very big and incredibly small. She heard her heartbeat, as well as the quieter heartbeat of her unborn child. And then she heard two more pulses. Opening her eyes, she witnessed steamy tendrils coalesce in the middle of the pool, two graceful heads emerging out of the whirling water.

The ash-colored hair and gray eyes were so much like her own that Briana could almost believe she was looking into a mirror, except this woman had eons of wisdom carved into her face, infusing her eyes with an intensity that Briana did not yet possess.

"My Queen," Briana said with an indrawn breath, dipping her head. "Grandmother."

"I have answered your call, Granddaughter."

The second head and chest to appear was less familiar, though Briana felt a connection with the being, more faerie than human.

"I am Queen Urelian. It is a joy to meet my descendant."

Catriona's corporeal form contrasted with Queen Urelian's floating translucence, which was as compelling as it was mystifying.

I should be freaking out right now, Briana thought, though her body felt relaxed and at one with these women.

"You have a problem," Catriona said.

"I have several, actually."

"How can we help?" Queen Urelian asked.

"Queen Catriona, I need to know where the runes are, and if you know what happened to the missing page of prophecy. If you happen to know a spell to control the Dar Morch, that would be lovely too."

The two queens turned to each other and began communicating without words.

I can hear you, Briana said, in the same silent language.

Yes, we know you can, and we will answer your questions. Queen Urelian nodded to Queen Catriona to begin.

The runes are on the Hill of Uisneach, Catriona said. *I wrapped them carefully in moss and tucked them between the stones of the sacred well. Not the one from the man they name Patrick, but another, smaller well. It was my hope that they would someday be found.*

Briana wondered why on earth Silas hadn't found them yet. Had he given up? Had he found them but decided living in the twenty-first century was to his liking, so he simply didn't find a way to return them? She needed to find out.

And the page of the prophecy? The Dar Morch spells?

Urelian looked to Catriona.

Although Queen Urelian crafted the spells, they were written into the Book of Leaves. *It was I who took them out of Uisneach, along with the runes.*

Why?

We were at war. Evil, under the power of the druid Shiall, was gaining control of the kingdom. I had no choice but to take the runes and any other potentially dangerous material, such as the Dar Morch spells, out of the kingdom. Had Shiall gotten those spells and control of the Dar Morch, we would be doomed. It was my hope that they would someday be found.

Did you ever plan on returning to Uisneach? How would anyone have known to find them?

Catriona smiled patiently.

The prophecy, my dear. As it was written, you are here, and someone has been sent to get the runes.

A never-ending circle, it seemed to Briana, but here they were.

The missing page of prophecy is there, as well. I put it in a trunk for safekeeping.

Does my grandmother know about all this?

I never told Caitlin about Uisneach, the runes or the prophecy because I didn't want to put her life in danger. In hindsight, that was a mistake.

Can you communicate this to her?

"No, dear heart, I cannot. But your Silas can. You must get a message to him."

What if she couldn't? *If you took the spells to Ireland for safekeeping, how was the Dar Morch released?*

All three queens looked to each other for answers. Urelian, the one who cast him into Scáil Meanoiche, answered. *I do not have any idea how that happened. It should not be possible.*

We believe the witch, Ealga, summoned him, Briana told her ancestors. *She's dead, so I suppose it doesn't matter how, if we get him back there. Oh, and do I really have to ride him to the Underworld?*

You should not have to ride him to Scáil Meanoiche, Urelian said, *but you will have to create a portal and have it open when you cast the banishing spell. And, it does matter how he got here, if Ealga was* not *the one to call him.*

Who else could it be?

Perhaps Lord Shamwa?

Briana paused. As far as Briana knew, he had no magic, so how would he have done that? But they really didn't know, so it was possible.

If it was Shamwa, he will soon be meeting the same fate as Ealga. Briana felt a power surge at the mere thought of it. They would destroy Shamwa. It was the only way Uisneach would ever be safe.

So, it's up to me and Silas to get these runes back and send the Dar Morch packing for eternity?

Both queens nodded. *It always has been, but now time is of the essence.*

Because Shamwa's destroying the faerie trees?

No, because the Dar Morch is on his way here, to Evalon.

Now?

Catriona nodded. *Go, Briana. Speak to the bard and help him find the runes.*

I will. One more question. Why didn't you come to me and tell me this before now? Why didn't you tell King Kailen?

Because you are the one with the power to create the portal that made it possible for us to talk.

There are many ways in which to create openings between worlds, grand-daughter. Coming here to this pool, summoning us with your pure intentions, that enabled us to join you.

I should bring King Kailen here to meet you.

Queen Catriona smiled. *Perhaps, someday you will be able to open a portal with him and we might speak to each other again.*

Oh, and by the way, you are going to be a great-great- however many times, grandmother.

You are with child?

Briana nodded.

And so, the queendom, or kingdom, Catriona said with a wink, *continues. Many blessings to you and your child.*

Briana could see Queen Urelian beginning to fade and knew their time was nearly up. They had provided the necessary information to handle the Dar Morch and finish the prophecy. The rest was up to her and Silas.

Power waned in her and the tattoos began to lose some of their glow. Before she could ask about the brown king, the queens disappeared beneath the water and Briana felt herself pulled back into the present.

She was resting on the ledge, supported by Cailleach and Teaguen.

"Wowzer!" she said, taking a deep, restoring breath. "That was incredible."

"What happened? Did you see the queen?"

"Two of them. Catriona and Urelian." At Teaguen's wide-open mouth and rounded eyes, she laughed. "So that's what shocked faeries look like. I'll tell you everything, but why are you two holding me up?" Fully recovered, she pulled herself out of the pool. She took the tunic from Cailleach and slid it over her head while Teaguen explained.

"Everything turned green and you seemed to be floating for a long time. and Then you began to slide underwater. Fortunately, you were close enough that we could support you against the ledge."

"Thanks."

She told them everything that happened, ending with an apology to Cailleach for not getting any answer to the question about the brown king.

Teaguen's cornflower eyes had gone distant and dreamy. "You really met Queen Urelian. I cannot believe it. What an experience that would be."

Briana realized that to Teaguen, it must be the equivalent of her meeting Princess Diana. However, the wonder of meeting the faerie rock star queen would have to wait. The Dar Morch, in his nefarious host, Shamwa, was headed their way. Somehow, they had to stop him.

"What do you need to do to connect with Silas?" Cailleach asked.

"Well, that's a first—you *wanting* me to connect with him." Briana was teasing but couldn't help but feel a twinge of resentment that suddenly it was okay to reach out to the man she loved so dearly, whom everyone had tried so hard to keep her away from.

"Don't be sassy, lass."

Teaguen was inspecting the cave for a comfortable spot for Briana so she could relax and prepare her mind.

"Relax! Are you kidding? Shamwa is on his way here, this very moment. How can I relax?" Shaking her head, she looked at the flat stone Teaguen had found. She followed the faerie to the spot and settled cross-legged in a meditation pose.

"Let me help get you started, High Lady," the faerie said, and sat opposite her, taking her hands. She began to breathe in a slow, peaceful rhythm. Briana looked into her eyes and saw the gentle blue of the soul-reflection pool. In moments, the pool was all she saw, and she looked into it, searching for another pair of blue eyes. "Silas," she whispered. "Can you hear me? Can you feel me? I need to talk to you."

At first nothing happened, and Briana felt a tremor of anxiety sneak into her mind. She imagined it floating away on a cloud and tried again. Gray obelisks rose up in an ancient circle. Bittersweet memory swelled. Surveying the scene, she found the abbey. Imagining two hearts, she called to him. *Silas, please hear me. Put down the barrier we built to our telepathy. I need to tell you something.*

Briana?

Silas. He was there. She knew he could hear her. *Hey, how are you? Wow, that's lame.* Something like static or confused energy rippled between the words. *Never mind. I'll just get to the point. Remember the words of the prophecy? From hill to hill. The runes are on the hill in the smaller well. Not St. Patrick's well, the small one.*

Briana?

She had no idea if he was getting the information, but she felt him and embraced the familiar energy and kept going. *The missing part of the prophecy and some written spells are in a trunk in my grandmother's house. We need that. Silas, please, if you can hear me, find these quickly and come home. We need you.* She paused and let her heart fill with every tiny shred of his energy she could collect. *I need you, Silas.*

Regretting the need to disconnect and deal with whatever new threat was on the horizon, she took the deep breaths needed to move out of the trance.

"I've done the best I could," she said rising. "I have no idea if he heard me, but I gave it my best. Let's get back to the cabin."

It hit her the moment she stepped out of the cave. She felt the Dar Morch as close to her as Silas had just been. "The Dar Morch is here."

CHAPTER THIRTY-SEVEN

HORE ABBEY

Silas, Hore Abbey, Cashel, Ireland

Silas sat on the edge of his bed, his head in his hands. He had no energy for anything, and he knew why. He'd last seen Orla four months ago. Yet the embarrassing and painful scene in her bedroom the night of the Christmas party still looped like a YouTube video in his brain.

I made right bags of it. I meant to protect her and I hurt her all the same. What a feckin' eejit!

He was going to make love to her. She looked up at him with such love and trust in her eyes and asked if he was sure. He stared back and the air left his body like a ship's sail on a windless day. In that moment, he understood he was motivated by purely selfish need.

He had pushed himself up and moved away from the bed, gulping in a breath and running a hand through his hair.

"You're kiddin', right, Silas? Please say you're just teasin' me. We're both half naked, you've got a condom in your hand and you're tellin' me you can't make love to me? This is not funny."

"I know," he said, sliding the aluminum package back inside the pocket of his slacks. "I'm sorry, Orla. You can't possibly know how sorry I am."

She shook her head. "I don't want to know how sorry you are. I want to know what your problem is. Briana? For Chrissake, Silas. She's married.

She's not even on this planet." She grabbed her blouse and yanked it over her head.

That wasn't true, but he wasn't about to argue the point.

"I had every intention of makin' love with you tonight. I've wanted to for weeks and tonight, you are so beautiful that it was all I could think of."

She threw her hands up. "Then what the feck happened?"

He knelt before her. "Orla, I *am* going home. As soon as I find the runes, I *will* leave and you deserve better than to have someone accept the gift of your body and your heart without givin' you all of themselves, and the world, in return."

"Is it your intention to live as a monk because the woman you love doesn't love you enough to give up her position and her supposed destiny as some kind of savior?"

He winced. "I don't know. I hope not, but I do know that I am not ready to commit to another woman and I never, ever want you to feel that you're second best."

"How gallant of you," she mocked him. "And how touchin', your loyalty to her."

He bit his lip.

She edged around him and grabbed his shirt from the chair near the door. Throwing it at him, she opened the bedroom door wider. "I think you should go, Silas. I'm done with you. I'm going to get back to work, focus on my education and career. You can chase after leprechauns, faeries and ghost queens all you like. Without me!"

He slipped the shirt on and headed out of her bedroom, but stopped in front of her. They were so close he could smell the mixture of perfume and desire from her skin. "I'm sorry."

"Don't," she said, and he cringed at the sound of tears barely held in check. "Just go."

He left. Since then, his calls and emails went unanswered, and he hadn't seen her in the pub for almost four months. School was in session, but she should've been at the hill on the weekends, and she was not. He'd been told curtly that she was taking a leave.

Missing her was no reason to torment her with repeated efforts to contact her or make amends. He needed to let it go and somehow find the energy to go on with his search. He fingered the warrior bone hearts he'd put back around his neck and looked at the photograph that had been returned to its place beside his bed. "Briana, help me. I don't know what to do."

It was more intuition that anything else that propelled him out of the house and onto the road to Tipperary. The Rock of Cashel towered up in the center of Cashel village. He drove past the Brian Boru Cultural Center and the road to the castle's parking lot. Just beyond Bailey's Hotel was the road to Hore Abbey, the magnet that drew him. Asking permission from the desk girl at O'Brien's Holiday Lodge to park, he locked up the car and hopped over the stone wall to the abbey. It was a fine day and the grass was dry beneath his feet. Briana had been right, the abbey in ruins was a very strange sight compared to the Shannon Abbey of his time. Wandering through empty rooms of moss-covered stone that were open to the sky reminded him of the sisters of Shannon Abbey going about their work and devotions, and their Abbess, who he was sure was connected to Shamwa's nefarious plot to overtake Uisneach. This did nothing to ease his loneliness.

He passed by the three panes of windows of the chapel where in his world, Mother Ealga had pretended to bless them. Stepping over an ancient threshold to what had once been the sisters' rooms but was now mere tumbled-down sections of walls, he found a spot where he could sit on the wall with a view to the castle.

Large as Cashel Castle was, it faded into oblivion as his mind conjured the standing stones that stood on that hill in Uisneach. Memory was a wonderful, painful thing that could bring a moonlit night to life in his mind and remind him of words spoken from the heart, of love and marriage to a woman he knew would never be his wife.

The world faded away around him, leaving only the stones in his vision. Words, a voice, entered his mind through a door he hadn't realized had been opened.

From hill to hill.

Briana? It was her voice he heard. Forcing himself to stay still and focus, he listened for more.

Silas? Hey, how are you? Wow, that's lame.

He smiled. *It's her! Oh, Maker, she's dropped the barrier! Briana? I'm here,* a mhuirnin. *Is somethin' wrong?* He reached out to her silently, hoping she could hear him.

Her telepathy was fuzzy, like talking on the mobile phone in an area of low reception. No wonder, it had been a long time since they'd used it. Or, maybe the distance between them made it more difficult. She was coming in and out, but he picked up several key words.

Hill of Uisneach... small well... missing prophecy... spells... trunk. And then, as though she were screaming, *Silas, please, if you can hear me, find these quickly and come home. We need you. I need you, Silas.* Initial joy at those words was quickly replaced with a sense of urgency and foreboding. Something *was* wrong, but Briana had been able to give him what he needed. He knew where to find the runes!

But, before he could complete this quest, he had to see Orla. He could not leave Uisneach without trying once more to heal the hurt between them.

CHAPTER THIRTY-EIGHT

RETURN TO DUBLIN

Green buses whizzed by, people crisscrossed the streets, lights blinked from green to red and roundabouts appeared, which required weaving in and out with other cars. A pedestrian stepped out into the street and Silas crushed the brakes.

If I can handle Dublin traffic, I can handle anythin' Uisneach wants to hand to me, Silas thought, reflecting on all that he'd learned of Briana's world. Some things were better left forgotten when he left here, but others, like the crossbow and information on how to make armor, would be a huge boon to Brath's army.

He wondered what Briana would think when he came home with a few of her treasures. He wondered what she would think of having her mother in Uisneach, if Katrina was of a mind to make the journey. And, of course, if she could get through.

He had so much to talk to her about. His time in her world had put them on a more even playing field and could only draw them closer together. Poking into his thoughts of Briana came an image of Orla with her bluebell eyes and... He shook his head. He now understood how Briana could love two men. His feelings for Orla were real, but his love for Uisneach and Briana greater. Briana had been right when she said Uisneach demanded much of her children. Leaving Orla and Finnegan and Caitlin would hurt.

With these thoughts running through his mind, it was in no time at all that he was parking near Trinity College. He walked across Library Square, pausing for a moment to appreciate the glorious sunset gilding the tops of the Campanile and the Old Library, while leaving the grassy square in long shadows. He would miss such easy access to learning. Books were in short supply in Uisneach because they lacked the technology of printing. It was sad that he could bring so little back, but maybe what he'd learned of military strategy would be helpful to his king and queen. *Maker, you'd think I already had the runes in me pocket and was headin' for Maine today. I've a way yet to that end.*

He maneuvered through the academic buildings to the dormitories where Orla kept a room with a couple of other students. Taking a deep breath and praying she didn't slam the door in his face, he knocked with more confidence than he felt.

"Come in," Orla called.

He took a second gulp of air and turned the knob. Orla sat around a table scattered with books and papers with three people he didn't know. Her blue eyes flared with pain that turned quickly to anger.

"Orla, can I speak with you?"

"Hey, Orla, you've been holdin' out on us. Who's your friend?" The question came from a tall, skinny blonde woman whose raised eyebrows indicated more than passing interest.

"He's just a guy from Tullamore," Orla said, without taking her eyes off him.

Her words, meant to hurt, hit the mark. "Can I talk to you, please. Alone."

She turned a way for a moment. The blonde said, "If you don't want to talk to him, Orla, I'll be happy to."

Orla's mouth turned down, but she nodded to Silas. "We'll go for a walk, then."

She grabbed a light jacket from the closet and led the way out of the apartment. Neither of them said anything until they were out of the building, as though being outside would make this conversation easier.

"I'm sorry, Orla, for what happened that night. I really am. I hate that things have been left this way between us. I want you to know that I truly do care for you. I never meant to hurt you."

She snorted. "You're such a gobdaw, Silas."

He nodded and let the insult linger a moment in hopes it would make her feel better.

"Why are you really here, Silas?"

"I know where the runes are, Orla. I expect to find them and be gone from Ireland within the week. I don't want to leave with you so angry at me."

"Angry at you? You scundered me beyond belief and you *did* hurt me. I'm sorry you came all this way to make amends. I wish you luck on your quest, but this is where we part."

With that, she turned and walked away from him, with not so much as a handshake. He watched her go, feeling like far more than a gobdaw when he saw her shoulders shaking and knew there was not a single thing he could do to stop her tears. He leaned against a maple tree outside the building and stayed for a while, hoping she would have a change of heart. Finally, he turned his car up the road to Tullamore.

CHAPTER THIRTY-NINE

A FATAL BREACH

Briana, Queen's Pool, Evalon, Uisneach

The Queen's Pool was no place for a stand-off with the Dar Morch. What if he could tap into that power?

"Here, Tuathla, put this around you," Teaguen said, handing her the invisibility cloak. The rest of them followed suit.

"Be careful going down the steps," Briana reminded them. "And leave a finger or two out, so we can see each other."

Epona went first, followed by Jonathan, Briana and Cailleach. Teaguen and Dara brought up the rear.

A sense of urgency pushed them faster than prudent. Briana stepped too quickly on a wet, mossy stone. One foot skimmed awkwardly over the rock and she felt her body follow. She grabbed for Jonathan. He swung his arm around in the opposite direction, hooking her miraculously by the waist, preventing her dive into the roaring waterfall.

"Thanks," she yelled.

"You're welcome," he yelled back.

Briana shuddered. Something was very wrong here. Her hair felt electrified, her gut tight.

Away from the roar of water, the din of distant battle could be heard. Briana looked up to the ridge.

"Don't even think it, Briana," Epona said. "You're going to the castle."

"How'd you know…"

"You paused. I'm quite sure you're thinking of heading to whatever is underway up there. Your husband would have my head if I allowed that."

Epona was right; they needed to get to safety and prepare for whatever was about to hit the fan. In less than a hundred yards, Briana's heart stopped. Galloping hooves thundered beyond the pine stand in front of them. She grasped Nua. Horses broke through the trees, carrying Brath, Sigel, Rippa, Sir Jameson and Sir Niall.

Briana's group threw off their cloaks to prevent the men from running over them.

Ruark skidded to a halt in front of Briana.

Responding from an adrenaline high, Briana joked, "Oh, honey, you're home."

Brath frowned. His eyes were hazel glints of alarm. "What in Maker's name are you doing out here?"

"Long story, but we need to get to the castle. Something's going on over that ridge," she said pointing north.

"No kidding. Our troops are battling a large unit of Gray Military and Shamwa knows you're here."

"How did they get through the faeries?"

"Don't know, but they did."

"Dar Morch magic?" Briana wondered. "Is Shamwa here?"

"I haven't seen him, but if he's come because he thinks you and I are here, then he is probably somewhere nearby. How's he moving without being seen is something I would really like to know."

"I been thinkin' on that, Sire," Rippa spoke up from his mount, a larger horse than Briana remembered him having. "I wonders if he used the invisible cloak he stole at the Howling Wolf?"

Briana was horrified. He might be anywhere around here.

"Kieran is leading the Winge and Taranian army in a barrier between here and the ridge," said Sigel. "The faeries will attack from behind. We should be able to contain the Grays, but I want you in that castle safe and out of Shamwa's reach."

Briana nodded. "Let's go, then. Wait! Cailleach, we should place a protection spell around us." She raised her hand, ready to cast the energetic spell.

"I've already tried. Something is blocking. I can't raise a lick of magic."

"I call on the wisdom and power of the tuathla." Briana frowned when her tattoo did not react. No sandalwood smell. No tingling in her body. Nothing. Something or someone was blocking their basic abilities. The Dar Morch?

The warriors encircled Briana and Cailleach. "Let's go!" Brath ordered.

They moved quickly and silently through the forest, until Briana could see the castle. Tree branches swayed and leaves danced softly in the gentle breeze. The waterwheel spun peacefully, bucketing water into the stream below. Serene. Safe.

Brath whispered for the men to inspect around and inside the castle.

"There's nothing of a threat here that we can see," Sigel said when they returned.

"Let's get the queen inside," Brath said, dismounting.

Briana and the rest of them followed. The horses, stamping and blowing, were left untied with a soft command from Briana to stay put.

They were feet away from the door when Dara growled. The front door to the castle opened. A soft *whoosh* and the doorway filled with the Herculean body of Lord Shamwa. He flicked away the remnants of an invisibility cloak and bowed politely in their direction. Cruel, blazing red eyes contrasted with a welcoming smile. "Nice castle you have here."

Brath nudged Briana behind him. Sigel and the knights moved of one accord with raised weapons, their blades glinting sun that filtered through the canopy.

Epona, sword raised, covered Cailleach.

There's no way he's here alone, Briana thought, scanning the forest with sharpened senses. A slight movement caught her eye above the waterwheel and a Gray Military soldier appeared out of thin air. Somehow, Shamwa had secured more than just one invisibility cloak. Briana wondered how many other warriors were surrounding them.

"This is crazy, Shamwa," said Brath. "You're surrounded by faerie warriors and the Taranian and Winge armies. You don't stand a chance."

The prime minister smiled. "Oh, but I do. I have the Dar Morch."

Suddenly Briana heard a snort and the fire-breathing black horse appeared between Ruark and Orion. Briana's breath caught in her throat.

Shamwa sighed. "Oh, Briana—oops, sorry, Your Majesty, those animals are the least of your concern right now."

Over the next ten seconds, warrior after warrior appeared around the perimeter of the forest, across the roofline of Kailen's castle and along the stream. A sound like wind chimes revealed Aya'emrys and one thousand golden faerie warriors with swords, bows and shields at attention, waiting for their moment.

Shamwa didn't seem concerned. He looked around at the royals and knights. "At the end of the day, only one of us is leaving here alive."

A Gray warrior now appeared above the waterwheel. He raised his bow, but was instantly dropped, by an arrow splitting through his skull, into the buckets of the device. A thud underneath the wheel and the man was spit out downstream, a ribbon of red trailing him. Briana saw Jonathan, his bow still raised, nock another arrow. She thought of Silas and bizarrely wondered which of the two of them was the better archer. The split-second thought was replaced by an explosion of activity. She and Brath were sandwiched between Shamwa, who raised a battle ax, and the knights.

"Nothing to do but fight, Bri," Brath whispered. "Stay behind me." She would have, except he was suddenly ripped away by a snaking vine that grasped his feet and pulled him down.

Briana stood exposed before Shamwa. She met his eyes. *I'm his target.* Nua rose from her side, almost of its own accord, ready to defend or kill, whatever was needed. Dara pushed ahead of Briana. Briana saw every detail around her with absolute clarity. Sigel beat back Gray Military. *His limp doesn't slow him down any.* Jonathan shot arrow after arrow into the warriors on the roof, dropping them one after the other. An arrow whizzed beside Briana from behind and found a target in Dara's neck. The hound yelped and fell sideways. Briana couldn't help him, trapped between Brath and Shamwa. Hot anger blazed inside her. The ex-prime minister stepped toward her, his axe still upright in his hand. Nua flashed. She stepped back as she caught Brath in the periphery, frantically tearing the vine away from his legs. A shaft of sunlight pierced through the trees. Briana tilted Nua slightly, catching the sunlight and glancing it into Shamwa's eyes, temporarily blinding him. It gave Brath the time he needed to free himself. Not long enough, though. Shamwa recovered and raised his ax again. Briana stood ready to counterattack. Dara, recovered from the hit, but wearing the end of an arrow, beat her to the attack and lunged into Shamwa, forcing him to swing down as Brath moved next to Briana.

"Run, Bri."

He leaped in front of Briana at the exact moment Shamwa's axe arced down, burying its blade in his chest. A rosette of blood slowly bloomed around the butt and shoulder of the weapon, spreading across Brath's shirt.

Briana screamed. The sound rang through the forest and for a split second, everything paused.

The black horse of Dar Morch trumpeted, and Briana faced the beast, her anguish put on hold long enough to deal with the threat. "You belong to me!" she roared, flashing her ring at the fire that was coming at her from his nostrils. Flame bent on itself and returned to its source. The horse reared up and then stood still, confused by the power around him.

Briana turned back to Shamwa to see a sword falling, intent on cleaving her in two. Nua shot up and stopped the trajectory. Briana held on for dear life as Nua fought to protect its queen. Shamwa reeled when Evalonian steel ripped down his shoulder and arm. Briana noted the brief glimmer of fear in his eyes when he realized he couldn't fight her and win. Maintaining sure contact with Nua prevented her from interrupting his next action. With a cocky grin, he whipped the invisibility cloak that lay at his feet over his head and vanished.

Let the knights deal with him, she thought, turning back to Brath, who lay crumpled on the ground in front of the castle. He breathed raggedly. His eyes were open and staring at Briana.

"I'm sorry, my love," he said faintly.

"Someone help me get him in the house," she bellowed, kneeling beside her husband and trying with every ounce of energy she possessed to bring magic to save his life. She prayed. She uttered incantations. She worked her hands over and around the axe, still in his chest.

"No, Briana. It's not going to work. Just lay here with me, please."

She looked around at the chaos still swirling around them. She needed help. He was so pale and breathing so poorly. "Aya'emrys, Teaguen," she called. "Cailleach. Someone, help us."

"Bri, please hold me. I'm cold."

Shit. Shit. Shit.

She lay down and pulled him into her arms.

Then Cailleach was beside them, tears streaming down her face. Aya'emrys appeared, moving his hands over Brath and uttering words in the faerie language. For a moment, Briana thought Brath's color improved.

Sigel broke through the circle of healers and stared in shock at Brath. "No."

"I wanted to see my son," Brath said weakly to Briana.

"You will see him," she replied, with pure determination. "You will see him, Brath, and watch him grow to be as strong a man as you are."

"Briana, I love you. I wish we had been given more time."

"Brath, I love you, too, and I want you to stop talking like this right now. You are going to live,; do you hear me? I will not let you die." She began her magical ministrations all over again, but a gentle hand stopped her.

"King Brath." Teaguen knelt next to them. "Would you like to see your son?"

Brath met her eyes and nodded. She took his hand and placed it on the slight bump of Briana's belly. "Close your eyes, and behold."

His hand felt so cold on her abdomen.

She knew the silence around them meant the battle was over, at least for the moment. She held her husband as his hand grew light on her belly and his breathing slowed. For several seconds it seemed to stop altogether. Her sound of anguish was met with a sound of awe from Brath. He opened his eyes and tears slid down his cheeks, but he smiled at Briana. "He's strong and good."

She nodded, choking back sobs that would only upset him.

"Sigel—I need you to witness something for me."

Sigel knelt awkwardly before his king, his face ravaged by grief, his scar bright red. "Whatever you want, Brath. I will do it for you."

"Take care of Briana. Protect her with your life."

"I will."

"She and Silas have my blessing. He will make her a good husband and be a good father to my son."

"Brath, stop. I love you. I don't want to be married to anyone but you. Fight for me, Brath. Fight for your son. Stay with us. Look at me, Brath. You can't leave me." Briana wailed her grief, knowing in her heart that nothing could save this man who lay in a crimson pool, his life force ebbing away before her eyes. His eyes clouded as the soul light left them, and his mouth slacked open. He was gone.

Panicked, she kneeled beside him and began chest compressions.

"What the hell are you doing, Briana?" Sigel tried to push her away.

"Breathe into his mouth," she said. "We can bring him back."

When no one moved, she did CPR as she'd been taught, breathing into his mouth and pumping his chest. "Someone help me!"

When Briana moved to give him breaths, Epona fell beside her and mimicked the chest compressions. Briana sealed her mouth over his, willing and breathing him back.

He did not move. Sweat dripped from Briana. He did not breathe, and finally, even she knew there was nothing more they could do. She collapsed across his chest, not caring if the entire Gray Military came down on them. Grief and rage poured out of her in fierce wailing. "No. No. Please Maker, don't let this happen. No more."

When Sigel finally pulled her off the king, tears had ceased, leaving ragged tracks down her pallid face. She stood and faced the ridge where Shamwa must have made his escape cowardly cloaked by invisibility.

"I am coming after you, and I am going to kill you, Shamwa, and when I do, it will be as slow and painful as I can possibly make it."

CHAPTER FORTY

REGALO NI MORTEN. REGALA GROHANED ETERO.

Ard Darach was cold. Briana was cold. She hadn't been warm since she watched Brath's beautiful hazel eyes turn milky white as the light of life left them. In the three days it took to get his body to the castle under the full force of three armies, she'd felt nothing but cold. Even the bed warmer tucked at her feet couldn't chase away the iciness that ran through her veins.

Deadly dreams had divided the night into movie clips: the queen's pool, bathed in green light, the two queens laughing from macabre mouths of sharp teeth. Shamwa standing over her with fiery red eyes, shouting, "Off with her head!" Brath jumping in front of her and melting in a scarlet pool.

She woke with wet cheeks. *He's dead. What does life even look like without him in it?* Rolling on her side, acutely aware of the absence of his warm, loving body next to her, she stared into the fire. *Please, Maker, take me too.* Her eyes caught the twitch of whiskers near the peat pile. She closed her eyes. She didn't want to talk to anyone, including Mr. Mouse.

"I know you're awake."

She didn't move.

"May I offer my condolences, Your Majesty?"

"Thank you." It was only polite to acknowledge his sentiment.

"I'd also like to offer my support in any way that might be helpful."

"I appreciate it, but there is nothing you can do. There's nothing anyone can do."

"I see, then."

He was quiet for so long she had to open her eyes to see if he was still there. He sat on his haunches, staring at her. Dara also stared at her with dark, mourning eyes.

"You must be in a great deal of pain."

"Which I would like to be alone with," she responded dully.

"Are you going to get up today?"

"No."

"Everyone is downstairs wondering what they are to do."

She rolled onto her back. "I don't care what they do."

"Might I remind you that you are the queen, and with the king gone, it is your responsibility to take his place and lead your people."

She uttered something rude, that only a mouse with excellent hearing would pick up on.

"That is no way for a queen to talk. I understand your grief, but…"

She bolted upright and slammed her hand on the bed poster. The sting felt good. "Do you? Do you really? I beg your pardon, but have you lost every person you ever loved? Have you sacrificed every bloody thing in the world to help that man restore this kingdom, only to have him snatched out from under your nose by someone or something that you're supposed to be able to control? Have you?"

"Not exactly, but…"

"Not exactly is right. I just want to die." She flopped back on the bed, pulling the covers over her head, unwilling to allow even the mouse to see her hot tears.

All she heard was a soft squeak and nails along the stone floor.

"What about the baby? Will you let him die with you?"

Her hand automatically covered the tiny swelling on her belly. Her son. Brath's son. He's strong and good, he'd said.

"He will be the king of Uisneach, but only if he lives to wear the crown."

She stared at the rodent. She should have let Mary O'Brien have at him with the broom. But he was right. Her responsibility did not end with Brath's death, as much as she might wish it so.

With a groan, she sat up and swung her legs over the bed, just as the door to her chambers opened. Gael tiptoed in until she saw Briana sitting up. Mr. Mouse squeaked and hurried now out of sight.

Briana and Gael looked at each other for a moment.

"I need to get dressed."

Gael nodded without saying anything and went to the wardrobe.

Briana leaned forward, putting her head in her hands, and stared at the floor. She felt a hand on her back.

"Your Majesty—Briana, I wish there was something I could say to help."

Briana shook her head. "There isn't, so let's just focus on the next thing I need to do. If you can help me do that, it's as good as anything else to be done."

"Whatever you need. Sigel is downstairs with the knights. I think they're wondering how you are." She held out a black and rose day gown. She remembered the times she and Gael agonized over which dress Brath would like the best.

Briana stared at it. "Brath liked that dress."

"There isn't a single dress in there that I've not heard him say you looked beautiful in, so one's as good as another."

She took the dress in her hand but immediately dropped it in her lap. "I can't do this, Gael." Dara whined and laid his head on her knee.

"Yes, you can. The first thing you do is stand up and let me dress you."

Half an hour later, she was at the door to the great hall, Gael at her side. She needed a moment to prepare herself for whatever happened next.

"She will be a great queen one day."

She heard Sir Cruahan's words and waited for the 'but' coming next. "It's just that she doesn't have a lot of experience, she's grieving, she's pregnant, and I'm not sure she's ready to lead alone."

She and Gael exchanged a startled glance.

"She's not alone!" Sigel barked. "I stand at her side. Anyone else care to join us?"

Briana heard chairs scraping against the floor. "Any other arguments, Cruahan?"

"Look, I respect Queen Briana and I'm not trying to rebel against her.

I just don't know how she'll manage right now. But, if you don't think it's a concern, then of course, I stand with you."

"What can we do to help her?" Sir Jameson asked quietly.

"We let her get through the funeral and we begin planning the next campaign."

"With or without her?"

"You know the queen as well as I do. Do you honestly believe she will not be itching to get to Shamwa?"

"She will," said Sir Thomas, surprising her. They must have just arrived. "But one of our responsibilities will be to guide her in that effort. Lord Marshall, you must encourage her to do this sensibly."

Briana shrank against the wall, looking at Gael. "I really can't do this."

"Yes, Your Majesty, you can." The firm press on her shoulder and the confidence in her eyes gave Briana a boost. Taking a deep breath, Briana pushed the door open.

Everyone stood at her entrance. Sigel pulled her chair out. She paused, staring at the chair beside it. Brath's chair. Empty. Cold.

"I'm sorry, Briana. I should've had someone take it out," Sigel said, seeing the torture on her face. He flicked a hand to one of the servants, but she shook her head.

"No, leave it. I think I might want it there for a while."

She sat and accepted a cup of tea, but waved off the food set before her.

"Sir Thomas and Lady Isabella, I'm glad you're here."

"Where else would we be, Your Majesty?" Lady Isabella said.

Briana was grateful that she did not add condolences. She would not be able to handle the constant expressions of sympathy.

"Where's Cailleach?" she asked.

"Preparing Brath's body for burial," Sigel answered, meeting her eyes.

"I see. And what are the proper protocols for a royal funeral?"

"Normally, a king would be prepared with special herbs and magic to lie in state for six days so the kingdom could come and pay their respects. Then he could either be entombed or carried into the sea by boat on a hero's funeral pyre. Since we're short on magic and Uisneach is not safe for travel, you can waive the lying-in period, if you wish."

She looked around the room. Everyone looked tired and sad. "It's too dangerous for people to travel to the castle now, so we'll have to skip the lying-in period. But I don't want anything else to compromise our honoring of him. We send this hero on his way at sunset tonight. Crows should be sent across the kingdom with news of his death so that our people can mourn. Teaguen, if you haven't done so already, I'd like you to inform King Kailen of Brath's death. He might wish to be here. Aya'emrys will help you at the portal."

The faeries tipped their heads and with a bow, left for the garden portal.

"Your Majesty," Epona stood. "The hero's sendoff requires a skilled archer to send a flaming arrow into the boat once it has set sail, to light the pyre." Briana searched the room until she found her squire. "Jonathan can do it. He is our most proficient archer."

The boy's eyes went huge and shiny. He shook his head, but said nothing.

"Is there anything else?" Briana asked.

"No, Your Majesty," Sigel said. "We'll take care of everything else."

She stood, and the room of people stood with her. *Maker, I wish they wouldn't do that.* "I'm going to help Cailleach."

Jonathan was at her side instantly. She started to dismiss him, but knew that would cause a ruckus. She was not likely to be allowed anywhere alone, anytime soon.

They were nearly to the keep, where Brath's body was being sheltered under guard and Cailleach's care, when the lad spoke. "Your Majesty, are you sure you want me to be the archer for this ceremony? There are older, more experienced men who should have the honor."

She never stopped walking. "It's not a matter of who gets the honor, Mr. Stark. It's who is most able to make sure that pyre lights with the first arrow. You and Silas are the only ones capable of that, and he isn't here. It is an honor, but it is also a duty that you must accept."

He looked down. "I hope I don't miss," he said, so softly she almost didn't hear him.

"You won't."

They stopped at the door of the keep. She had to go in, but her heart began to pound. Brath was inside and she didn't know if she could see him again like that. Jonathan stood stalwartly beside her.

"Do you want me to go in with you, or wait here?"

"You should probably stand guard here, Mr. Stark. Thank you."

He pushed the door open, leaving her no choice but to enter.

Cailleach looked up from her work with eyes dark and shining from grief and the sacredness of what she was doing.

Briana was thankful she did not ask her if she was sure she should be there. She simply reached for Briana's hand.

Pine and bergamot scented the air. Herbs she had come to associate with her husband were the oils that Cailleach was using to anoint him. She stood next to Cailleach and looked down at the man who had been such a large presence in life, and was glad to see that none of his dignity had been reduced in death. She touched his cheek, still stubbly from a day's worth of growth. He was still a king.

"He should be shaved," Briana said.

"Would you like to do that?"

She nodded. Cailleach handed her the razor and some oil. Briana lovingly went about the work of making her husband's face as smooth as he liked it. His skin was cold, but she welcomed the feel of it against her hand. She noticed little things, like the cinnamon strands of his hair that mixed with mahogany and caramel. She traced his jawline with her fingertip, finding a tiny mole that she'd only discovered a few weeks ago. She slid the blade over the contours of his face and remembered every smile, frown or laugh that had drawn her in like a moth to a flame.

Finishing her ministrations, she turned to the witch. "Cailleach, can I have some time alone with him, please?"

"Of course. I'll be just outside, if you need me."

Briana pulled a chair next to Brath's body and sat down facing him.

"I'm sorry, my love," she said. "I should have been able to stop him with magic. He was trying to kill me, not you." She sniffed and wiped her eyes. "We should've had armor." Guilt was like a knife in her chest. "If I hadn't forgotten to ask the queens about the brown king. Maybe, if we'd known, we could have protected you better." All the if onlys rang shrilly in her mind until culpability was replaced with resolution.

"Brath, I want you to know that I will do everything in my power to raise your son to be as good a king as you were. I will teach him everything you taught me. Well, Sigel and I will." She felt a flutter in her belly. It was too soon to feel movement from the child within, but it seemed the child's spirit wanted to acknowledge his father.

She lay her head on his chest, unaware that she was crying until her cheek slipped across the wetness on his skin. "How could you leave me? I need you. Please, Brath, come back. I can't do this by myself."

"He's gone, Briana. We have to keep going."

She hadn't heard Sigel enter until he spoke, his voice husky but firm. He pulled a chair beside her and they sat together mutely, staring at the empty vessel of the man whom they had both loved so much.

"I didn't want to love him."

"I know you didn't. But I'm glad you did."

"Because of me, he died."

Sigel twisted around to take her hands in his. "Briana, because of you, he was released from a timeless bubble. You rescued him from that cursed prison and gave him life." He let that sink in before continuing. "You know, the first night we spent on the road after the apple orchard attack, I knew that the prophecy was true and that you were exactly the right woman for Brath. Even knowing how you felt about Silas, I knew you and Brath would be good together. I have never met another woman who had the intellect, the wit or the passion to be a fitting match for him.

"The prophecy has unfolded exactly as written. Brath's death was written in the stars a long time ago. As, I am willing to bet, is your monarchy. But the more important truth in what has happened is that Brath loved you with all his heart and he did what any devoted husband would do when his wife and child's life were threatened. He protected you. His death is on Shamwa, not you. You harbor no responsibility for this. But, as Maker is my witness, you will have justice."

They sat a while longer. It would be the last time she could be with Brath like this. The next time she saw him would be when he sailed away into the night, forever a hero. Finally, she stood, and Sigel stood with her.

"Are you ready to go?"

"Yes." She leaned down and placed a final kiss on Brath's cheek. "Good night, my love."

They walked out of the keep together, but Briana broke away from Sigel and headed toward the blacksmith's shop.

"What are you doing, Briana?"

"We will have armor."

❦

Waves layered themselves against the shore in readiness to receive the small boat that would carry King Brath to eternity. The evening sky was a banner of purple and orange with tiny, starry dots beginning to glitter into another night of celestial guardianship.

One thousand golden warriors, an equal number of crow soldiers and the entire Taranian army lined in formation across the cliffs overlooking the sea. Briana stood on the beach surrounded by her closest friends, the knights, and household staff. Sigel and King Kailen flanked her on either side. Brath, dressed in royal splendor, his sword resting across his chest, lay still in the center of the pyre built by the knights to carry their king into the long night. Stoic, tearless expressions of grief chiseled every face.

A collective gasp rolled over those gathered when a brilliant heavenly light streaked across the horizon, its long, fiery tail heralding the beginning of the hero's journey.

Of course a comet would appear, Briana thought, with a hint of a smile.

"Borach a lorien Uisneach, regalo do maliani, Borach Brath Taranian, neerah shanna ghomara donnalei." Captain Aya'emrys' crisp pure voice began the faerie lament, honoring the king who was so determined to bring unity between Uisneach and Evalon.

Behold a man of Uisneach, of royal heritage, Behold Brath Taranian, the first of his name, destined for greatness.

Ancient memory roused an understanding of the faerie language in Briana's mind, filling her with soul-deep longing. When the entire army of Evalon joined in the lament, a chill snaked down her spine. The barely controlled sob she heard from Sigel weakened her knees.

"Dienar, te sughar a fiial to preashan an nadar. Dienar te pighanna."

Born to lead a people to peace and unity. Born to fulfill a prophecy.

"Hi ghrohan an morten a pighanna a fiial. Regalo ni morten. Shoen maliana grohaned. Regala grohaned etero."

He lived and died a hero of the people. The king is dead. May his legacy live on. Long live the queen!

When the requiem ended, the deep throb of a single drum began to beat and the Winge and Taranian armies took up a chant:

"Behold a king, a hero king.
Forever more a legend.
Behold a king, a hero king
For glory he was destined."

The chant went on several rounds as Sigel and Briana, accompanied by Dara, carried a wreath of holly, hawthorn and ash into which was sewn the white weasel, the Taranian insignia, and laid it across his chest. Dara nuzzled Brath's face and whined. Briana remembered the first time he'd met Brath and growled. It seemed he too, had fallen for the king.

Rippa took up where the chant ended.

"Let the mountains and the sea, the grasses and the sky
Sing the name—Brath Taranian—first of his name,
Son of Barclay Taranian, third of his name,
Grandson of Barclay Taranian, second of his name,
Great grandson of Barclay, first of his name,
Great-great-grandson of Banniman, first and last of
his name,
Husband of Briana Brennan-Taranian, first of her name.
King of Uisneach, the Five Blessed Realms:
Dromdara,
Tynan Ibor,
Appleduir,
Cedarmara,
Evalon.
Having honored his responsibility to the prophecy
Having given his sword and his heart in honor of
kingdom and family.
Having brought unity between the realms and the faerie

kingdom of Evalon Let his name be remembered in ages
to come.
A great king and friend to all people and beings.
Let his legacy and bloodline live on in his descendants
Let the ocean, under witness by the stars, take his body
and Maker receive his soul."

The knights stepped forward in unison and surrounded the small vessel, pushing it into the waiting waves.

The boat bobbed farther and farther from shore, carrying the man who had stolen Briana's heart against her will, but treated it with nothing but love. She took a step forward, as if to go after him. Sigel curled his arm around her waist, preventing the desperate act. They leaned into each other for strength and watched the boat being carried over the ocean swells. The sound of slicing air was followed by the fiery tip of an arrow over her head and straight out to sea. Hitting its mark, the arrow lit the pyre. Small flames turned into a giant ball of light, burning brightly, carrying Brath to a place beyond the horizon.

Rippa's words of lament were accompanied by strangled sobs and muffled tears. Darkness eased its cloak over the beach. People started the lonely walk back to the castle.

Finally, it was just Briana and Sigel left, standing in darkness, gazing out at the tiny orange speck on the horizon. Tearless, they waited until even the speck disappeared.

The lord marshall turned and pulled Briana in his arms. She felt the wetness of his cheek on her head. "We will survive, little warrior, and finish what he started. Your son will lead a kingdom at peace and rich with magic."

Briana wrapped his words in a protective cocoon for a time when she could fully appreciate them. For now, everything in her was fighting the desire to walk into the ocean to join with her husband. She cupped her palm over her belly. She had to stay behind. Brath's son must live.

CHAPTER FORTY-ONE

THE RUNES OF EVALON

Silas, O'Brien cottage, Tullamore, Ireland

Silas nearly dropped his cup of tea when a loud knock at the door startled him. "Come in."

Katrina swept in, followed by Caitlin, both clearly agitated.

"Something's happened," Katrina blurted out. "I did a card reading this morning and there are kings and queens literally falling out of the deck, along with the Journey card."

"Katrina, you know very well that the Journey card could represent any change. It could even mean Briana is coming home," Caitlin said, though she didn't sound convincing.

Katrina sat on the couch and pushed her hands against the sides of her head. Her voice barely above a whisper, she answered, "Then how do you explain the Seven of Vessels and the Blasted Oak?"

Silas sat beside her and laid a hand on her shoulder. "What do they mean, Katrina?"

"Mourning and death."

Quietly as they were spoken, the words fell like an axe on Silas' ears. In his head he heard Briana saying she needed him, her voice urgent and ominous.

Katrina grabbed both of his hands. "Silas, you have to find the runes. I don't believe there is any time to waste."

"I know where they are," Silas said as calmly as he could, though he was worried. "They are on the hill in Finnleaseach's Well."

"How do you know?" Caitlin's eyes were alight with excitement.

"Briana told me."

"Briana!" Katrina exclaimed. She shook her head. "How on earth…"

"Apparently she let down her barriers at a time when I was pretty open meself. She also told me where to look for the missin' pages of the prophecy." He held off telling her about Briana's urgent call to come home; Katrina was already anxious enough without that information. "We need to go through that trunk again." He led the way back to the closet in the bedroom and pulled out the white trunk. He unlocked the silver latch again and lifted the lid.

"Silas, we've already been through this. There was nothing here," Caitlin said.

"We look again."

He handed them the shawls, jewelry and other treasures until it was empty. Running his hand over every seam and piece of fabric lining turned up nothing. He sat back on his heels and sighed, staring blankly at the trunk. "She clearly said to look in the trunk."

"Have you turned it over?" Finnegan said, from behind them.

"Uh, no," Silas said, suddenly feeling foolish. Re-securing the latch, he pushed the trunk on its side and saw the obvious line along the edge of the cleats on the bottom. He grinned sheepishly up at Finnegan.

"It's okay, lad. I only just thought of it." He handed Silas his pocket knife.

Using the small blade to pry along the edge, he separated the wooden base and heard everyone gasp behind him when several books and papers fell out of the hidden compartment.

"This explains why it seemed so heavy," Silas commented, as he accepted a book from Katrina. He cracked the book open to a page with a drawing of a well. "That's Finnleaseach's Well! I've walked past it dozens of times but it doesn't appear to be anythin' you could get into, never mind hide somethin' in."

"And yet, that would be the perfect place to hide something," Katrina said.

"Aye, it would."

"Oh!"

"What is it, mother?"

Caitlin's voice went soft and her eyes turned dreamy. "I think this might be part of the prophecy you were searchin' for, Silas." She handed him a parchment with ancient words on it. "Do you know what it says?"

"Aye, I do," he whispered, scanning the page through eyes that were misting over. He cleared his throat.

> "Royal hill and royal womb, runes seek to bind.
> A new day brings new hope.
> For sake of babe and holy quest,
> The cat must now return.
> The Wheel begins to turn once more,
> Druid, crown and faerie, three become the one,
> Cheerful celebration.
> Evil met with golden arrow,
> Snow brings happy season.
> Peace and glory, magic lives, five kingdoms now
> are one."

"That's beautiful," Katrina said. "Do you understand it?"

Silas looked up at her, not bothering to wipe the tear sliding down his cheek. "I believe you are going to be a grandmother," he said to Katrina, and turning to Caitlin, added, "and a great-grandmother. And I need to go home."

Katrina stared blankly for the space of three seconds before comprehension dawned on her. "She's pregnant?"

"Well, if she isn't already, she will be. Her destiny is to bear the next king of Uisneach."

"Or queen," Caitlin chirped, a wide grin lighting her face.

"You said you have to go home," Finnegan said. "Does that mean you're the cat?"

"She used to call me her great cat."

Katrina bit her lip. Silas saw her conflict between wanting to be happy about the baby and not wanting to hurt him.

"Well, looks like we have somethin' to celebrate," he said. "My queen and king are goin' to have their first child," he said cheerfully, trying to ease her mind.

"It's more important that we get to the runes." Katrina said. "What do we need to do?"

"It's Sunday," Silas answered, "which means no one will be on the grounds. I can get in and dig around without anyone noticin'. I'll go have a wee look."

"I'll come and help you," Katrina suggested.

Silas shook his head. "It will be harder to hide two people, if it comes down to that. You might want to look through these journals to see if there is anythin' else of importance. However, Finnegan, if you wouldn't mind droppin' me off, that would eliminate the need for any cars parked out front. I'll call you on my cell phone when I need you to pick me up." If I don't call in three hours," he paused. *What should they do if he didn't call? He couldn't risk them getting into trouble over this.* He blew out his breath, "If I don't call in three hours, call Orla and see if she'll come to find me."

They nodded solemnly. Although Silas hadn't shared any specifics with them, they were aware that he and Orla had a falling out.

⬦

Silas watched Finnegan drive away before squeezing between the gate and the hedge. He wandered up the hill, staying close to the hedgerow until he was out of sight of the road. He sprinted most of the way across grass still wet from the rains of the last several days to the trees near the fort, and then followed a line of hedges until he came to the spot where a wooden marker identified Finnleaseach's Well.

Stepping through scrubby bushes, he came to the edge of the stone-lined well and kneeled on slippery, lichen-covered stones. He reached into his pocket for his cell phone, meaning to set it aside in case it fell out while he was searching around. It was gone! *Great. How am I to call Finnegan? Ah, shit, I'll worry about that later.* Luckily, he still had the collapsible shovel and flashlight Finnegan gave him. He laid that on the ground and stretched out on his stomach at the edge of the well.

The water was several inches deep from the recent rains. Grabbing the flashlight, he focused its beam along the inside stones. Moss dripped with water from the rocks, making everything shiny. He turned the flashlight downward. His breath caught at a flash of greenish-blue. He leaned forward a bit more. Reaching out, he could almost touch whatever it was, and his breath came faster as he realized what he might have just discovered. Another inch was all he needed to touch the colored stone. Stretching with a groan he was almost… The rock crumbled underneath his belly and before he could stop himself, he was tumbling down, miraculously ending upright in six inches of water—on his bad leg.

He let out a screech at the pain that shot up his leg to his hip. *Maker, please don't let me have broken this again.* Gingerly, he lifted his leg, relieved when it moved without difficulty. Not broken. *Thank you.* He gave himself a minute to orient to his surroundings and realized that he would have to find a way to climb out later. He fished around the bottom of the well to find the flashlight and gave thanks when it worked, waveringly, but enough to find what he was looking for. Another bloody miracle. An almost giddy giggle escaped as he touched the smooth, blue-green surface of the nuggets. Wedging the light between his teeth, he trained it on the area he needed to work in. Using his fingers, he dug around the moss and mud that surrounded the runes and one by one, pulled out twelve small stones, each with a different symbol carved into it. He leaned against the wall behind him and stared at the ancient Runes of Evalon.

Hot tears stung his eyes. "I've done it. I've found them. Thank you, Briana, for showin' me where to look. I'll bring them to you as soon as I can." The last of the light died and he looked skyward. "Now, there's the little matter of gettin' out of here."

He pocketed the stones and grabbed hold of two larger stones above him and lifted his leg to find a foothold in the wall. Ouch! His leg hurt like hell, but he had to climb. Hefting his weight up he cleared the ground for only a few seconds before his foot slipped on the wet wall. He tried twice more with no success. "Am, I goin' to find the runes only to die in this hole?"

"I doubt it, though you likely deserve to," Orla called from above. Áed perched jauntily on her shoulder as both peered down at him.

"Hello Silas," the wee man greeted him. "What are ye doin' down there?"

"Sweet God, I'm glad you're here. Can you get me out?"

"Well, maybe we can use this." She held a coil of rope over the well opening and began to whirl it around. "Or, we could call for help with this," she said, showing him the cell phone he'd dropped.

"Okay, I feel fool enough, if you don't mind. Are you goin' to throw me the rope or not?"

"Be nice, and I might. However, I doubt I could hold it while you climb, so I'm thinkin' I should tie it to one of these trees. Do you happen to know how to tie an anchor hitch knot? It might take me a bit to figure it out."

"Orla, please. I'm standin' knee deep in water, me feet are froze and me legs hurt like the devil. I've scrapes on me head and I just want to get out of here."

Áed laughed hysterically, but Orla's head disappeared, and in a few moments, the rope was tossed down.

"Okay," she said, reappearing. "It should hold you."

He caught a foothold and climbed up the wall, ignoring his leg's protests of pain. At the top, Orla reached under his arm and helped pull him over the edge.

Standing, he took a deep breath and started to hug Orla. Her expression told him that was not a good idea.

"Thank you," he said instead.

She nodded. "Any luck, while you were at it?"

He fished in his pocket for the runes and held them out to her. Even in the fading light, their brilliance was remarkable.

"Looks like Connemara marble," she commented. "Do they do anythin' special?"

"Not that I can tell, but I do recognize these markin's as Uisneachan. These are the runes, Orla."

"So, you'll go home now." Her voice held a note of acceptance. "Silas, I was wrong to reject your friendship. I'm the one who's been a wanker about all this, and I want to apologize. I went to your place, but Katrina told me you'd come here, so I thought I'd see if I could help."

"I wish I could hug you, Orla, but I'm afraid you'd thwack me over the head, and it already aches."

Her smile was bittersweet, but she held out her arms and he wrapped her in his.

"It would never have worked out between us, would it?"

"Orla, I do care for you, very much. If things..."

She stepped back and touched the warrior bone hearts around his neck. "If your heart wasn't already bound to someone else. She's a lucky woman, Silas O'Mara, to have a man as fine as yourself love her. If my only role in your life was to help you find the runes and save your kingdom, then it is a privilege to do so."

There were many things he thought of saying, but knew they would sound hollow. Instead he hugged her close. "Thank you, Orla. For everythin'. Could I impose on you once more, to take me home?"

"Yes, please, get us home, lass." Áed had been invisible until now. Silas wondered at his rare moment of insight.

Back in Tullamore, they went straight to Caitlin's house to share the discovery.

Everyone took a turn holding the runes, admiring the ancient symbols and closing their eyes in hopes of feeling something. Katrina and Caitlin both said there was a warmth to them, but that was the extent of any magical emanations.

"Now, we can truly celebrate," Finnegan announced, lifting a bottle of Dew.

Four glasses were poured and raised. "To Silas and Orla, for perseverin' through a difficult quest and saving a kingdom. *Slàinte!*"

Silas looked to Orla and saw her smile fixed in place. "Well, Uisneach is not quite saved yet, but we are one step closer," Silas said quietly, hoping that their victory wasn't throwing salt in her hurting heart.

After Caitlin's open-mouthed yawn, Silas and Orla wished them a good night.

"Would you want to come in for a bit?" Silas asked her, hoping she would say yes.

"I would, for a bit."

Inside, she poured them another drink while he put the runes in his bedroom in the nightstand drawer for safekeeping.

"Have you seen Áed?" he asked when he came out.

She shook her head. "No, and that doesn't bother me a bit. I certainly hope when you leave, he doesn't decide to hang around my place."

"Aye, well, there is that still to be decided, isn't it?" asked Áed. Silas and Orla both groaned, hearing the clurichaun's voice from the corner of the room. "What's to happen to me?"

"I'll just be usin' the bathroom now," Orla said, grinning, leaving him to deal with the angry wee man.

"You promised to find me a wife."

Silas settled himself on the couch, drawing the throw pillow across his lap and settling in for what could be a long argument.

"I did not promise you a wife, I promised to teach you how to get a wife yourself."

"Either way, yer leavin', and I have no wife."

"Where do you even look for a wife around here?"

"There's places."

"Áed, here's what I can tell you. Go to those places, don't drink, and be nice. That is how you find a wife."

"Don't drink? Are you serious, man? You drink and ye have women crawlin' all over you."

Silas ignored the snigger he heard from the other room. "I handle me liquor better than you do."

"Silas, I think I should head home. It's gettin' late." Orla appeared from the bedroom.

In the time it took for Silas to look from Orla to Áed, the clurichaun disappeared.

"Are you okay?"

"Yeah. I'm really happy for you, Silas. It's been a rocky road, but you did it." She hugged him, then left.

Some of the cheer he'd felt faded with Orla's leaving. He looked around the room, but finding no evidence of irritating beings, he turned the lights off and headed for bed himself.

He undressed and slid into bed, turning Briana's picture toward him. Staring at the image, he wondered if he could reach her again. *Briana? Hey, are you there? I did it. I found the runes. I'll be home soon.* Nothing happened. It was probably too much to hope for. *Wait a minute. Could the runes provide a little extra punch to connect us?* He slid the drawer open and pulled out the bag with the runes it. Dumping them on the bed, he was shocked to find one missing. Searching through the drawer didn't produce it. Nor was it under the bed. He dressed and searched the apartment.

A sick feeling crawled into his gut. Rewinding from the point he and Orla returned to his apartment, the one thing that stuck out was that she used the bathroom and then left abruptly. Would she have taken one, and why? To prevent his leaving? Maker, he hated to think it of her, but there was no other explanation.

He grabbed his keys and left for Orla's house. There was no other way to deal with this than in person.

⪥

A light was still on in her house. He dragged himself up the walkway to her door and knocked. He had to repeat it twice. When she answered, he was disconcerted by her red-rimmed eyes.

"Orla," he said softly, "you've been cryin'?"

"What do you think, Silas? Why are you here?"

He swallowed hard but pushed forward. "Orla, one of the runes is missin'."

"Missin'?" She looked confused.

"Yeah, it's gone. I put them in the nightstand in my room. After you left, I was goin' to have another look at them, but found one missin'."

He watched her eyes change from sadness to confusion to outrage.

"I see. You think I took one, then?"

"You were the only one who went in there, Orla. What am I to think?"

He watched her jaw clench and eyes narrow. "And you didn't think maybe the wee, vile leprechaun had somethin' to do with it?"

"He was with me."

Guilt ripped through him as her eyes welled with tears and she grabbed

485

on to the door post. "I would *never* do that to you, Silas. I cannot believe you would think it of me."

"What am I to think, then?"

"Try this. I saw you had put her picture back on the nightstand and realized there was never going to be a chance for you and me. I left because I didn't want you to see me fall apart."

An owl hooted somewhere nearby, providing the only noise in the horrific silence that lay between them.

"I did not take it, Silas. I imagine Áed did. Whatever. Don't call me again. Don't come here again. I'm done with you."

The slamming of the door in his face was followed by the laughing hoot of the owl.

CHAPTER FORTY-TWO

RIVERS OF SORROW

Silas opened the front door of his cottage to the disturbing vision of Áed splayed out on the couch pillow, crying his eyes out. A bottle of whiskey lay tipped over on the coffee table, next to the clurichaun's small cup, a small river of amber liquid running down the leg of the table. The room reeked.

"What in God's name are you doin'?" Silas demanded, angry that now, after he'd accused Orla, the wee man might have had something to do with the missing stone.

"I know I'm drinkin' too much, and I need to stop."

"And, pray tell, what's brought about this epiphany?"

Áed reached out a hand and Silas clenched his teeth. The missing rune lay sweet as you please in the center of his gnarly hand.

"I just wanted ye to stay. Yer the only friend I have. And ye promised to help me find a wife."

"Áed, the only thing keepin' you from findin' a wife is your nasty attitude and your drunkenness. You need to change your ways. Even if I could take you with me to Uisneach, you wouldn't find a wife as long as you behave as you do."

The little fellow looked down at his hand and pushed the rune closer to Silas. "I'm sorry, man. I shouldn't have taken this. Is Orla mad?"

"What do you think? I just accused her of takin' it. Áed, I could murder you right now!"

"I said I were sorry. I'll apologize to yer lady."

"Áed, do us both a favor and stay away from her."

The clurichaun looked so contrite that Silas nearly relented. "Just go pass out somewhere, would you. I need to make me own apologies."

In a wink, the wee man disappeared. Silas picked up his phone and punched in Orla's number but received only her voice mail. "Orla, please call me. I need to talk to you. I've made a horrible mistake and I want to apologize. I'd come over, but I'm pretty sure you'd slam the door in me face."

He ended the call and looked around the room. What needing doing next? While cleaning up Áed's mess, he remembered he had a job to quit. Grabbing his jacket, he headed for Seamus' Pub. The evening was fair, and it felt good to walk some of the heat out of his system.

Being a Monday night, there was hardly a soul in the pub. Indie pop music played from a CD. Seamus poured a pint for Silas and slid it across the bar.

"What's on your mind, man? You look like a pup that's been staked outside in the cold."

"I feel it. The long and short of it is that I need to go back to the states in a hurry. I hate to do this to you, but I'll have to resign."

"You'll be comin' back, won't you?" Seamus leaned against the edge of the bar, frowning.

Silas had thought of an explanation on the way over and answered smoothly, "Don't think so, Seamus. Been a family emergency, and I doubt I'll be returnin' to Ireland anytime soon. I'm grateful for the chance you gave me to work here, and I'll not forget you, nor Rebecca. Where is she, anyway?"

"Off to Dublin with her mother. She'll be sorry not to say good bye."

They chatted a few more minutes while Silas finished his beer. Then he left. Darkness had fallen, but the night remained dry and the moon showed half her face. A rare heaviness of heart kept Silas at a slow wander up High Street. Pausing under the Irish flags at Eugene Kelly's, he searched within for the source of his anxiety. It wasn't just the argument with Orla, though he was upset about how things were going to be left between them. Briana was in trouble. He felt it in every part of him. She might be pregnant, but something was wrong and more than anything he wanted to be home, to help her, whatever the problem was.

He neared the bridge over the grand canal. A streetlight illuminated a solitary figure leaning on the cement post in the center of the bridge. The woman's head was bowed and her shoulder's shook. *Bloody hell, she's brave to be out here alone again.* He sighed and approached carefully.

"Orla," he said quietly, when he was a few feet away.

Her head whipped up and she backed away. Shadows swallowed her as she stepped out of the light.

"Orla, please, I was wrong to accuse you and I am more sorry than you can know."

She shook her head. "I'm not mad, Silas. I would have thought the same thing and honestly, if I had thought to take a rune to keep you here, I might have. That's not why I'm cryin'."

"Why, then?"

"Why do you think, eejit? I don't want you to go." She looked down at the ground for a moment and then lifted her head. When she stepped forward, the streetlight illuminated her ravaged face. "I love you, Silas. The thought of never seein' you again kills me."

The heavy heart he'd been feeling became a millstone that threatened to drag him into the canal. He almost wished it would. This was exactly what he'd feared from the very beginning and yet, he'd carried on as though this day would never come. "Orla, I..."

She put her fingers to his lips. "Please, don't say anythin', Silas. I couldn't bear it. I have no intention of tryin' to hold you back in any way. You've been crystal clear from day one that you couldn't get involved with me. This is entirely me own folly. It just hurts, is all."

"I hurt too, Orla. I can't imagine not seein' your beautiful face again and never hearin' your voice swearin' with poetic elegance."

She laughed. "Is that supposed to be a compliment, then?"

"Well, Orla, you have a wonderful way with words and a brilliant mind. I'll miss you terribly."

She nodded. "I'll miss you too, Silas."

He stepped closer and watching her carefully, took her hand. She squeezed his fingers and they turned toward the canal, holding hands, watching in silence as its water flowed beneath them, under the bridge and away from Tullamore.

Silas felt the energy change between them, felt a calmness steal over them. "Orla, if you're ever in Uisneach, look me up."

She chuckled. "You never know, I might just find a way. But I don't think your queen would like that very much, now, would she?"

"Well, she's married, isn't she?"

CHAPTER FORTY-THREE

HOME

Katrina and her parents shared a tearful farewell, certain that they'd never see each other again. Silas discovered a part of his heart didn't want to leave Ireland at all, while another couldn't get to Maine fast enough. He'd be one step closer to Uisneach and Briana, but he was leaving so much behind. In some ways, it was a death for them all. Silas had even commented to Katrina on the flight back to the states that perhaps that was what she'd seen on the cards.

Katrina's attorney, Robert O'Shaughnessy, met them at the Portland Jetport with some unexpected news.

"You won't need to sell the house, Katrina. I'll be t'e caretaker, so to speak, and we'll rent it out as a vacation home. T'is way, should you return, you'll have a place to live. It's all legal and aboveboard, I assure you."

"I trust you, Robert, but I need to sell the house to pay you for the *other* legal arrangement."

Silas knew she meant his legal identification. Her entire life had been turned upside down for the sake of Uisneach and for love of her daughter.

"Och, I'll keep half the rents as repayment, t'e other half to be put in trust, in case you need it. I look at it t'is way, I'm doin' me part for t'e mother country."

Debbie met them at Katrina's house with a warm meal and her four-month-old son, Wesley, jabbering happily away in his baby carrier.

"He's a handsome lad, Debbie," Silas said, bending over the little one and letting him grab on to his fingers, one of which he put in his mouth.

"No, Wesley, he's not your next meal."

"It's all right, Debbie. I've washed me hands." He studied the boy and felt an ache in his heart. Briana was probably going to have one of these wee creatures soon, if she hadn't already. A baby she created with Brath. He was happy for them, of course, but couldn't help wondering if he would ever have a wife and child. He'd just left his best hope behind. Orla remained a large part of his consciousness, even as he planned for the attempt to get through a tree to Uisneach.

Night had fallen. The dishes were done and Wesley was waxing cranky.

Debbie sighed. "I guess it's time to get the little man to bed, but I really hate to leave." She gave Katrina a sorrowful stare. "I may never see you again. And with you gone, it will feel like for sure I'll never see Briana again."

"You never know what the future may bring, Debbie," Katrina replied with a wink, "but remember, always, that you are in our hearts and will never be forgotten."

The two women hugged, and Silas was about to hug her as well, when she reached into her pocket and pulled out an envelope.

"You said you'd give this to Briana for me."

"I did, and I will," he said accepting that heavy envelope.

"There's pictures of Wesley in there," she said. She pressed her lips together.

"It's okay to cry," Katrina said, her own eyes moist.

Debbie shook her head. "I don't want to leave blubbering. That's much too Briana a thing to do."

It took over a week to finalize everything and pack a couple of large backpacks with things they wanted to take with them. Silas had gone out daily to check for a door in the tree. Every time, the tree looked like every other spring oak in the forest, with new leaves just beginning to unfurl. How would they know when it was time to go?

He woke on a Saturday morning with an odd feeling in his stomach and a tremor-like energy circuiting his spine.

"Katrina! It's time," he hollered, throwing on jeans and a tee shirt. He raced out to the kitchen, where Katrina was in a frenzy herself.

"It's time," he repeated.

"I know. I woke feeling strange and just knew today was the day."

He saw nothing to indicate excitement or happiness that today she would enter a new world to be reunited with her daughter. Instead he saw uncertainty and fear. Her hands shook when she handed him a cup of coffee. Her lips trembled when she stopped biting them. He took a breath.

"Do you still want to go, Katrina?"

"Of course," she said. "I'm just nervous."

He understood. Portals were not an everyday experience for either of them, and truth be told, he was nervous too. "We'll make it through. Maker has gotten us this far. I doubt we'll be blocked now. But, would it be awful to hope for a bit of breakfast before we go?"

Doing something normal seemed to soothe her. Silas had no problem putting down three eggs, bacon and a muffin. Katrina picked at her meal, but the tremors stopped, and when the dishes were done, she hoisted her backpack and turned for Silas to adjust the straps.

"We're bringing half the house with us, Katrina," he joked, hiking his own pack a little higher on his back. "Ready?"

Katrina looked around the house, at the pictures of her family, and the furniture and household items that probably held strong memories. A tear escaped as she nodded and turned toward the door. "I need to go before I can't."

They made their way down the drive and across the street. Silas held Katrina's hand as she stepped through the opening in the stone wall.

"I hope any nosey neighbors assume we're hiking Mt. Battie," she said.

Silas' stomach dropped when they got to the tree and it was as it had been every other day. No magical portal greeted them. No change in the tree whatsoever. Surely, they hadn't both misinterpreted their feelings. Even now, the feelings of urgency and immediacy were almost more than he could bear. His gut told him it was time. His heart could not imagine waiting one more day.

Quickly fishing the runes out of his pocket, he laid them at the base of the oak. When nothing happened, he wondered what else was needed. Inspiration came in the form of words from the prophecy that he'd memorized. Closing his eyes, he repeated them.

"Royal hill and royal womb, runes seek to bind.
A new day brings new hope.
For sake of babe and holy quest,
The cat must now return.
The Wheel begins to turn once more,
Druid, crown and faerie, three become the one."

He expected to see a change in the tree when he opened his eyes, but there was nothing different. Katrina paced back and forth, tears welling and on the verge of spilling over. She needed something to do.

"Katrina, do you have your cards handy? I wonder if they might give us a clue as to what we need to do. Maybe you can call upon Cailleach to help. She's had a connection to you in the past."

She turned her back to him so he could release the pack. Digging through the side pocket, she found a set of cards. Taking some deep breaths, she shuffled the deck. The action put her into a calmer state. Laying out five cards in a spread meant to identify and overcome obstacles, she turned them over one by one. The first card was the Tree of Life. She grimaced. "Yes, it would be a tree that is our obstacle," she said. "What can we do about it?"

The second card was the Queen of Bows. Briana. Her concern and her hope. "Come on Briana, help us open this door," Katrina whispered.

Briana, we need you to help us, Silas said in his head, hoping that his urgency would lower the barriers to their telepathy and reach her.

Next, she laid down a Queen of Arrows. Taking a deep breath, Katrina nodded in self-awareness. "I need to let go of my fear and ambivalence about leaving. It's blocking the way." She hesitated, allowing herself to fully acknowledge the feelings. "I'm coming, Briana. I will be there for the birth of my grandchild."

Silas choked when he saw the next card. The Seer. A mediator to all the elemental forces. However, it wasn't the hooded woman who startled him, but the arrow-headed shaft, illuminated and nearly rising out of the card. He remembered the dagger Katrina had wrapped in her pack.

While he was thinking of this, she laid down the last card, The Green Woman. "All I can think of here is that it is feminine energy that will ensure success. Like the Lady of the Lake, who brought King Arthur his powerful sword, she is the energy behind his success."

Swords. King Arthur. Successful endeavor. Suddenly Silas remembered Aislin's words, "ye'll need to rely on someone else's power to accomplish the task before ye."

Smiling, he spoke with the calmness that came from knowing exactly what to do. "Katrina, pull out the dagger, if you would."

Silas received the package and solemnly unwrapped it until the beautiful steel carved with runes glinted in a sudden ray of sun that seemed to focus directly on it.

Silas held out the dagger, still partially swaddled in its cloth. "Katrina, I believe once you touch this, the way will be clear for us to go, but I also think you have to be absolutely sure you want to make the journey. You are the one who must summon the portal."

She stared at the blade, then lifted the dagger from its wrapping.

They felt the instant shift in the air around them, watched in rapt fascination as the oak tree grew. Leaves unfurled to maturity and branches dipped, heavy with acorns. A green door appeared in the trunk, with ancient carvings and a silver handle. Katrina grabbed at her heart. "I have to go to her," she said, trancelike. Silas stepped forward and took the handle, pushed the door open. He peered into the darkness without any trepidation about taking the first step. Feeling Katrina hesitate behind him, he turned.

She was looking back at her house. "All our memories are there. Everything familiar and safe is in that house." She turned back to Silas, who reached out a hand.

"Come with me, Katrina. Your daughter waits on the other side."

She met his eyes and nodded. "And what waits for you, Silas?"

He grinned, his eyes alight with joy. "Home."

The End

GLOSSARY

Áed (ed): Irish name for the clurichaun

a ghrá (uh hraw): my love

Ail na Mireann (ahl mwir en): the stone of divisions (the Catstone)

ainmhithe (anya ve hi): creature

a leanbh (lan uv): child

a mhuirnin (uh war neen): sweetheart

art (art): mountain

a sonuachar (uh sun uh khar): my true spouse or soul mate

a stor (uh store): my treasure

Ayvinn (a vin): Irish mythic banshee

banjaxed: broken, wrecked

Banrion (Ban-reen): queen

Bebinn (Bevin): female name

Beltane (Bel tane or Bel tanya): Celtic festival in May

bennacht (ben ocht): blessing

bodhran (bo-ran): Irish drum

Cailleach (Kyle-yock): witch

cath (ca): fort

ceartais (kair tis): justice

Cennétig mac Lorcain (kin-sig-mac-lor-can): the name that was modernized to "Kennedy"

chancer: dodgy character, not trustworthy

chisler: young child

clurichaun (Kloor-i-kan): a very naughty type of leprechaun

craic (crack): fun, good times

cumhacht (koo at): power

Dáil Éireann (dool erin or doyle erin): Lower House of Parliament in Ireland

Dian Cecht (Dion Set): god of healing for the Tuatha Dé Danann

Dar Morch (Dar Mork): evil fantasy figure based on real Irish mythological figure

Eire (air-u or air a): Ireland

Fianna Fáil (finna fall): The Republican party of Ireland (conservative)

Fine Gail (fina-gale): the moderate party of Ireland

Finnleaseach's Well (finn le och): a sacred well on the hill of Uisneach

Fir Bolg (fear bullug): ancient tribe of Ireland around the same time as the Tuatha Dé Danann

gobdaw: dumb person who hasn't got it together

gombeen: fool

Imbolc (imbug): Celtic festival of spring, St. Brigid's day

langers: drunk

Leanach (Lee a nock): plains in Uisneach

Lough Ennell (lock Ennell): a lake in County Westmeath

Lugh (loo): Irish warrior god/king of the Tuatha Dé Danann

Madb (mauve or may uv): female name

Máire O'Braoin (maw ra o breun or o brian)

Manannán mac Lir (man a non mac leer): Irish sea god associated with both the Tuatha Dé Danann and the Fomorians

mo chroi (ma kree): my love

Nuada Airgetlam (Noo-a-da tha AR-gid-lawv): first king of the Tuatha Dé Danann, known as "Silver Hand"

òichte (e hye): night, darkness

oision (oy sheen): legendary poet of Ireland

rath: fort, ring fort

Rathcroghan (rath crawn or croahn): fort of Cruahan. One of the six royal sites of Ireland, believed to contain an entrance to the Underworld.

ríocht (rot): kingdoms, realms; an Uisneachan form of chess

rún (roon): mystery or secret

Samchea Molloie (sam-chee mol oy): male name

Scáil Meanoiche (skaw or skaw-I mi-ahn-ee-heh): dark shadows. The underworld

sídhe (shee): supernatural race of beings comparable to faeries

slàinte (slawn): to your health, cheers

slàinte mhaith (slawn cha wa): good health to you

Srah Castle (Shra): 16th century castle in Tullamore, now in ruins

smooring: banking a fire in a hearth

Taoisech (tee-shock): Irish prime minister, the leader of the parliament

Teaguen (Tee gin): a faerie of Evalon

Tir fo Thuinn (cheer fo hin): land under the sea

Tuatha Dé Danann (too-ah day don-an): children or people of the goddess Danu

Tuathla (Too uh la): a princess of the People (the faeries)

Tuathal Techtmar (too uh hul tek mar): ancient high king of Ireland from around AD 56

Tynan Ibor (Tinin i bor): kingdom in the center of Uisneach

uisce beatha (ish-ga-ba-ha): "water of life"—refers to Irish whiskey

Uilleann pipes (ill-yin): Irish bagpipes

Uisneach (oosh-nay): mythical place and geographical center of Ireland

Urelian (ur el e an): fictitious name for ancient queen of Uisneach

Some terms or names in this book are fictitious or based loosely on Irish words. Please note that regional variations in spelling and pronunciation abound in Ireland. As much as possible, I held to pronunciations consistent with Ulster.

ABOUT THE AUTHOR

For Heidi Hanley, reading and writing are like breathing. On her 50th birthday, she got serious about turning her passion for writing into a goal to publish. The result was *The Prophecy*, Book One of the Kingdom of Uisneach series. *The Runes of Evalon* is the second book in the series. Heidi lives in New Hampshire beside the Connecticut River with her husband and a Scottish terrier. She has enjoyed a career as a Registered Nurse, Interfaith minister and currently serves as a Hospice chaplain. When not working, you will find her reading, sneaking away to Maine, or in the garden with the birds and faeries.